Scoundrel
Ever After

DARCY
BURKE

For Janice

The baskets in chapter eight are for you.
And they're filled with gratitude and love
(instead of apples and chicken, though you can have those too).

SCOUNDREL EVER AFTER

Once upon a time there was a very bad boy...

Ethan Jagger will do anything to leave his illicit past behind and take his place as a gentleman in Society. Success is within his grasp until his boss discovers his double cross and frames him for murder. As if running from the law and the outlaws weren't bad enough, he must protect an innocent young lady from the very cutthroats who want him dead. Worst of all, however, is the dangerous attraction that sparks between them.

Who met a very nice girl...

London only thinks of Audrey Cheswick as a wallflower—if they even think of her at all. She's tried to find satisfaction—if not happiness—as a spinster-in-waiting, though her intrepid spirit yearns for a grand adventure. But when she runs away with England's most wanted criminal, she learns adventure comes with a price—not just her reputation or her virtue, but her heart.

Love romance? Have a free book (or two or three) on me!

Sign up at http://www.darcyburke.com/readerclub for members-only exclusives, including advance notice of pre-orders and insider scoop, as well as contests, give-aways, freebies, and 99 cent deals!

Want to share your love of my books with like-minded readers? Want to hang with me and get inside scoop? Then don't miss my exclusive Facebook groups!

Darcy's Duchesses for historical readers
Burke's Book Lovers for contemporary readers

Scoundrel Ever After
Copyright © 2014 Darcy Burke
All rights reserved.
ISBN: 1939713943
ISBN-13: 9781939713940

Book design © Darcy Burke.
Cover design © Elizabeth Mackey.
Cover Image © Period Images.
Copyediting: Martha Trachtenberg.

❀ Created with Vellum

CHAPTER 1

*E*than Jagger ran like hell. Every swing of his arm pumped blood from the knife wound in his bicep and brought a fresh burn of agony. Still, he couldn't stop. Stopping meant capture. Capture meant the hangman's noose.

He didn't chance a look back. Though he couldn't yet hear them, he knew the Bow Street Runners were closing in. Wounded as he was, Ethan wasn't sure he could outpace them. St. Giles was still too bloody far away.

He almost stopped cold. He couldn't go to St. Giles. Despite his allies, and he had more than a few, everyone in the rookery would know Gin Jimmy was after him. And if they had to choose their loyalty, and they did, they'd award it to the man who could cause them the most harm: Gin Jimmy. Pursued by the law *and* the outlaw: Ethan was well and truly buggered.

There was no help for it. He had to get out of London and figure out what to do next. To do that, he'd need to get to one of the hiding spots where he kept his emergency funds. The closest one—and more importantly in the opposite direction of St. Giles—was in Berkley Square, which meant he had to double back.

But first he had to elude the Runners. He veered left onto a narrow street. And ran straight into a whore.

She grasped his arms to steady herself. Her hand closed around his wound. He sucked in air and white lights speckled his sight.

"Ho there!" She drew her hand away. "Wot's wrong with ye?"

Lamplight from the wider street up ahead filtered back into the alley, but it was too dark for him to discern much of her features. He could, however, tell she was studying her hand. She had to have felt the blood seeping from the gash Gin Jimmy had given him scarcely a quarter hour before.

Aware that this pause was allowing his pursuers to gain on him, Ethan pushed her aside so he could slip past her down the alleyway.

"'Ey now, there's no need to be rude!" she shrieked.

Ethan didn't spare her a glance as he hastily set off once more. But then a very large man stepped in his way. "Ye shouldn't be rude to me trollop."

Bloody fucking hell. Ethan did not have time for a prostitute or her pimp. However, before he could take off running once more, the pimp stepped so close to Ethan that he could smell the man's filth as well as the gin he'd swilled earlier.

"'Is arm's 'urt," the woman said.

Ethan braced himself, expecting the pimp to hit or grab him in the arm, but the hulking bloke only leaned in closer, sticking his face a mere inch from Ethan's. "Jagger?" he asked.

It didn't surprise Ethan that the pimp knew him, though the recognition was not reciprocated. One didn't rise as far as Ethan had within the criminal ranks without developing a reputation and a . . . following.

"Yes, Jagger. Now, back off." He kept his tone even, yet commanding.

The pimp stepped back, and Ethan inhaled fresher air. His pulse was slowing, which meant he'd been motionless too long. The Runners were going to be on him.

"Ye don't spend as much time at the flash houses as ye used to." The pimp's tone carried an edge of skepticism that Ethan didn't like. "I hear ye've taken up with a diff'rent class o' folk, and that ye might not even go by Jagger no more."

Ethan didn't have time or patience for the man's inquiry. His arm was killing him and if he didn't start running again, Bow Street would be upon him. "I need to be on my way. Move aside."

Ethan made to dash past, but as he stepped to the side, the pimp's arm shot out and he grabbed Ethan's bicep. With a howl, Ethan spun and sent his fist into the pimp's jaw. He would've followed up with another jab to his middle, but Ethan couldn't make his right arm work.

A shout of "There he is!" came from behind. Damn everything to hell. The Runners had found him.

The pimp had been momentarily surprised by Ethan's blow, but he recovered quickly and threw a fist toward Ethan's gut.

Ethan danced away, barely missing the hit. "Those are Bow Street Runners, you imbecile. We need to move!" Whatever the pimp's motive, he wouldn't want to be detained by Bow Street. None of their class ever did.

The pimp straightened, his body angled toward where Ethan had come from.

"Hold there, Jagger!" one of the Runners called. Teague. He'd been hounding Ethan for years, but particularly during the last fortnight. Ethan didn't mean for him to catch him now.

Jabbing his elbow out toward the pimp, Ethan took off running.

"Catch him!" Teague shouted. "Or find yourself in trouble!"

The pimp's hand closed around Ethan's bicep and dragged him to a stop. Agony spiraled up and down Ethan's arm. "Sorry, mate."

No. Ethan refused to go down like this. With a surge of energy, he threw off the pimp's grip and punched him in the jaw again. The pimp was slightly more prepared this time and angled his head away, though Ethan still caught a piece of him.

Then the Runners were on them.

Ethan moved quickly, pulling his knife from his boot and squaring off before all three men could get to him. Suddenly a high-pitched squeal filled the air as the prostitute jumped on Teague's back and began to beat him about the head. Ethan would've thanked her for her support if he hadn't needed to dispatch the other two blokes.

He glanced around the narrow alley, gauging his options. A half dozen or so wooden crates were stacked to his right. But they were the only relief from the bricked walls rising up on either side of the close.

The pimp rushed at him, but Ethan flashed his knife, which slowed the other man's attack. Ethan didn't want to cause him damage—the bloke was only trying to save his own hide—so he snatched up one of the crates to use it as a weapon instead of his knife, which he kept tucked into his left palm. He lifted the crate as the pimp came at him again. Ethan brought the box down over the man's skull. The pimp stumbled backward as the crate splintered.

The second Runner rushed at him like a flash, his truncheon raised. Ethan pulled his arm back, but the truncheon hit his wrist hard enough that he dropped his knife. Swearing, Ethan skittered backward. He rubbed his wrist in an effort to banish the pain as he cursed the loss of his weapon.

The Runner eyed him warily. He kept a firm grip on his club, keeping it elevated. "Just come along with us now, Jagger. I don't want to have to hurt you."

Though he'd lost his knife, Ethan thought he could disarm the Runner. Even so, Ethan doubted his ability to take down all three men—the prostitute surely couldn't overpower Teague, though she was managing to keep him occupied. Still, Ethan had to do what he could to escape. He held his hands up and speared the Runner with a direct stare. "I'll go with you."

The Runner didn't appear convinced. He edged forward slowly, tentatively.

When the Runner drew close, Ethan kicked him in the knee. The Runner went down, colliding with the pimp who'd been shaking off the remains of the broken crate. They landed together in a tangle of wood pieces and flailing limbs.

Ethan lunged forward. He snatched the truncheon from the dazed Runner and waved it in his face. "I'm going now, and you're letting me."

"Jagger, hold." Teague had finally gotten free of the hissing prostitute. He held the woman by the hair.

"Ye go on then, Jagger," she said, gritting her teeth as Teague tugged at her scalp. "Don't worry none 'bout me. I can take care o' meself."

Given her spitfire demeanor, Ethan didn't doubt it. But he wouldn't leave her to Teague.

Ethan skipped back several steps, lest the downed Runner or the pimp decide to reach out for his ankles. "Let her go. Then let *me* go and I'll get Gin Jimmy for you."

That had been his original goal: Take down the man who would ensure Ethan never broke free of his past. However, he had no idea how he'd manage that when tonight's plan had been a total pissing failure. Still, he had to try. It was the only chance he had.

Teague took a step forward, dragging the woman along with him. "I'd be much obliged, but that doesn't erase what you've done. You'll answer for your crimes, Jagger."

"Which ones?" There were far too many to count. Far too many that Ethan would just as soon forget.

Teague's glare was menacing. "Murdering Wolverton. Conspiring to kill Lady Aldridge."

"Is that all?" Ethan drawled, injecting a false carelessness into his tone.

"For now."

In a fluid movement surely born of years of practice, the prostitute turned toward Teague and kneed him square in the bollocks. Teague released her as he crumpled to the cobblestones. She cast a glance back at Ethan. "Run, Jagger!" Then she took off herself.

Ethan didn't need further urging. He turned to go, but a hand wrapped around his ankle. The pimp had disentangled himself from the other Runner. His meaty fingers grasped at Ethan's boot. Ethan brought the truncheon down on the man's wrist. The pimp howled with pain and withdrew his hand. Ethan sped from the alley as if the very devil were licking at his heels.

And he supposed he was.

Ethan had eluded the law for more than a decade, and he only needed to do it a little while longer. Until he could get out from under Gin Jimmy and get on with the life he'd begun to taste. A life where he could be Ethan Locke—better yet, Ethan Lockwood—and hold his head up as a member of the precious ton, even on its fringes. Not because he cared about them, but because he wanted to stay close to his brother.

As Ethan raced up the new Regent Street, he looked back to see if any of the men were pursuing him.

Nothing yet. Still, he kept up his pace until he was panting and his side began to ache.

A few moments later, he turned onto Conduit Street and the energy that had dulled the pain in his arm began to ebb. His steps were flagging, and the burn in his bicep reached a crescendo. Wincing, he reluctantly slowed to a fast walk. He looked behind him, ever aware that the Runners or even the pimp were likely chasing him. He should have taken a less traveled path, but he was desperate to get to Berkley Square—and to his stash of money—as quickly as possible.

That thought spurred him on. He dug deep, searching for the perseverance that had guided his survival for over a decade, and picked up speed again. He had to navigate traffic to get across New Bond Street, but it was late and he was lucky. With his goal nearly in sight, he pressed himself even faster, so that by the time he cut into the Berkley mews, his entire body was thrumming with exertion and pain.

It took every ounce of strength he had left to vault the wall into the garden where he'd hidden his money. He slumped back against the stone, its coldness seeping through his layers of clothing and offering a slight respite from the heat of his activity.

The garden was dark, but pale light flickered in a few of the windows of the house. No matter, as no one would notice a shadowy figure climbing a tree. *The fucking tree.* Climbing that was going to hurt.

Inhaling a shuddering breath, Ethan pushed himself away from the wall and put one foot in front of the other. He just had to get his money and then he could be on his way. A much-needed rest—maybe even inside the house—for an hour or so tempted him, but he wasn't sure he dared. At the very least, however, he should find something to bind his wound.

At the base of the tree, he set the Runner's truncheon on the ground. He winced as pain radiated from his sliced arm. How the hell was he supposed to pull himself up? Damn Gin Jimmy to hell and back.

Heaving out a frustrated breath, he reached up with his left hand and found a handhold. At least Jimmy hadn't wounded his stronger arm.

Ethan pulled himself up and flinched as pain sparked anew. He stepped up into a vee and exhaled. He couldn't use his right hand to climb, so he put his left up again and slowly made his way to the hollow where he'd stashed a bag of money the last time he'd gone up the tree. He nearly smiled at the recollection.

His gaze flicked up a few feet to where he'd entered the house on two other occasions. He'd climbed in Miss Audrey Cheswick's window for secret waltzing lessons. He shook his head at how ridiculously *normal* that sounded—save the secret part. How he yearned for such simplicity as dancing lessons or paying court to some young woman. Not that he'd courted Miss Cheswick. He was in no position to court anyone. And he wasn't even sure he wanted to.

He pulled the bag from the hollow and cradled it in his left arm. Though he was content with its weight, he opened it and stuck his hand inside to feel the notes and coin within. Relief and comfort at having his hard-earned money, however, didn't take the edge off the pain shooting up his arm. Definitely time to find some sort of bandage. Once inside, he'd also nick a bottle of brandy or whisky or whatever the hell he could lay his hands on.

Cinching the bag tight, he tucked it back in the tree. There was no way he could carry it and climb, so he'd have to fetch it on the way down. He gritted his teeth for the final ascent. It was only a few feet, but he had to stretch to reach the window. He only hoped the sash wasn't locked.

He pulled himself up to the branch and thought about which hand to use to hold on to the tree and which hand to extend for the sash. However, before he could make up his mind, a pale face appeared in the window. He nearly fell out of the tree.

The sash came open and the stricken expression of Miss Audrey Cheswick sent a shaft of fear straight to his gut.

"Mr. Locke," she said. "Thank goodness you've come. There are men in the house!"

Shit. "What sort of men?"

"I can't say, but they don't mean well. There was a tussle in the foyer." Her eyes were wide with fright. "I'm afraid for our butler."

Men in her house on this night of all nights couldn't be a coincidence. But why? They hadn't trailed him here unbeknownst to him, had they? But no, it wouldn't be Bow Street. They would've treated the occupants of this house, including the retainers, with respect. These had to be men of a different sort.

He leaned forward with his right arm because he didn't trust it to hold on to the tree. "Help me."

She took his hand and pulled. Then gasped. "There's blood on your arm!"

"I know." He clutched the window ledge. Clenching his teeth against the pain, he took his hand from the tree while keeping his feet braced on the branch. Then he hauled himself up over the ledge and into the room.

He sank down to the floor. His breath came in deep pants as he closed his eyes in sheer agony.

"I hear them in the corridor," she whispered.

Ethan opened his eyes. There'd be time to nurse his pains later. God, he hoped there'd be time.

He pushed himself up with his left hand. He touched her shoulder, and she turned her head back to look at him. The coals burning low in the grate cast a faint glow over her frightened features, made her eyes glimmer like aquamarines. Ethan put his finger to his lips, then crept past her toward the door.

Pausing with his ear against the wood, he listened intently. Low voices. Footsteps. Two men. One large, one not as large. Something shattered, like glass or pottery. A man swore.

"Watch yerself," a voice hissed. "Which room do ye s'pose is 'ers?"

They were here for her. *Why?*

Sweet Christ. This was an entanglement he didn't need right now.

Miss Cheswick thrust a pistol into his hand.

He stared at her. Especially when he realized she was holding one too. "Where in the hell . . ." he mouthed, then shook his head. It didn't matter where she'd gotten them. "Do you know how to use that?"

She nodded.

It seemed the fairer sex was bent on saving his arse tonight.

"What the devil's going on here?" came a loud booming voice. Not one of the invaders.

Ethan pressed against the door as she crashed into his back, presumably in an effort to get around him.

"Grandfather!"

There went their advantage. She reached around him and wrenched open the door. The sound of a body hitting the floor greeted them as they rushed into the corridor. Light from a sconce illuminated two burly thugs standing over an elderly gentleman in his nightclothes.

"Grandfather!" Miss Cheswick tried to rush forward. Ethan moved in front of her to block her progress.

But it didn't matter. It turned out she could shoot a man just fine right where she was.

~

*A*udrey gaped at the fallen man for a brief moment before recalling the reason she'd shot the bounder in the first place: her grandfather. Her intent to rush forward was blocked by Mr. Locke tackling her to the floor. They landed in a tangle of limbs, his face a mere inch from hers. Then he rotated his body so that he was on top of her. The sound of a bullet lodging in the wall behind them eradicated any outrage she might've felt.

But then she didn't actually *feel* any outrage. At least not toward Mr. Locke.

His gaze met hers, and his mouth was pressed into a grim line. Before she could ask if he was all right, he leapt up and launched himself toward the man who was still standing.

Audrey crawled over to her grandfather. His face was ashen, his eyes closed. Audrey clasped his hand—warm and alive. She exhaled and shot a glance at the second criminal, who was lying next to her grandfather.

The criminal's eyelid crept up, revealing a bloodshot eyeball. His lip curled. Audrey screamed.

Mr. Locke spun toward her. He looked at Audrey, his features tight.

"He's conscious!" She inclined her head toward the ruffian, who was now trying to right himself on the other side of her grandfather.

In a quick, superbly fluid move, Mr. Locke pivoted. His hand shot out and wrapped around the wrist of the criminal who was still on his feet. Mr. Locke shook the man's hand, apparently trying to wrest the knife from the other man's grip.

Wait, what had happened to the gun she'd given Mr. Locke?

Audrey glanced around frantically, finally seeing the weapon lying near the open door to her bedroom.

Mr. Locke sidled toward her until their arms were nearly touching. "I didn't think this was a simple robbery gone awry. You tell Gin Jimmy I'm a step ahead of him and I always will be."

And who was Gin Jimmy? Audrey forced herself to focus on the moment, to keep her pistol trained on the criminal.

The criminal on the floor groaned and reached for his cohort. "Help me."

"Shoot him!" Mr. Locke's elbow grazed her arm.

"No!" The standing criminal held up his hand. "We'll go." He grabbed the other's collar and pulled him up.

The wounded man wobbled to his feet. "We can't jes' go, Jimmy wants 'er."

Mr. Locke's hand covered hers and before she knew it had snatched the pistol from her. He aimed and fired, but his movement had given the men enough time to throw themselves out of the way. Rather, for the one criminal to throw himself to the floor and pull the other one back down with him.

"Go! Go!" The stocky ruffian shoved his cohort toward the stairs.

Mr. Locke moved toward them, his knife raised.

Audrey grabbed his arm and pulled. "What are you doing?" she whispered. "Let them go. We need to help my grandfather." She glanced at his bleeding arm. "And you."

He tugged his arm free of her grasp. "I can't let them escape. You heard what he said about you."

She lunged toward him and wrapped her hand around his arm again. This time she thrust her body forward into his path too. "Just what do you plan to do, kill them?"

Mr. Locke blinked at her, his long, inky lashes very briefly shuttering the gray of his eyes. He sealed his lips together, but she couldn't tell if it was due to his wound. He had to be in an enormous amount of pain after the way he'd just exerted himself.

The criminals scrambled down the corridor, their awkward movements making a clamor. Mr. Locke tried to push past her, but she held her ground. "Let them go, please."

He muttered something that sounded like a curse. He stopped trying to move past her, his body slumping.

She tightened her hold on him. "You need to sit down. Go on back to my room." She took a step and tried to guide him.

He straightened slightly. "I'm fine."

As he staggered toward her bedchamber, Audrey rushed to her grandfather, who was still unconscious on the floor. She kneeled and touched his neck. He was warm, his pulse strong. The opening and closing of drawers sounded from her bedchamber.

She stood and hurried inside to find Mr. Locke going through her dresser. "What are you doing?"

"Looking for bandages and liquor."

"Don't be ridiculous. I don't keep those things in my bedchamber."

He looked sideways at her. "Why not? You kept a pair of pistols in here."

Heat crept up her neck. "You need to sit." She hurried toward him and perched him on the edge of her bed. The entire situation was beyond scandalous, but Audrey didn't let such nonsense bother her. She went into the small dressing chamber adjoining her room and came back with a length of toweling, which she used to dab at his wound.

She couldn't see the actual wound beneath the layers of his coat and shirt. He was going to need to take his clothing off. The heat that had crept up to her face a moment ago now snaked its way much, much lower. She gently shook her head to eradicate such tri-

fle. "How did you learn to fight like that? You don't belong to Lord Sevrin's fighting club, do you?"

Mr. Locke gaped at her. "How do you know about
that? First pistols—and you're a damn fine shot—and
now this. Are you *trying* to shock me tonight?" He
gasped, which she took to mean that her ministrations
had probed a particularly painful spot.

She flashed him a weak, regretful smile. "Sorry.
Here, press this on your arm while I go find supplies."
She turned to go, a dozen tasks running through her
mind, but he clasped her elbow with his good hand.

His gaze was blisteringly intense. "Find something
here. I need to leave."

She frowned at him; his face had gone a bit ashen.
"That's absurd. You need care and rest. Furthermore, I
need to see what happened to our butler and other
staff, check on my grandfather, and send someone to
fetch Bow Street—" She stopped talking because he got
up from the bed and made his way, somewhat errati-
cally, toward the window.

A groan from the hallway drew their attention. Audrey rushed to the door and could hear Mr. Locke following. She hastened to her grandfather's side as his
eyes fluttered open.

"Audrey, dear?" His voice was rough.

"Grandfather, are you all right?"

"My head." He groaned, and his eyes closed for a
long moment.

Audrey wiped a hand over his brow. "Grandfather?"

His eyes opened again. "I'm here, gel, I'm here." His
brown gaze fixed on her and then moved past her.
"Who the devil is that? The brigand who hit me?"

Audrey looked back at Mr. Locke who stood at the
threshold to her bedroom. His features were drawn
tight—presumably with pain.

"Is that a pistol?" Grandfather drew Audrey's attention once more. "Did you shoot him, dear?"

The sound of running footsteps prompted Audrey to turn her head. Her maid, Thorpe, rushed down the corridor. "Your lordship!" She dropped to her knees beside Audrey. "I'm so sorry, Miss. I heard the men come into the house and I hid in the linen cupboard. I came up here as soon as I heard them leave!"

"Please, help Grandfather." Audrey glanced back at the doorway to her room. Mr. Locke was no longer there, and the unmistakable sounds of him trying to do something foolish, like climb back out of her window, drifted from her chamber. "I'll be right back." She leapt up and dashed into her bedroom. Sure enough, Mr. Locke had one foot thrust out the window. She rushed to him. "What are you doing?"

"Leaving." He grimaced as he grasped the tree branch with his right hand and angled his body out of the window.

"Why? Wait, who's Jagger? Was that criminal referring to you?"

He pulled his other leg outside. "Yes. I'm Jagger, but don't ask me anything else. I won't put you in danger. Aw, fuck." His shoulders slumped for a brief second. "You're already in danger. Goddamn that Gin Jimmy."

She'd heard plenty of coarse language before, but it never failed to make her blush. "Who's Gin Jimmy?"

"I told you not to ask me anything else." He gave his head a fierce shake. "Never mind, you have to come with me. It's not safe for you to stay here."

"Why not?"

"You heard what they said. They were here for *you*. And they'll try again." He glanced down at her robe. "Throw something on."

She was actually already dressed beneath her robe. She discarded the outer garment and dared to look at his reaction. He gaped at her pantaloons, open waistcoat, and shirt. She hurriedly pulled on her boots, which she'd stashed beneath her bed.

She hesitated a moment—she was worried about Grandfather. But he seemed fine, and Thorpe was with him. Still, Audrey ought to tell him she was leaving. And how would that go? *Grandfather, I'm running off with Mr. Locke because some man called Gin Jimmy wants to take me.* That sounded rather absurd. Perhaps she should leave a note . . .

"Audrey!"

She snapped her gaze up and saw the urgency in Mr. Locke's eyes. No time for a note. Besides, she'd left a note last time and that had only ruined things.

He pierced her with a sharp stare. "You come with me now or you stay. I can't protect you if you stay."

He wanted to protect her? Something inside of her unfurled and spread warmth to every darkened corner of her soul. She went to the trunk in the corner and grabbed the hat, cravat, and coat she'd put away earlier.

When she reached the window, he'd already started climbing down the tree. He grunted with the movement and she realized she still didn't have a bandage for him. She grabbed a second cravat and followed him out the window. Surely she had a minute to tell her grandfather she was leaving . . . But he'd try to stop her and she *wanted* to go. She *needed* to go. This adventure was exactly what she wanted, what she'd been looking for, and it would irrevocably change her life. A life she barely tolerated.

She heard a muffled sound and looked outside. Mr. Locke or Jagger or whatever his name was had fallen to the ground. He needed her. Grandfather had the staff—Audrey refused to think anything bad had happened to them—and Mr. Locke had no one at present.

Audrey thanked God for her above-average height as she reached for the tree and swung herself out the window. It was a challenging move, but she managed to get herself onto the branch, though she dropped her coat, hat, and the cravats. The white linen fluttered to the ground in a graceful series of swaying arcs.

"Throw that bag down!" he called up to her. "It's in the tree."

Audrey's foot nudged a bag tucked into a small hollow between the branches. She picked it up, heard the jingle of coin, and dropped it next to him on the ground. Then she shimmied her way down the tree, grateful that she was, indeed, dressed like a man. The disguise would also help, but she'd forgotten the wig she usually wore over her dark brown curls.

By the time she reached the base of the tree, Mr. Locke had righted himself and had slung the bag over his uninjured shoulder. He was also armed with a truncheon, which he must've left outside before coming up. Why had he climbed to her room in the first place?

"Let's go." He took off across the garden, moving much more efficiently than he had in the last several minutes. Maybe the fall had done him good.

Audrey plucked up her coat and pulled it on. Then she shoved the hat on her head and stuffed the cravats into the pockets of the coat. She ran after him, stopping when she reached the stone wall separating her grandfather's small rear garden from the alley that led to the Berkeley mews.

Mr. Locke turned and looked at her. The dull light of the half-moon offered just enough illumination for her to see his shadowed features. "Can you climb the wall unassisted? I'm not in much shape to help you."

She nodded. "I'll be fine. But can you do it? Tell me how I can help."

The wall was six feet tall, but there were foot and handholds in the rock.

"I'll go first," he said. He handed her the bag and truncheon. "Hold these, and then toss them over when I get to the other side."

"Please be careful."

He hesitated briefly, his gaze inscrutable in the near darkness. Then he turned and climbed over the wall, far more easily than she would have imagined possible in his currently wounded state.

"Throw the bag and the truncheon!" he called.

She tossed the club first, heard it hit the ground. Then the bag, but it made a different sound, as if he'd caught it. She tried to find the same hand and footholds he had, but her efforts took longer. When she finally pulled herself up and over the top of the wall, she was breathing heavily. She swung her body down against the other side and tried to find a foothold, but a hand on her buttocks surprised her. She squealed and let go, falling to the ground feet first.

She spun about, ready to take Mr. Locke to task for touching her in such an intimate fashion, but bit the reprimand back. What did she expect? She was taking off on a midnight adventure with a man she barely knew. An adventure she'd tried and failed to execute two years ago.

Excitement thrummed through her along with a hundred questions. "Now what?"

"You follow me and keep quiet." He turned, the bag slung over his shoulder once more, and rotated the truncheon in his grip.

"Wait." She hurried up beside him. "Tell me where we're going. Shouldn't you go home and take care of yourself?"

"I can't go home." He started forward.

She kept pace with him. "Why not?"

He stopped short and faced her. "Let me clarify one thing straightaway. There will be no questions. Do you understand?" His tone was dark, clipped, almost . . . sinister. He didn't sound anything like the charming man she'd taught to dance on two occasions.

A bead of fear slithered along her spine. He'd known those criminals—rather, they'd known him. Jagger.

What the devil was going on? What sort of adventure had she just agreed to?

I can't protect you if you stay.

Though this seemed a dangerous endeavor and every schooled and rational part of her screamed to return home, she couldn't banish the desperate words he'd uttered. The implication—that she was vital, important—sparked something deep inside of her. He made her feel like she was someone worth taking a chance for. And *no one* had ever made her feel that way before.

She nodded once at him, steeling her will. He turned and continued on toward the mews. When they drew near, he moved her into the shadows cloaking the area surrounding the massive archway that led into the courtyard.

"What are we doing here?" she whispered without thinking. No questions. She pressed her lips together in silent self-reprimand. "Sorry. Forget I asked."

He made a sound that reminded her of a muffled laugh. Before she could wonder what had provoked his sudden and surprising sense of humor, he said, "We're going to steal a phaeton."

Though loath to leave her grandfather's side, she crawled over to it and grasped it firmly.

Mr. Locke was still fighting the other criminal. Meanwhile the one on the floor was trying to get up. Blood was visible on the shirt beneath his coat, spreading out from a wound on his right upper chest.

The knife clattered to the floor, and Locke's opponent punched him squarely in the arm where he was wounded. Mr. Locke groaned, his knees bent, and for a quick, frightening second, she thought he was going to fall down. He staggered backward and managed to keep his footing.

Audrey didn't hesitate. She leapt to her feet and stepped toward them, around her grandfather. "Stop!" She leveled the pistol at the criminal who was stalking Mr. Locke. "I'll shoot you like I did your friend. Or, you can leave."

"Letting them leave isn't wise," Mr. Locke said, sounding breathless.

Audrey's toe came into contact with the knife the men had been fighting over. She kicked it toward Mr. Locke. Then she scooted toward him and addressed the criminal once more. "Help your friend up and get out."

Mr. Locke swiped up the knife with his uninjured arm. "Miss Cheswick, shoot him. *Please*."

Audrey hadn't thought before firing earlier, but now that reason had returned, she couldn't bring herself to do it again, not if there was a chance she could avoid it. Still, she kept her gaze fixed on the intruders. "I'd rather they just leave."

"For Christ's sake, they're here to—" Mr. Locke stopped short. "Why are you here?" He asked the standing criminal, a stocky fellow with a grizzled face.

The man's small, pale eyes, one of which was beginning to swell—a likely product of his quarrel with Mr. Locke—squinted. "I think ye know, Jagger."

Audrey frowned. Who was Jagger?

CHAPTER 2

*E*than knew he was shocking her, but couldn't seem to stop himself. And why bother? They were on the run, both from Bow Street and Gin Jimmy's gang. There would be plenty of shocks coming her way.

She pulled him against the corner of the archway. "You can't steal a phaeton!"

He put his finger to her lips. "Keep your voice down. How do you suggest we get out of town without a vehicle?"

"We're leaving London?" She shook her head. "Sorry, I have to ask questions. And don't tell me I can't. You're not kidnapping me, after all; I came of my own accord."

He hadn't meant to growl at her about asking questions, but he'd needed to think. They had to leave town. His usual havens were out of the question—every single one was known by at least one person who would claim loyalty to Gin Jimmy. There was a slim chance they'd defer their loyalty to Ethan, but it was a chance he couldn't take. Not with Audrey.

Christ, what was he doing with her?

Trying to save her life.

"Can you at least save your questions for later?" He

pressed her back against the brick wall and peered around the corner into the courtyard. There'd be maybe five stable lads on hand at this hour, most of them sleeping. All of them, if they were lucky. Ethan, however, feared his luck had run out.

He exhaled as he pressed his head back against the cool brick. His aches were many—his arm, his legs from running, his head from the entirety of this ruined night. All of his careful planning to lure Gin Jimmy from the rookery so that Bow Street could arrest him had been for naught. The criminal overlord had gotten away and in the process had learned that his right-hand man—Ethan—had worked to bring him down. Shit, Ethan's life wasn't worth a farthing. Especially not in London where everyone, lawman and criminal alike, would be searching for him.

He brought his head back around and looked at Audrey. It was difficult to discern every nuance of her expression in this light. He spoke in low tones. "You must heed everything I say now. No questions, no behavior that will draw unwanted attention." His gaze dipped over her manly costume. "You make a lousy gentleman, particularly with your hair sticking out like that." He reached up and lightly tugged one of the curls drooping against her neck.

She pulled the hat down more firmly on her head and notched her chin up. "I neglected to grab my wig."

He shook his head. He had plenty of questions of his own for later. "Keep your head down and lean on me. Can you play drunk?"

She hesitated, then nodded.

He doubted her. "Have you ever *been* drunk?"

"No. Unless you count having two glasses of sherry at Michaelmas."

At any other time, he would've laughed. "Just stumble and make indeterminate noises now and again."

"I can do that."

He smiled at her, appreciating her pluck. He put his uninjured left arm around her and drew her against him. His right arm continued to ache, but he'd relegated the pain to the back of his mind.

She stiffened slightly as she came against him, then relaxed. In fact, she slumped against him and he had to prop her up.

"Perhaps you could merely try to *look* incapacitated instead of actually *being* incapacitated," he whispered down at her. "I'm having a hard time supporting both of our weight in my wounded state."

She immediately corrected her posture, pulling herself away from him, but still keeping close as if she were leaning on him. "Give me a pinch or something if I'm hurting you."

Yes, Miss Audrey Cheswick was a most intrepid young woman.

He moved around the corner into the courtyard. A couple of lanterns glowed, offering just enough light for him to select their quarry, though he could probably do just as well in the dark. He'd come to these mews often as a lad and knew them nearly as well as the rookeries.

There were no stable lads about, but they wouldn't be far off—either slumbering in an empty stall or gathered around a table drinking from a bottle of this or that.

He led her to the first alcove, but it held a coach. And the next one contained a brougham. He paused and leaned against the brick again. Hitching up horses was complicated with two good arms. How in the hell was he going to manage it with only one? He leaned down, tucking his head beneath her hat, and spoke softly against Audrey's ear. "I don't suppose you know how to hitch horses to a vehicle?"

She angled her head, trying to look at him, but he

pressed her back against his shoulder. "Don't," he whispered. She needed to keep her head down to continue their ruse. Furthermore, turning to look at him would've brought her mouth dangerously close to his. It was bad enough his lips were against the delicate shell of her ear. Worse, his nose was full of her tantalizing scent—something floral, but with a bit of spice. She smelled clean, fresh, not like the women of his acquaintance who used fragrance to draw one's attention away from their lesser attributes.

"Not very well," she whispered in response to his question.

He could work with that. He pushed away from the wall, intent on finding a smaller vehicle. The sound of horses' hooves and wheels over cobblestone drove him back against the wall. "Shhh," he hissed as the carriage —or whatever it was—drew near to the courtyard.

A stable lad dashed into the center of the cobblestoned area to greet the vehicle, a jaunty two-seat cabriolet.

Perfect.

Ethan grinned against her ear. "No need. We'll take that one."

A tiger jumped out of the terribly fashionable cab, its two-person seat shielded from the elements by a dark blue cover. He exchanged words with the stable lad and then took off hastily across the courtyard back the way he came. *Even better.*

The stable boy led the horse and vehicle toward the opposite side of the courtyard. Ethan pulled his arm from around Audrey's shoulder and drew a few coins from his bag. "Wait here."

He set his bag and truncheon down beside her, then strode purposefully across the cobblestones to where the boy was leading the vehicle toward an empty stall. The boy would unhitch the horse, store the vehicle, and take care of the livestock. Or, he would if Ethan didn't have other plans.

"'Evening there," Ethan said warmly. "That's quite a piece." He nodded at the cabriolet.

As expected, the boy regarded him suspiciously. He cocked his ginger head to the side. "Who're you?"

As a lad, Ethan had offered to help the stable boys, give them a reprieve from their duties—free of charge. They'd tottered off to have an ale or play some cards upstairs, while Ethan had taken the vehicle out for a wild ride. Such a ruse wouldn't work in this instance. Ethan couldn't pass himself off as a poor young boy looking for a brush with finery. Instead, he said, "I'm a friend of his lordship's," and hoped the owner of the cabriolet was in fact a peer.

"What're ye doing 'ere?" The boy's question was laced with doubt. He kept his hand on the horse's lead.

"He bade me meet him here for a midnight ride. It appears he forgot."

The boy seemed to relax slightly. "Not surprised. 'E takes this thing out at all hours. Couple o' times 'e's been passed out inside when the tiger drops it off." The boy laughed commiseratively.

Ethan smiled. "Sounds like him. I don't suppose you'd mind if I took it out anyway?"

The boy's brow furrowed and he scratched his head. "I don't want no trouble."

"It'll be fine." Ethan grabbed the boy's hand, startling him, and dumped the coins into his palm. "It'll be our secret. I'll be back in an hour or so."

The boy stared at the coins. It was more than he'd make in a week. "Right ye are." He released the horse, touched his forehead, and ambled across the courtyard to a dimly lit room in the back corner.

Ethan moved fast. He pulled the horse around and looked to see if Audrey had watched the exchange. She was already stepping out of the stall they'd been hiding in, carrying his bag and truncheon. *Good girl.*

When she got to the cabriolet, he helped her up into it and then climbed in, wincing, beside her. He hadn't planned it, but was glad to be on her right so that she wouldn't jostle against his wound. Plucking up the reins, he turned the horse and drove them out of the courtyard.

She looked sideways at him from beneath her too-large hat. "How did you manage that?"

He steered the cab toward Piccadilly, past Devon-shire House. "Money."

"You gave him some money and he just let you take this?" She sounded incredulous. How innocent and naïve she was. People would do just about anything for money, but he wouldn't spoil her illusions. Not yet.

"I told him we were only going for a short ride."

She pulled her coat more tightly around her. "You lied."

"I did what I had to." Lying was the least of his crimes. What would the guileless young lady beside him think if she knew the depths of his wickedness? He kept his gaze fixed straight ahead as he turned the corner onto Piccadilly. The traffic was more congested here, but not terrible. It would lighten up as they traveled west.

"Do you have a destination in mind yet or are you driving blindly? I should like to know where we're going."

"Questions, questions. I'm not precisely sure of where we'll end up. We're getting out of London before those men can find you again."

She exhaled loudly, a sound of profound relief. "That's undoubtedly for the best. I hope it won't take terribly long to get there. Your wound needs attention."

He looked sideways at her. The small lanterns hanging from the sides of the cover offered a faint glow that streamed over her pale face. She was looking forward, her hands wrapped about herself. "Are you cold?" he asked.

"A bit, yes."

He reached down and pulled a flap up to cover her knees. "It's not much, but it's better than nothing."

She settled it more firmly across her legs. "Thank you." After a moment, she tried again. "Do you have a specific location in mind?"

Hell no, just out of London. He'd take them out the Knightsbridge Highway. There were plenty of inns where they could stop for the night. Two gentlemen on their way out of town. He glanced at her, wondering if she could even pass for such a thing. But apparently she already had—or had at least tried to. His curiosity was piqued.

They made their way past Hyde Park in silence. Ethan worked to keep himself upright. He felt weakened, exhausted. He blinked furiously and stiffened his spine.

"Mr. Locke," Audrey's voice rang out clear and startling after the length of quiet, "or should I call you Mr. Jagger?"

"I prefer Locke." He actually preferred Lockwood, but he wasn't quite there yet. His half-brother, Lord Jason Lockwood, might finally be willing to claim him as blood, but would he share his name?

"Is Jagger your real surname?" she asked softly. "Your mother's name?" She knew what everyone knew —that he was a bastard, Lockwood's bastard brother.

He didn't want her to know that name, and not because of his illegitimacy. If she knew even a fraction of the things Jagger had done . . . she'd never look at him with kindness again. "Yes, but as I said, I prefer Locke."

She was quiet a moment. The dark night enveloped them as they drew away from the park. "I have a lot of questions." She turned her head to look at him. "Beginning with why you came to my window tonight."

Best to stay with the truth, or at least a partial version of it. "To tend my wound. You were the closest person I knew." *And my money was stashed in your tree.*

"And how did you sustain the wound?" She looked across him, her gaze fixed on the bloodied tear in his coat. "Did a knife do that?"

"You know your weapons," he said wryly. "I have questions for you as well." Deflection was an old and welcome tool. "How does a proper young lady like you know how to fire a pistol? And why do you keep two of them in your bedroom?"

She withdrew her hand from his arm and thrust it into the pocket of her coat. Then she snapped her gaze forward. "I grew up in the country with two much older brothers and too many male cousins."

He noted she only answered one of his queries, and only barely. Just as he didn't wish to be pressed, he would allow her the same courtesy.

Silence descended once more, for a good ten minutes. Finally, she breached the void. "Are you in some sort of trouble?"

A fair conclusion for anyone with average intelligence, and he knew Audrey Cheswick well enough to know she possessed quite a bit more than that. "Perhaps." Time for more deflection. He reached his arm around her and pulled her against his side to pool their warmth. "We'll be there soon." Ethan would stop at the first inn he felt was far enough away from town.

"It's just . . ." Her voice was laced with something cold and brittle, a sadness tinged with disbelief. "I've never shot anyone before. I hope he'll be all right."

Ethan swallowed a laugh. She wouldn't find any humor in the situation, while he couldn't help but be amused by her concern for a criminal. "You shot him near the shoulder. He might have trouble with his arm for a while, but if he takes care of it, he'll be fine." Back on the street enforcing Gin Jimmy's will within the week, probably.

"You think so?" Her frame relaxed against his. "I'm pleased to hear it. I would hate to think I killed a man."

"You do realize he knocked your grandfather unconscious? And was going to kidnap you to God-knows-what fate." Ethan knew what fate, but he sure as hell wasn't going to outline it for her.

She stiffened. "You're right. I refuse to feel badly for him. Maybe he won't be able to use his arm well again. That would serve him right."

Ethan smiled into the darkness. "What a little cutthroat you are."

Just then, a man on horseback moved into the road, forcing Ethan to slow. The lights from the cabriolet illuminated the cocked pistol in his hand and the nasty leer on his face. "Stand and deliver, mate."

Ethan clenched the reins. *Fucking highwaymen.* Ethan considered running the man down, but the cabriolet wasn't a particularly heavy vehicle. The sound of a pistol cocking to his right made the final decision. A second brigand had ridden up beside them and was close enough that his shot wouldn't miss.

Audrey inhaled sharply and grabbed Ethan's elbow with both hands as if she were holding on for her life. His mind scrambled to think of how to defend her. He had the knife he'd taken from the criminal at Audrey's tucked into his boot, but he missed his familiar blade and wished he hadn't had to leave it behind in the alley. He shook his head to refocus, a problem he'd never encountered before tonight. But then he'd never had to protect a young lady before.

He also had the truncheon, which was tucked beneath his coat beside him on the seat.

"Follow what I do," he whispered urgently toward Audrey. He held up his left hand, which dislodged her grip, as well as her hat as his fingers grazed the brim. "We don't have anything for you." Not true, but there was no way he'd relinquish his bag of money, which sat on the floor of the cabriolet between their feet.

"We'll jes' see 'bout that," the highwayman to his right said.

The other one steered his horse toward them and came around to Audrey's side. Her hat had fallen to her lap, revealing her hair and face and leaving no doubt as to her sex. Ethan didn't like the way the man leered at her.

Ethan's pulse thrummed hard and fast in his veins. He wished she had a pistol to fire. The highwaymen wouldn't stand a chance.

The highwayman next to Ethan spoke again. "Pull the flap back. Slow or my friend," he nodded toward the other highwayman, "will jes' as soon kill yer bird."

Ethan's blood started to boil. He steeled himself and hoped Audrey could handle what he had to do.

He eased the cover back, exposing their legs by degrees. Audrey's tension and fear seeped into him like cold and damp on a harsh winter night. As he pushed the flap down toward their ankles, he slipped the knife from his boot and thrust it up beneath the cuff of his coat. The steel was icy against his wrist, the hilt a welcome weight against his palm.

"Wot's 'at?" the man near Audrey asked. "Looks like a bag. Toss it 'ere then."

"I don't have the strength," Ethan said, infusing his tone with pain and weakness. He held up his right arm so the highwayman on his side could see the bloodied tear in his coat. "I'm hurt. You'll have to come get it."

"She can toss it."

"Faint!" Ethan muttered, barely moving his lips.

A beat passed and then she let out a shriek before collapsing against him, her eyelids dropping.

"Fer Christ's sake. Jes' get it, Tim!" the brigand on Ethan's side called.

The highwayman slid from his horse and stepped onto the side of the cab. "We should take the gig. Never seen one this fancy." He leaned down to pick up the bag, and Ethan made his move.

He reared up and slashed at the man's neck with the knife. Blood spurted across Audrey's pantaloons and the man slumped upon her feet. Her eyes flew open and she screamed.

Ethan shoved her down, her head coming within inches of the bleeding highwayman at her feet, just as his partner's pistol discharged behind Ethan. The bullet grazed his right shoulder. With a cry, he turned and launched himself from the cab. His body connected with the highwayman, knocking him from the horse. They landed in a heap on the opposite side of the animal, near the ditch beside the road. The beast whinnied and skipped away.

Ethan gripped the knife and rolled onto his knees. The brigand was also trying to come up from his back, but Ethan was a bit faster. He lurched over the highwayman and aimed the knife for his jugular, but the man brought up his hand, earning a nasty gash across his forearm.

Another scream from the cabriolet drew Ethan's attention, allowing the highwayman to roll away. Dammit, if he wasn't distracted, the thief would be dead by now.

Ethan reared up and reached for the man, but he was already on his feet. He took off running. As Ethan made to go after him, he glanced back at the cab to check on Audrey and saw a slight figure—a boy who was maybe working with the highwaymen or maybe not—jumping down with Ethan's bag in his hands. The boy spared Ethan the slightest of glances and took off running. *With his money.*

Cursing, Ethan ran after him, but with his twice-wounded arm and the bruises he'd just sustained from attacking the highwayman, he was too slow. The boy was already disappearing into the dark night. Uttering another, much louder, curse Ethan stalked back toward the cab. Christ, Audrey! She'd screamed a second time. Had the boy hurt her? Why had Ethan been more concerned with the money than with her?

Shame washed through him as he found the strength to run back to the cabriolet.

She stumbled onto the road as he arrived, his breath coming hard and fast. Her eyes were huge in the lamplight, her face nearly white. "He's . . . he's . . . he's dead." She clapped her hand over her mouth and rushed to the side of the road.

She bent over, but Ethan couldn't be certain if she was sick. Torn between going to her and disposing of the body in the cabriolet, he decided he'd better do the latter before attempting the former.

He moved slowly to the other side of the cab, stopping briefly to reassure the horse, who'd been astonishingly calm throughout the encounter. Ethan's experience with the animals wasn't extensive, but he knew a horse attached to a vehicle of this caliber would be a well-trained beast. Thank God for that.

The highwayman was sprawled on the floor, his feet dangling over the edge of the cab. He was on his side, a pool of blood beneath his head. His eyes gazed sightlessly at the night sky. Ethan felt no remorse. In his life, the tenet of "kill or be killed" was more than an idea; it was reality.

He pulled the lifeless body out of the cab. His muscles screamed in agony at the exertion required to wrestle the large man to the ground. Then Ethan dragged the highwayman to the side of the road and pushed him over into the ditch.

When he turned around, Audrey was standing near the coach. "Why did you kill him?"

"He would've killed us."

"Would he have? Maybe if you'd given him the bag, they would've gone about their way and left us alone."

Ethan shook his head. "No, they wouldn't have. At best, they would've taken the money and you. I saw the way they both looked at you." With lust and violence gleaming in their eyes.

She brought her hands to her mouth and clenched her eyes shut.

Though agony poured through him, Ethan forced himself toward her. "Miss Cheswick. Audrey." He had no experience in soothing a distraught young woman. "He was a very bad man. A criminal." Like Ethan. He took her hands away from her face. "Look at me."

She opened her eyes slowly, revealing wariness in their depths. She averted her gaze from him and spoke softly, but firmly, "I want to go home."

He couldn't take her home. And if she went home, she'd be a sitting target for Gin Jimmy. He opted for deflection again. "Just stand here and look at the stars. Do you see Aquila, the eagle?"

She tilted her head back. After a long moment, she exhaled. "Yes."

"Good. Tell me what else you see."

He hurried back to the ditch where he pulled the highwayman's coat from his body. He glanced back at Audrey and saw that she was watching him. He pointed to the sky. "What else?"

She snapped her head back up. "I see Cygnus, the swan, and Delphinus, the dolphin."

"Excellent. Cygnus is one of my favorites." He rushed back to the cabriolet with the coat, one sleeve of which was already rather bloody. He used the rest to wipe up as much of the blood on the floor of the cab as he could.

She was quiet as he moved past her to dispose of the ruined coat, which he tossed atop the corpse. When he turned back toward her and the cab, he was suddenly and thoroughly spent. His vision blurred. His knees shook. He barely kept a grip on consciousness.

He must've swayed, because the next thing he focused on was her coming toward him.

"Are you all right?" she asked. She clasped his good arm and only just stopped from grabbing the bad one.

No, but he didn't say that. Nausea swirled in his gut. Tossing up his own accounts didn't seem like such a bad notion all of a sudden.

"We need to get off the road." She pulled him toward the cab and helped him climb up.

"I'm supposed to be helping you," he muttered.

"It's a bit late to act the gentleman, isn't it?"

Nothing she said could've stung more. He'd tried very hard to be a gentleman. It was all he bloody wanted. But it was impossible when trouble was intent on finding him. If tonight's plan had been successful, he'd be at Lockwood House toasting the arrest of one of London's worst criminals and he'd be free of his old life.

Instead, he was fleeing London with two holes in his arm and was subjecting a perfectly lovely young woman to atrocities she should never experience. Yes, it was altogether too late to be a gentleman.

He landed in the seat with a loud exhalation.

She climbed up and sat beside him, casting a look of distaste toward the floor. She didn't, however, break down, once more affirming his estimation of her intrepid spirit. "How's your arm? Should I drive?"

Ethan cradled his injured arm and winced. "Do you know how?"

"I used to drive our gig in the country. It had two horses, so this has to be simpler, doesn't it?" She picked up the reins.

Ethan wanted to argue, but he was too overcome with pain and exhaustion. He just wanted to close his eyes.

The last thing he heard was another shriek.

~

*A*udrey barely kept Mr. Locke from toppling from the cabriolet. She wrapped her arms around him and pulled him toward her, trying to be careful of his arm, but in the end, she feared she'd caused him more pain.

But now he was slumped toward her. She peered at his face in the lamplight. Dark circles, accentuated by the pallor of his skin, had formed beneath his eyes. Eyes that were closed.

"Mr. Locke?" She shook him gently. "Mr. Locke?"

He was utterly unresponsive.

She let him go, careful to angle him against her, and leaned back against the seat. Panic seared through her. Where was she to go? She couldn't stay here. One of the highwaymen had run off. He might decide to return with reinforcements.

Get a hold of yourself, Audrey. You are not a simpering featherwit.

She turned sideways and shook him again, this time more firmly. "Mr. Locke. Wake. Up." In the absence of smelling salts, she did the only other thing she could think of: She slapped his cheek.

His eyes shot open. "Ow."

"Sorry, but I had to wake you." She smoothed her hand against his stubbled cheek. The dark growth of his beard was visible. She ought to find his appearance shocking; instead she was oddly intrigued by the scratch of the hair beneath her fingers.

"No, my arm." He groaned again and cradled his wounded arm with his good one.

"You may return to your unconscious state as soon as you tell me your plan. Where am I to drive?"

His head rolled back against the seat and he closed his eyes. His pale throat was elongated above the twisted knot of his cravat. He looked a gentleman, despite his unshaven state, but he'd done things tonight she doubted most gentlemen could—or would—do. "An inn," he said weakly. He tried to sit up, but barely moved. His breath came in sharp gusts, like he'd run a great distance.

He pierced her with his intense gray stare, eyes she'd looked into before as she'd taught him to waltz. She'd wondered why he hadn't learned before, but had been too shy to ask. It would join the list of questions she'd formed tonight.

"Be careful. Not all of the inns are . . ." His head lolled back against the seat and his eyes shuttered once more.

"Not all of the inns are what?" She willed him to open his eyes again, to answer her, but he didn't stir. His chest rose and fell with his breath, rapidly at first, and then slowing to a sleeping rhythm.

She repositioned herself on the seat and picked up the reins again. It took a few tries, but she managed to get the horse moving. The road was dark as pitch and rather uneven. She was glad Mr. Locke was unconscious because the constant bump and jostle would've caused him no small amount of pain.

Her mind traveled over the course of the night. She'd started it with scandalous behavior—a quick glance down at her gentleman's costume affirmed that —and she was ending it in much the same manner. If anyone knew that she was alone with Mr. Ethan Locke, she'd be completely ruined.

As if it mattered. What sort of marriage prospects did she have? None. Her parents would be horrified; she'd scandalized them before, but that would be the extent of things. Oh, she supposed she wouldn't go to any more balls or parties, but what was the point of them anyway? She propped up the wall and visited with her small circle of friends, things she could do anywhere, anytime.

Should she turn back to London? No, she wanted to find shelter as soon as possible, and there was nothing behind her for a few miles. However, returning home meant she could preserve her reputation. Her stomach roiled, not with the same gut-wrenching sickness the dead highwayman had provoked, but with a gripping tension that accompanied thoughts of the life that awaited her in London. The life she'd tried so hard to appreciate and succeed at, and she'd failed miserably on both counts.

Yet when she thought of the last hour, her body thrummed with exhilaration—dead highwayman notwithstanding. She flinched. What sort of person did that make her? She'd shot a man, committed larceny, and witnessed a murder. No, surely it wasn't murder since Mr. Locke had been defending her.

And what sort of person was Mr. Locke? He'd fought off the intruders at her house, orchestrated the theft of the cabriolet, and saved her from the highwayman. She couldn't fault him for any of those things, only the manner in which he'd done them. And yet, she was invigorated by him.

The cabriolet moved forward. Away from London. Away from the life she didn't really want. A sense of rightness settled over her. Whatever happened now, things would be different. She relaxed into the seat and smiled softly. The one thing she would do upon arriving at the inn would be to draft a short note to Grandfather, assuring him of her well-being. She didn't want him to worry, but neither did she want to give details about where she was or why.

The sound of hooves clopping in the dirt drew her

to sit up straight and search the darkness. She prayed to God it wasn't another highwayman. Where on earth was an inn? She needed to get off this blessed road!

The horseman came into view. And rode straight into the center of the road, just as the highwayman had done.

CHAPTER 3

*L*ight blistered the backs of Ethan's eyes. He turned his head to try to evade the intrusive glare and promptly groaned at the shard of pain that sliced through his temple. Tentatively, he opened his eyes. He stared at the ceiling over his head, registered that he was in a bed, and that his arm was on fire.

Memories of the previous night rushed over him. *Audrey.*

He pushed himself up, wincing with the pain the movement wrought. A thorough scan of the room revealed it to be empty. It was narrow, with two slender windows on either side of his bed. A small table and a rough-hewn chair sat before the hearth, which held a smoldering fire. Though sparse, the space appeared clean and well-kept. And completely foreign.

Where was he? Was Audrey near? God, he hoped nothing had happened to her. He didn't remember a thing after dragging the body of the highwayman from the cab.

He swung his legs over the edge of the bed. He still wore his breeches, but the rest of him was quite bare, save the bandages covering his right bicep and shoulder. Who had tended his wounds? More importantly, who had removed his clothing?

The door opened and Audrey stepped over the threshold. She carried several garments folded over her arm. Her gaze connected with his and she smiled. "Good morning!" she said cheerily, as if she hadn't seen things last night that no proper young lady should.

And she looked like a proper young lady this morning—gone was her gentleman's garb. A simple gray frock hung a bit loosely from her frame, and it was too short for her taller than average height. Her hair was pulled up haphazardly. Errant curls tumbled here and there. She looked fresh and lovely, not at all like she'd been to hell and back the night before.

She set the clothing on the chair next to the table and bustled toward him. "You shouldn't be up."

"Where are we?" he croaked, as if he'd spent the night drinking too much gin in a flash house.

She waved at his feet, directing him to put them back on the bed. However, she kept her gaze fixed on his face. "An inn. Don't you remember?"

He complied and brought his legs back up, though he kept them atop the coverlet. "Should I?"

Her brows gathered in an adorably perplexed expression. "You seemed at least semiconscious, but perhaps you weren't." She fluffed up the pillow. "You should lie down."

"May I have something to drink first?" He had no intention of lying down.

"Certainly, I should have thought of that straightaway." She went to the table, where there was a pitcher and a cup. She returned to him with water, which he drank greedily.

He handed her the empty cup. "Thank you."

She kept her gaze focused on his face. He recognized that his lack of attire was completely scandalous to someone like Audrey. The gentleman he was trying to be urged him to put on a shirt, but the wounded animal he currently felt like didn't give a damn.

"What happened last night? I'm assuming I lost consciousness. How did you get us here?" Shit, they didn't have any money since that boy had stolen his bag from the cab. How was she paying for this?

She turned and went to the chair. When she came back, she handed him a shirt. "Maybe you could put this on?" Her gaze dipped to his bare chest and dainty little roses bloomed in her cheeks.

Ethan leaned back against the wall behind the bed. A jolt of satisfaction shot through him. Audrey was a beautiful woman, intelligent, and able to handle herself. In any other circumstance he'd tumble her into the bed. Just then a stabbing pain in his arm reminded him that tumbling of any kind might be a few days off.

He took the proffered shirt. "I'm not sure I can raise my arm up to get this on. At least not without help."

Her blush deepened. "I can help you."

He sat forward from the wall and drew the shirt over his head. Thrusting his left arm into the sleeve was no problem. He looked at her and she helped lift his right arm and slide it into the shirtsleeve.

"I don't suppose you helped me out of my clothes last night?"

She pulled the shirt down his back and stepped quickly away from the bed. Her maidenly sensibilities were charming. "Yes, with the innkeeper's wife's assistance. We had to burn the clothes, however."

"Yet, you found new ones, as well as lodgings, and treated my wounds—"

She cut him off. "Yes, *wounds*. Why didn't you tell me you'd been shot?"

"If you recall, we didn't exactly have time for idle conversation. I was terribly distracted by those foul highwaymen—and that lad who stole my money." He peered at her intently. "I'm afraid to ask how you're paying for this room and my care."

Her eyes widened and he belatedly realized his comment could have been taken in a rather perverse way. He added, "I didn't mean to suggest you're doing anything untoward. You are, I'm certain, above reproach."

She glanced away. "Clearly not, since I fled London with you." When she returned her gaze to his, she revealed a quiet dignity in the depths of her blue-green gaze and he knew in that moment that he was right— she *was* above reproach. And not just by Society's standards. She was a good and honest person at heart. The type of person who should run screaming from the likes of him.

"I had money in a purse sewn inside my pants," she said.

His mouth sagged open for a moment before he snapped it closed. "Your pants. Why the devil were you even wearing pants? And why did you have money sewn into them? Thank God you did."

"Yes, thank goodness I did, though I suspect the Bow Street Runner would've paid for our lodgings."

Ethan's blood ran cold. His legs itched to run. He mentally calculated how quickly he could finish dressing and get out of the inn. Except he didn't know the layout, which put him at a very distinct disadvantage. Any criminal worth his salt knew every way to escape a building before he entered it. "What Bow Street Runner?"

"The one who was thankfully patrolling the highway last night. I encountered him after you fell asleep, and he guided us to this inn."

And not directly to Bow Street? Ethan relaxed, but only slightly. "What did you tell him?"

She blinked at him, appearing a little uncertain, perhaps because he'd asked that question in a rather ferocious tone. "I said we were attacked by highwaymen."

He modulated his question this time. "What did you tell him about us?"

"Oh!" She flashed a beguiling smile that did odd things to his belly. He found her quite attractive, but it was more than that. He didn't like it. "I told him my name was Mary St. Clyde and that you were my brother, Algernon."

"Algernon?"

She lifted a shoulder. "To be fair, I only called you Al."

"What a god-awful name." That she'd taken the time to come up with aliases and even a nickname for him only proved her cunning and courage. He looked away from her. "Smart girl." *Dangerous girl.* "Why'd you lie?"

"I thought it best to protect my identity for now. My reputation will likely be ruined, but then I have no intention of returning to my life in London, so it really doesn't matter." She squared her shoulders as if in response to some silent conversation going on inside of her. He wanted to ask what she intended to do, but she continued before he could open his mouth.

"The Runner was kind enough to lead us to this inn, which he knew to be reputable. You'd cautioned me about the inns, but I'm afraid you slipped from consciousness before explaining. The Runner said some of the establishments along the highway are in league with the highwaymen, is that what you meant?"

"Yes." And with Gin Jimmy. "Where are we exactly?"

"Hounslow."

Jimmy's reach extended at least this far, which meant they needed to get back on the road. And go where? His experience with the country was limited to a few summer visits to his father's estate in northern Oxfordshire. But they couldn't go there, his brother's mother lived there and she was ill. Plus, she despised Ethan like fire hates water.

He looked back to Audrey who was watching him expectantly. "Where's the Runner now?"

"I don't know," she said. "He guided us here and was going to go back to take care of the dead highwayman." She cringed and looked at the floor. "Sorry, I had to tell him what happened, that you'd killed him defending me. I know he was a terrible criminal, but he at least deserves to be buried."

Is that all she thought a terrible criminal deserved? If she knew how terrible he'd been . . .

"You look worried." She took a step toward the bed. "He's coming back to talk to you. Do you think we should tell him the truth?" Her shoulders slumped. "I suppose we should."

"No." He spoke without thinking, but there was no other answer. The truth would reveal his true identity —that of a notorious criminal—not only to her but to Bow Street, which was already looking for him in order to charge him with the murder of the Marquess of Wolverton and for organizing the death of Lady Aldridge. Ironically, they were two crimes he hadn't actually committed. No one would believe that, however. No one save his brother, who'd only just decided to trust him last night. That thought gave Ethan a very small amount of relief.

"You still haven't told me why you needed to leave London. Or why you were climbing up the tree outside my window."

And he didn't plan on answering those questions now. "Assuming I'm identified as the man who was in your house last night, I think it's fair to also assume Bow Street will think I've kidnapped you. For that reason alone, I should prefer to avoid not only Bow Street, but also the entirety of London."

Her eyebrows—slender brown swathes that made

her forehead impossibly elegant with the way they swept over her incredible eyes—slanted down. She shook her head once. Definitively. "That doesn't address why you were climbing the tree outside my window."

"Perhaps you'd care to tell me why you were wearing men's clothing?" Her eyes widened and she shook her head again as definitively as before. "Then I guess we're both going to keep a few secrets."

She exhaled, then went over to the window. Her long fingers parted the curtains and she looked down. He remembered those fingers entwined with his when she'd taught him to waltz. He longed for those fingers—

She dropped the curtain and abruptly turned. "He's back."

~

*M*r. Locke swore again. He swore an awful lot, more than any other gentleman of her acquaintance, but then she had to consider whether he was truly a gentleman. She wouldn't really know unless he unveiled his secrets, and since she wasn't willing to share hers, she couldn't blame him for guarding his.

He climbed out of bed, grimacing in pain as he pushed himself to his feet.

She rushed to his side. "Let me help you."

"We need to leave. Now."

"Sit, I'll get the rest of the clothing." She hurried to the chair and grabbed what the innkeeper's wife had found besides the shirt—a coat, a cravat, and fresh stockings. She handed him the latter and then realized he couldn't put them on with his wounded arm. Taking them back, she kneeled before him and pulled the first one onto his left leg. She tried not to pay any attention to his bare calf. Or the fact that her bare fingers were

touching that calf. Mostly, she tried not to pay attention to how much she enjoyed it.

When both of his stockings were on, she went to
grab his boots, which were at the end of the bed. She
set them before his feet and helped him draw them on.

"This is bloody awkward," he breathed. He stood up
from the bed and worked to tuck in the hem of his
shirt. "Go and see if he's still outside."

She went to the window and looked back down into
the courtyard. "There are two men on horses, but neither one of them is the Runner. There are also two
empty horses being held by a groom."

Another curse, this one quite colorful. "Help me
with the coat."

She dashed to assist him, again guiding his right
arm into the sleeve. "The innkeeper's wife didn't have a
waistcoat." Belatedly, she realized she could've given
him the waistcoat she'd been wearing, but after Audrey
removing her purse from the pants, she'd traded the
costume to the innkeeper's wife for the garments she
was now wearing. She'd also borrowed a needle and
thread, and had stitched the small purse to the top of
her stocking. On second thought, her waistcoat
wouldn't have fit his broad shoulders.

With his one good arm, he wrapped the cravat
around his neck so that it hung loose. "Do you know
where the back stairs are?"

"I don't."

He grasped her hand and pierced her with his devastating gray stare. "Tell me everything you know about
this establishment. How many doors, how many floors,
how many people might be about."

She swallowed. He was looking at her so . . . expectantly. No, that wasn't wholly accurate. There was an
intensity about him, the same he'd displayed last night
in every situation they'd encountered. Again, she wondered about his true nature.

She searched her brain for whatever details she could recall from their late arrival the previous night, or rather, quite early this morning. "There's a door to the rear yard. But I don't know another way downstairs besides the main staircase—we're on the second floor."

He'd gone to the window while she'd explained what she knew. "Is it a large inn? How many rooms?" He pulled back the curtain and swore violently. He spun about and marched toward her. "Time to go." He snagged her elbow and propelled her toward the door.

She went along, her veins icing at the desperation in his tone. It wasn't fear, but he was clearly anxious to leave. Which made her anxious.

He paused in the corridor. "Which way?"

"Right."

Voices sounded from that direction—not close, but there nonetheless.

"Left, then." He let go of her elbow and strode down the hallway. His boots made very little sound as he moved, and his gait reminded her of a cat stalking its prey—soft, but surefooted. "You didn't answer me before. Is this a large inn?"

"I suppose. I think she said they had ten rooms of varying size?"

"They must have a servant staircase." He stopped at a door and cracked it open. Then pulled it closed. He moved to the next one, on the opposite side of the hallway from the first, and did the same. Again, he closed the door and moved on. At the third door, he pushed it wider. She came up behind him and saw that it was a narrow staircase.

He glanced back at her. "Quietly," he whispered, bringing his finger to his lips.

Light from a small window illuminated the stairs. He descended swiftly, but stealthily. She closed the door behind her and followed close on his heels, trying to keep her steps as light as his. They reached the door at the bottom. He pulled it open slowly until the barest gap separated the door's edge and the frame. He peered through the slim space.

Audrey's breath hitched, her ears strained to pick up the faintest sound, and sweat dotted the back of her neck.

He angled his head toward her. "Which way is the common room?"

She thought about the layout. "Left. Maybe thirty feet."

He nodded slightly, then pulled the door wide. He grabbed her hand and turned right. He stopped at the first door on the right and turned to look at her. "How much money do you have?"

"A bit."

"Give me a guinea." He was asking for money at a time like this?

"A *guinea*? What for?"

"Just give me the bloody guinea."

She withdrew her hand from his and lifted the skirt of her borrowed dress. Aware she was revealing far more of her leg than she'd ever allowed a gentleman to see, she quickly withdrew the coin from her purse and dropped her skirt. She deposited the guinea into his hand.

Wordlessly, he curled his fingers around it and opened the door. He tugged her into the chamber, a room slightly larger than the one he'd awakened in upstairs.

He glanced around the room. "There's no one here." Then he rushed toward the window and threw open the sash. "Come on. Quickly."

She joined him near the window. "You were expecting someone? It's nearly noon. I'm sure the traveler left long ago."

"Damn, I didn't realize it was that late. You should've said so."

She didn't care for his scolding tone. "Pardon me, but you didn't ask."

He gestured for her to precede him from the window. "Just climb out the window, so we can be on our way."

Right. Escape. Or, she could stay here and return to London with the Bow Street Runners. She wanted to know why he was running, but the question died on her tongue when she looked into his eyes. The desperation and anxiety she heard in his voice was mirrored there.

He muttered something under his breath and clambered out of the window, albeit awkwardly since his arm wouldn't quite cooperate. Lines of pain creased his face.

"Wait," she said softly before following him. She wasn't going to let him go off alone. Besides, she'd left London with him for a reason. This was the adventure she'd always wanted, the life-changing escapade that would satisfy her soul.

He lightly massaged his wounded bicep. "Where's our cab?"

Technically speaking, it wasn't *their* cab, but she didn't think now was the right time to remind him of that. "It's in the stables on the other side of the courtyard." Another foul curse. She couldn't help herself this time. "You do realize you're in the presence of a lady?"

He peered at her askance. There was a subtle lift to his lips. "Who wears gentleman's garments, stashes money about her person, and can fire a pistol better than most men. Despite all of that, yes, I realize." He held out his hand. "Are you still with me?"

She slid her fingers through his. "Yes."

"Then let's go." He led her from the back yard area to a low stone wall. It took little effort to vault the impediment, but he groaned with the effort nonetheless.

She hated that he was hurting. "You shouldn't be out of bed."

Once they were both on the other side of the wall, he took her hand again. "I can't stay back there."

"Dare I hope you'll tell me why at some point?"

"Something tells me you'll dare plenty." The look he threw her was both dark and seductive. It heated the depths of her belly.

She looked away just as a shout came from behind them—from the inn. They both stopped and turned to look, but didn't see anyone. There was more shouting, but she couldn't make out what they were saying.

He let go of her hand. "We need to run."

Without waiting for a response, he took off across the field. She worked to keep up with him, which was difficult in her dress. Why had she changed clothes? If she'd known they were going to be dashing about the countryside, she wouldn't have. She let go of his hand so she could hike her skirt up and allow her legs more freedom with which to run. And she had to flat out sprint to keep up with him.

How was he moving so quickly? He'd been grievously injured the night before, and he hadn't eaten anything today. By all accounts, he should be exhausted and feeble. Instead, he was running as if his life depended on it. Perhaps it did.

Audrey chanced a look back at the inn and saw a few figures in the rear yard. "I think they're coming," she huffed.

He didn't turn his head, but increased his pace as he dodged to the left where there was a hedge. He ran along it, and she thought he was trying to find a way through so they could get on the other side in order to shield them from their pursuers.

At last there was a space where the foliage wasn't as thick, but it wasn't really large enough for an adult to fit through. He came to a stop and parted the branches. "Go on."

She was breathing heavily, and pitched slightly forward due to the hitch in her side. Unlike him, she'd had a good-sized breakfast a couple of hours ago and she felt every bite of it like a rock in her stomach. "I can't fit through there, how can you?"

"Go!" He spoke softly but urgently, and his eyes were the color of winter storm clouds.

She pushed her hands through to separate the branches and stuck one foot into the shrub. Then he shoved her and she fell on the other side of the hedge in an awkward heap. She clamped her jaw shut lest she voice the jolt of pain in the leg she'd landed on. He came through next, barely sidestepping her before taking off again.

She pushed herself up and regained her bearings. Dirt and mud clung to her dress, but she didn't take the time to tidy herself. Mr. Locke was already running toward a building several hundred yards away. She picked up her skirts again, still breathing hard from the last sprint, and took off after him. Light raindrops fell against her bare head, and again she wished she'd retained her gentleman's clothing, especially the hat.

It seemed to take a lifetime to finally reach the building, a dilapidated stable belonging to an equally dilapidated cottage situated beyond the stable. Mr. Locke was already inside grabbing implements to . . . saddle a horse? She looked around, but didn't spy any animal at all, let alone a horse.

She glanced outside and saw four men running across the field. There was no door to shut and lock, it was just an open doorway. She stepped further into the interior, toward Mr. Locke. "They'll be here in another minute."

He didn't respond, nor did he look at her. He exited the building through a doorway on the other side. Audrey followed him quickly, her boots kicking the straw and dirt beneath her feet.

The doorway led to a small enclosure, where a single horse grazed. Mr. Locke was already in the process of bridling the animal. Once he had the bit in the horse's mouth, he threw a blanket over the beast's back and finally turned to Audrey. "You can choose to stay. All I ask is that you lead them away from me."

"And how shall I do that when I don't know where you're—we're—going?" She considered staying, she would be a fool not to, but the pull of the adventure was too strong. Or perhaps, the pull of her old life was simply nonexistent. "No, I'm going with you."

The unmistakable sound of their pursuers entering the stable prevented further conversation. Mr. Locke put his hands together and boosted her onto the horse, then she helped him clamber up behind her. He groaned, and she imagined the movement must have hurt him greatly.

"Can you take the reins?" he asked against her ear.

It would be difficult with no saddle to help her keep her seat, but his support helped. "Hold on to me."

His arms wrapped around her middle and his chest pressed against her back. She clicked her tongue and dug her knee into the horse's flanks just as the men came into the yard.

"Stop, Jagger!" There was that name again.

The gate to the enclosure wasn't open. Audrey hadn't jumped a horse in a long time. "Hold on tight!"

Mr. Locke's arms squeezed her midsection as she vaulted over the fence. She felt him slide away from her as they arced over, but then he slammed against her as they hit the ground. She pressed her knee into the horse again and urged her faster. Shouts and curses sounded from behind them, but faded quickly. Exhilaration and joy swept through her as she left their pursuers behind.

Several minutes later, she allowed the horse to slow to a less frantic gallop.

"What are you doing?" Mr. Locke asked. His breath tickled her neck. "They'll go back to the inn and get their horses and continue their pursuit. We need to put as much distance between us and them as possible."

"We can't run the horse that fast indefinitely, best to conserve her energy. Isn't that right, sweet girl?" Audrey patted the horse's neck.

Mr. Locke grunted in response.

"How's your arm?" she asked, concerned that he'd reinjured himself with all of that exertion.

"Awful. But it's better than the alternative. Where are you going?"

"I don't know." She glanced up at the gray sky, trying to discern the position of the sun and therefore the direction they were headed. The light rain had stopped, but it looked like a stronger downpour might be coming. "North, maybe? It's going to rain again soon. We should find shelter."

"We aren't stopping. Change direction."

She turned the horse west. She was quiet a few minutes, straining to hear if anyone was pursuing them. She knew Mr. Locke had turned his head several times trying to ascertain the same. "Is there anyone coming?" she finally asked.

"Not yet."

She had no idea where they were going, besides vaguely west, maybe southwest actually. There was no sign of a road, but she figured he preferred to stay away from them anyway. "Are you going to tell me why you're running from Bow Street?"

"It's a long story. A misunderstanding."

"That's not terribly reassuring." Had she fled London with a criminal? It was certainly beginning to seem like it. "You can trust me—haven't I proven that?"

"I don't trust anyone."

It was a simple statement, and one that could be disregarded as the declaration of a man who was weary with fatigue and the effects of his wounds. However, his tone reflected a conviction she felt into her bones. "That sounds very lonely."

"It is." His grip around her waist loosened and he sat back from her, though it would've been impossible for them to not be touching in some way. His hips were still snug against her backside, and his chest was close enough to her back that she felt his heat.

She didn't want him to feel lonely. "Well, you aren't alone anymore, and I'll tell you again that you can trust me. I hope you will. However are we going to get on if we can't trust each other?"

"Get on? Just what do you think we're doing?"

She had no idea, she just knew it was better than what she *had* been doing. "You have no plan whatsoever, do you? Luckily for you, I do."

"You do?" He couldn't have sounded more incredulous, which suffused Audrey with a mixture of irritation and pride.

"I do. We're about two days from Wootton Bassett."

"What's a Wootton Bassett, some sort of dog?"

She smiled in spite of the situation—which she had no means of classifying. "No, a town. I know people who live there and we can at least get decent clothing and rest for a while to get you healed. I would prefer to stop sooner, but I doubt you'll agree to that."

"You're a very smart young woman. The distance of Wootton Bassett from London sounds perfect." He fell silent a moment. When he spoke again, his voice was low and vibrated through her like a song. "Why are you helping me?"

As he asked, he sounded equally as incredulous as he had a few minutes ago, but there was something more. There was a disbelieving quality that was perhaps at the root of his distrust. "Because you helped me.

You saved me and my grandfather from those men. And you let me come with you." She felt him shaking his head behind her.

"Probably a foolish decision."

"Why?"

"You really have to ask?" Scorn laced his tone. "Bow Street is already after me, and now I've kidnapped a young lady."

"You didn't kidnap me."

"I doubt they'll see it that way."

"They *will* see it that way. I had the inn post a note to my grandfather telling him I was safe." She felt him tense behind her and rushed to say, "I didn't tell him where we were going or who I was with. I've made that mistake before."

"What?" Was there a bead of respect in his question?

Her lips curved into the softest of smiles. "I ran away with the blacksmith's son two years ago."

"Good Christ, you didn't."

"I did." She sighed, exhaling the regret she always felt when she thought of the ill-fated venture. "Unfortunately, I left a note and it didn't take my parents too long to find us at an inn."

"Were you eloping?"

"No, I wasn't in love with him, nor was he in love with me. We were friends who wanted different lives. I didn't want to be married off to some rich lord I didn't like, and he didn't want to become a blacksmith."

"So you simply ran away." Again his breath tickled her neck, causing a shiver to cascade down her spine. She tried to keep herself stiff, lest he become aware of her reaction to his proximity.

"We had a plan—we were going to America. My mistake was in telling my parents that in the note. They were able to track us to an inn on the way to the coast where we'd planned to book passage on a ship." Memories of that awkward evening crowded into her mind, but she pushed them away.

"Who financed this excursion—you or the black-smith's son?" He asked the question in a way that inferred he already knew the answer. Damn him for asking, for reminding her of her poor judgment.

The familiar heat that accompanied recollections of her failed adventure crept up her neck. She was glad he couldn't see her face. "I did."

"And what happened to the blacksmith's son?"

Her jaw clenched, but she forced the words out. "My parents let him go off to America—they paid his passage."

He pulled his hands back from her waist so that he only barely gripped her sides. "How convenient for him." He splayed his palms against her ribcage. Though the shift in his touch was subtle, she felt suddenly and wholly *caressed*. Then his mouth was close against her ear, closer than it had ever been. "If I ever find my way to America, he'd best watch his back."

There was no quashing the appreciative tremor his words provoked within her. She only hoped he didn't feel it.

CHAPTER 4

Though they were tired and hungry, Ethan had forced her to ride to the outskirts of Reading. They'd found a small inn where they'd pretended to be a young couple by the name of Miller. Such a ruse had required them to rent just one room, which also happened to be all the tiny facility had to offer.

Ethan liked the place because it was on a quiet lane with an easy escape route. Their bedroom faced the road and he left the window open so he could hear anyone approach.

Dinner had been a simple affair of beef and potatoes, but both he and Audrey had satisfied their hunger. Then they'd retreated to their chamber, a small square room with a bed, a fireplace, a spindly table with implements for washing, and one chair.

Audrey strode directly to the pitcher on the table and poured water into the washbasin beside it. "Time to tend your wound. Sit." Her tone was so adorably commanding that he allowed himself to be managed.

The chair was situated near the fire, which had been stoked by the innkeeper while they'd eaten. His arm was sore, but he'd become accustomed to the dull ache, and it was better than the sharp pains he'd endured last night as he'd fought to keep them safe.

She came to his side and helped him out of his coat. He winced as the garment moved over his injuries. She'd tied his cravat before they'd gone into the inn earlier, and now he unthreaded the linen and pulled it from his neck. She took the cloth from him and set it over a hook on the wall where she'd hung his coat.

Now his shirt would have to come off. He looked up at her standing beside his chair. Her gaze was focused on the hearth behind him, giving proof to the discomfort she felt. But what was causing her discomfort? It could be any number of things, and he had no indication she shared the undeniable attraction he felt in her presence. What a bloody nuisance that was too. This entire escapade would be a damn sight easier if he didn't like her or find her alluring. He wished he could put her at ease, but the fact was he needed her help. "You'll have to assist me with my shirt again."

She nodded imperceptibly. "Put your left arm up." He did as she bade and she eased the garment up his arm and over his head so that only his right arm was still encased. Then she slid it from him without causing him even the slightest discomfort.

"Well done." He looked up to find her watching him.

Her cheeks pinked. Then she snapped her gaze to his arm as she worked to undo the bandage she'd affixed that morning. Presumably. He had absolutely no recollection of anything she'd done.

She pressed lightly at his flesh, causing him to bite his cheek and to question why he hadn't asked the innkeeper for a bottle of brandy. "I think the poultice the innkeeper's wife used last night is working. And she was kind enough to give me a small jar." She pulled the medicinal from her skirt pocket.

He looked over at the wound—or wounds; he actually had two, he recalled—seeing them for the first time. His eyes widened in surprise. "I slept through someone sewing my flesh together?"

"Not exactly." She went to the basin where she dipped the edge of a towel into the water. When she returned, she cleaned around the stitches of the knife wound. The gunshot's graze looked like it had barely pierced his skin, for a long, red welt was all that remained.

She opened the jar and smoothed some of the liniment over his injuries. "You swore even worse than you do when you're conscious. You condemned both me and the innkeeper's very pleasant wife to a fate worse than hell. I shan't repeat the specifics."

This made him feel a bit better, or maybe it was the slight humor playing about her lips. "How long do the sutures need to remain in? And who will take them out?" He didn't fancy trying to cut them out himself.

She retied the bandage around his arm, her slender fingers working deftly. "She said maybe as long as a fortnight, but that I would be able to tell, and she told me how to remove them."

"I see. And how did this estimable woman come about her medical knowledge?"

She peered at him, her aqua eyes luminous in the firelight. "You don't trust anyone at all, do you?"

"No. But you admit it's odd to find a woman with the ability to stave off putridity from setting in. That knife wound cut fairly deep, did it not?"

She grimaced as she tied off the bandage. "It did. We were very fortunate that she was able to help you. Don't question a gift from Fate."

He wouldn't, particularly in his current predicament. "I should like more of them."

"Wouldn't we all?" she murmured. She moved away from his chair and stood before the fire. "There's only one bed."

He knew this would be a problem, but didn't care to sleep in the chair or on the floor. His entire body was aching and sore from the events of last night and from spending all day riding a horse. He hadn't ridden that much since his father had taken him to his country estate, and that had been fifteen years ago.

"It's big enough for both of us," he said. "I promise to keep my hands to myself. It's not as if I can move very well."

She glanced at him, her gaze briefly landing on his bare chest. She wrung her hands, then smoothed them down the folds of her skirt. Apprehension and anxiety radiated from her and filled the tiny room.

"I'll sleep on the floor." She didn't look at him. "You should take the bed."

"Horse—" He caught himself before swearing again. He really needed to stop doing that around her. "Nonsense. There's a blanket at the edge of the bed. Roll it up and put it between us as a barrier. Will that suffice?"

She snuck a quick glance in his direction. "I suppose." She still sounded doubtful.

What he was about to ask wasn't going to help matters, but it had to be done. "I, ah, I'll need your help removing my boots."

Her head snapped up. "Oh." She came toward him and he prayed she wouldn't kneel at his feet. He recognized he was attracted to her, but he hadn't taken things further in his mind. He hadn't allowed himself to feel outright desire. But then, dear God, she kneeled, and for the first time, his body tightened with lust in her presence. He forced himself to look away and steeled his nerves for her touch.

Her fingers wrapped around his calf and drew the boot from his foot. Then she repeated the action on the second leg and quickly stood. By the time he dared look at her, she'd retreated to the other side of the bed and was busily rolling up the blanket.

After she'd placed the barrier in the middle of the bed, she crawled beneath the coverlet. "Sleep well," she said as she turned to her side.

He was about to ask why she was sleeping fully clothed, but decided even he wasn't that much of a brute. She was a chaste young woman and he would let her be.

For the hundredth time, he asked himself what the hell he was doing with her. She *was* a chaste young woman whom everyone probably thought he'd kidnapped. Or at least Bow Street would think that. What did anyone else know of her disappearance? Dread curdled his gut.

Did his brother think he'd kidnapped her? They'd only just reached some sort of accord. Ethan hoped Jason would give him the benefit of the doubt. Logically, however, Ethan had to ask why he would. Ethan had given Jason very little reason to trust him and had made it clear he couldn't trust anyone in return.

Jason's fiancée, Lydia, was Audrey's closest friend. She had to be overwrought with worry. He grimaced against the twinge of regret. He wished there was a way he could communicate to them what had happened and that Audrey was safe, but he daren't send any correspondence. Bow Street was too close.

Ethan stretched his legs out and slid down the chair until the back of his head rested against the top.

For the first time in over a decade, he had no firm plan. His father had died when Ethan was ten, leaving him and his mother with nothing save the small house he'd purchased for her when Ethan had been born. The house would've been a decent legacy, if his mother hadn't sold it to settle debts. When she'd joined his father in death four years later, Ethan had been cast into the world alone with only his mother's former lover, Davis, to guide him. With no money and no prospects, Ethan had consented to train as a thief-taker at Davis's side. Until Ethan had been forced to choose his own life over Davis's.

Ethan had spent the years since living by that creed

—survive at any cost. He still lived by it, or he might not have killed that highwayman. An image of Audrey's terrorized expression stole into his brain. He squeezed his eyes shut to banish it. He'd tried to change, dammit. He wanted to change. He'd established a relationship with Jason, the only family he had left, and he wanted it to continue. It was the whole reason he'd executed the failed plan to take Gin Jimmy down. The permanent removal of Gin Jimmy was the only way Ethan could be truly free of the criminal life he regretted.

Disgust knifed through him. The future he wanted with Jason was gone. The minute Ethan set foot back in London, he would be arrested for murder, tried, and likely hanged. Or, mayhap Gin Jimmy's men would get to him first and his fate would be far worse. Since neither option was acceptable, that left leaving the life he wanted behind.

But for what? Jaunting around the countryside with Audrey?

He pushed himself up from the chair and went to the bed. She was still on her side with her back to him, the coverlet pulled to her ears. Her dark curls were drawn up, but several of them had escaped their pins. They lay in stark contrast against the ivory pillow beneath her head. He longed to loop his finger through one of them and satisfy his curiosity regarding its softness. Since the days of their secret waltzing lessons, he'd admired the beauty of her hair, which seemed to have a mind of its own with the way it unerringly escaped from any proper style.

He lay down on the bed and stretched out his aching muscles, save his arm, which wouldn't put up with such activity.

She was a proper young lady. Who'd escaped London with him, and had opted to continue along with him for the sake of adventure. Had she really tried to run off to America? He could imagine her sailing for an unknown land, her hair exhibiting a similar independence and working its way completely free from its reins, blowing haphazardly and beautifully in the salty breeze. He could join her, start anew in America.

What a load of horseshit. He was Ethan bloody Jagger. No, *Lockwood*. Son of a viscount and brother to a viscount. He was not going to run off with his tail between his legs. He wanted the life he deserved, the life he'd just begun to taste at his brother's side.

He turned and looked at Audrey sleeping. And imagined the life he might've led if his father hadn't died. Or if his mother hadn't died and left him with nothing. Or if Davis hadn't recruited him. Or if he hadn't so easily and thoroughly allowed himself to be corrupted.

Looking back, it seemed everything was destined to happen as it did. No matter how much he wanted things to be different, he couldn't change who he was, who he was likely always meant to be: a criminal.

∽

*A*udrey awoke just after the sun rose. She wasn't typically an early riser, but she also didn't typically share a bed. With anyone, let alone a *man*. The barrier she'd placed between them was still in place. She peeked over it. Mr. Locke was on his back, his good arm flung above his head, his dark lashes fanned against his cheeks. She stared at those lashes, marveling at how long and luxurious they appeared, completely unfair for a man to possess. Audrey wished hers were that spectacular. Instead, they were just brown and somewhat nondescript. Like the rest of her.

In repose, Mr. Locke looked younger. His ink-dark hair was thick and in need of a trim. His beard was longer still, and Audrey was surprised to find she still found it attractive. Despite the growth of hair, his chin was squared and strong. He might look youthful in sleep, but he also exuded a power and magnetism that was undeniable. At least to her.

Mr. Locke's eyes shot open and he was suddenly on top of her. He'd rolled like quicksilver, pinning her to the mattress.

She gasped—both with surprise and with the shock of his masculine body pressed atop hers. He was hard and muscular, and for the first time in her life she felt dainty and impossibly feminine.

His gray eyes focused on her, but she couldn't immediately discern what he was thinking. Then his brow arched and he drawled, "Good morning" without sounding the least bit apologetic.

"I beg your pardon," she said, trying desperately not to blush in his presence for the thousandth time.

He stared down at her, studying her face. His hands were on either side of her head while his hips were settled firmly against hers.

She squirmed beneath him, which only served to heighten the closeness. Shards of heat sparked between her legs, and made her want to invite him to do more.

He rolled off her, gently, so that his hips brushed hers as he retreated to his side of the bed.

She jumped up, eager to put space between them. "Was that necessary?"

He massaged his bandaged arm. "We're in a precarious situation. I'm on my guard."

"You thought I posed a threat?"

"Not you exactly. I didn't immediately process who you were. Forgive me if I'm not used to waking up beside beautiful young society misses." He swung his legs off the side of the bed.

He thought her beautiful? Warmth suffused her. He'd paid her similar compliments when she'd taught him to waltz, had flirted with her, but she'd written it off as a gentleman's charm. He was ridiculously handsome, and men who looked like him flirted with everyone. Well, everyone except her.

She fetched his shirt and helped him don the garment, working to keep her gaze averted from the muscles rippling in his back and chest and arms. He had muscles everywhere. It was very disconcerting. Once he was covered, she took a deep, sustaining breath. Much better.

She brought his boots over and tugged them up his calves after he'd stuck his foot inside. "I'd best tie your cravat again." She slid the linen around his neck and adjusted the collar of his shirt.

He stared at her intently, his eyes boring into her with a heat she felt all the way to her toes. Was it purposeful? Was he flirting with her again? She wasn't sure she could bear it. No one had ever flirted with her until him.

She dropped her gaze to the cravat her clumsy fingers were trying to knot. "Please don't look at me like that."

"Like what?"

She chanced a glance at him and was sorry for it because his gaze had only intensified, if that were possible. Plus, he'd arched his brow again in that frustratingly provocative manner. "Oh, never mind." She knew she mumbled, but she deeply regretted drawing attention to her discomfort. The constant blushing was bad enough.

She finished her work as quickly as possible and helped him don the coat. At last, they were ready to leave.

"What about your hair?" he asked.

She'd been so flustered, she'd forgotten all about her own toilette. Of course her hair would be a disaster, but she had no brush and she'd lost more pins than she had left. A small glass on the wall revealed a completely disheveled mess. She now doubted the veracity of his flirtation—he was surely bamming her. No one would find her attractive, least of all a man like him.

She pulled what pins remained out of her hair and looked about for a place to set them.

He appeared beside her with his palm open. Three hairpins were already lying there.

She looked up at him. "Where did you find those?"

"In the bed." The mere mention of the word bed threatened to send heat up her neck again, but she managed to keep it at bay. "I'll hold the others while you make repairs. I'm sorry you don't have a brush." The fact that he sounded genuinely apologetic only made things worse. Why did he have to be so gentlemanly when she was perfectly aware he was probably no gentleman?

She deposited the pins in his hand. "Thank you." Trying to work her hair into a serviceable knot was nearly impossible, but she managed to secure it, at least for now. Doubtless, when they got on their way, it would begin its inevitable descent.

"Ready?" he asked, going to the door.

"Yes." She followed him out of the room and down the narrow stairs to the small common area.

The innkeeper's wife greeted them and offered them a modest repast of potatoes, ham, and bread. When they were finished and preparing to leave, she approached Audrey with a small bag. "This is for your luncheon," she said warmly. "And I also have these for you." She handed Audrey a bonnet and a . . . brush.

Audrey glanced at Mr. Locke, who was conversing with the innkeeper near the front door. He'd procured these things for her, she was certain of it.

"And don't worry," the innkeeper's wife said, "your secret is safe with us. No one shall know the Millers passed through. I realize Miller isn't likely your real name." She winked at Audrey and gave her a quick hug.

What sort of secret had Mr. Locke told them? Audrey set the bonnet atop her head and tucked the brush into the food bag. "Thank you for your kindness." She turned and joined Mr. Locke.

He opened the door for her and they stepped out into the overcast morning. "What's that?" he asked, nodding toward the bag.

"Food from Mrs. Hodges. Thank you for asking for the bonnet and brush."

He looked at her askance. "How did you know that was me?"

"How else would she have known?"

He shrugged, moving toward the lean-to where their horse was stabled. "Maybe she was just observant."

Audrey stared after him. "Are you saying it's obvious my hair was in want of a brush?"

He turned. "Are you trying to make me into a villain?"

She cringed internally. *Wasn't* he a villain? "What story did you tell them?"

"What we agreed to, that we were a young married couple."

The untied ribbons of her bonnet lifted in the breeze. "That can't be all you said. Mrs. Hodges told me not to worry, that our 'secret' was safe."

He exhaled and came toward her. He took her hand and pulled her toward the lean-to. "We need to be on our way."

"You're not going to tell me what you said, are you?"

"What does it matter?" He let go of her hand when they got to the lean-to.

She wanted to know the truth. She felt fairly certain by now that he was a criminal. He had to be. Why else would he run from Bow Street? And why else would he

keep the truth from her? More importantly, if she believed he was a criminal, why was she trusting him?
She'd given him a portion of her funds the previous
night so he could pay for their lodgings. Had he used it
all? He hadn't given her any of it back.

"Where's the rest of the money I gave you?" she
asked, her suspicion getting the better of her.

He took the bag from her and tied it to the back of
the horse, which was now sporting a saddle. "I had to
use it all."

She was glad she hadn't given him the lot. "Why?"

He untied the horse and led her into the yard. "The
lodgings, your accoutrements, the saddle, and a second
horse, which we'll need to have someone return at
some point. I couldn't afford to buy her outright." He
inclined his head toward the lane.

A boy was leading another horse toward them. He
came into the yard, touched his cap and handed the
lead to Mr. Locke.

"Thank you, lad." Mr. Locke gave him a penny and
the boy turned and ran back the way he'd come. "Actually, *that* was the last of the money."

She eyed the second horse. "Why did we need another mount?"

"I thought we'd make better time if we rode sepa-
rately. And I thought you might appreciate your own
horse—with a sidesaddle—you're a very fine
horsewoman."

Another compliment and another flush of pleasure.
She had to admit it was probably safer—at least for her
sensibilities—if he wasn't pressed behind her. "Thank
you."

"May I help you up?"

She tied her bonnet beneath her chin. "Yes, please.
Does she have a name?"

"I was told she's called Athena." He boosted her onto
the horse and climbed atop the one they'd stolen the

day before. "We'll have to keep referring to this one as 'girl,' I suppose."

Audrey felt bad about stealing the first horse, and felt much better that they'd paid for everything today, even if it meant their funds were running low. And she was also glad he'd done the paying instead of resorting to thievery. Maybe he wasn't truly a criminal after all. "Do you think we could return your horse to that farmer we, uh, borrowed it from?"

"I suppose." He didn't sound as if he'd given it any thought. "To be honest, I don't even know how we'll get anyone to return your horse."

Had he lied? "But you told them you would. Return it, I mean."

"I did, and I will try." He gave her a hard look. "Sometimes life doesn't work out the way we plan."

She was well aware of that. Still, she felt a bit uneasy.

As they rode out of the yard, he turned to her and said, "Mr. Hodges gave me directions on how to get to Wootton Bassett. Without taking the main roads of course."

Of course. Surely Mr. Hodges had found that odd. Suddenly she was quite fed up with him withholding information. "Why is Bow Street chasing you? I think I've a right to know what I'm fleeing."

"*You're* not fleeing anything." He kicked his horse into a trot.

She followed him and easily caught up. She wasn't going to let him ignore her questions again. Perhaps she could try another way to learn his closely-guarded secrets. "I've been thinking about you. You clearly know how to steal. I wonder if you stole a lady's heart. You're certainly charming and handsome enough."

He looked over at her. "Very amusing."

"Of course, Bow Street wouldn't actually pursue you for such nonsense. So maybe you stole something else."

He was looking forward once more, but she could make out his scowl in profile.

She continued on her path of inquiry. "Or perhaps it was some other crime entirely. Perhaps you exhibited public drunkenness."

"Haven't we all? Save you of course, unless your two sherries at Michaelmas induced you to run amok in public."

She smiled. "What about blasphemy? You certainly like to swear a lot."

"Are you having fun?"

"In the absence of your forthrightness, I have to make my own assumptions." And yes, she *was* having fun. "I know! Adultery. As I said, you're too handsome for your own good."

"Fine." He slid her an embittered glance. "If I tell you something, will you stop?"

She'd been hoping to divert him, but that was proving to be difficult. "That depends on what you tell me."

"When I was a lad, I was called 'Pretty Boy.'" His tone held a weary scorn that provoked her to laugh.

She looked over at him. Yes, he had a pretty face, but his attraction was so much more than that. He had a presence about him—of authority and arrogance, of intelligence and wit that gave him an aura of power, as if he was in absolute control of any situation. "Can I call you Pretty Boy?"

He turned his head and their gazes connected. She chilled at the ice in his eyes. "No, you may not," he said. "I hated that nickname. No one ever took me seriously." He slowed his horse to a stop, and she did the same because she was absolutely compelled by him.

"Would you like to know how I got rid of that nickname?" he asked softly. Dangerously.

A shiver curled in her belly. "Yes." The word was barely a whisper.

"As a lad, I worked in a theft gang. When I was fifteen, I was tired of being discounted because of the way I looked. I wanted power. Prestige. Respect. So I killed the leader of the gang and assumed his place. No one ever called me 'Pretty Boy' again."

CHAPTER 5

As the sun began to set, Ethan looked over at Audrey. They'd barely exchanged words since he'd told her about killing Four-Finger Tom, and that had been hours ago. They'd stopped briefly for lunch and here and there for personal reasons, but for the most part, they'd ridden relentlessly. He wanted to put as many miles between him and London as possible. But then what? Hang around Wootton Bassett until when? Forever? His skin itched at the prospect of set-tling into a tiny village in the middle of the countryside.

"Are we going to stop soon?" Exhaustion weighted her tone, and her posture was that of a person who was tired of sitting atop a horse. Ethan knew this because he was certain it mirrored his own.

He was weary, sore from being in the saddle so long, and his arm ached almost unbearably at times. He wanted to stop, but there was no village in sight. "I don't know if we'll find a place to stay before it gets dark. We may just have to make do with something else."

She moved her horse closer beside him, walking them side-by-side. "What does that mean?"

"It means we may need to sleep wherever we find shelter. Provided we even find any."

She didn't respond and kept her face directed straight ahead. He ought to apologize for frightening her earlier. He had frightened her—he was certain of it. He'd admitted to not only thievery but murder.

He'd been considering what to do, trying to formulate a plan. Taking her out of London had been a gut reaction. Yes, she'd been in danger from Gin Jimmy, but Ethan wondered if he couldn't have asked Jason to ensure her safety. He was sure his brother would've agreed. If only Ethan had trusted him. Or even thought of trusting him. Christ, having an ally—a true, blood ally—was going to take getting used to.

He glanced at Audrey again, wilting in her saddle. His future was as uncertain as ever. She was a burden he couldn't really afford, and he'd done what he'd set out to do—he'd gotten her out of London. He didn't expect Gin Jimmy or Bow Street, who likely couldn't spare a Runner for a merry chase, would follow them this far out. Ethan's mind kept returning to the obvious solution: as soon as they reached Wootton Bassett, he'd leave her with her friends—she'd be safe this far from London—and be on his way.

At last, a small building came into view. It sat at the edge of a large enclosure with a dozen or so sheep grazing in the golden rays of the setting sun filtering through the mottled clouds.

"Will that work?" she asked, eyeing the shelter.

"Let's find out." He kicked his horse into a canter and stopped at the edge of the enclosure. He dismounted, his wounds protesting angrily with the movement. His legs wobbled, like they were made of pudding. He tied the horse to the fence and climbed over to investigate the building.

It was small, maybe twelve by fifteen feet, with three walls and support posts along the open side that faced the pasture. The dirt floor was littered with hay. Unfortunately, there were no blankets, but if they kept riding in search of something better they might not find anything else. This was, at least, shelter.

He limped back to the fence, Christ, his arse was sore. She was still in the saddle. Smart girl. He didn't really want to get back on his horse now that he was off.

"It's a shelter with a dirt floor." He'd slept in worse.

"Do you think we'll find anything better?"

He glanced at the rapidly darkening sky. "Probably not before the sun sets."

"Then we should stay here." She was already sliding off her mount, before he could rush to her aid. Not that he would be much help with his arm. Some gentleman he was turning out to be.

He wanted to hit something or yell at someone. Those were the ways he typically expended his frustrated energy. Definitely not the actions of a gentleman. But hadn't he well and truly botched that effort? There was no hope for him now. If he returned to London, he'd be hanged. The best he could hope for was to start over somewhere else unless he wanted to take his chances with Teague and the rest of Bow Street. The glaring answer was hell no, but hadn't his life changed? He had his brother he could call upon, and perhaps even Lord Daniel Carlyle, a viscount who was a former magistrate. Ethan had saved his life once—and the life of his wife. Would he come to Ethan's aid? Though he owed Ethan at least one favor, if not two for past assistances, in Ethan's experience people didn't help each other unless there was something in it for them, and Ethan had nothing to offer any of them.

Audrey tied her horse beside his, then removed the food pack from her saddle and came to the fence. It was only four feet high, so she handed the bag to Ethan and then hoisted herself up and over. Her skirts caught, but Ethan flipped them over so she could jump down unhindered.

"I'll take care of the horses in a minute," Ethan said, following her into the shelter.

She surveyed the interior and then turned toward him. "I suppose it's better than nothing. I'll set out some food." She held her hand out for him to return the food bag.

"Don't bother." He pulled a small hunk of cheese from the bag before transferring the pack to her. "I'll just eat before I tend the animals."

Her eyes tentatively met his. "Is this how it's going to be? You tell me you killed someone and that's it? I've done everything you've asked. Indeed, without me, you'd be God-knows-where since your money was stolen."

He arched a brow at her. "You assume my money would've *been* stolen had you not accompanied me."

She blanched. He bit back an apology, hating that he'd grown soft in recent weeks. But why, hadn't he *wanted* to change? If he wanted to shirk the mantle of his former life, what better way than to show kindness, especially to her of all people? "Pardon me," he said softly. Yes, she deserved at least that. And a modicum of honesty. "I think you'll be safe in Wootton Bassett. I can't believe Gin Jimmy would follow us this far from London."

She clutched the bag and stared at him. "Are you planning to abandon me?"

His temper—frayed by travel, his wounds, and most importantly, the lack of a plan—threatened to blow apart. He wiped his hand over his brow and scrubbed at his eyes for a moment. When he looked at her again, she was still watching him but there was a wariness in her gaze. "I'm not abandoning you. I got you out of London, and Gin Jimmy's men won't leave the city. These people in Wootton Bassett are your friends. Staying with them is much better than a life on the run."

"And then what? I'm to stay there forever? Alone?"

He cringed at the disappointment in her questions. He hadn't meant to . . . what, give her hope? For what? He leaned toward her, narrowing his eyes. "What would you have me do? As you so accurately surmised, I'm a *criminal*, not a gentleman who's going to whisk you away to some fantasy life."

She drew the bag closer to her chest, maybe as protection. Or maybe she just wanted to hold on to something because she felt completely adrift, which was precisely how he felt. "I don't think you want to be a criminal."

He'd never really *wanted* to be. But it had been better than begging. Or dying. "I killed that boy because I had to. His was marginalizing me to the point where I would've been excised from the gang."

She blinked. "Excised?"

"Killed."

"You had no choice?"

"Not if I wanted to live, Audrey." It was the first time he'd used her given name in a moment that hadn't involved them defending their lives and he liked the way it tasted on his tongue. "I lived on the streets. After my mother died, I had no one to turn to, no one to care for me. I made the most of my life with what I could."

That life seemed so far away, like someone else's existence.

"You have that chance again now," she said softly. "You can change what you are, who you want to be."

He'd been trying to, before this Wolverton mess. "All I ever wanted was to bring my brother pain. To hurt him the way he and his mother had hurt me."

The pain in her eyes had warmed to empathy. At least he thought it might be—he couldn't be certain since he'd only rarely been shown any. "Why?" she asked.

There was no reason not to tell her. It wasn't a secret, and it didn't mean he trusted her. The facts of his life were just that—cold facts that he couldn't change. "When my mother died, I had nothing. No one, save her final protector." An image of Davis's gray and desperate expression just before the hood had fallen over his face on hanging day swam before Ethan. "But he was a criminal, and I'd been raised to be a gentleman. I was supposed to go to Oxford." The pain of his lost dreams superseded the agony in his arm.

"I went to Jason and his mother, begged them to take me in. She laughed in my face. Then spit on me." His left hand involuntarily curled into a fist.

"Jason didn't intervene?"

Ethan's answering laugh was hollow and dark, just like his husk of a heart. "Why would he? He hated me almost as much as she did. She threw me back into the street and I had no choice but to take Davis's protection. Which meant working with him as a thief-taker."

Her brow furrowed. "That's not a terrible thing."

"It is when he's setting up the thefts and sending the thieves to prison or worse. And when he planned to use me in the same fashion."

"What do you mean?" The horror in her question matched the familiar sense of betrayal that roiled in his gut.

"He was being investigated and had to deflect suspicion from himself. He set me up to take the fall for him, but I figured that out, and he's the one who swung."

And that had been the beginning of Ethan's downfall. From there, he'd joined the theft gang run by Four-Finger Tom. After taking that over, he'd gained respect and power. Soon after, he'd begun to work for Gin Jimmy's crew, working his way up over the years until he'd become one of Jimmy's most trusted men.

Audrey set the bag down and moved toward him. Her eyes were soft, caring. No one had ever looked at him like that. Not even his mother when he'd been a young boy. He couldn't bear her concern. He didn't deserve something so pure. He backed away. "I'll take care of the horses."

"Wait." She touched his arm and it was like the jolt of energy one experienced just before a fight or a theft. But a thousand times better. "I can't imagine the life you've led, what you've overcome . . ."

He didn't want her pity, and he didn't deserve her understanding. "No, you can't imagine. And this is why we'll be parting ways. I'm a criminal and that's all I'll ever be." The knowledge speared through him until he wanted to retch.

She pressed her fingers into his forearm. "Why were you learning to waltz? You were behaving like a gentleman. All of London thinks you're the charming, longlost half-brother of Jason Lockwood."

"Aren't I?" He extracted his elbow from her grip. "I *am* the long-lost brother of Jason Lockwood, but rest assured: I'm no gentleman."

～

*L*ater that night, Audrey huddled into the corner of the sheep barn. She'd curled into a ball on her side, facing the pasture where the murky shapes of distant shrubs and trees along the perimeter rose out of the near darkness. The moon was faint, its glow dimming and brightening as clouds drifted across it.

She ought to close her eyes and try to sleep, but she was too cold. Shivers racked her body intermittently, but there was no help for it unless she wanted to snuggle up with Mr. Locke. Right now, she wasn't sure he was someone she wanted to snuggle *with*.

He'd taken quite a long time to deal with the horses. When he'd finally returned, she'd already eaten and had replayed his revelations dozens of time in her head. She could scarcely believe all he'd told her, yet it made sense, given everything she'd seen him do. No gentleman would know how to steal a cabriolet or fight the intruders in her grandfather's house or kill a highwayman. Then again, no gentlewoman ought to know how to fire a gun, much less shoot a man. Yes, appearances could be deceiving and she would try not to judge.

At last she closed her eyes. If she didn't sleep, she'd be miserable tomorrow, and they needed to make good time to reach Wootton Bassett. She thought of a fire and a warm bed. And a bath. How divine that would be.

She turned over, thinking it might be better to face the wall, where her warm breath might bounce off the wood and at least her nose wouldn't be frozen. It was pathetic reasoning, but it was all she had.

A few minutes later she nearly jumped out of her skin when something came over her shoulders. Her eyes shot open and she turned her head to see Mr. Locke tucking his coat around her. He turned to go.

"Don't." It wasn't fair that he should sleep in his shirtsleeves. She knew it was horribly improper, but what place did propriety have when one was freezing? "Sleep here. We'll share the coat."

He hesitated. "I don't think that's wise."

"Nothing I have done in the past two days has been wise. Don't make me start now."

His soft chuckle gave her a burst of warmth. "If you insist."

"I do." She held the coat up to let him under it.

He settled down behind her and inserted himself beneath the edge of the coat, leaving most of the garment covering her. She felt his heat, but he wasn't as close as he'd been when they'd ridden the same horse. "Move closer for heaven's sake. I want to be warm, don't you?"

"You're a managing chit, do you know that?" He slid closer until his chest pressed against her back. "Better?"

"Much." His heat was already seeping into her. He'd tried to threaten her earlier. By all accounts she should be frightened of him, but she wasn't. He made her feel protected and secure. She'd heard the pain when he'd recounted his youth, and she wanted him to experience the sensation of knowing that someone cared what happened to him, that someone wanted to keep him safe. "How's your arm? I wish you would've let me check it earlier." He'd insisted it was fine, but she knew he was just trying to increase the distance between them.

"I'll let you check it when we arrive tomorrow, all right?"

"Or, I could take a look at in the morning."

"I want to be on our way as soon as it's light."

So they could get to Wootton Bassett and he could dump her there. That gave her tomorrow—and tonight—to convince him otherwise. "What will you do when you leave Wootton Bassett?" Her breath hitched as she awaited his answer.

"Even if I knew, I wouldn't tell you."

"I think you should stay. Just for a bit. You need to rest your arm." Her brain seized on a way to keep him from leaving. She turned to look at him. "You can't leave until after I take your stitches out. You'll need to stay for at least a week."

The muted light from the moon cast a halo about his head and made his features barely visible. The edge of his mouth ticked up. "I will?"

"Yes. I insist."

"You do like to manage," he murmured. "But no, I won't stay that long. I'll find someone to remove my sutures."

"It doesn't sound as if you have a plan. Why not stay until you do?"

He was quiet a moment, perhaps considering. "If I tell you I'll think about it, will you let me sleep?"

It was as much as she could expect. She'd continue her campaign tomorrow. "Yes." Another idea struck her. "What am I to tell Miranda and her husband? That I just came for a visit by myself? Or will you wait to leave until after you've met them?" Maybe then it would be harder for him to depart.

"It's probably best for everyone if I don't meet them, don't you think?" He shook his head. "No, don't answer that. I'm afraid of what you think. It's much easier and cleaner if I see you to your friends' house and be on my way before making anyone's acquaintance."

Audrey deflated. He sounded resolute. Still, she could try to come up with some other plan tomorrow. For now, exhaustion was starting to get the better of her. She turned to her side so that her back was against his chest once more.

She listened to his breathing, deep and sure, and let it flow through her until his proximity and heat lulled her body into relaxing. As sleep threatened, she voiced just one more thing. "I know you want to leave me in Wootton Bassett, but if you decide to go to America, I hope you'll take me with you."

He did nothing to indicate he'd heard her, which was just as well. Likely, he would have reconfirmed his plan to drop her off and behave as if the last two days had never happened. As if the last two days hadn't altered her life in the most unchangeable of ways.

Her body twitched as sleep claimed her.

CHAPTER 6

*A*s dusk fell the next day, Ethan glanced over at Audrey. He was glad they were riding into Wootton Bassett at last. She looked tired and had every reason to be, considering how little he'd allowed her to rest the past two days. They'd been awakened just after dawn that morning by the sheep farmer who owned the barn they'd been sleeping in. He'd damned their souls as he'd run them off. Ethan had expected Audrey to be upset, but she'd been quite pleasant all day. In fact, she was bewilderingly cheery toward him. His revelations hadn't sparked fear, disgust, or worst of all, pity. She treated him much the same as she'd done when he'd been her waltzing student.

His gaze again strayed to her riding beside him, as it had many times during their journey. He'd studied her greatly, the subtle turn of her nose at the very tip, the graceful sweep of her brows, the supple curve of her lips. She appeared so elegant, despite the hopeless creases in her gown and the absolute ramshackle mess of her hair trying to fight its way from beneath her bonnet. Elegant and composed. Maybe it was the way she carried herself. Or the commitment she'd demonstrated to this adventure she'd chosen. Or the way she hadn't run screaming when he'd revealed he'd murdered someone.

And he'd expected her to. It was why he'd done it. She'd been flirting with him, dammit, and he was already too attracted to her. Nothing good could come from their association and once he settled her in Wootton Bassett, it would be at an end. He'd post a letter to Jason asking him to ensure her safety when she returned to London and he'd enclose a letter for Carlyle. The man owed him, and Ethan would collect. Carlyle would find a way to protect her until Gin Jimmy realized Ethan was gone for good.

A chill settled at the base of Ethan's neck. He'd never planned his life around the welfare of someone else. It was a bloody nuisance. And yet, he'd bound himself to her—at least temporarily—when he'd snuck into her house for waltzing lessons.

If you decide to go to America, I hope you'll take me with you.

Her request had kept him up long after she'd fallen into slumber. He'd actually *considered* what she said. Fleeing to America where he *could* be Ethan Lockwood. And she could be . . . What could she be? His wife? The dream he'd long envisioned of somehow regaining the life that had been stolen from him had never included domestic bliss.

That dream had started to become reality when he'd entered Society several weeks ago as Jason Lockwood's long-lost bastard brother. People had been titillated by his mysterious background and his charming disposition, which was at such odds with Jason's reputation as a potential lunatic who hosted notorious vice parties, a reputation Ethan took credit for creating.

Ethan had done a good job displacing Jason from Society years ago when he'd accidentally scarred his face in a fight. Then he'd ensured Jason's staff had fled his town house, declaring him mad like his mother. Jason's marital eligibility had promptly disintegrated and he'd been left with nothing but a frightening reputation, which he'd turned into one of scandal and decadence when he began hosting London's premier vice parties.

But Ethan didn't want that revenge anymore. Instead, he and Jason had begun to claim the brotherhood they'd lost amidst the wreckage their parents' hatred had left. That was more valuable to Ethan than he'd ever dreamed anything could be. To feel a sense of belonging, of rightness . . . He wanted that. And he couldn't get it in America, which meant he had to find a way to make it happen in London.

"I'm not sure where Bassett Manor is located." The lilt of Audrey's voice broke into his thoughts. Bassett Manor was the estate where her friends resided.

"Shouldn't be too hard to find," he said as their horses walked onto the High Street. "How many estates can one little village have?"

"Actually, there's another nearby, Cosgrove."

Bloody rich people. "Let's just have a look, shall we?"

They rode up the street past some shops and a pub. Several coaches were parked in front of a large building. As they came closer, music drifted from the open doors.

Lanterns from the coaches and from the building illuminated the area and allowed him to see her face more clearly. She was smiling. His heart did a little trip, as if it had missed a beat.

"Can we listen, just for a minute?" she asked, guiding her horse to the side of the street.

He followed her and dismounted, his body protesting with its various aches and pains. He tied his horse to a post and helped her down. While he secured her mount beside his, she moved to the side of the building where a window was open and tapped her foot to the music.

They ought to find Bassett Manor, but he couldn't deny her a moment's joy after their grueling journey. Nor could he deny himself the joy of watching her.

The music stopped and then started again, but with a slower tune. A waltz.

She turned toward him. "Have you been practicing?"

He had, in fact. With some of the lightskirts at the Crystal, the flash house where he kept his primary lodging in St. Giles. They hadn't been nearly as skilled or graceful as Audrey, but he'd closed his eyes and done his best to imagine her in their place. He realized he had the opportunity to enjoy the real thing. Perhaps the last such opportunity he'd ever have.

He went to her and offered his most courtly bow. "May I have the honor of this dance?"

She curtseyed in return. "You may."

He clasped her hand and splayed his palm against her back as he swept her into the dance. He'd practiced enough to make the steps without counting, but he still worried about stepping on her toes, as he'd done the first time she'd taught him.

"You *have* been practicing. And with excellent results. You dance divinely, sir."

He resisted the urge to nuzzle the graceful column of her neck. "I had an excellent teacher."

"You seem the perfect gentleman." Her tone had been light but now took a darker, more serious turn. She looked at him again with that infinitely warm and sympathetic gaze that threatened every wall he'd built around himself. "I'll say it again, you can change what you are, who you want to be. Who you want to be *with*."

He knew what she was asking. Temptation hovered before him just as surely as the promise of brotherhood was luring him back to London. Both were a risk and he was no stranger to risk . . .

"Ethan." Her voice drew him back. Had she called him by his Christian name? No one save Jason had called him that since his mother had died. He'd been "Jagger" nearly as long as he could remember.

The music seemed to fade from his ears as he looked into her eyes. He slowed until they were no longer waltzing. She touched his cheek. His smooth, unscarred, pretty-boy cheek.

"Did you know I gave Jason his scar? I wish it had been the other way around."

She shook her head. "Why?"

He smiled wryly. "A menacing facial disfigurement would've suited my lifestyle far better than his."

She brought her other hand up and cupped his face. "Don't wish that. Don't."

A part of him knew what she meant to do before she did it, but he was paralyzed by her touch, by the soft look of understanding and empathy in her gaze. And by God even if he could've moved, he wouldn't have. He wanted her lips on his.

She kissed him, her mouth pressing against his with an innocence sweeter than any delicacy he'd tasted during all of his decadent years as Gin Jimmy's right hand. During that time, Ethan had evaded death countless times, always with a fervor for life and an absolute refusal to surrender, but right now he thought he might welcome his maker, for nothing could be closer to heaven than her. Nor had he ever wanted anything more.

He wrapped his other arm around her and drew her up against him. Her tall, lithe body fit into his with sweet precision, as if their coupling was ordained by God himself. A silly notion, for God wouldn't have paid any attention to Ethan Jagger.

Her hands moved from his face to the back of his neck. He took the action as an invitation and slanted his head. With his lips, he applied pressure to her mouth, coaxing, teasing. He held her close, anticipating she might flinch as he licked along her lower lip. She surprised him again by clasping him more tightly. Her lips parted in another invitation he couldn't refuse.

He slid his tongue into her mouth. Cautiously, so as not to frighten her, he swept along her interior, relishing her velvety softness. She was hesitant, allowing him to kiss her but not responding in kind. It wasn't enough. He wanted her to give what she was getting, to share in the rapture he felt.

He skimmed his left hand up her spine and fingered the curls that had escaped their pins and grazed the back of her neck. They were as soft and silky as he'd imagined. He wanted to twist his hands in them as he probed her mouth. And why not? He might never get this chance again.

He speared his fingers into her hair beneath her bonnet until he palmed the back of her head. Then he deepened the kiss, stroking his tongue into her mouth with mad possession, demanding her response.

Now she flinched. Or did she shiver? Whatever she did, she didn't pull away, and that was all he needed. He tugged at her hair, pulling her head slightly back and arching her neck. He nipped at her lower lip. "Kiss me, Audrey."

He'd looked at her shuttered eyelids as he'd spoken. Her eyes flashed open, their aqua depths sparkling like jewels. She stared at him the barest moment before pulling his mouth back to hers and doing exactly as he'd instructed.

Her kiss wasn't perfect and it wasn't graceful. Her teeth grazed his as their mouths connected, but the ferocity with which she clutched him to her and pressed her tongue into his fired his need better than any lustful imagining. But she was no dream. She was real and wonderful and everything he never knew he wanted.

He massaged her scalp as he plundered her mouth. The kiss burned through him. His cock grew hard as it

had been the other morning when he'd rolled on top of
her. That he could explain away as a typical morning
problem. But he could no longer deny he wanted Audrey. He wanted her naked and moaning beneath him.
On top of him. Every way he could have her.

Her fingers dug into his neck. She copied him and
nipped at his lower lip. His lust roared and he pulled
her head back farther, exposing her neck, then put his
open mouth on her flesh. He sucked and nibbled beneath her jaw, then licked a path to her ear. He'd just
lightly closed his teeth over her sensitive lobe when a
cough behind him froze his desire.

"Oh my goodness, is that Audrey Cheswick?"

~

udrey's eyes flew open and she stepped
backward. Ethan let her go—there was no point
in trying to think of him as anything other than Ethan
now—and her knees wobbled. She managed to focus on
the couple gaping at them from maybe five feet away,
standing between them and the street. She recognized
them of course, as they were the people she and Ethan
had come to find.

"Lady Foxcroft." Audrey strove to keep the apprehension from her tone. She curtseyed, as one would do
in the presence of the daughter of a duke. Then she repeated the action for her husband. Though he wasn't a
peer at all, he still deserved a curtsey, she reasoned.
"Mr. Foxcroft."

"Good evening, Miss Cheswick," Mr. Foxcroft said.
He gave both Audrey and Ethan a thoroughly assessing
perusal. "You are, ah, a bit underdressed for the
assembly."

Audrey and her friends had known Lady Foxcroft as
Miranda before she'd been expelled from London two
and a half years prior for exhibiting scandalous behav-

ior. Her exploits had, in fact, inspired Audrey to launch her own ill-fated adventure with the blacksmith's son.

Miranda smacked her husband playfully on the arm. "Fox, they are clearly not going to the assembly. Otherwise, they wouldn't be skulking about the window. What *are* you doing out here?"

The fear that had shot through Audrey when she'd heard the cough returned tenfold. She glanced at Ethan and hoped she didn't look as panicked as she felt. He, on the other hand, looked calm and cool, not at all as if they'd just shared an incredible embrace that had been tragically interrupted.

"We're actually looking for you." Ethan smiled and the effect caused Audrey's knees to wobble again. The man possessed devastating charm when he wanted to, and probably even when he didn't. "We're, ah—"

"Eloping," Audrey said, sidling closer to him and putting her arm around his waist. There was no sense hiding what they'd been doing. And really, what else were they going to tell them? Their plan, rather, Ethan's plan, had been to simply drop her at Bassett Manor and leave her to explain how she'd gotten there. However, now that they'd both encountered the Foxcrofts and they'd been caught in an embrace, it seemed a new plan was in order.

Miranda and her husband looked at each other, doubt clearly etched on their faces. Her mouth curled into a confused moue. "You came here on your way to Gretna Green?"

"Something like that," Ethan said smoothly, moving away from Audrey. "We've come a long way. Might we go to Bassett Manor for a bath and perhaps a meal?"

Miranda straightened. "Of course! We only just arrived for the assembly, but we'll have the coach take you home."

Fox looked at her, his mouth lifting in a half-smile. "Shouldn't we go with them? For propriety's sake?"

"Why bother? They've clearly been traveling alone." Miranda glanced at Audrey who was certain her face had turned a vivid scarlet. She gave her a commiserative smile. "Sorry, dear." Miranda touched her husband's arm. "I'm sure they want to get cleaned up. We'll see them later. I refuse to miss the quarterly assembly." She turned to look at Audrey and Ethan. "You see, my husband is the finest dancer in all of Wiltshire."

Audrey didn't think it would be seemly to argue that Ethan was, in fact, the best dancer in all of England. Probably because her opinion had more to do with his kissing than his actual dancing skill.

Mr. Foxcroft scrutinized Ethan. "Gretna Green, you say? You're a bit out of the way if you've come from London." His gaze raked over them again and he clearly wondered why they were dressed as they were—Ethan in an incomplete suit of clothing and Audrey in an unfashionable, ill-fitting sack. Thank God she at least had the bonnet to mask her disastrous hair, though she suspected it was a catastrophic mess after the way Ethan had tangled his hands in it. Heat bloomed in her belly and she tried desperately not to think of their kiss. Rather, *kisses*.

Ethan's features were placid, his smile benign. "As I said, it was something like that. We're not on our way to Gretna Green."

Audrey recognized what he was doing; he'd done it with her the past few days. He acted as though he was answering questions in a polite fashion, but in reality he didn't impart the information one was looking to ascertain. Then again, he'd also outright ignored her questions or told her plainly that he wasn't going to answer them. She decided this was a better tactic.

"Might we discuss this later, Foxcroft?" Ethan asked. "I'd like to see Miss Cheswick to Bassett Manor right away."

"Certainly, and it's Fox."

Ethan held out his hand. "Ethan Locke."

Miranda offered her hand to Ethan, who pressed a kiss to her glove. "Fox, you remember, he's Lord Lockwood's brother."

Ethan smiled broadly. "Indeed. We, ah," he glanced at their horses, "have mounts that will need to be tended."

"We'll send a couple of grooms to collect them when the coach comes back to retrieve us. Fox?" She inclined her head toward the coachman.

Fox shook his head at her, then went to direct the retainer. When he returned he said, "Everything is organized. The coachman will take you to Bassett Manor straightaway."

"Thank you."

Miranda went to Audrey and linked arms with her. "Pardon us, gentlemen." She moved her away a few steps and whispered, "What the devil are you doing here with him?" Her gaze dipped over Audrey's form. "And just look at you. Good Lord, what happened?"

"It's a dreadfully long story. I'll tell you about it later." *Which will give me time to figure out exactly what to say.* "However, if you have clothing we might borrow . . ."

Miranda waved her hand. "Of course. Just ask my maid for whatever you need." She turned and led Audrey back to where Ethan had moved to stand near the coach. "See you later!" She waved, then dragged her husband into the assembly.

Ethan, meanwhile, helped Audrey into the coach and climbed in after her. They started moving almost immediately and the rumble and sway of the vehicle, and its delightfully cushioned seats, were a welcome respite from horseback.

Ethan sat on the seat opposite her. The lantern inside the coach showed the firm set of his jaw and the lines around his mouth. "That was unfortunate," he said.

"Them catching us? Yes." She'd been about to say the kiss had been anything but; however, she decided it might be better if they didn't discuss it. Not when Ethan looked annoyed. "Are you angry?"

His features relaxed slightly and he leaned his head back so that he was looking at the ceiling of the coach. "No. I just have to readjust my plan." He lowered his gaze and directed her a half-amused, half-frustrated look. "They think we're eloping."

"What else was I supposed to say? They saw us . . . you know." Audrey scooted toward the corner where the lantern light didn't quite penetrate, in the hope of shadowing her flaming cheeks.

He pulled the curtain aside and looked outside. "I don't know. I suppose we'll simply tell them tomorrow that we've changed our minds. I'm sure they'll agree to come up with a story that will preserve your reputation."

"My reputation is beyond preservation." She had no remorse about this, but recognized her family would be devastated. However, there was nothing she could do about it now. "My grandfather knows I left with you."

He dropped the curtain and sat back. "If everyone thinks I kidnapped you, your reputation could be salvageable."

She laughed, but it was hollow. "You don't really understand Society, do you? I could tell them all you stole me away in the night but didn't lay a hand on me. No one would believe that. Besides, I won't let anyone think you kidnapped me, because you didn't."

A long moment of silence stretched between them before she continued. "Let's just tell them we're going to America together. Then we can leave after your arm is healed."

"And actually go to America? My life—my brother—is in London, Audrey."

"You left London. In quite a hurry too. Won't Bow Street be waiting for you when you return?" How she longed to know why they were pursuing him.

"Probably."

This time the heat in her face was due to anger. "Why won't you just tell me what happened? It can't possibly be worse than killing someone, and you've already admitted to that."

He rubbed his hand over his eyes. "Audrey, please don't ask me. I've told you far more than I've ever told anyone." He lowered his hand and settled a dark glare on her. "Don't make me regret that."

She leaned slightly forward "People would help you. Your brother and Lydia. Me. And we know other people."

"Your faith in people is astounding." The disbelief in his tone filled the coach with a sour air. "You assume there's a way to help me without even knowing what I've done."

She folded her arms across her chest. "You see why it would be so much easier if you would just trust me?"

"What's easy for you is bloody impossible for me. I can't do what you're asking."

Weariness from the past few days of travel and from doing battle with him on this issue made her droop back against the seat. "No, you *won't*. There's a difference. I only hope someday you'll find a way to see it."

CHAPTER 7

*E*than was grateful he hadn't had to endure an interrogation from Fox last night. When he and Audrey had arrived at Bassett Manor, an ancient pile of stone that looked as if it was undergoing much-needed refurbishment, they'd both been shown immediately to their rooms. He'd enjoyed a meal and a bath in his chamber and had forced himself to fall into bed, where dreams of chocolate corkscrew curls and aqua eyes tortured him all night long.

Now, however, the stark light of a bright October morning streamed through the hall windows, and as he stepped into the breakfast room, Fox was already seated at the table.

"Good morning," Fox said, smiling. He indicated the sideboard, which was stacked with food. "Help yourself."

Ethan goggled at the amount and variety of items. There were ham and kippers, potatoes and turnips, eggs, bread, and cheese. It was an awful lot of food for Fox and his wife and their guests.

Fox interrupted Ethan's cataloging of the menu. "Miranda wanted to have a proper breakfast for you. I told her it was too much."

"Perhaps." Regardless, Ethan was hungry and would

do his best to put a dent in her array. He piled a plate high and joined Fox at the table.

Fox eyed Ethan's plate. "Perhaps *not*." He popped a bite of toast into his mouth. Then he sat back in his chair. "So, you're not exactly eloping to Gretna Green. Pardon me, I have to ask."

Ethan understood. It was why he'd planned what to say. He only hoped Audrey would cooperate by crying off before they went anywhere. Otherwise, he'd have to be the one to leave her, and he didn't want anyone thinking she'd been abandoned—she deserved better than that. "No, we're headed to Plymouth where we plan to take a ship for America."

Fox shot forward in his chair. "The devil you say. That's quite a departure."

Ethan shrugged. "I'm the bastard son of a viscount. My prospects are likely better there."

Fox settled back in his chair. "Your prospects are whatever you make them. I can see the benefit of starting in a new place, of establishing yourself. However, it's not as if you wouldn't be accepted here. I suspect you'd gain entry into more places as Lockwood's bastard than I do as a legitimate nobody."

Ethan scooped up a spoon of potatoes. "You're not a nobody. You're married to the Duke of Holborn's daughter. That will gain you entry anywhere."

"You know what I mean. Before Miranda, I wasn't fit to clean the man's boots." Fox's mouth twisted wryly. "Believe me, he told me so."

Ethan swallowed. He understood what Fox was trying to say, and didn't disagree with him. In fact, Ethan had counted on his ability to claim a place in Society despite his illegitimacy. He was, as Fox had pointed out, the son of a viscount. That counted for something and while it wouldn't give him carte blanche, it would likely allow him to do just about everything he wanted.

Which was what? Attend house parties? Take tea with London's elite? Obtain a voucher to Almack's? He nearly choked on the bite of kippers he'd just taken. So maybe not Almack's, the horror, but he thought he might like a house party or two. His last few days on horseback had been painful, but he'd recalled the lessons he'd taken as a lad, the promises of riding with his father, of joining him on a hunt, and he'd begun to revisit the dreams he'd thought long destroyed. Dreams that were still likely unreachable, given his problems with both Bow Street and Gin Jimmy.

"You should come with me to the orphanage today," Fox said. "I'll show you what we do there."

Ethan was surprised to find he was actually tempted to stay for a few days. He told himself it was because he was tired and he wanted to rest his arm, but there was something appealing about spending a day or two with Audrey before he left. Or at least today. Since she hadn't left her room yet this morning, there hadn't been an opportunity to organize their plan. He might as well accompany Fox to his orphanage. "Yes, show me your orphanage."

Fox pushed back from the table and stood. "Excellent. I'll meet you out front when you're finished."

Ethan nodded and welcomed the peace of enjoying his breakfast the way he so often did: alone.

Little more than a half hour later, Fox steered his cart up the long drive to Stipple's End, a monstrosity of a building that was equally as ancient as Bassett Manor, but less stately in its appearance. Ethan didn't know much about architecture, but even he could recognize the house had been renovated many times over the past centuries.

He didn't bother censoring his reaction. "How old is this place?"

Fox chuckled as he steered the cart around the building to a stable area in the back. "Six hundred years. But that's just the original building. The various enlargements happened at different times."

Ethan surveyed the peaks in the roof, part of which appeared to be newly repaired. "And you said it's been in your family nearly as long as it's been in existence?"

A boy maybe twelve years old rushed to meet them. Fox handed him the reins as he climbed down. "Thank you, Charlie."

Ethan stepped out of the cart and joined Fox as he made his way toward the back of the house.

"We've run the orphanage for nigh on four hundred years, beginning when Stipple's End came to the Foxcroft family by way of marriage," Fox continued. "My forebears didn't need two houses and sought to use the extra one to help the children in the district. It started as a school, actually, but gradually became an orphanage." Fox held the back door open and gestured for Ethan to precede him into a narrow hallway.

Ethan walked inside and sniffed as a strong odor assaulted him.

Fox strode past him. "They must've already started painting. We've done a lot of improvements over the past couple of years. The roof fell into the great hall two years ago."

Ethan followed him into a massive great hall. "That sounds expensive."

"Quite. Luckily, I married Miranda. She inherited a property that makes an income, and I've been able to make improvements at Bassett Manor so that it's now starting to earn a better income."

"You married her for her money?" Though it was a typical occurrence, Ethan was surprised to hear Fox say so.

Fox pivoted to look at him. "Hell no. I married her because she's Miranda. That she improved my financial state is simply a happy accident."

Ethan felt a pang of alarm. Fox had fallen in love

with her. Like Jason had fallen in love with Lydia. Christ, love was all around him. What if that happened to him—with Audrey? Falling in love had never been something he considered and now . . . there couldn't be a worse time. If he'd needed a reason to get the hell away from Audrey, he had one now. Not that he was actually in danger of falling in love with her. He *was*, however, in danger of falling in lust.

"Bernard, you're off to an early start this morning," Fox said, moving toward the boys who were painting.

A tall lad, probably fifteen years old or so, turned. He held a round brush in his hand and had been applying whitewash to the wall. "Good morning, Fox. I hope you don't mind. I wanted to get this done today, if possible."

"Why would I mind your industriousness?" Fox clapped the boy on the shoulder. "Locke, this is Bernard, he's been with us since he was what, four years old?"

Bernard nodded. "Nearly ten years."

Ethan's curiosity was piqued. "How did you come to be at Stipple's End?"

"My father was in the navy, but he didn't come home. My mother passed and the vicar—we lived in Swindon—sent me here."

Ethan knew what would've happened to the boy if the vicar hadn't stepped in. He thought of all of the children in London who ended up in workhouses or on the street. He didn't know which was worse. He knew with certainty, however, that Stipple's End was far better than either of those alternatives.

Fox moved around to watch two younger boys who'd gone back to whitewashing. "Painting the walls in the great hall is the final step in the long renovation. Miranda wanted to hang wallpaper, but I convinced her that whitewash was the smarter choice in a facility full of children. You're doing a fine job, boys."

One of them, an apple-cheeked lad who couldn't be more than nine or ten and whose hands were covered in whitewash, flashed him a grin.

Fox nodded toward Ethan. "Come, I'll show you the library, the only room I've allowed Miranda to decorate."

Ethan trailed him along a corridor past a grand staircase. He couldn't stop thinking of the boys and the incredible opportunity they'd been given in coming here. "What happens to the children when they leave here?"

Fox took a right through a doorway. He turned back to look at Ethan. "Bernard has taken quite an interest in the refurbishment. We had an architectural firm from London here and Bernard was fascinated. I'm going to send him to school in a couple of years—he's only thirteen though he looks older, I know—and then he's going to apprentice with them."

Ethan nearly stumbled over the edge of the carpet as he moved into the library. That an orphan would be able to make so much of his life was astounding. "This is a remarkable place, Fox." While he was impressed and amazed, he doubted the orphanage would've taken him. At fourteen, Ethan had been too old for anything but a workhouse. "Do you have an age limit for those you take in?"

Fox tipped his head right, then left. "Somewhat. It's more of a judgment call. I can tell if someone is too set in their ways to benefit from what we do. We teach them rudimentary skills such as how to speak and eat properly, how to conduct themselves in different situations. It seems like they ought to know such things, but you'd be surprised at what we take for granted in our station."

If only Fox knew the "station" Ethan had been living in, that he knew all too well how different things were for the lower classes. He'd not only been taunted for his good looks, he'd been ridiculed because of his upper-class way of speaking and his manners. He'd worked hard to dirty his language and comport himself in a less formal fashion before he'd established himself.

Ethan glanced around the huge room lined with bookshelves. "The orphans have access to all of this?"

"Yes, I transferred all of the books from Bassett Manor here after my father died. It made more sense to have them accessible for the children. I just borrow the books I want and return them when I'm finished."

His own private lending library. Books were one of the things Ethan had missed most since his father's death. Ethan possessed a passion for reading, but when his mother had sold the house Lockwood had purchased for her, she'd also sold the books. Ethan read when he could, but the life of a master criminal hadn't allowed him such luxury. That's one thing he would do when he regained his life as Ethan Lockwood: He'd have his own goddamned library.

He strolled to the bookshelf and ran his finger along the spines. He inhaled deeply, trying to catch the whiff of parchment and ink, of knowledge and joy. "How did you manage all of this? You inferred that before you married Miranda, you were in financial difficulty. Yet, you managed to keep two estates running and support," he turned to look at Fox, "how many children?"

"It varies, but we currently house forty-nine. We've been able to take in more since I married Miranda. She insisted."

"She now shares your dedication?"

"Vociferously. Hell's teeth, you should've seen her when she was first forced to work here as penance for her scandalous behavior." Fox's eyes crinkled as he smiled. "She was completely out of her element. Still, she bewitched me from the start."

Ethan turned back to the books, picked up a thick volume, and flipped through the pages, relishing the weight of the tome in his palm. He glanced up at Fox. "This is your whole life then? The orphanage?" A noble enterprise.

"And our own family. You haven't yet met Alexander—our son. He's only a year old." Fox gave his head a shake. "He already has everyone wrapped around his finger, just like his mother. He'll be here later this morning, I imagine."

Ethan looked up again, once again surprised. "He spends time here with the orphans?"

Fox's answering stare was cool. "Yes. I grew up with the orphans, and I consider myself the better for it."

Ethan snapped the book shut. "I meant no offense. I was merely startled to hear that you would allow your son to mingle with them. Most gentlemen would not."

Fox inclined his head and seemed to relax slightly. "I'm not most gentlemen. I'm barely a gentleman at all. Remember, I'm just Montgomery Foxcroft, farmer and orphanage owner. Who happened to marry the daughter of a duke."

A vision of Ethan in such a life flashed before him. Could he settle into a situation where he was a country gentleman with a wife and retainers, people who depended upon him? He had underlings who worked for him, but it wasn't the same. On several occasions, they'd turned against him or simply left his employ for a better offer. There was a degree of loyalty, but money and the promise of power always won out. Ethan imagined it was different in Fox's experience. "You've built quite a life for yourself here. It's enviable."

"You hope to do the same in America?" Fox turned toward him and leaned his shoulder against the bookshelf. "Forgive me, but I'm curious as to why you would elope in the first place. Did her parents refuse your suit because of your parentage?" Fox's lip curled in distaste.

Ethan appreciated the other man's compassion, but he wasn't going to divulge any information he didn't have to. "Audrey and I prefer to start our life some-where new. She's long wanted to go to America." That part, at least, was true. Surprisingly so. Ethan could still scarcely believe she'd tried to run off with a black-smith's son. She was either terribly adventurous or ex-ceedingly foolhardy. Ethan recognized those qualities in himself. They were why he'd become a successful criminal—one had to possess a bit of both if one wanted to reap the greatest rewards.

Fox was quiet a moment, perhaps trying to decide whether he would press Ethan for a better answer. Ethan gave him an unwavering stare, daring him to question him further.

With a subtle nod, Fox pushed away from the book-shelf. "If you want to confide in me about anything, I promise you the utmost discretion. America is an aw-fully long way to go, but I suppose the opportunities there are incomparable—for the right people. I hope you and Miss Cheswick are the right people." He straightened. "Come, there's more to see, if you're in-terested. You can take the book if you want."

He did. "Thank you." Ethan tucked the book under his arm and accompanied Fox from the library. Fox's words bounced around his brain—America *was* an aw-fully long way to go. Could he and Audrey start over somewhere closer? Somewhere that would allow him to at least see his brother from time to time?

Alarms pealed in his brain. What the hell was he doing planning *anything* with Audrey in mind? It was all a lie, a fabrication they'd told the Foxcrofts to ex-plain their being here. They had no future, no relation-ship, no reason to be together. The sooner he got away from her, the better. For everyone.

CHAPTER 8

*A*udrey wasn't an early by any account, but she'd slept rather late that morning. The fresh clothes the maid had left were of the construction that allowed Audrey to dress herself. A boon, because she was eager to see Ethan as soon as possible. Though she hurried through her toilet, dealing with her hair without assistance was a particular chore. When she finally decided she was presentable, she made her way—achingly thanks to several days in the saddle—downstairs. Her haste had been for naught however, when she found the breakfast room empty save for Miranda sitting on the floor with her young son.

Miranda smiled up at her. "Good morning, I trust you slept well."

Panic rooted in Audrey's gut and made her feel shaky. She didn't want to make small talk. "Yes, thank you. Has Mr. Locke come down yet?" She practically held her breath waiting for the answer. He wouldn't have left without saying good-bye . . .

"He and Fox are at Stipple's End. If you'd like, we can go for a visit. Just let me take Alexander up to the nurse for his nap."

Audrey recalled that Stipple's End was the orphanage they operated. If Ethan was there, Audrey definitely wanted to go. "That would be lovely. I'll have a quick breakfast."

Miranda scooped her son into her arms and brought him to Audrey. "Say hello to Miss Cheswick, Alex."

He held his hand out toward her, his fingers splayed. "Ba!"

Audrey couldn't help but grin at him in return. "Ba!"

His lips spread to reveal two teeth peeking from the bottom of his mouth. "Ba!"

Audrey moved her head forward so he could touch her cheek. Instead, he grabbed at her hair and pulled a curl free. "Ba!"

Miranda laughed. "We could play this game all day, but you probably want to eat and Alex needs to sleep. Help yourself to the sideboard and ring the bellpull if you need anything—one of the footmen or maids will attend you."

Audrey nodded as they left and went to serve herself. Her mind immediately returned to Ethan and what they were going to do next.

They.

They weren't going to do anything. He was going to leave her here and she was going to what, return to London? She had to convince him to take her with him. At the very least, she wasn't ready for her adventure to end. At the very most, she'd persuade him to trust her and she'd find a way to help him with his Bow Street problem.

While she ate, Audrey pondered how she might get through to Ethan. She also wondered if he'd appropriately cared for his wounds. She'd given him the jar of ointment last night, but had no idea if he'd actually applied it.

As she was finishing up, Miranda returned carrying bonnets for both of them. She handed one to Audrey.

"Thank you for lending me the dress and this bonnet." She set it atop her head, grateful to have something to contain her wayward hair, and tied the ribbons beneath her chin.

"It's no trouble. That dress is from when I was carrying Alexander. I thought the larger bodice might fit you a bit better, though I'm sorry it's so short. But then you're quite tall."

"It's lovely." Audrey ran her hand along the soft cotton day dress. It was pretty, and most importantly, serviceable.

Miranda chuckled. "Not quite what we'd wear in London, is it? I'm a far cry from the young woman who gadded about London without a care for her reputation. Motherhood changes a person drastically. And I suppose my first taste of it came when I worked at Stipple's End two years ago during the summer I was banished from London."

"I remember that. You'd been caught on the Dark Walk at Vauxhall?"

Miranda tied the ribbons of her bonnet. "People weren't supposed to know."

Audrey stood from the table and joined her in leaving the breakfast room. "Lady Lydia Prewitt is my dearest friend. I'm afraid I know many things that people aren't supposed to know." Lydia had spent the last several years as one of the ton's premier gossips, at the behest of her chaperone, London's *premier* gossip, her harridan great-aunt.

"I see." Miranda's lips pursed, and Audrey had the sense that Miranda didn't perhaps care for Lydia. But then many people didn't. However, they didn't know the real Lydia who was kind and witty and the most supportive friend Audrey could ask for. Perhaps now that Lydia was out from under her aunt's control and had decided to build a future with Jason Lockwood, people would see her for who she really was.

"Lydia isn't a bad person. She was the victim of terrible circumstances because of her family. Surely you can understand that?" Audrey knew that Miranda's father, the Duke of Holborn, was a cold and fearsome autocrat. Miranda's sister-in-law, Olivia Sinclair, was a friend of Audrey's, and Audrey had heard a tale or two about the duke's cruelty to his children.

Miranda eyed her cautiously. "I can. And I value second chances. The people here gave me one. They taught me what was truly important in life. Coming here—being exiled—was the best thing that could've happened to me. I thank God every day that I was foolish enough to be sent to the country. It's funny how a poor decision can turn out to be the very thing that makes everything fall into place."

Audrey acknowledged that her decision to accompany Ethan hadn't been well thought out, and only time would tell if any good would come of it. She'd wanted an adventure, something that would fill her with excitement and purpose, instead of detachment and ennui. She blinked. It was already exciting. And she'd felt great purpose in taking care of Ethan's wounds, in helping him to escape, even if she hadn't realized that was what she'd been doing. If he would only trust her, she would do everything in her power to help him. She knew in her heart that he wasn't the monster he purported to be, that he was trying to change. Why else would he have been trying to establish himself in Society?

"Audrey, however did you meet Mr. Locke?"

"Through Lydia, actually. She and Lord Lockwood will be announcing their engagement shortly, I imagine." If they hadn't already. Lydia had planned to tell Lockwood that she loved him and propose marriage to him, if necessary. He'd already asked her—quite publicly—but she'd frozen amidst the stares and expectation of the entire ton, and hadn't responded. She regretted her silence, and his humiliation, to her very bones. Audrey was certain she would make it up to him. They made a surprisingly perfect couple.

Miranda paused a moment as they strolled into the large entry hall. "Indeed? I'm shocked to hear Lockwood is going to marry. What about his vice parties?"

"He's giving them up."

Miranda laughed. "That will disappoint a good number of gentlemen."

"Probably." Audrey averted her gaze and continued toward the front door. She knew far more than most about those parties. With the exception of Lady Philippa Sevrin, Audrey was the only young, unmarried woman to ever attend one. In actuality, she'd attended four, including one on the night she'd left London with Ethan.

"So, Lydia has found love with England's most scandalous rogue, and you've found it with his illegitimate brother?" Miranda shot her an amused glance. "Why did London have to get so interesting *after* I left?"

Audrey couldn't contain a laugh, but then Miranda was laughing too. Though a sobering thought was at the back of Audrey's mind—she hadn't found love with Ethan. What, then, had she found?

Miranda opened the door—Audrey had learned from the maid the previous evening that they didn't have a butler, just a housekeeper, a cook, a small complement of maids who performed various tasks, and only a few footmen who also worked in other capacities such that a retainer was rarely stationed at the entry—and led Audrey into the late morning sunshine.

"What a marvelous day," Miranda said, looking up at the blue sky, marred by just a few drifting clouds. She turned to Audrey expectantly. "Now, you must tell me why you're eloping. Is it because Mr. Locke is illegitimate?"

It was an easy explanation. But would her parents really care? Audrey was nearly four and twenty. They might be happy to marry her off to a bastard. After all, he was the son of a viscount and that was certainly better than a blacksmith's son. "Yes. They're disappointed in my choice."

The coachman drove toward them and brought the vehicle to a halt. He opened the door and assisted first Miranda, then Audrey inside. During the brief, ten-minute trip to Stipple's End, they discussed parental disappointment and how they would be far more understanding of their own children. Audrey only hoped she'd have the chance to be a parent someday.

At Stipple's End, a round-faced woman in an apron greeted them at the door with a broad grin. "Good morning, Miranda." Her face immediately fell. "Where's Alexander?"

"He's napping. Millie promised she would bring him over later." Miranda turned to Audrey. "They hate it when I come without the baby. Audrey, this is Mrs. Gates, Stipple's End's headmistress. Mrs. Gates, this is my friend, Miss Audrey Cheswick."

Mrs. Gates inclined her head. "A pleasure to meet you, Miss Cheswick." She opened the door wide and gestured for them to enter.

"And you." Audrey stepped into a massive hall pungent with the smell of whitewash. The far wall was about half painted, but it looked like they'd stopped in the middle.

"What happened with the painting?" Miranda asked.

"An impromptu picnic in the apple orchard," Mrs. Gates said. "It's such a lovely fall day and who knows how many more we'll get. Plus, the children wanted to pick apples before the rest are harvested next week. Fox and Mr. Locke are with them."

"Then that's where we'll go." Miranda smiled as she linked arms with Audrey and led her through the great hall, then down a narrow corridor to a door that led into the rear yard. They veered left and went down a hill toward the orchard. The midday sun warmed Audrey's shoulders through the linen of her borrowed gown.

The sounds of children playing and laughing wafted toward them. A small group was playing a game in a clearing, while others were climbing trees. A man, whom Audrey was fairly certain was Ethan, stood on a ladder against a tree.

He balanced a basket full of apples on his hip as he climbed down the ladder. At the bottom, he turned. His gray eyes glinted in the sunlight and seemed to heat as they settled on Audrey. "Miss Cheswick," he murmured.

Audrey moved closer and kept her voice low. "You should probably call me Audrey. Since we're supposed to be eloping." She looked at him with raised eyebrows, urging him to comprehend.

He inclined his head. "I see. *Audrey.*"

The single word slid into her chest and wound to her extremities, stroking her like an intimate caress. She recalled they weren't alone, even if it suddenly felt as though they were. "Miranda brought me."

Ethan's gaze moved to Miranda. "Hello. Thank you again for your hospitality." He flicked a glance down at his costume, a gray coat topping a pair of dark blue breeches. The coat was a little wide for his shoulders, but the color suited his black hair and light gray eyes. He wore a simple cravat, which was more than what Fox had donned—his shirt was open at the collar. He came around the tree with another basket of apples and set them near his wife.

Fox dropped a kiss on Miranda's cheek. "You are as lovely as the day is bright."

Miranda rolled her eyes. "My husband, the poet." She gave him a look that clearly held some sort of personal, intimate meaning. Audrey returned her attention to Ethan, lest she intrude.

But averting her gaze to Ethan offered no solace, for he was staring at her with an intensity that was going to set her face on fire. "Why are you looking at me like that?" she whispered urgently before thinking better of it.

"We're supposed to be a couple, aren't we?" He took her hand, their bare fingers touching and igniting sensations Audrey felt all the way to her core. He lifted her hand and kissed the back, his eyes never leaving hers.

Despite the warmth of the sun, shiver after shiver raced up and down her spine. "Should you have been climbing the ladder? What about your arm?"

"It's much better." He spoke softly. "More importantly, I don't want them to know I'm injured. Too many questions."

She understood. "Did you put the poultice on it?"

"Yes, *Nurse*." His gaze danced with merriment and she was reminded of her flirtatious waltzing partner instead of the dangerous criminal.

"Come and have some chicken," Fox said, indicating a blanket bedecked with several hampers of food. "There's a special basket for us adults."

Ethan let go of Audrey's hand, which would've been disappointing, if he hadn't immediately slid it to her lower back to guide her to the blanket. Audrey practically floated there. She didn't remember the last time a gentleman had paid her such singular attention. Probably because it had never happened.

They situated themselves on the blanket while the children continued their antics around them. Normally, Audrey would've been interested in their games and laughter, but she couldn't tear her attention away from her enigmatic companion. It seemed she didn't need to try very hard to pretend they were a couple.

Miranda dished them up some chicken and, naturally, apples, though she gave Audrey a lighter portion, likely since she'd only eaten breakfast a short while ago.

Audrey didn't care, she wasn't the least bit interested in food.

Fox turned to Audrey. "Locke tells me that you and he are going to America."

Miranda gasped. "*America?* Why?"

Fox laughed. "Pardon my wife. She once held Wootton Bassett in the same esteem."

She playfully smacked his arm. "At least it's still England. And I came around. I can't imagine living anywhere else now."

"I imagine you'd do the same in America if we went together. After all, it's not where you live, but who you're with that really matters."

Miranda's eyes locked with her husband's and her lips curved into a beatific smile. "I couldn't agree more."

Neither could Audrey. Which was why she was willing to go to America with Ethan. Had he really told Fox that, and had he meant it? She slid him a glance. He was eating a chicken leg, seemingly oblivious to the topic. But she knew him better than that. He paid attention to everything.

Miranda turned to look at Audrey. "What will your family think of that?"

Audrey lifted a shoulder. "They'll have to grow accustomed to it."

Miranda exhaled. "They will. My parents did." She flashed Fox a commiserative grin. "Although, you needn't go all the way to America to avoid your family. Wootton Bassett is far enough removed that I needn't tolerate my parents and they needn't suffer me or Fox. It's a splendid arrangement."

"I suppose we could stay in England," Audrey said. Except they weren't even actually eloping. She was all but certain he was preparing to abandon her here. Why then had he told Fox they were going to America? It must be part of some ruse—hopefully he planned to clue her in. She glanced at Ethan, but he was watching the children who were rolling down the hill.

"I hope you'll consider it." Miranda's eyes widened and she leaned toward Audrey and touched her arm. "You could even settle here. We'd love to find someone to help us with the orphanage. It just keeps growing and there's so much to do. What do you think, Mr. Locke?"

Ethan's focus was still on the children. "I haven't done that—rolling down hills—in ages."

Audrey stifled a smile at Ethan's complete—and typical—lack of response to Miranda's inquiries. Normally, Audrey found this behavior infuriating, but in this instance it was surprisingly endearing. Maybe because she suddenly wanted to roll down the hill. With him.

"Then, we'll have to partake." Fox stood up and held his hand for Miranda. "Come, dear wife."

Miranda took his hand and got to her feet.

"Since I'm wearing a borrowed costume, I feel as though I must ask if I may join in," Ethan said, standing.

As fun as it looked, Audrey didn't think it would be good for Ethan's arm. At all. "My dress is also borrowed. I'd feel terrible if we ruined the clothing." She tried to send Ethan a pleading glance to silently tell him to sit back down.

Fox shook his head. "It's no bother. And consider them yours. We won't send you on your way without provisions." His eyes hooded for a moment. "Nor will we ask why you didn't have any to begin with."

But it had been noted. Audrey stood up in an effort to battle the sudden uneasiness she felt.

Miranda pretended to scowl at him. "Fox, be nice. It's not as if we haven't ignored propriety."

Fox pointed his finger at her. "*You* ignored propriety. I tried very hard to court you properly."

"Fine." She lifted her chin and gave him a haughty look. "Either way, *be nice* and mind your own business."

He held his hands up in defeat, then swatted her backside as they turned toward the hill. Miranda threw her husband a flirty, provocative glance. Audrey snuck a look at Ethan to see what he thought of their romantic play, but he was busy brushing a speck of something from his sleeve.

He looked up and registered her, arching his brow in silent question.

"What about your arm? You really oughtn't roll down that hill."

"What am I to say?" He touched the small of her back again and urged her to follow Fox and Miranda.

"Just tell them you fell off your horse or something."

He chuckled. "No. My riding skills are poor enough without adding that lie."

"You like lying." At his dark look, she added, " You at least like avoiding the truth." And he was rather good at it.

He peered sideways at her. "Maybe I just want to roll down a hill with you."

"Hurry up!" Miranda called from the top of the hill.

They hastened their pace and joined Fox, Miranda, and the boy who was leading the activity.

"Philip," Fox said, "we need an adults-only race."

Philip, a boy of maybe thirteen or so, grinned. "You heard Fox," he shouted to the children. "Move aside so our elders can have a go."

Fox cringed at the word elders, but only shook his head with a small smile. "How does this work? First one to the bottom wins what?"

"First pick of Mrs. Gates's cakes this afternoon at tea," Philip said.

Fox tapped his finger against his mouth. "That won't work for us as we likely won't be attending tea."

"The winner gets to determine our after-dinner entertainment this evening," Miranda said with a mischievous glint to her eye.

Fox leaned toward Audrey and Ethan. "We can't let her win, else we'll be subjected to charades or some such nonsense."

Miranda crossed her arms. "You have no idea what I have in mind."

Audrey had her own ideas about the sort of after-dinner entertainment she might prefer, but none of it included their hosts.

"I'll take care of winning," Ethan said with a determined set to his mouth. Audrey had seen him look like that many times before. Miranda didn't stand a chance.

Philip moved back from the top of the hill. "All right then, assume your positions. Just lie down on your side facing the slope."

The children gathered around Philip, their faces eager. Some moved to stand near Fox at the end, clearly interested in how he would fare.

Audrey lay down on the grass on her side. Then she turned her head to see Philip.

"Ready? Roll!" Philip brought his arm down.

Audrey pushed herself and rolled a few feet before stopping. The slope wasn't that steep at first, so they had to work to keep rolling. She propelled herself forward and tumbled a few more feet, laughing as the shouts and cheers of the children spurred her onward. She held her arms close to her sides and threw herself down the hill. The ground fell away as she hit a steeper section and her rotation picked up speed. Her equilibrium went completely sideways as she rolled faster and faster. She closed her eyes to keep the swirling images of ground and sky at bay. Then she landed against something firm, yet very warm.

She opened her eyes and found herself staring into clear gray. In rather close proximity. So close, she could feel his heat.

And see the tight set of his features.

Alarm washed through her. "Are you all right?" She hoped he hadn't ripped out his stitches.

"I think so." His voice was tight, thin. "That was, however, ill-advised. I should probably listen to you in the future."

Audrey would remind him that he said that. "Yes, you should. Although, I must commend you on re-fraining from cursing."

This elicited a laugh of such warmth from him that Audrey couldn't help but laugh with him.

"Believe me," he said, "it took a great deal of effort."

"Did you do that for me or for the children?"

His gaze was steady, direct. Soul-stirring. "The children can't hear me."

For her, then. She nearly forgot they were in the middle of broad daylight in sight of dozens of people and leaned forward to kiss him.

He shook his head and pushed himself up to a sit-ting position. "Not here," he murmured.

"Not here" perhaps meant someplace else. She could hardly wait.

With a grimace, Ethan got to his feet. Audrey scrambled up. Fox and Miranda were twenty or so feet away, laughing. The children were chanting, "Fox won! Fox won!"

"Damn shoulder," Ethan said. "I should've won."

Audrey wished she could check his wounds. She hoped he hadn't disturbed the sutures. They weren't due to come out for several more days. "You're swearing again."

He shot her an apologetic glance. It was a first, and caught her off guard. But she recovered quickly in order to take advantage. "Why did you tell them we were going to America? You're not really planning on doing that are you?"

His answer came swiftly. "No. They're coming," he

whispered. He wrapped his good arm around her waist and drew her close. "Well rolled, Fox."

Audrey leaned into Ethan. Though she knew there was no future for them, she gave herself up to the ruse. For today she would pretend to be Ethan's fiancée. And she would cherish every moment of it. Tomorrow—forever—would come soon enough.

CHAPTER 9

As the winner of the rolling contest, Fox had chosen dancing as their after-dinner entertainment. To have an adequate number for dancing, Miranda had invited two other couples. The Knotts, Rob who was Fox's steward and his wife Felicity, were longtime friends of Fox's. Beatrice Stratham was Miranda's distant cousin—her parents had taken Miranda in after she'd been exiled from London. Beatrice's husband, Donovan, was a former MP who'd lost his seat after admitting to accepting bribes. Miranda had told Audrey that Fox had been instrumental in exposing Stratham, which, understandably, made for a strained relationship between the two men. However, since their wives had become close, they suffered each other's company when required.

Ethan escorted Audrey from the dining room. "What sort of dancing will there be?" he whispered near her ear.

She leaned toward him. "A lot of the kind I believe you termed 'silly.'" That had been during their first waltzing lesson.

"I haven't the slightest idea how to do anything but waltz."

She patted his arm as they entered the drawing

room. "You caught on to waltzing fairly easily. I'm sure you'll do the same with country dancing. I'll make sure Miranda and Fox call the first dance and we'll go last. That way you can see how it's done."

He gave her a sidelong glance. "I'll just nod and pretend I understand what you're saying."

Audrey smiled at him and laughed softly. "You can *pretend* you know how to dance as well as I pretended to be drunk when we borrowed that cabriolet. You'll be as fine as you look." She dipped her head to hide the blush that stole up her cheeks. She couldn't help herself; he *did* look fine. He'd been outfitted in a splendid costume that fit him well enough for her to wonder if someone had made alterations to his clothing as Felicity Knott had done to Audrey's gown. She'd added a flounce to the hem of one of Miranda's old dresses so that it now suited Audrey's height.

"Thank you," he said, addressing her embarrassing comment. "However, I'm certain I pale in comparison to your brilliance this evening."

Now her blush was for an altogether different reason. Thankfully they were summoned for the dance. She gave him an encouraging look and led him to the makeshift dance floor.

Over the next half hour, Ethan made an extraordinary effort to keep up. If anyone noticed he'd never performed a country dance in his life, they didn't say so.

Stratham, a somewhat short—shorter than Audrey anyway—but attractive fellow smoothed back his dark hair. "I say, Locke, been awhile since you danced?"

Or at least, they *hadn't*.

Ethan shot the former MP a scalding look, but quickly masked it. Not that Stratham would have noticed. He spent most of his time fawning over his wife, who was expecting their first child.

A small array of refreshments had been laid out, and

the gentlemen now took an opportunity to enjoy a glass of spirits. Beatrice and Felicity were discussing her impending motherhood while Miranda came to Audrey with a slight grimace. "I have to beg your pardon for Stratham. He can be a bit of a blurter."

Audrey nodded understandingly. "It's all right. Ethan doesn't dance very much, and when he does, it's typically a waltz. Like the other night at the assembly."

Miranda flashed a smile. "Is that what you were doing?"

Audrey's face heated, much to her chagrin, but she was a hopeless cause when it came to subduing her self-awareness.

"I must beg your pardon," Miranda said, touching Audrey's arm, "I didn't mean to embarrass you."

"It's all right. I've a terrible habit of blushing. All the time. It's a nuisance." She'd almost said "bloody nuisance," speaking of terrible habits. Ethan was apparently leaving his impression.

"How long do you think you and Mr. Locke will stay before you continue on to America?" Miranda wrinkled her nose. "My apologies, but it's just so far away. Like I said this afternoon, I just don't see why you need to go that far. Why not go to Gretna Green and then come back to England?" She cocked her head to the side and smiled softly. "You could come back here, in fact."

"What do you mean?"

"Fox was telling me about Mr. Locke's interest in the orphanage. He seems like a man looking for his place in the world. And we really would love to find some people—the right people—to help us enlarge the facilities at Stipple's End. Imagine being able to help even more children."

Ethan was interested in the orphanage? Audrey was surprised by this. More than surprised. She was intrigued. "You'd let us come to stay? To live?"

Miranda patted her arm. "It's something to think about." She looked over at Felicity and Beatrice, who were coming toward them.

Audrey forced a smile as she tried to push the conversation to the back of her mind. It was difficult—Miranda had given her more than *something* to think about: She'd given them another option.

However, it included one crucial aspect she and Ethan had never discussed, and one she wasn't even sure either of them wanted: marriage. She liked Ethan and was attracted to him, but there were so many things she didn't know about him. Put that with the things she *did* know, and she had to admit a future with him seemed unlikely, no matter how wonderful he made her feel.

She just had to convince him to stay. Perhaps time would make things clearer?

～

*L*ater that night, Ethan eased out of his shirt. Undressing had been easier with Audrey to help him. He could've accepted the offer of a valet from Fox, but had declined. He'd tried using one when he'd entered Society several weeks ago, but it was an unusual thing to become accustomed to, and the notion just hadn't stuck. Perhaps that was because the man Ethan had employed was a criminal like him. He hadn't wanted to invite an unknown into his inner circle. It seemed he couldn't even trust someone to take care of his clothing.

Furthermore, a valet provided by Fox would've seen his wounds, and Ethan didn't need to explain stitches to a retainer who would blather it to all and sundry. He knew servants, and they were a gossipy lot.

He had, however, asked for a basin of hot water so he could bathe. Barefooted, he padded to the glass in the corner to scrutinize his wound. It had bled a bit, leaving a small, dark stain on the bandage, but it thankfully hadn't seeped through to his shirt.

After unwrapping the bandage and dropping it to the floor, he prodded at the flesh. It didn't look angry and it was feeling better, though the hill-rolling had been agony. He'd been cursing his foolishness all afternoon, through dinner, and throughout their post-dinner entertainment.

Ethan didn't remember when he'd had such a wonderful time. He hadn't thought of Gin Jimmy or Bow Street or his brother or anything but keeping up with Audrey and learning several new dances—country dances, which he'd never imagined he'd enjoy and which he'd never remember on the morrow. Though he might not recall the steps, he'd remember the evening forever.

Damn, it had felt good to be normal, if only for a day. He was sorely tempted to stay another day, but he worried it would turn into another and another. Still, would that be so terrible?

Miranda's invitation for them to remain and help with the orphanage, though likely spoken in fun, actually held appeal. He'd never imagined he could be happy anywhere but London, but seeing the difference Fox made to so many young people gave him pause. When he thought of the boys he could help—boys from London that he could bring here and educate . . . They'd be safe from London's crime and grit, from the temptations that would inevitably lure them to a life of bitterness and regret.

A life like Ethan's.

A gentle click had him reaching for the knife in his boot, but he wasn't wearing anything on his feet. He turned from the glass and instantly relaxed at the sight of Audrey creeping into his room.

He hurried to the door and closed it swiftly, leaning

against the wood and peering at her, garbed in a dressing gown wrapped tightly about her middle. The gown barely reached her ankles, giving him the opportunity to appreciate her naked feet. Pity there wasn't more of her to see.

She immediately fixed her gaze on his arm. "I came to see to your injuries." She took his hand and dragged him to the fireplace where a fire burned brightly. The day had been warm, but the night had turned quite cold.

Ethan allowed himself—happily—to be managed by her. Perhaps his perfect day wasn't over after all.

She looked at his knife wound and frowned. "There's dried blood."

"Hardly any. I'm fine."

With a mild scowl, she went to the basin with its now-tepid water and dabbed a cloth into it. She returned to him and cleaned around the stitches as best she could. "Does that hurt?"

"No," he lied. It actually hurt a little, but it was nothing compared to the pleasure elicited by her fingers stroking his skin.

"Where's the poultice?"

"The drawer in that table next to the bed."

She fetched the ointment and spread it on his wound. She drew a length of cotton from the pocket of her gown. "I brought you a new bandage." She wrapped it around his arm and secured the ends. "There. No more rolling down hills." She gave him a sincere, but captivating stare.

He held up his hands in surrender. "You win. Thank you for coming. I suppose you should go back to your room."

Her eyes narrowed. "Not so fast. You owe me an explanation. You told me you didn't have time to stay here, that you needed to be on your way. And then you go and tell Fox that we're eloping to America. I'm not going to let you evade my questions. Not this time."

She was so resolute, so adorably perturbed, he almost wanted to prolong her irritation. But even he wasn't that cruel. "I had to tell Fox something."

She edged backward from him. "You plan to leave, then?"

He frowned. He didn't want her to go. "I must. At some point."

"Why?"

He couldn't give her all the answers she wanted. It was one thing to confess to killing Four-Finger Tom. That had been more than a decade ago. He wouldn't tell her he was wanted for killing the Marquess of Wolverton, particularly because he hadn't done it and he was afraid she wouldn't believe him. She liked him. She looked at him in a way no other woman had ever looked at him, and dammit she was like sunlight to his blackened soul. She didn't want anything from him, save his trust. Ironically—tragically—it was the one thing he just couldn't give. "It's complicated."

"It doesn't have to be," she said softly, lowering her gaze to the carpet that cushioned their feet before the fireplace. When she raised her face once more, her eyes were so clear and blue-green, he thought he might be looking out at the sea. He'd seen it twice. Just last spring when he'd gone to Cornwall for a prizefight, and as a boy when his father had taken him to Brighton. That life was barely a memory, and yet after a day like today, it seemed within his grasp.

She straightened her spine and clenched her jaw. "Why did you take me with you?"

Because Gin Jimmy had sent men to take her. They thought she was important to him. And, dammit, if she hadn't been then, she sure as hell was now. The best thing he could do for her, though, would be to leave her so that Gin Jimmy would think he'd tired of her. He never kept a woman long, so it made sense that Ethan would discard her at some point.

But what of Bow Street? It was one thing to start over in Wootton Bassett to avoid an irksome family as Lady Miranda had done, but something altogether different to escape charges of murder. Sooner or later, he was going to have to deal with that.

"I took you with me to protect you from those men who came to your house." He watched her intently. "You remember what they said—that they'd come there for you."

She suddenly looked very tense. "Who were they?"

"Men who work for my employer, Gin Jimmy. He's a lord of crime, Audrey, a very bad man."

"Why did they come for me?"

As always, he considered how much to reveal. In this case, he didn't think it would harm her—or him—to know the truth. "They think you mean something to me. I suspect they saw me sneaking into your house when you gave me waltzing lessons." Which meant they'd been following him for weeks. How long had Gin Jimmy suspected Ethan of turning against him? Or had he simply been keeping tabs on Ethan, who'd been sent into Society to keep an eye on the widow of one of Gin Jimmy's "inside men," an earl who, for a price, had identified opportunities for theft within the ton. That widow had ultimately been killed, a murder Ethan was also being charged with.

Audrey's eyes rounded briefly before she turned to look at the fire. "I see. But you think I'm safe here, so you can continue on and I'll stay? That's what you planned isn't it?"

There was no point lying to her. She deserved the truth—at least as much as it pertained to her. "Yes, I think you'll be safe this far away from London. I planned to ask you to cry off. Then I'll leave."

She threw him a sad smile. "That's magnanimous of you. However, it won't spare my reputation."

He couldn't keep himself from edging closer to her. "You knew your reputation would be damaged the minute you stepped outside your window."

"I did. And I'd do it again." She turned to face him, just a mere foot or so away. He could reach out and touch her, but he didn't dare. She deserved so much more than he could give.

"Ethan." Her eyes turned soft. "I would do it again. I don't want to go back to London—even if I could and it sounds as if it's not safe for me there, at least not yet and maybe not ever? I don't really understand how this is supposed to work. But you said you could protect me, so," she took a deep breath, "take me with you."

His heart hammered, sending reverberations of want and need through his body until they settled in his groin. Women had begged him for all manner of things: favors, his attention, money. Never had they asked for his company in so earnest a fashion, as if their very peace depended upon it. Still, he couldn't allow her into the darkness that was his existence. Not now, and, to echo her words, maybe not ever.

"I can't."

"Why not? You said I'm safer with you. Keep me safe. Let me do the same for you. I don't think anyone has cared for you. I do. I will."

The room swayed a moment and his knees felt as though they might give way. He could scarcely bear what she was offering, and yet his soul hungered for it like nothing before.

She stepped before him and cradled his cheek. "Don't turn me away. I want to come with you—of my own accord. There is nothing for me anywhere. I've never felt as alive as I do with you. Together, we can figure out whatever we need to figure out. Or," she smiled crookedly, "we can actually go to America and be whoever the hell we want."

She'd cursed. For him.

Ethan crushed his mouth over hers in a blistering kiss. He didn't want to coax or invite her, he wanted to own her, to tame her, to bring her completely under his control. When he decided he wanted something, he conquered it fully, and he wanted Audrey.

He thrust his hands into her hair, knowing it would tumble from its pins with the barest of effort. He wasn't disappointed. With a gentle movement of his fingers, her curls cascaded over his hands and down her back. Violets and honey filled his senses.

He plundered her mouth with his tongue, pleased when she met him thrust for thrust. Her hands clutched at his neck as she pressed herself into him. She was taller than any other woman he'd held, which meant she fit against him in ways no other woman had. His cock burned against her hip. He adjusted her, pulling her so that he was between her thighs. He drifted one hand down her back and splayed his hand across her backside, drawing her tightly to him.

She moaned softly. Ethan continued to devour her mouth as he brought his hand around to the front of her dressing gown. He slid his hand beneath the fabric, wondering if—hoping that—she was naked beneath it. But she wasn't. Her chemise prevented him from connecting with her bare flesh. It was just the interruption he needed for sanity to gain a foothold in his brain.

He pulled away abruptly and stepped back. "Audrey," he croaked. "You should return to your chamber."

"I don't want to." She untied her dressing gown, but stopped short of slipping it from her shoulders. She was trying very hard to be seductive and brave, but he saw the underlying tremor of apprehension.

Christ, she was a virgin. Ethan didn't *do* virgins. Not since he'd been one, anyway. That had been an awk-

ward affair when he was fifteen. From then on, he'd
sought out more experienced partners. Yet, he felt certain none of them would hold a candle to Audrey.

"Audrey, you must. Your reputation might be
tainted, but I will not be responsible for actually ruining you."

"What if I told you I was already ruined?"

He thought of the blacksmith's son and her aborted
escape to America. Her behavior with him over the past
several days did not indicate a woman who was comfortable with a man on an intimate level. "I wouldn't
believe you."

Even as he said it, he was less sure. Had something
happened with the blacksmith's son? He suddenly
wanted to get on a goddamned ship and find the prick
on the other side of the world.

Her frame relaxed slightly, and so did his. "I can tell
you want me. Why can't I stay?"

He couldn't keep from laughing, loving her honesty.
How strange and pleasant the world would be if people
were as genuine as her.

"It's best for everyone." He reached out and tied her
robe closed, his hands lightly shaking as they grazed
her hip. He wanted so desperately to tear every strip of
fabric from her body and worship her in the golden
glow of the fire. "You deserve a better life than running
with me."

She splayed her hand against his chest, and his will
faltered. "You don't have to run." She was killing him.

He kissed her again, more gently this time, but still
with all the need he'd suppressed for as long as he could
remember. Forever, probably. He could relent. Relinquish the control he relied upon to keep himself apart,
safe, alone. It was why he didn't trust anyone to get
close. They'd all left him or hurt him or both. If there
was one thing he'd learned it was that nothing was permanent. Nothing. At least not for him.

He tore his mouth from hers. He put his hands on her shoulders and pushed away from her, backing up several steps before he could change his mind. "Go. Please."

"I won't cry off." She elevated her chin and gave him a challenging stare. "You'll have to be the one to do it." She knew he didn't want to, was trying to call his bluff. She turned and left, her curls taunting him as she went.

He stared at the closed door for a long time. It was unfortunate she didn't realize that no one forced him to do anything. Why then, was he considering it?

❧

*A*udrey had a maid wake her early the next morning. She didn't want Ethan dashing off before she rose. When she arrived downstairs, however, she learned he'd accompanied Fox to the orphanage to help him with some repairs. Worried he might try to leave her at Bassett Manor, she hurried to join them.

During the short ride to Stipple's End, she relived Ethan's kisses. And his rejection. She'd been disappointed that he'd turned her away, but she also knew how painful it had been for him to do so. She smiled, hoping she'd started to convince him they could be better together than apart.

Upon arriving at the orphanage, she was relieved to find him and Fox working on a section of fence. Around a sheep pasture. She smiled at the irony, given where they'd slept two nights ago.

The remainder of the morning passed in a blur as Audrey assisted Mrs. Gates with various duties around Stipple's End. It was nearly luncheon when Mrs. Gates asked her to oversee the children in setting the table. When Audrey was finished, she made her way to the kitchen to see if she could help serve the food.

Audrey halted just outside the door at the sound of

Rob Knott's voice. "The man said he was from Bow Street, that he was looking for a man called Jagger or Locke."

"Bow Street?" Fox said, his tone rising with surprise.

Bow Street was here? Audrey couldn't breathe. She didn't want to alert anyone to her presence, but more importantly, she just couldn't seem to draw air into her lungs.

"Unfortunately, Stratham overheard the man and offered that he'd met Locke at Bassett Manor, that he's your guest."

Fox swore. "Pardon me, Mrs. Gates. Stratham's a menace."

"Did you know Bow Street was looking for Locke?" Rob asked.

"No, I didn't." Fox sounded dismayed. "I'll go and speak with him. Rob, is the Runner on his way?"

"I don't know," Rob said. "As soon as I realized Bow Street was looking for him, I came straight here."

It was all Audrey needed to hear. She tore out of the building and stopped short. Miranda and three girls were just dismounting from their horses in the stable yard. Audrey could scarcely believe her good luck. She hurried over.

Miranda handed her reins to one of the boys who were learning how to groom. "Audrey, are we late for luncheon? I lost track of time, I'm afraid. The girls were doing so well today."

"No, you're right on time." Audrey eyed Miranda's mount. "Do you mind if I borrow one of the horses? I need to fetch Ethan and I turned my ankle, so I'd prefer to ride." The lie fell off her tongue with surprising ease.

"Not at all, take mine," Miranda said.

Audrey wasn't sure she wanted to take Miranda's horse. What if she and Ethan left immediately? She was still only borrowing the creature, but the length of the loan was currently indeterminate. "I'll just take this one." She took the reins of the nearest animal.

"That's Posy. She won't give you any trouble."

Audrey led her to the block and mounted. "See you in a bit!" She rather doubted that was true and felt a pang of regret that she was perhaps leaving without a proper thank-you or good-bye. She smiled at Miranda. "Thank you. For everything." Then she turned Posy and raced for the sheep pasture.

~

*E*than drove a nail into the fence, the effort and exercise soothing him in a way he'd never expected. It was so different out here—the quiet, the smell of earth and grass, the simplicity. He wasn't sure he liked it, but he didn't hate it. He did, however, like feeling needed and that he was making a positive impact. By repairing a fence at an orphanage? He scoffed at himself. He could do better than that.

In London, he did what he could. He tried to look out for young boys, and while it was typically too late to dissuade them from crime, he did his best to teach them how to take care of themselves. He schooled them in ways he'd never been taught, and he hoped he made some small difference.

Except in the instance of Oscar. He'd been a young lad, small for his age, orphaned—or so he'd said. He could easily have had parents who were either too drunk to care for him or had pushed him out because they had too many other mouths to feed. At nine, he would've been deemed old enough to take care of himself.

He'd turned up in one of the flash houses and would've been put to work as a prostitute, or he might've joined up with a young theft gang. He'd tried to pick pockets, but hadn't been very adept. Ethan could see that he was going to fail and likely end up in gaol or worse. So Ethan, who'd been relatively young at the time, just seventeen, had taken the boy out of London to a vicarage.

Ethan had earned sufficient funds to pass himself off as a gentleman. He'd convinced the vicar that the orphaned Oscar would make an excellent groomsman or gardener or anything the vicar could train him to be. He'd then given the vicar a sum of money large enough to ensure he couldn't say no. But as it happened, the money hadn't been necessary. The vicar's wife had brought them tea and upon hearing what Ethan had proposed had wept. They'd been unable to have children of their own and she saw Oscar as a gift from God. It had been the happiest day of Ethan's life.

Upon returning to London, however, a few of his cohorts had suspected what he'd done. It had made him look soft and weak. He'd never indulged that sort of fancy again. And now, here, amidst Fox's kindness and benevolence, his lack of action weighed on him.

The sound of an approaching horse made him look up. A lone rider was coming toward him down the road that ran beside the sheep pasture. The back of Ethan's neck tingled, but he shrugged the sensation away. It could be anyone.

The brim of his hat shielded his eyes from the sun, but he squinted nonetheless in an effort to make out the rider. As he drew nearer, Ethan's blood ran cold as recognition hit him. *Teague.*

Ethan tensed to run, but the horse would overtake him quickly. His mind raced. He didn't want to be dragged back to London to the noose. Unfortunately, that seemed suddenly inevitable. Unless he could take Teague down.

Teague led his horse through the gap in the fence— the gap Ethan and Fox had been repairing—and stopped. He withdrew a pistol from his coat and pointed it at Ethan's heart. "Finally found you."

Ethan fought to keep the panic at bay. His fingers clenched around the hammer. Its presence gave him a modicum of comfort. "You came an awfully long way. Most people would've given up. In fact, I didn't realize the Runners even came this far out." He was satisfied that he sounded calm, unaffected, but then he'd spent years perfecting such deceit.

Teague slid from his horse, but kept his gun trained on Ethan. "I'd follow you to the ends of the earth. Particularly now that I have you away from your protective army, and I've charges to lay against you to boot."

"Ah yes, the charges. You've been working so hard to find something. The irony here is that this is one crime I am not guilty of."

Teague's lip curled. "I saw you standing over Wolverton's body with a bloody knife. It doesn't get much more damning than that."

Ethan couldn't argue that, but he hadn't killed the marquess. "It was Gin Jimmy. You know Wolverton controlled a theft ring. He worked for Gin Jimmy, just like Aldridge did."

"And Wolverton ended up dead, just like Aldridge." Teague cocked his head to the side. "You're Gin Jimmy's right hand. You were there. It's logical you would carry out his bidding."

Logical, yes, but he hadn't done it. Ethan gritted his teeth. "I'm guilty of a lot of things, but this isn't one of them."

Teague's dark eyes glittered in the midday sun. "Do catalog them for me so that I may increase the charges against you. Shall we start with my sister?"

Ethan expected nothing less. "There was nothing illegal about what happened with your sister. You can't fault me for her choices."

"The hell I can't. She died because of what you did to her."

A stab of regret pierced Ethan's gut. Janey Teague had been a nice girl once. Just as he'd been a decent boy. That she'd chosen a dangerous life instead of fighting for whatever opportunities her brother had found wasn't Ethan's fault. At fifteen, they'd been each other's first lovers. He'd liked her, liked having someone he could be intimate with, but their relationship hadn't lasted long. She was young, beautiful, and possessed a wealth of charm. Lured by the promise of fame and fortune, she'd left Ethan to become some man's paramour. Years later, when she'd fallen out of favor and had found herself back in Ethan's world, she'd tried to use their former association to gain entry into Gin Jimmy's favorite flash house, presumably to draw Jimmy's eye. However, she'd been turned away and months later, Ethan had heard she'd died of drink. Teague blamed him for her death since she'd told him on her deathbed that Ethan had been the one to ruin her.

Ethan gripped the hammer and calculated whether he could use it to disarm Teague. "I was a lad and she was more than willing. And *she* left me—I had nothing to do with her later choices. I am sorry for her death, but if I hadn't been her first, she would've found someone else."

"You rotten piece of filth!" Teague spat.

"I'm not going with you," Ethan said quietly. He tested the hammer's weight in his hand. "I didn't kill Wolverton. You're going to have to fight me."

Teague shook his head. "Drop the hammer or I'll put a bullet in you. That'd be a shame since I'd prefer to watch you hang. The other Runner will be here shortly. We'll shackle you and take you into town where we'll get a cart to transport you back to London."

Ethan's blood turned to ice. The sound of hooves

beating against the earth reached his ears and his stomach clenched. The other Runner.

"As I said. Here comes Lewis." His mouth contorted into a snarl. "Now, drop the hammer."

Ethan glanced at the road, but there was no horse. Then he saw it racing down the slope from the orphanage. It was sidesaddled and there was a skirt flowing against the horse's flank. *Audrey.*

Relief poured through him and he sought to distract Teague so he could gain the upper hand. He grinned toward Audrey. "It's not Lewis."

Teague turned, his brow knitting. Ethan lunged forward and used the hammer to knock the pistol from Teague's hand. The weapon fired into the air, and Teague's horse darted off.

Teague spun toward him as Audrey bore down on them. She ran her mount at Teague, who fell to the side before he could be trampled.

"Ethan!" she called, bringing her horse to a halt beside him. "Get on."

He wanted to tell her to get off the horse so he could leave alone, but how in the hell was he going to ride a horse with a sidesaddle? He climbed up, awkwardly, behind her and she maneuvered the animal out to the road. She kicked the horse to a full run.

He wrapped his arms around her waist and held on, grateful that she was an excellent horsewoman. Or so he thought. He really had no expertise in the matter.

Her head was bare, her dark curls blowing against his cheeks, evidence perhaps that she'd dropped whatever she was doing and come to his rescue. While part of him thrilled at this notion, the rest of him was cold and dead. She shouldn't be here with him. She should be back at Bassett Manor where she could be safe.

After a short while, she slowed the horse.

His insides twisted frantically. "Must you slow down?"

"I can't run Posy that hard for too long."

Posy? He looked up at the sky and tried to gauge their direction. Southeast of Wootton Bassett, he would guess. What was he going to do with Audrey? "You can't come with me anymore."

She shook her head. "I'm not leaving you. I still have money, and you don't. You need me."

He'd been alone as long as he could remember. Teague had just reminded him of that. "I don't need anyone. And I'm fairly certain your informing that farmer the other morning that we were on our way to Wootton Bassett is how Teague found me." She'd made a simple mistake, and if he wasn't such a prick he wouldn't have thrown it in her face. But he needed her to go back, and maybe if she stopped liking him, she would.

"I'm sorry. But I'm not leaving you." She was quiet a moment, but he sensed she wasn't finished. "The Runner—Teague?—he followed you an awfully long way. Will you now tell me why he means to arrest you?"

They'd come to a copse of trees, a perfect place to take cover if need be. Audrey brought Posy to a stop.

"What are you doing?" Ethan hissed near her ear.

"Stopping." She turned her head to look at him. "I just saved you back there, something I've been doing for days now, and you still won't tell me why Bow Street is chasing you all over England. I deserve to know the truth."

Ethan glared at her, hating that she'd helped him, even as he felt relief and gladness that she really should go with him now. Teague had found him, so there was a chance Gin Jimmy's men might not be far behind. Ethan's irritation at his lack of control over the entire situation took hold of his emotions. He slid from the horse, needing to think for a moment. "I never asked you to help me."

"I'm not leaving." She followed him, albeit gracelessly, and landed against him. She clasped his arms to steady himself. He cringed as her fingers bit into his wound. She pulled her hands away. "Sorry." Her eyes hardened. "No, I'm not sorry. And I'm not letting you go alone."

The sound of approaching horses drew them both to turn. Two riders were bearing down on them, and judging from the way their pistols were pointed, they were either more Runners or worse—Gin Jimmy's men.

CHAPTER 10

*E*than shoved Audrey to the ground and fell on top of her. So much for her being safe out here.

The report of a pistol sounded. Ethan braced for pain and exhaled when there was nothing. He glanced back and saw one of the men climbing down from his horse, while the other was still riding straight for them. Posy whinnied and ran off.

Ethan rolled off Audrey and dragged her up. "Move!" He ran with her to the trees and pulled her behind a thick trunk. "Can you climb one of these?"

She turned her head to look at him and squeezed his hand. "I'm not leaving you."

He leaned his head back against the rough wood. "Christ, you're impossible. You'll be safer up there."

"I can't let you fight both of them. They have pistols."

"Jagger, there's nowhere else to run," one of the men shouted.

Ethan peered around the trunk. A lanky fellow with his pistol cocked moved into the copse. The second one wasn't visible. Probably reloading his pistol, if he was smart.

Ethan slid the knife from his boot. If he'd learned anything from his years preserving himself, it was to act fast and act sure. He stepped out from behind the tree and launched his knife at the man with the pistol. The blade drove into his flesh just beneath his collarbone. He managed to fire, but the shot came nowhere near Ethan or Audrey.

The lanky man staggered and dropped to his knees, his eyes wide. Ethan ran to him and withdrew the knife. Then he pulled the man's head by his hair and sliced his throat with a quick flick of his wrist. He dropped the corpse to the ground and spun about before the second man could surprise him, but he hadn't reappeared.

Ethan moved cautiously toward where they'd stopped their horses. The animals were grazing carelessly, oblivious to the danger around them. But then *they* weren't in danger.

Shit, Audrey.

Ethan pivoted and rushed back toward the tree where he'd left her. Too late.

The second man, a thick-chested brute, had Audrey by the waist. He clutched a pistol against her side, but the real threat was the blade pressed to her throat.

"Come with me, Jagger, an' I'll let yer gel go."

Audrey's skin had gone deathly gray. Her wide, aqua eyes were fixed on Ethan.

Ethan clutched the knife in his hand and considered his options, not one of which was leaving with this prick. That didn't mean he wouldn't play along. "How do you want to do this?"

"Drop the knife," the man said, "then get down on your knees."

"You going to kill me or take me back to Gin Jimmy? That is why you've come, isn't it?"

"Ye're a smart lad, but then we all know that."

"You won't be able to take him alone," Audrey said, her voice sounding small but strong. She never failed to surprise Ethan with her bravery.

The rogue grinned and moved his mouth far too close to Audrey's ear. "I don't plan to. There's another pair of gents just behind us."

Audrey flinched. Ethan's patience was wearing thin. He wanted to end this. Now. But if he missed . . .

The man's grin turned into a malevolent sneer. He dug the knife into Audrey's neck until a drop of blood appeared. "Drop the blade, Jagger."

Ethan didn't hesitate. He threw the weapon and prayed his aim was true. The knife speared into the man's jugular. His eyes rolled and he stumbled backward.

Audrey swayed. Ethan rushed forward and caught her. "I have you!" He looked into her eyes and tried to give her some strength. But he couldn't stay with her. Not yet.

He squeezed her arms and dashed to where the man had fallen to the ground. His eyes stared at the treetops, and his mouth sputtered as blood leaked from between his lips.

Ethan pulled his knife from his neck. Blood spilled from the wound, staining the dirt beneath him in an ever-widening pool of black-red.

Ethan wiped the blade on the man's coat and re-placed it in his boot. They needed to get out of there in case there really were two more men coming. He wasn't sure he believed that, but wouldn't take the chance.

He walked back to Audrey, who'd turned to watch what he'd done. He lightly clasped her arm and drew her away. "Don't look."

He guided her quickly through the trees, silently cursing that they had to walk past the other dead man. She kept her gaze focused straight ahead.

"On the brighter side of things," he said, "we have two saddled horses to take us where we're going."

There was no question now that she had to come with him.

She pulled her arm away from him. "I'm not going with you." She didn't make eye contact, but maintained her vacant stare. She'd changed her mind?

"I'm afraid you must. You heard him. There are more men coming."

"I'll ride back to Wootton Bassett. It's what you want, isn't it?" She'd sounded so resolute in the copse—frightened, but still brave. Now, she sounded defeated. Broken.

Ethan hated himself more than he had ever thought possible in that moment. But what choice did he have? He couldn't let those men hurt her. Or take him.

He grabbed her shoulders and forced her to look at him. "You're coming with me. I had thought you'd be safe this far from London, but clearly that's not the case. We need to keep going."

"Fox will see to my safety once I get back."

He used his sternest voice, knew that he wasn't helping matters, but they didn't have time to debate this. "You're not listening to me, Audrey. Get on the horse." He pulled her to the nearest one and tried to push her to get on.

She resisted, elbowing him in the process. "Let me go!"

He'd shocked her, like that night on the road near Hounslow when he'd killed the highwayman. She'd work through this and accept it as necessary, just like she had before. At least, he hoped she would.

He slid his hands on either side of her head and flattened her back against the side of the animal. "Audrey." He pressed his fingers gently against her scalp. "You're not thinking clearly. I know that was traumatic. But I had to kill them. It was that, or let them kill me, because that's the only other way that would've ended."

Emotion finally entered her eyes, dark and soul-piercing. "Why won't you go back to Wootton Bassett? Bow Street is a better alternative than having to kill to stay alive."

He wouldn't argue with her that fighting for his life was second nature, that he'd rather kill a thousand of Gin Jimmy's hirelings than take his chances with the hangman's noose.

Why he finally decided to be honest with her, he didn't know. He just knew he needed her to come with him and he'd do anything to make that happen. He leaned closer and stared into her eyes. "Because I'm wanted for murder and I've no wish to dangle from a rope."

~

*A*udrey endured the next day and a half with barely a word to Ethan. They'd ridden well past dark the previous night, but the moon had lit their way to a small inn on the outskirts of Bath. Ethan would've preferred to sleep in a barn again, but they'd had to change horses. They'd ridden theirs too hard for too long. So they'd found a coaching inn where they'd replaced their mounts—which included acquiring a ladies' saddle for Audrey—and slept for a few hours.

That early morning stop seemed forever ago, though it was only dusk of the same day. They'd just skirted the town of Glastonbury—they avoided entering any place that was too populated—and Ethan had informed her a while ago that they'd stop when they reached Street, a small village a few miles away. He still didn't trust her enough to share their ultimate destination. If he hadn't been so purposeful in their travel, she might've doubted he even had one.

Weariness overcame her and she closed her eyes as her mount plodded along. She'd slept last night, early this morning really, out of pure exhaustion, but the images of the men Ethan had killed permeated her dreams. She didn't really blame him, not when he'd done it to save their lives. The part she couldn't quite process was the ease with which he'd done it. He'd thrown that knife as if he'd done it every day of his life, and he'd shown the same remorse one might when one squashed a fly, which is to say none. And now she knew the truth of his escape from London: Bow Street wanted to arrest him for murder. She'd been too stunned to ask for more information, too overwhelmed by the events that had transpired.

"You're not falling asleep are you?" His voice, coming from her right, jolted her eyes open.

"No."

"I know you're tired. We're nearly there," he said.

"To Street, but where after that? I wish you would tell me. I won't tell anyone."

His mouth pressed into a tight line. "I can't afford for you to let it slip by accident."

She glared at him. "I'm not a simpleton."

"I didn't say you were, but you're also not skilled in deception."

She thought of the times she'd fooled everyone at Lockwood House into thinking she was a man. "I'm better at that than you think."

He cast her a sidelong glance. "Indeed?"

"Don't ask me about it. I'll be as closemouthed as you." She actually took solace in having a secret to keep from him. "Don't think that your revelation yesterday has softened my temper."

"I wouldn't dream of it." He sounded amused, the blighter.

She was so bloody tired of his half-answers and cheeky attitude. She drew her horse to a stop. He rode a few yards in front of her before stopping and turning back.

She walked her horse up beside him. "Did you

commit murder? Aside from yesterday. And the high-wayman. And that boy you killed when you were younger." Four people. He'd killed at least four people. She shouldn't be surprised if there were more.

"Are you asking me if I did what Bow Street is accusing me of? No, I did not."

Some of the tension leaked out of her, causing her frame to wilt a little. Instinctively, she believed him, but why? What cause had he given her to trust him? He'd kept her safe, protected her at the greatest of costs. But he still wouldn't open himself to her.

"Why should I believe you?" She held up her hand to stop him from speaking, though realizing he likely wouldn't have said a word—at least not on that subject. "Never mind. I don't care to know. I only want to get wherever we're going. Do you want to leave me there too?"

His jaw clenched as he stared at her. At length he finally answered. "I don't know."

Maybe he didn't have a destination. He hadn't before. "Do you even know where we're going?"

"Yes. Very far from London. Someplace I hope you'll be safe."

She tried to conceive of where he might take her, but then how would she know anything that went on in his secretive mind? She was surprised to hear that he even knew of anyone or any place outside London, let alone "very far" away. "You thought I'd be safe in Wootton Bassett."

His stare turned into a glower. "For now, we need to keep moving. I'll figure out what to do when we get where we're going."

She'd had enough of his cavalier behavior. "*You'll* figure out what to do. Am I not to be consulted?"

He tore his gaze from hers. "Dammit, Audrey, I'm trying to do what's best for you."

She sharpened her tone. "My parents have also tried

to do what's best for me—in their opinion. I think *I* should like to decide what's best for me. That's the reason I came with you."

He glanced at her, but his expression was unreadable. "We need to find a place to stay." He kicked his horse forward. Since she didn't want to linger in the middle of nowhere, she followed him. "To conserve money, we can't stay at an inn every night. I'd like to find a cottage or a house that might take us in. A vicarage would be good—they're keen on helping others."

That made sense. "You plan to simply ask for lodging?"

"You're expecting a child, and we can't travel anymore today."

"What?" It was a good thing she was on a horse, because if she'd been walking, she would've tripped.

He shot her as sidelong glance. "We want them to take pity on us. Do you have a better idea?"

No, but that didn't mean she had to like it. Two days ago, the idea of pretending such nonsense would've made her laugh. She'd enjoyed faking their engagement in Wootton Bassett. She'd never felt more alive, more *wanted*. "And why are we traveling on horseback with nothing but the clothes on our backs?"

"I'm your brother and I'm helping you escape your abusive husband."

Her brother. So much for a sham romance. She looked over at Ethan. He looked like a farmer in his floppy hat, but beneath the brim was the visage of a hard man, a criminal who'd seen and done unspeakable things. His kisses had enthralled her, but what more could he promise her? He'd done her a great service by sending her back to her room the other night, and if she were smart she'd welcome any space between them.

They passed the gates to a wide drive. Audrey looked up and saw a manor house atop a hill. It was stately and beautiful with the setting sun coloring the windows a burnished gold.

They rode another few minutes before Ethan's sharp voice drew her attention. "Audrey." He inclined his head toward an intersection with a narrow lane where a man was watching them.

The man stepped into the road. Ethan's hand drifted toward his boot. Hoping to avoid another violent act, Audrey rode past Ethan and engaged the man. He looked to be past thirty, with ragged hair, and an untrimmed beard. His clothing was in good condition, but a bit dirty. He tipped his hat at her, which she found encouraging.

"Good evening, kind sir," Audrey said as Ethan rode up beside her.

"Evening, miss." His gaze darted to Ethan.

"I'm Miss Hughes." Belatedly, she realized she was supposed to be married. Oh well. "This is my brother."

Ethan inclined his head. "We're looking for a place to stay for the night."

"I expect so." The man looked up at the darkening sky. "Not many places to stay in Street."

"We're a bit low on funds, as well," Ethan said. "Perhaps you can direct us somewhere with a tendency for generosity."

The man nodded. "Can't rightly think of such a place. But you're welcome to stay with me. I'm Peck. I live in the hermitage at Versant House."

That must be the manor house they'd passed. Audrey had known of a few hermits at grand houses, but had never met one. "Thank you for your kindness."

Ethan looked over at her, and she could tell from the set of his mouth that he wasn't convinced they should accompany the hermit. Audrey thought it was the best they could hope for. The hermit wouldn't tell anyone about them. It would afford them a level of anonymity they likely wouldn't find anywhere else.

She stepped her horse closer to his. "Come, brother. The hermit seems a kindly fellow, and he's all alone."

With a subtle nod of his head, he seemed to get her meaning. "Very well." He looked down at the hermit. "Lead the way."

"'Tisn't far." He led them down the narrow path for perhaps a half mile, before cutting through some rougher terrain to a small clearing nestled in a grove of trees. He gestured to a small stone structure. "My humble abode."

Humble indeed. It boasted a single room and a dirt floor, though at least it had a hearth.

The hermit gestured toward the trees. "Just tie your beasts up. I can't offer lodgings for them, but there's fresh grass, plus an apple tree and a stream over yonder." He pointed opposite the way they'd come.

Ethan climbed off his horse and Audrey followed suit. He took care of tying them up and unsaddling them, then used his hands to brush his mount as best he could, while Audrey did the same for hers. Meanwhile, the hermit had gone into his little house.

"What the hell is a hermitage?" Ethan asked.

He'd never heard of one? But why would he have? "Some large houses like the one we passed keep hermitages—small houses or even caves. Most are follies, but this one is real. It seems Versant House keeps a live hermit."

His eyes widened in horror. "What does that mean —*keep*? Is he a pet?"

She shook her head, smiling at his reaction. "No. He likely prefers to live on his own and in the elements. Some landowners employ a hermit to provide a sort of entertainment for their visitors."

Ethan paused in brushing his horse. "I don't understand."

Audrey chuckled. "No, I don't imagine you would. It's an odd situation, really, though it's not as popular as it once was, according to my father. As I said, in many cases there is just a hermitage, an abode like that one that looks rather charming and fanciful. However, sometimes there's an actual person who lives there to give truth to the myth, bringing the fantastical to life."

Ethan shook his head, appearing altogether perplexed. "I will never understand the eccentricities of the wealthy. He's paid to live out here alone because it might amuse the landowner and his friends?"

"That's about right." Though when he said it, the notion did indeed sound absolutely ludicrous. "It suits the hermit fine, so it's not a hurtful arrangement."

"I understand." He sounded as if he really didn't.

Audrey finished brushing her mount. "I'm going to pick apples for the horses. They should eat something beyond grass." Both had been grazing since they'd been tied up.

"No, let me. I'll water them too."

Audrey watched him pick his way through the shrubbery and wished they could go back to the way they'd been in Wootton Bassett. Rolling down a hill seemed so far away. It was part of the adventure she'd longed for, but she realized it was only a piece of it. This, now, fighting for their survival is what she would've done had she made her way to America. Was it what she truly wanted? It could be, with the right person. But was Ethan the right person?

"I have rabbit stew for dinner." The hermit's voice startled her from her thoughts. "Come inside." He beckoned her from the doorway.

"My brother's gone to get apples for the horses." She glanced back toward the way Ethan had gone.

"He'll come in when he gets back."

Nodding, she went into the small hermitage. She'd been in one once, but it had been a folly while this was a real home. The interior was dark, with a single window on the opposite wall. A fire sparked in the hearth, its heat permeating the space to make it quite warm. There was a narrow bed in the corner and a single chair with a rickety table.

"I don't have enough seating, but the rug is comfortable enough." He gestured to the oval carpet placed in front of the hearth. "His lordship likes to give me things he doesn't need anymore."

Not very many things it seemed, but it was better than nothing. She sank down to the carpet and curled her feet to the side. She pulled her bonnet from her head and immediately felt her hair slump to the side in rebellion against the few pins she had left tucked into the curly mass. "You're happy here?"

Though she'd explained the arrangement to Ethan, she wasn't sure she didn't share at least a portion of his surprise at such a situation. Particularly the living outside and alone, which she supposed was the crux of it.

"Oh yes," the hermit answered, kneeling before the hearth to spoon the stew into three bowls, which once again looked like castoffs from the manor house. "Solitude suits me just fine, but I do appreciate company now and again." He smiled at her warmly, then handed her a steaming bowl. He fetched three spoons from a small cupboard in the corner and gave her one. "Where are you and your brother headed?"

Ethan would want her to be noncommittal. She tried to mimic the way he danced around questions. "We're just passing through." Though Ethan had given her a concrete story to tell, she found she didn't even want to pretend such an awful existence. "My brother is going to be a teacher at a boys' academy, and he secured a position for me as housekeeper for the headmaster."

"He really is your brother then?" The hermit glanced at her skeptically.

Audrey dropped her gaze and filled her spoon with the aromatic stew. "Yes, he is. I'm quite proud of him."

"Mr. Hughes," the hermit said, "come in and join us."

Audrey turned her head to look at the doorway. Ethan stood in shadow, the twilight casting a faint glow around him. He looked rugged and handsome, and she envisioned him living the life of a hermit in the more glamorous hermitage she'd seen before, with its columns, arched doorway, and multiple sparkling windows. Could he live like that? Would he want that?

Ethan moved inside and sat down beside Audrey on the carpet. He set his hat near the hearth and plucked up his bowl of stew and the third spoon with a nod of thanks to the hermit. Ethan shot Audrey a questioning glance, but she couldn't comprehend what he was asking. Had he overheard the story she'd told? If not, she'd best inform him.

"My brother Wendell is going to be an excellent teacher," she said. "He's quite good at motivating young lads."

Ethan's nostrils flared, but that was the only indication that he was perhaps surprised or dismayed. Too bad. She was tired of taking only his directives. She'd chosen to come on this adventure and she'd been through quite a lot. If she wanted him to be a teacher instead of her fleeing a violent husband, he could play along.

"What will you be teaching them?" Peck asked before spooning stew into his mouth.

Audrey watched Ethan and wondered what he would say. He'd said he was supposed to attend Oxford and had sounded bitter about not going. Perhaps making him a teacher hadn't been very thoughtful of her.

"A variety of things," he said smoothly. "Though Greek is my favorite." He said something in what had to be Greek, drawing Audrey to look at him in surprise. He was watching her with that edge of arrogance that never failed to heat her belly. "'Education is an orna-ment in prosperity and a refuge in adversity.'"

Peck grunted. "I was fortunate enough to learn to read, but I don't speak any languages beyond my native tongue."

Ethan leaned slightly forward. "How does one be-come a hermit?"

"I suppose it must be different for everyone, but if you make enough mistakes and ruin enough chances, there's not much left to do."

Audrey studied Ethan for some sort of reaction, but he'd gone back to eating.

Peck finished up his stew, drinking the dregs from his bowl, and wiped his sleeve across his mouth. He stood and put his bowl and spoon on the table. "Just set your dishes here. I'll wash them in the stream in the morning. I'll be going out to hunt now. Make your-selves comfortable and leave whenever you wish."

Audrey blinked at him. "You hunt at night?"

"There are many creatures that only inhabit the shadow hours." He grinned. "Tasty creatures."

Ethan nodded and laughed. "Right you are."

Peck took a blanket from the end of his bed and set it next to Audrey. "I have just this one extra covering, but it's better than none. Sleep well."

After he'd gone and closed the door, Audrey turned to Ethan. "Why did you laugh? What do you know of nighttime hunting?"

"Plenty. The best game come out after the sun goes down. We hunters know this." The gleam in his eye made her shiver. What could he possibly hunt in London?

She thought about what Peck had said about why he was a hermit, about mistakes and ruined chances. Mis-fortune had driven Ethan to a criminal life, something he would not have chosen otherwise. "You seem to have more in common with the hermit than I would've thought."

"Mmm." He spooned the last bit of stew into his mouth. "Are you finished?" At her nod, he took her bowl and deposited their dishes atop the table. "Why did you tell him I was a teacher? What happened to the story we planned?"

"'We' didn't plan a story. *You* did. I didn't want to be pregnant or abused." She stretched her legs out in front of her. "Anyway, where did you learn to speak Greek?"

He stood beside the table and looked into the fire. "I didn't. My father had several favorite quotes."

"Would you have liked to learn Greek?"

He shrugged. "I don't know. I had a tutor who taught me Latin for a time, but I've forgotten most of it."

A life interrupted by tragedy. That he was still here, still fighting for his survival was a testament to his self-discipline. She didn't know much about the life he'd led but imagined he was someone important. Why else would men have followed him so far from London? "What sort of criminal are you?" she asked softly. "You said Gin Jimmy was a lord of crime. What are you?"

He turned his head to look at her. The firelight danced in his eyes. He shrugged out of his coat and folded it up, then placed it on the carpet that covered the dirt near the hearth. "Your pillow, my lady. You take the blanket as well."

He wasn't going to answer her. Again. She wanted to shout in frustration. She settled for glaring at him, but he wasn't paying attention as he untied his cravat, pulled off his waistcoat, and made his own, smaller, pillow.

She ought to check his wound, but she was too annoyed. Besides, they'd left the poultice at Bassett Manor so there was nothing to do except inspect it. He'd begun to scratch at it, she'd noticed, which meant the wound was healing. Or so the innkeeper's wife had told her.

He lay down on the carpet, his head on his waistcoat. She did the same, using his coat as her pillow and drawing the threadbare blanket over her. She was careful to keep at least a foot between her and Ethan. Then she rolled on her side, putting her back to him for good measure.

"I'm Gin Jimmy's right hand. Or I was until I tried to double-cross him."

Her breath hitched and she held it, trying to be extra quiet in case he said something more. When he didn't, she rolled over and looked at him. His eyes were open, staring at the beamed ceiling.

"What did you do?" Fear for him quickened her pulse. No wonder men had followed him so far from London. If he'd gone against this crime lord, he would have enemies.

"I wanted to be Ethan Lockwood." His mouth quirked into a wry smile. "A stupid dream, I realize now."

"It's not stupid. And it doesn't have to be a dream." She scooted closer to him. "You *are* Ethan Lockwood, aren't you?"

He turned his head and looked at her. The searing gray of his eyes nearly burned her with their intensity. "I am who I am, Audrey. I'm a criminal who is wanted for murder and I doubt there's a way I can redeem myself. I can't seem to go even a couple of days without having to kill someone."

She heard the pain and regret in his tone and longed to soothe it all away. "I'll help you, however I can."

His features hardened. "There's no helping me. Any regret I feel at killing those men is because of you. I regret bringing you along and exposing you to my depravity. But know this: I don't regret killing them. In fact, I revel in it. I rose to become Gin Jimmy's right hand because I am smart and cunning and above all ruthless. Don't ever forget that, and don't ever think I'm someone I'm not. I am the hermit, Audrey. A solitary monster who's chosen his lot and must endure it."

She exhaled then, having held her breath through all he'd said. She wanted to argue with him, to again say it wasn't too late to change, but so far he hadn't listened.

He looked back at the ceiling. "Go to sleep. We've still four or five more days of travel until we get to Beckwith."

Beckwith? The name was familiar . . . Lord Sevrin's estate in Cornwall. Where her friend Philippa lived.

Ethan put his back to her, signifying an end to their conversation, and perhaps their friendship, if that was what it had ever been. She rolled to her back and stared at the wood crisscrossing above her. At least he'd finally revealed some of himself, and he'd told her where they were going. A minor victory, but she'd celebrate it since it was the only one she had.

CHAPTER 11

*T*he hermit Peck awoke early and departed the tiny cottage. Ethan opened his eyes after he left. He'd turned toward Audrey in the night. Now, he watched her sleep, her long, dark lashes fanned against her cheeks. The fire had died down, but still cast enough heat that her cheeks were pink and lovely.

He'd watched her sleep every night that they'd been together. The two nights he'd spent apart from her at Bassett Manor had been cold and lonely. He'd been annoyed at how quickly he'd grown accustomed to her company. He was right about being the hermit—he'd lived a solitary life for far too long and it galled him to rely on anyone else, let alone want to.

Did he want to rely on her? Trust her?

The temptation was there. She was so earnest in her desire to help him, to understand him, to vindicate him. All of it was so misplaced. He didn't deserve that, especially from her. Which was why he'd continue to keep her at arm's length no matter how badly he'd softened toward her.

And he had.

She occupied his thoughts as they rode each day and crowded his dreams every night. She was beauty and goodness and he desired her so badly he nearly shook with it. He was no better than a rutting beast. She wanted to improve him, and he wanted to shag her. Proof that he wasn't worthy of her.

He just needed to get through the next handful of days until they reached Beckwith. Then he could deposit her with Sevrin, who would keep her safe. He'd take his leave and return to London to attempt to clear his name. How would he do that? Teague would stop at nothing to ensure he hung for killing the Marquess of Wolverton. And Ethan had made it easy for him. For Christ's sake, Teague *had* found him standing over the dead body with a bloody knife. Ethan wiped his hands over his eyes and cursed his stupidity, as he'd done countless times since that night.

He'd crafted an elaborate plan in which Wolverton would be exposed as the head of a theft ring that preyed upon the elite of Mayfair, while at the same time appearing to have double-crossed Gin Jimmy, which would lure the crime lord out of the rookery. That last part had been the most difficult to manage. Jimmy stayed close to his usual haunts, where he was safe and protected. Getting him out of St. Giles so he'd be vulnerable had taken careful planning. But Gin Jimmy had learned that someone had set him up.

Ethan had tried to puzzle out how that had happened. He could only reason that Jimmy had arrived at Wolverton's too late that night, after Bow Street—whom Ethan had anonymously tipped off—had already infiltrated the marquess's home. Instead of being at Wolverton's when Bow Street had arrived, he'd showed up after the fact. Probably, Bow Street had ignored Ethan's tip to conceal themselves until after they'd apprehended the crime lord and consequently, Jimmy had seen them at the house.

It made sense that Jimmy had then gone on the hunt for Wolverton, finding him at Lockwood House during one of Jason's notorious vice parties. Jimmy had killed one of Jason's footmen, donned his livery to pass into the party unnoticed, then killed Wolverton. Ethan had gone onto the terrace just as Wolverton lay dying. The marquess had told Ethan that Jimmy was dressed as a retainer. Then Ethan had caught sight of the knife Jimmy had used. The hilt had been engraved with the letter J, which Ethan knew meant Jimmy, but which could also be interpreted as being for Jagger. He'd picked it up, intending to remove it from the scene, but that was when Jason and then Teague had come onto the terrace and discovered him.

In the eyes of Bow Street, Ethan was a murderer. It didn't help that they'd also wanted to charge him with the death of Lady Aldridge, who'd died of opium poisoning at the hands of Jimmy's underlings. Her husband had led a second Mayfair theft ring and had been killed last spring when he'd been in danger of being caught by a former magistrate. Jimmy didn't want Aldridge or his widow telling the authorities about the intricate theft rings he'd built among London's Upper Ten Thousand.

Audrey's eyes opened and she blinked several times before focusing on him.

He tried to read her expression, but couldn't. "Good morning."

"Good morning," she murmured. She sat up abruptly. Her hair had come completely undone, as it usually did in her sleep. The dark curls cascaded past her shoulders. She put her hands up and patted the mass.

He gathered up the pins on and around his coat and handed them to her. "Here. I don't see a glass, and judging from the length of Peck's beard, I presume there isn't one."

She held her palm flat to receive the hairpins. "I daresay you're correct." She smiled at him, and it was at moments like these that he wondered if he could truly choose a normal life. With her.

He shook off the ridiculous fancy and got to his feet. "I need to run outside."

He took his time conducting a rudimentary toilet in the narrow stream running seventy or so yards away from the hermitage. He wondered if he'd run across Peck, but didn't.

Perched on a rock, he leaned over and splashed water on his face. The sound of a gunshot nearly launched him into the creek. He leapt up and raced back toward the hermitage. If Jimmy's men had found them again . . . He nearly tripped in his desperation to get to Audrey.

As soon as he reached the clearing where the tiny cottage was settled, he stopped short. Four young dandies were circled around with their rifles. Peck and Audrey stood near the doorway to the cottage.

Everyone looked safe and whole. Ethan's heartbeat began to slow.

One of the dandies turned. "This your brother, then?" He took in Ethan's damp hair and shirtsleeves. Ethan hadn't bothered to don his waistcoat or any of his other garments yet, while these men were decked out in their best hunting attire. Their finery grated on Ethan. His clothing and accoutrements back in London rivaled anything they were wearing. He might be a god-damned criminal, but he was the best-dressed one in London.

Audrey had managed to tame her hair into a sedate style. Dressed in Miranda's dark blue gown that was too short for her, she looked like an inferior miss in hand-me-down clothes. Ethan detested that far more than his own inadequate costume. In different circum-stances, he would gown her in the finest silks and drape her in jewels.

"Yes, this is my brother, Wendell," Audrey said.

"Wendell, these gentlemen are out for their morning hunt."

"I heard the gunshot. I trust they're not hunting hermits." He didn't bother masking his glower. What manner of idiots were they to be firing so near to the hermitage?

"No, no," one of them answered jovially. "Just a misfire!" He didn't seem to notice or perhaps he didn't care about Ethan's annoyance, which only served to irritate Ethan even more. Everyone paid attention to his reactions. It was generally accepted that agitating Jagger wasn't beneficial for one's health.

Ethan cut through the group of gentlemen and went into the hermitage. He quickly donned his waistcoat and simply tied his cravat. He pulled on his thoroughly rumpled coat as he walked back outside.

"If you weren't such a delightful young lady," one of the men was saying to Audrey, "I'd be inclined to report Peck's behavior to my father."

"What sort of 'behavior' is that?" Ethan asked, again not sparing the effort to keep the bite from his question.

"Having guests. We don't pay him to entertain."

One of the other men snorted. "That's precisely why you pay him. To entertain us. And I'm *thoroughly* entertained by Miss Hughes." He dropped a lascivious gaze at Audrey's chest and it was all Ethan could do not to toss his dagger into the man's throat.

"Ah, Wendell, we should perhaps be going," Audrey said, touching his arm and drawing his murderous glare away from the man who'd offended her. Audrey's gaze connected with Ethan's and she widened her eyes to perhaps communicate with him to stop. Though Ethan wanted to eviscerate the man who'd ogled her, he recognized such foolishness, though satisfying, wouldn't aid their cause.

He forced a smile at the dandies, his lips threatening to break under the exercise. "Don't blame Peck. He merely took pity on us as we were traveling through. It was quite late and my sister is in a rather delicate condition."

He slid a glance at Audrey, whose face had paled. "Come, Sister, it is time for us to depart." He went to their horses and loosened them from their tethers. Then he helped Audrey to mount.

Ethan offered his courtliest bow to the hermit, and pointedly ignored the others. "Thank you for your kind hospitality." He swung himself up on his horse and led Audrey from the clearing.

They weren't able to ride side by side until they reached the main road. Audrey wasted no time in riding abreast of him. "Why did you say that about my condition?"

"I wanted to mitigate any trouble our visit might've caused Peck." And attempt to make her less attractive to their lewd attention.

"I don't think it caused any trouble."

"You heard what that fop said. He considered telling his father that Peck had somehow overstepped his role of hired hermit." Peck was little better than a slave, it seemed. They weren't so alike after all. Ethan enjoyed absolute freedom. He could do whatever he wished whenever he wished.

His body slumped as if he'd been kicked in the gut. No, he couldn't. He couldn't simply tell Jimmy he was through being his right hand, that he wanted to be a proper gentleman in Society as Ethan Lockwood. Jimmy would never let him go, would never free him from his criminal obligations. It was why Ethan had orchestrated his plan to bring him down in the first place. Only then would he be truly free.

Ethan and the hermit were exactly the same. Men who'd chosen a life in the hope that it would be an improvement, only to find they were little better than serfs of old.

"I'm not sure they really meant any harm," Audrey said.

His hands tightened on the reins. "You might have if you'd noted the way they were looking at you."

She snapped her gaze to his, then nodded, understanding his meaning. "I didn't realize. No one ever looks at me like that."

I do. He bit back the words before he uttered them. There was absolutely no reason to encourage an attraction between them.

They rode a few minutes in silence. "Peck said he put some bread in the saddle bag for us," she noted. "I hope those gentlemen didn't mean him ill. He really is a kind soul."

A kind soul. How Ethan longed for her to think of him in that way. Could he be kind? He'd tried to be. He'd gone out of his way to try to save people in recent months, risking his own neck in the process. Not only had he not had a hand in Lady Aldridge's death, he'd tried, unsuccessfully, to persuade her to leave London, to remove her from Jimmy's reach. And now, seeing how far Jimmy was willing to go to get his way, he had to ask himself—would it have helped? Ethan wondered if he'd even have a chance at life if he went back to London. Clearing his name was one hurdle; surviving Jimmy's death warrant would be a far more dangerous one.

He had another choice. He could go to America and start over. It wasn't what he'd planned or what he wanted, but what if Audrey went with him? She'd seemed not only open to the idea, but even enthusiastic about it. She'd tried to do it once, after all.

He looked over at her, her gaze fixed straight ahead, her posture tall and regal in its bearing. She might've agreed to go with him once, but now? After all she'd seen at his hand and everything he'd revealed?

He wanted to nurture a sliver of hope, but he didn't know how. The life he'd chosen had led him to abandon such worthless sentiments.

∾

*F*our very long days later, Audrey followed Ethan into the tiny inn where they'd secured a room in Lostwithiel. It would be their last stop before reaching Beckwith.

Audrey had never been so happy to arrive some-where. Her body was exhausted and her mind equally so. Keeping Ethan at arm's length took a great deal of mental effort. They'd both adopted mutual avoidance tactics, but she'd no idea if it came easier to him or not. It certainly seemed as though it might. They ate meals in relative silence, traveled in absolute silence, and ex-changed mere pleasantries upon retiring each night and awaking each morning. It was, upon reflection, the an-tithesis of the adventure she'd hoped for.

Since the hermitage, anyway.

Prior to that, it had been one life-changing event after another. The question was, in what way? Her life was unalterably different, which meant she'd have to figure out what to do once she arrived at Beckwith. She knew what she *couldn't* do, and that was return to the life she'd been living before Ethan Locke-Jagger-Lock-wood had waltzed into it. Which left spinsterhood, per-haps retiring to her own hermitage, or if she really wanted to embrace her ruination, lead the life of a demimondaine. She smiled to herself at that absurd thought.

"Audrey?" Ethan nudged her arm, dislodging her from her musings.

"Yes?"

"We have a room, albeit a very small one just beneath the roof. The innkeeper is preparing it now. I also requested a tub of water."

Audrey nearly squealed with delight. They'd spent the last two nights in a barn and a lean-to. She was just grateful to have a bed tonight—everything else was extravagance.

"Thank you."

His gaze lingered on her a moment. Though their relationship had cooled, the attraction between them had not. Every night, she fought to keep space between them, and every morning she woke up curled against his heat.

"The innkeeper said we could go through there," he gestured to a doorway on the other side of the staircase, "and take our supper."

Audrey nodded before preceding him to the small dining room where they enjoyed a delicious repast of mutton stew and the best ale she'd ever tasted.

Ethan apparently agreed. He said, "Our host is an accomplished brewer. He'd be one of the most popular ale makers in London." It was the sort of innocuous conversation they'd shared since leaving the hermitage. Audrey was weary of trying so hard, so she only nodded.

His forehead creased. "Are you tired?"

She arched her brows. "Aren't you?"

He chuckled softly. "I think I'm making a bad impression on you. You're turning sarcastic. If I'm not careful, you'll become cynical too."

"I doubt that. I'm far too optimistic."

He drank the remainder of his ale. "A remarkable trait." He fixed her with a dark stare. "Don't lose it." He wiped his mouth with his serviette and stood. "Are you ready to go up? I'm sure the innkeeper is finished by now."

"Yes."

He performed the duty of footman and pulled her

chair back so she could stand. She turned her head to look at him, but he'd gone back to avoiding looking at her.

They trudged up two flights of stairs, the latter set being very narrow and close. They had to duck their heads the last several steps lest they knock against the ceiling.

The room really was tiny. They could only stand straight in the very center where the roof peaked. There was no fireplace, but several lanterns cheered the space. Best of all, there was a tub of water from which steam curled into the air. It wasn't large enough to bathe in, but there was sufficient water for both of them to share.

"You go first," he said.

She glanced around the chamber. The basin sat on the floor, and aside from it and the lanterns, there was a pallet in the corner. Her belongings—the various items Ethan had procured over the last several days, including a second hairbrush and bonnet since she'd left the first ones at Bassett Manor and a spencer that offered at least a modicum of warmth during the cool nights—sat in one corner. The innkeeper must have brought them up from her saddlebag, something else Ethan had mysteriously obtained.

The space and furnishings were definitely meager, but Audrey thought it grand after their recent lodgings. Still, there was no privacy. She supposed she could ask Ethan to go back down to the dining room, but the innkeeper's wife had bustled in as they'd left, presumably to clean it up for the night.

"I'll just lie down on the pallet and look at the wall," he said. "I promise I won't peek."

She trusted him not to, which was probably foolish, given all she knew of him. Even so, he'd always proven to have her best interests at heart. "I'll be quick."

She went to the basin and kneeled beside it, putting

her back toward the bed. She hesitated until she heard what sounded like Ethan lying down. To confirm that, she turned to look. He'd discarded his coat and waistcoat at the foot of the pallet, along with his cravat.

Satisfied that the situation was as private as it was going to get, she unhooked her dress. Thankfully, it was a garment she could remove without the assistance of a maid. It felt wonderful to divest herself of it and her corset entirely. And though she ought to put both back on before going to bed, she didn't think she could.

She dipped one of the small towels the innkeeper had left into the water and scrubbed her face. The cloth smelled vaguely of rosemary, which only added to her comfort. She closed her eyes and imagined she was home. But that actually had the reverse effect. She didn't want to be home. She wanted to be right here.

She glanced back over her shoulder at Ethan. He wasn't facing the wall anymore. He'd rolled toward her and was watching her.

Her breath became trapped in her lungs. "You promised you wouldn't look."

His gaze didn't waver. "You trusted me?"

She narrowed her eyes at him, but without heat as she recognized this was the banter she missed sharing with him. "You've given me plenty of reasons to believe I'm safe with you. In every way."

He flopped onto his back and looked at the ceiling. "I'm a scoundrel, Audrey. Forevermore. You make me . . . No, I'm still a scoundrel."

She made him what? He'd never tell her if she asked, so she didn't bother.

She longed to peel her chemise from her body and wipe away the days of travel, but wasn't sure she dared. If she kept her back to him, he wouldn't see anything . . . intimate. Provided she only took the chemise down part way. Gathering her courage, she wriggled her arms from the capped sleeves. The garment pooled at her waist. She didn't dawdle, but completed her toilet as quickly and thoroughly as possible given her partially dressed state.

When she was finished she set the wet towel to the side and pulled the chemise back up over her arms. Only then did she brave a look back at Ethan. He was unabashedly watching her again. Scoundrel indeed.

The water drying on her flesh should have chilled her, but heat pooled in her belly and swirled through her. Her skin tingled beneath the chemise and her nipples hardened to stiff points. She turned away from him once more in the hope of dousing the pull between them. Perhaps she was going to have to don her other garments again after all.

"I'm finished." She stood and moved away from the basin, careful to keep her back to him, though there wasn't really any place she could retreat to.

She heard him rise from the pallet, felt the air shift as he moved past her. She snatched a blanket from the bed and wrapped it around herself. Then she snuck a glance at Ethan. He'd also kneeled next to the basin. He drew his shirt over his head and the lanterns cast a golden glow across his muscled back.

She forced herself to sit on the bed with her back toward him. The deprivation did nothing to ease the want burning in her core.

"Audrey?"

His voice jolted her to an even greater sense of awareness. Had he somehow read her thoughts? Of course not, that was impossible.

"Yes?" Her voice sounded much too high.

"I believe it's time for my stitches to come out."

She turned toward him and looked at the wound. It appeared pink and quite healed. Yes, the stitches could likely come out. But she didn't have a blade.

Even as she thought it, he pulled his knife from his boot. Then he removed his footwear and slid it toward the wall. He sat down next to the basin. "Will you bring one of the lanterns?" There was one near him, but two would provide better illumination.

She swallowed, trying not to stare at his bare chest. Or at his face, so handsome and cold, yet dearer than she would've thought possible. She'd grown quite fond of this man, despite his faults, or maybe because of them.

She picked up the lantern nearest the bed and carried it to the basin. She kneeled beside him. He held the knife in his palm, offering it to her. Her fingers grazed his flesh as she took the blade. It was lighter than she imagined. For some reason, she'd thought a weapon that had killed would feel heavy, oppressive.

It would be tricky to slide it beneath the sutures without puncturing his flesh. Anxiety pricked her neck. "You must be careful not to move."

His eyes bored into hers. "I shall be a statue."

Who apparently planned to stare at her.

"Please don't look at me like that. I'm nervous enough."

He looked mildly surprised. "Why?"

She tested the unfamiliar knife in her hand. "I'm not a surgeon."

His mouth softened, and it transformed his face. She realized then that he held himself in a different way when he was her charming waltzing partner, as opposed to the brutal criminal. That he could change from one to the next in the space of a breath filled her with awe—and trepidation.

"You'll do fine. Just go slow." He touched her hand lightly. "And if you nick me, do not fret. I will have deserved it anyway."

She wanted to argue with him, no one deserved pain, but more than that she wanted to get this over with. Steeling herself, she slid the blade beneath the thread and gently sliced it up. The knife cut clean through the thread. She exhaled and set the weapon down, glad to be done with it. She plucked the stitches through his flesh as quickly as she dared.

He sucked in a breath, and she froze. "What is it?" she asked.

His lip curved up. "It tickles."

She moved rapidly to finish. It wouldn't do to have this turn into something else. She was sorely tempted by him, but he'd made his motives clear. She was a hindrance, and he would've left her behind already if he hadn't felt beholden.

She pulled the last of the thread through his flesh just as his hand came over hers. The heat of his fingers seared her. She tried to pull away, but he lifted her hand, took the thread, and tossed it away.

He pressed his lips to her fingertips. "Thank you."

The touch of his mouth sparked her desire. What had been curling through her, tempting her, roared to life. Maybe it was the closeness of the room or the enticing flicker of the lantern light or the sight of his bare, golden flesh—all of it, she decided. Whatever the reasons, she picked up a towel and wetted it, then drew it over his chest.

His inhalation sounded like a crash amidst the quiet. It jarred her and her hand froze against him.

"Don't stop." His voice cracked. She hadn't the courage to look at his face. She barely had the courage to continue what she was doing, but she'd started this dangerous game and wanted to finish it.

She cleansed his chest and shoulders, taking particular care to wipe away the tiny specks of dried blood that had come loose from the removal of his stitches. Aside from that wound, he had several scars scattered about. There was a particularly long one that stretched from his collarbone over his sternum. She wanted to ask how he'd sustained these injuries, but didn't want to disrupt the quiet connection that flowed between them.

The scratch from the highwayman's bullet was merely a faint red line now. Soon it would disappear completely. Would the memory? Would their time together fade as day becomes night? She didn't want that. She would remember their time—remember him—to the end of her days. It was suddenly imperative that he never forget her.

"Turn." She sounded strong, commanding. She chanced a look at his face. His eyebrow arched in that damnably attractive manner that set her heart to fluttering.

He scooted around so that his back was to her. She continued his bath, dunking the towel into the basin and scrubbing his back. She attended to his neck, her fingers itching to trace the tendons there. To kiss the hollow behind his ear.

Heat flushed her face and she was glad he couldn't see her. But then he turned. She lowered her head. "Your feet?" she asked softly.

He stretched his legs out and she cleaned his legs from the base of his breeches his toes. It was the most intimate act she'd ever performed. By the time she was finished, she was breathless and warm. She wanted to throw the blanket off her shoulders, but to do so would expose herself, and potentially her want. Could he see her desire?

She looked at his face again, tentatively, and bit down on the inside of her lip at the naked lust in his eyes. She had very little experience with such matters, but it was the way he'd looked at her that night at Bassett Manor. No, it was even more intense, she decided.

She set the towel down and told herself to go to the pallet. But she didn't move. She simply gazed at him, at the strong line of his nose, the arc of his cheekbones, and the three days of growth on his face since he'd last shaved. He looked wild. Utterly untamable. Devastatingly handsome.

At last, she moved, reaching for the edge of the pallet. He moved too. His arm snaked around her waist and drew her back to him. He looked at her for the briefest moment, and his eyes said all that was necessary: *I want you.*

His mouth found hers with a desperate hunger. The blanket fell from her shoulders as she clutched at his biceps and pressed herself against his heated chest. With only her chemise to separate them, she felt him in a way she never had—his warmth, his strength, his power.

One of his hands held her fast, splayed against her lower back, while the other tangled in her hair and scattered her pins to the floor. He combed his hand through her curls and palmed the back of her head, holding her captive to his mouth and tongue.

But he didn't need to, for she was a willing participant. She met his kiss with eager licks and longing suckles, applying what he'd taught her the last time.

He moved his hand down the side of her face to her neck. He stroked his thumb along the underside of her chin, coaxing her mouth to open even wider so he could devour her more fully. She'd never felt more vulnerable or more seductive.

Then his mouth left hers and moved to her neck. His hand drifted downward and settled gently over her breast. She tensed, but he didn't press her. He merely laid his palm over the mound as his lips and tongue worshiped her neck.

She closed her eyes and cast her head back, unable to hold herself upright as her body melted in his embrace. His hand at her back gave her support while his mouth gave her ecstasy. Gradually, she became aware that his hand had closed over her breast—slowly and with great care. His fingers teased her nipple. A moan sounded and she realized it came from her. His mouth moved lower, taunting her flesh and driving her need ever higher. He cupped her breast and then she felt his tongue against her sensitive nipple. The linen of her chemise kept him from touching her flesh directly, but she wasn't sure it mattered. Sensation drove through her, coaxed her to arch into his mouth. She gasped, her hands moving to clutch the hair at the base of his neck.

He pressed her breast upward, squeezing her almost roughly, but divinely as he drew her nipple to an even harder peak. Her core pulsed as a wild craving swept through her.

"Lie back." His words pierced the sensual haze that had settled over her. She felt herself falling backward toward the pallet. Not falling exactly, because his hand was guiding her. He managed to situate them onto the bed, his hand never leaving her breast.

He paused above her and she opened her eyes. She wanted this, wanted him. But he was right that she deserved better. She'd turned her back on her former life, but that didn't mean she had to settle for what he was offering her—which wasn't enough. Their physical attraction was unlike anything she'd ever known, an intoxicating remedy for her hungry soul. She wanted more than that, though—she wanted him to open up to her and she wanted his trust. She wanted more than he could give.

She put her hand to his chest and pressed. "Ethan."

He let go of her breast and an icy chill rushed over her. "Forgive me." He sat up and turned away, then handed her the blanket that had fallen from her shoulders.

She pulled the quilt over herself and moved to the far edge of the pallet. "Forgive me as well. I didn't mean to encourage you."

"You are blameless in this." His voice sounded

strained. He got up and pulled on his shirt, then his boots. He plucked his coat up.

She leaned up on her elbow. Her body was still thrumming with desire. It would be so easy to call him back, but she wouldn't. "Where are you going?"

"Out. Get some sleep. We'll leave early so we can get to Beckwith as soon as possible." He turned and left.

She stared at the closed door for a long time. Tomorrow their adventure would end. Tomorrow she would fight to move forward, to encapsulate her time with Ethan into a neat package she could recall and at which she would smile fondly. Tonight, however, she would weep for the future she could never have.

CHAPTER 12

*A*s usual, Ethan woke early. Instead of torturing himself by watching Audrey sleep, he left the pallet and readied himself. He crept down the steep, narrow stairs to the door that led to the corridor and then to the next set of stairs leading to the ground floor. He made his way to the room where they'd taken last night's meal and encountered the innkeeper.

He was a slight, seemingly frail man, but Ethan believed his unassuming appearance masked a core of steel. He'd insisted on taking care of their horses last evening and had seen to their bath—without the aid of footmen. He squinted at Ethan. "Ye're up early."

"We have a lot of miles to cover today." It was all he would say. He'd been careful to conceal their direction. Bow Street could still be behind them, particularly if Teague had managed to somehow figure out their destination. Ethan had considered the possibility that Teague might trace them to Beckwith, but he didn't have any better ideas of where to go. He thought Audrey would be safe with Sevrin. He was the only gentleman of Ethan's acquaintance who'd held his own among the criminal element.

The innkeeper nodded. "I'll have a luncheon made up for you to take along."

"Thank you." Ethan chose his words carefully. "Might I confirm your discretion about our being here?"

The man laughed, a low, gritty sound that reminded Ethan uncomfortably of his former mentor, Gin Jimmy. "Not your sister, eh?"

Ethan pressed another coin, one of the last they had, into his hand. "I appreciate your help."

"I hope ye'll do right by her. I'll go and get yer horses." He left the room via the kitchen situated at the back of the dwelling.

Ethan could spend the rest of his life trying to make Audrey's dreams come true and he doubted he'd ever come close to doing "right" by her.

The innkeeper's wife plied him with toast and ham. She grinned when he asked for a mug of ale—plus a flagon to take with them. "My husband makes the finest ale in Cornwall."

"Maybe in all of England," Ethan said, smiling at her in return.

The creak of the stairs drew him to turn from the small table where he'd taken his breakfast. Audrey appeared, her bonnet and hairbrush in hand, her hair half up.

She patted the back of her head. "I couldn't find all of the pins."

The innkeeper's wife returned with Ethan's ale and clucked her tongue upon seeing Audrey. "Come with me, dear. I'll set you to rights." She held out her hand and led Audrey back through a doorway.

Ethan watched the gentle sway of Audrey's hips as she followed the innkeeper's wife. His mind was suddenly full of images and sensations of her—the silk of her hair, the curve of her breast, the heat of her hips as he'd moved against her on the pallet. If he didn't curb his thoughts, he'd need to excuse himself as he'd done last night. His left hand was a sorry replacement for what he craved, but it was all he had. The alternative—surrendering to temptation—was inconceivable. That would cross a line they couldn't come back from, and Ethan wouldn't do that. One of the things that had ensured his criminal success was knowing when to stop before a critical error caused irrevocable damage.

A short while later, Audrey emerged from the doorway. Ethan instantly recognized the London miss who'd taught him to waltz. Her hair had been neatly coiled and she wore a fresh gown, one that actually suited her height. The style of the gown was a few years old, but its pale green color accentuated her eyes, making them appear more jade than aqua. An ivory ribbon was threaded beneath her breasts, emphasizing their delicious fullness. Again, her bearing reminded him of someone who was untouchable—at least to him.

He couldn't contain his reaction. "You're so beautiful."

She blushed, and he realized he'd missed her bouts of shyness and embarrassment. Why had they become less frequent? Because they didn't talk as much, or was it more than that? Had he ruined her innocence?

The innkeeper forestalled anything further when he stuck his head into the room. "The horses are ready."

Ethan looked to Audrey, who was tying the bonnet beneath her chin. The innkeeper's wife bustled in carrying Audrey's spencer, which Ethan had nicked from an inn three nights ago.

She smiled at Audrey as she helped her don the coat. "Here you are, dear. Take good care of yourself then."

Audrey gave the woman a quick hug. "Thank you again for the gown."

"I'm pleased to have found someone to wear it."

Audrey nodded, then turned to leave. Ethan gestured for her to precede him and worked to remain stoic as she passed, despite the desperate urge he felt to reach out and touch the small of her back.

They stepped outside into the dark, gray morning. They'd been blessed with mostly dry weather for their journey, but the sky looked as if it might drench their hopes for one more decent day.

Audrey raised her face to the sky. "I daresay those are rainclouds."

"We should get moving." Ethan helped her to mount her horse and climbed on his own.

They made it an hour before the rain started. It was, at least, a placid rain that would take some time before it soaked them. Hopefully it would stay that way.

"What is your plan when we arrive at Beckwith?" Audrey asked. "I want to be sure I play along with whatever Banbury tale you're going to tell."

He deserved that. He'd required her to go with whatever he determined, though she seemed to enjoy tweaking his plans from time to time—like with the hermit. "I'm going to tell him the truth, that you escaped London with me for your own safety."

She stopped her horse and gaped at him. "The truth?"

He deserved that too. "We need to keep moving." When she started forward again, he continued, "I have to tell him the truth," at least about that, "in order to keep you safe. He needs to know that Gin Jimmy wanted to take you to get to me."

"'Wanted'? You mean wants. I doubt his plans have changed."

"Perhaps not, but I'm hopeful he hasn't bothered to follow us this far from London." Especially after what Ethan had done to the men he'd already sent—but Ethan didn't say that out loud. "I'm also hopeful that he'll realize you won't be good leverage against me after I leave." He waited for her reaction, but she was quiet and the edge of her bonnet shielded her face from him. Christ, when had he cared what anyone thought of what he did or what he said? The irritation he tried to stir up didn't even spark. That man was gone—at least with regard to her. He cared what she thought of him.

Finally she said, "Where will you go?"

Once he would've avoided her question. He still considered doing so, but in the end he was tired of the wall he'd constructed. With her he could be himself. Couldn't he? Of all the people he'd come to know in his life, hadn't she been the most patient, the most kind, the most forgiving? "I don't know. Probably back to London. I can't keep running." And he couldn't keep her in a perpetual state of danger.

She shot him a sharp look. "But you'll hang."

A chill settled into his bones and made his teeth ache. His damp clothes suddenly felt like they were coated in ice. "Jason will help me." He hoped. God, could he really ask? He couldn't even recall what it felt like to solicit assistance. Reliance and expectation were for weaker men.

"I'm glad you're going to ask him. I'm also glad you're telling Lord Sevrin the truth." Her voice softened. "I think you'll be glad too."

Ethan spent the rest of the day brooding, even after the clouds parted and the sun dried them. The air had changed and the wind carried the not-too-distant scent of the sea, which he recalled from his last visit here. It was late afternoon when he finally broke the silence. "We're nearly there. Maybe another mile."

"You've been here before, haven't you?"

He nodded. "Last spring. My pugilist was to compete in a prizefight."

"But it ended up being Lord Sevrin, did it not? Philippa told me about it."

He hadn't realized she and Sevrin's wife were on such intimate terms. That could prove difficult, though it seemed as though Philippa hadn't shared what he'd done. If she had, Audrey never would've gone along with him. He shoved the thought away, unwilling to give it his concern. He had far weightier things to consider, such as how in the hell he was going to simply walk away from her.

He'd spent the bulk of the day fantasizing about leaving with her. Going to America, or anywhere really, and starting a life where no one knew the names Jagger or Lockwood. He had enough money stashed here and there to take them wherever they wanted to go as well as to set them up in at least a modest lifestyle. But then what would he do? Farm? Learn a trade? He thought of Fox, and while the farming seemed beyond Ethan, the orphanage management held a surprising appeal.

However, obtaining his stashed money was another problem altogether. Perhaps Sevrin and Jason could help him with that too. That he was actually considering it and that he was prepared to solicit even more support made his head spin. Bloody hell, he'd changed on this journey.

He slid a glance at Audrey's profile. His chest ached when he looked at her. Just as he didn't want to ponder any difficulty with Lady Philippa, nor did he want to think about why Audrey made him feel that way.

At last they rode up the drive to Beckwith. Audrey looked up at the impressive house, which was a converted medieval fortress. It wasn't in the best repair, but its placement on a bluff overlooking the bay was enviable. The weather in Cornwall was typically warmer and more pleasant than London. Ethan had enjoyed his stay in the nearby town of Truro.

"Was it a castle?" Audrey asked.

"I think so." Ethan had obtained only a few details from some people in Truro. Sevrin hadn't been terribly conversational during Ethan's visit. Though Ethan had tried to make amends to the viscount, he wasn't completely certain their arrival would be welcome. Now that they were here, he was having second thoughts.

They stopped in the shell-covered path just before

the front entrance. Ethan dismounted and helped Audrey do the same. He offered his arm, as a gentleman ought. She looked at him quizzically, as if such an action were bizarre, and he supposed it was. He hadn't behaved in the most gentlemanly fashion.

He'd try to make it up to her in the time they had left. The chill he'd been fighting off all day returned, sending ice down his neck. He didn't want to think about leaving her. Not yet.

He rapped on the door and it was instantly opened by a tall, young footman. Ethan vaguely recognized him from his last visit. "Good afternoon, we're friends of Lord and Lady Sevrin. Would you please tell them that Mr. Ethan Locke and Miss Audrey Cheswick have arrived?"

The heavy sound of boots falling across marble drew Ethan to look past the footman. Sevrin appeared in the entry hall, his dark brows drawn into a scowl. "What the bloody hell are you doing here?"

❧

*A*udrey tightened her grip on Ethan's arm. Lord Sevrin did not look pleased to see them here. Or at least Ethan. Sevrin hadn't seemed to register Audrey's presence at all.

"Might we come in?" Ethan asked pleasantly. He stepped over the threshold, forcing the footman to move back, without waiting for a response.

Sevrin stopped in the center of the entry and finally looked at Audrey. "Miss Cheswick, are you all right?" He returned his angry gaze to Ethan. "You didn't kidnap her, did you?"

Ethan's eyes narrowed. "Does she look kidnapped?"

Audrey moved forward toward their host. Hopefully he would be their host. Where else would they go? They were nearly out of funds and if she had to sleep in a barn again, she might cry. "Lord Sevrin, I am here of my own choosing."

All of the stories they'd told over the past days flitted through her brain, but Ethan wanted to tell the truth. The notion still bemused her. What had changed? She glanced at Ethan, but his features were still hardened in a mask of irritation. "Mr. Locke hasn't kidnapped me. In fact, he's saved my life multiple times."

Sevrin put his hands on his hips and stared at Ethan. He didn't look as if he believed Audrey. "I'm sure he only had to save your life because he put it in danger."

Just then Philippa came into the hall behind Sevrin. "What's going on?" She stopped short and gasped upon seeing Ethan, then her mouth formed an O when she saw Audrey. "Audrey!" She rushed forward and drew her further away from Ethan. "Ned, close the door, please."

The footman complied, but kept a wary eye on Ethan. Ethan stepped to the side, his gaze moving from Sevrin to Audrey. She detected the tiniest crack in his fierce composure—a slight wrinkle in his forehead.

Audrey put her hand over Philippa's. "I'm fine. We had to escape London. It's a dreadfully long story. Might we sit down and discuss the matter?" She longed for a glass of something that would warm her insides.

"Of course." Philippa linked her arm with Audrey's. "Come with me." She turned and led Audrey from the hall, but looked back over her shoulder at Ethan.

Audrey also turned back and watched the men stare at each other a long moment before Sevrin put his hands to his sides and then gestured for Ethan to precede him.

Philippa helped Audrey out of her spencer and took her bonnet, both of which she handed to Ned, who had followed them. "Will you have Mrs. Oldham prepare the chamber in the north wing for Miss Cheswick?"

The footman nodded and retreated from the room.

It was impossible not to notice that she hadn't given instructions for Ethan's comfort.

"Philippa," Audrey said, "Mr. Locke will also require a bedchamber."

Philippa threw a heated glare at Ethan. "I'm not certain I want him staying in my house."

"Please," Audrey said, squeezing Philippa's hand, "we've come such a long way, and he's recovering from being wounded."

"Which I'm sure he deserved." Philippa shook her head. "I'm sorry, Audrey, but I can't imagine why you've willingly traveled across southern England with a criminal like Jagger."

Philippa knew him as Jagger? Audrey's neck prickled with unease. "I told you, he saved my life. I was in danger in London." And Sevrin had been right, it *was* because of Ethan. Those men had wanted to take her because they thought she meant something to him. Which she didn't. Her unease grew until she felt cold and hollow.

"You were correct, Sevrin." Ethan's deep voice cut through the tension clouding the room. "She was in danger because of me. I brought her here because it's the farthest—and more importantly safest—place I could think of."

"It wasn't all that safe for me when you came last spring." Philippa's tone dripped with scorn. Audrey had never heard her friend talk like that, not even when she was bemoaning her parents' scandalous affairs.

"I've apologized for that repeatedly. And I took care of the matter." He shot Sevrin a dark glance.

"By having Swan killed?" Philippa turned to Audrey. Her golden brown eyes were distressed, but earnest. "You don't know anything about this man. You may have met him as Ethan Locke in London last month, but he's a criminal."

"I know that." But what did she really know? He'd

been mistreated by his half-brother and Lockwood's mother, and because of that had been driven to a criminal life. He stole and killed with ease and had become an excellent dancer. He was also angry and frustrated because his plans had not worked out the way he'd envisioned. "He's trying to reform himself."

Philippa glanced at Ethan. Her lips pursed. "That may be, but he's got an awful lot to reform. I can't let you think he's a decent person. He may not have kidnapped you, but he abducted me on two occasions, and a third time one of his men took me."

Audrey gaped at her. She'd no idea any of that had occurred. She looked at Ethan. His gray eyes were cold. She expected him to look furious, but his features were devoid of emotion.

"Yes, I kidnapped Lady Philippa." He moved to a sideboard with several bottles of spirits and splashed some into a glass. "I needed a prizefighter and I wanted Sevrin. I tried inviting him to come see me, but he responded by soundly beating two of my men. Proof that all men possess a degree of vicious intent." He lifted his glass in a silent toast toward a glowering Sevrin, then took a hearty drink.

His controlled response befuddled Audrey. She opened her mouth to ask why, but Ethan continued. "I used Philippa to gain Sevrin's cooperation. Not once, but twice. I had my men take her from a house party outside London and bring her to Sevrin's fight. That way I could be assured that Sevrin would do his very best to win."

Audrey's limbs felt weak. Her brain struggled to process what he was telling her and why it seemed worse than what she already knew of him. Kidnapping couldn't be worse than murder, could it? But all of it together . . . "Why did you want to win?" It was the only question her mouth could seem to form.

"I always win. At least I did until I had to flee London." Now his tone darkened and the fury she'd glimpsed in the hall resurfaced. "I told you I was ruthless, Audrey. I told you that you deserved better."

Yes, he had. But she'd clung to her belief that he wanted to change, that he'd been trying to. There was so much more to him than what he showed on the outside.

He looked at Philippa, his expression taking on a hint of remorse. "The only thing I regret is bringing Swan with me when I came for the fight. I had no idea he'd planned to abduct Philippa—something he never would've done if not for me. Without me, he wouldn't have even known of her existence, let alone had occasion to be in her presence."

Audrey shook her head. She was glad he regretted that, but it couldn't be the only thing. He had at least half a lifetime he should want to repent, shouldn't he?

Audrey was vaguely aware of Philippa stroking her back. It was supposed to be comforting, but her mind was in too much turmoil to relax. She locked eyes with Ethan, who'd gone back to appearing detached. "You told me Gin Jimmy was a bad man. But so are you."

His stare was unrelenting. "Yes, I am."

And there it was. The cold, stark truth from him at last.

She shouldn't have been surprised, and maybe she wasn't, but hearing him say it brought reality into the cocoon she now realized she'd constructed around them—or at least around herself where he was concerned. She looked away from him, unable to bear her foolishness in trusting him another moment. "Philippa, will you take me up to my room?"

Philippa gently guided her the way they'd come. Audrey paused as they passed by Ethan. "Thank you for bringing me here. I'm sure you'll understand when I say it's best if I remain while you continue on. Our association is finished."

CHAPTER 13

Years ago, when Ethan had taken to the streets, his life had gotten darker. Since then, he'd lived in a constant state of gray where there was no clarity, no right or wrong, just existence. But with Audrey, he'd glimpsed a brightness he'd never known, a glimmer of hope, of happiness. Now, hours after she'd ended their . . . whatever it was, total blackness threatened.

Ethan looked around the small, sparsely furnished room Sevrin had consented to give him. Though it was lit only by the dying fire and a single candle, Ethan could still catalog its modest furnishings: bed, armoire, chair. It didn't even have a view of the bay—but it was all Ethan deserved from him. Actually, it was probably more than that.

Dinner had been simple, but delicious, delivered to him by the housekeeper, Mrs. Oldham, three hours ago. Ethan had asked her where he might go for a bath. She'd pursed her lips at him, indicating she'd already judged him a scoundrel, and told him that her son, Ned the footman, would take care of it. After dinner, he'd brought up enough water for Ethan to bathe himself in a better fashion than he had since Bassett Manor.

Ethan had spent the intervening time lying on the

bed, contemplating his next move. He'd leave for London tomorrow after sending an advance letter to Jason—provided he could even convince Sevrin to do it. Ethan had foolishly underestimated the power of the man's memory—and more importantly, that of his wife.

Lady Philippa held him in the lowest of opinions. Could he blame her? He'd given her no reason to like him and certainly no reason to trust him. In retrospect, he should've perhaps chosen someplace else to go, but no, this was the best place for Audrey. Sevrin would keep her safe, and she was as far from London as he could get her without putting her on a boat that would take her across the world.

Ethan jumped up from the bed, where he'd been staring at the ceiling. He needed a drink.

He grabbed the candlestick and made his way downstairs to the great hall. A fire still burned in the huge grate at the end of the room opposite the stair-case. Ethan glanced around, but the room appeared to be empty.

He went to the sideboard and poured himself a glass of whisky and downed half of it in one gulp. He tucked the bottle beneath his arm, and carried his candle and glass through the great hall to a smaller chamber with expansive windows. The night was dark, but Ethan dropped onto a settee and stared at the blackness, thinking it mirrored what he felt inside.

He wasn't sure how long he sat like that, but on his third glass of whisky, Sevrin came into the chamber. "I see you helped yourself to my liquor," he said.

Ethan gestured toward the bottle, which sat on a low table before him. "Join me."

"How magnanimous of you to invite me." He left and came back with a glass, which he promptly filled. He picked up Ethan's candlestick from the table and lit two lamps, then took a chair near Ethan's settee. "You oughtn't drink too much. You want to be on the road early, don't you?"

"Yes," Ethan said. They'd discussed his departure earlier.

Sevrin sipped his drink. "I won't try to detain you, but you should know that I've written to Lockwood and informed him of your arrival. My footman took the letter into town to be posted first thing tomorrow."

Ethan was mildly surprised, but shouldn't have been. Everyone would, of course, treat him like the criminal he was. "I wish I'd known. I was going to ask you if I could post a letter to him. I'd like him to be aware of my return before I arrive."

Sevrin arched his brow. "You're actually going to go back to London? I admit I didn't believe you when you told me earlier." He shook his head. "A murder charge . . ."

Ethan shrugged and tried to appear nonchalant, though his insides were an anxious mess. He didn't remember the last time he'd felt as if he wasn't in absolute control of his life. "I told you, I didn't murder Wolverton; Gin Jimmy did. There has to be a way to prove it."

Sevrin rested his elbows on the arms of his chair. "If you're vindicated, will you go back to your life of crime?"

Strangely, this line of inquiry made Ethan more uncomfortable than discussing the murder charge. Maybe because this was what meant most to him. Or, because he doubted his dream would come to pass. "I'd prefer not to. I'd rather resume my place as Ethan Locke."

"Does Lockwood know this?"

"Yes." It had been a source of conflict between him and Jason, though Ethan believed he'd finally convinced his brother that he was trying to lead a new life. Granted, that had only been *after* he'd told him the truth about what he'd been trying to do—bring down Gin Jimmy so he could leave his criminal life for good.

Would his plan have worked if he'd trusted Jason sooner, as he'd repeatedly asked Ethan to do? Ethan downed a healthy swig of whisky.

Sevrin was watching him guardedly, like a hawk circling its prey, or a thief identifying his mark.

Ethan took a deep breath and then a massive leap of faith. "I lured Gin Jimmy out of the rookery so that Bow Street would arrest him as the mastermind of several theft rings, including one run by the Marquess of Wolverton. I made sure Jimmy learned that Wolverton had told Bow Street that he was behind the rings and that he'd orchestrated the deaths of Lord and Lady Aldridge."

Sevrin's eyes widened briefly. "He killed Lady Aldridge? I thought she died of laudanum poisoning."

"She did, but it was due to Gin Jimmy. He wanted me to make sure she died, but I couldn't do it." He looked out at the black night, regret swirling in his gut.

Sevrin leaned slightly forward. "You couldn't kill Lady Aldridge?"

Ethan shook his head. "I tried to save her." He'd worked to persuade her to leave London, but she'd refused to leave the house she and Aldridge had spent most of their time together in. She'd been devastated by his death last spring. Though Ethan hadn't caused the earl's demise, he also hadn't been able to stop it, which served to bring out every shred of guilt Ethan had worked to bury over the years. It was perhaps this guilt that was driving him to face Bow Street. That, and Audrey. He wanted to deserve her, though he feared he never would.

Sevrin settled back against his chair. "What changed? You were—to use your own word—ruthless, in our dealings with you. I still want to punch you every time I see you."

Ethan didn't doubt it. "I wouldn't try to stop you, despite your deadly hook." Sevrin had hit him once, and it had been enough for Ethan to want to never be on the receiving end of his fist again.

Sevrin fixed him with a direct stare. "What happened? You were a king—or so it looked to me when you brought me to your den. Why would you want to leave that?"

Ethan laughed, but it sounded empty, even to his own ears. "Everyone licks my feet because they're afraid. I never know who my friends are." He couldn't bear Sevrin's scrutiny another moment so he studied his whisky. "I don't have any friends. When you agreed to fight for me, I thought . . . I imagined we might've been friends. If things had been different." He looked up at Sevrin. "I regret what I did to you—and even more what I did to Philippa. Seeing you together . . . your love for each other." He took a fortifying drink. "I didn't want to be alone anymore."

"A criminal with a heart." There was a touch of something in Sevrin's voice—disbelief, wonder? "I didn't know such a thing existed."

Ethan scowled. "I don't have a heart, just a growing conscience. I don't like doing what I have to do. I never really liked doing it, but I didn't have much of a choice." He lifted his gaze to Sevrin's and stiffened his spine. "Besides, I was bloody good at it."

"There's the Jagger I know," Sevrin said softly.

Anger sparked through Ethan. He banged the glass down on the table in front of him, his body quickening into fight mode. "You know *nothing*. I've more wealth than I can spend, and I command the respect and admiration of a good many men."

Sevrin set his glass down also, and he leaned forward, his nostrils flaring. "Do you want that, or do you want to be a gentleman? You can't have both—at least not the way you've made yourself."

"Don't you think I fucking know that?" Ethan stood as he shouted, fury grinding through him. He went to the window and rested his forehead against the cool glass. It soothed the ragged edges of his temper. He closed his eyes. "I don't want to be a criminal anymore. Problem is, it won't let me go."

"Because of this charge from Bow Street."

Yes and . . . "No. The things I've had to do since I took Audrey out of London." He turned from the window and released the anguish stored deep in his bones. "I've had to steal. I've had to kill. To keep her warm and well and safe."

Sevrin's eyes glittered. "That's not being a criminal. I would do anything to protect Philippa." He dropped his gaze for a second. "Though I understand feeling guilty. I've spent many years battling that emotion and I still wonder if I'll ever truly defeat it." He looked up again. "Fortunately, I have Philippa at my side to help me."

Nothing he said could've gutted Ethan more. He turned back to the window. It was ironic that he'd finally found someone he wanted to trust, who he wanted to trust him, and that her importance caused him to commit acts that ensured she never did.

"Are you in love with her?" Sevrin's question hit Ethan in the back like a dagger.

Ethan tensed, but didn't turn. He had no idea what romantic love felt like. He'd loved his mother and his father, but in an adoring, childish way. "I don't know. I don't love anyone."

"Not even your brother?"

He'd grown very fond of Jason in the past few weeks. They'd reached a brotherly accord, a kinship Ethan had never imagined, but love? "I don't know. Maybe."

"You said you stole and killed for Audrey in order to keep her safe. She's clearly important to you. Would you have done those things if she hadn't been at stake?"

Ethan tried to think but couldn't find an answer. He honestly couldn't imagine being without her now. Consequently, he couldn't answer the question. So he said the only thing that filled his mind. "I don't want to leave her."

Sevrin came to the window and stood a few feet away. "I left Philippa once because I thought it was the right thing to do for her. I made a decision that affected her without discussing it with her first. It was the worst decision I ever made. Thankfully she's much smarter and braver than I am and came after me."

What was he saying, that he should talk to Audrey first? Just like he should've talked to Jason weeks ago, shared his plan, solicited his aid. But that took trust, something he never gave. Yet he'd have to give it to Audrey if he wanted any kind of future with her. If she'd even have him. "You heard Audrey. She doesn't want anything more to do with me."

"Then go back to London and see how leaving her feels. I'm willing to wager you'll figure it out by the time you hit Plymouth." Sevrin shot him a look that clearly told him he was an idiot if he left. "Whatever you decide, I promise we'll keep Miss Cheswick safe."

Ethan wanted to fix him with his most imperious glare, one that wouldn't brook any failure, one he used on his men all the time. But he was too overwhelmed with trepidation and uncertainty. All he could manage was to say, "Thank you."

~

*A*udrey dismissed the young maid Philippa had sent to help her prepare for bed. She'd almost forgotten what it was like to have assistance with her clothes and her hair—such as it was. Thankfully, her curls were in much better condition since taking a bath. The maid had brushed the heavy mass until it was nearly dry. It ought to have relaxed Audrey, but she was as tightly wound as she'd been hours ago when she'd left Ethan downstairs.

She'd known he was a criminal, had seen him kill firsthand. However, the things he'd revealed tonight had been far more personal. He'd hurt people she knew and cared about. It made everything he'd done, everything he was, far more real.

A slight rap on her door made her tense even further. She got up from the chair by the fire, her legs feeling like brittle wood, and made her way slowly to the door. "Yes?"

"It's Philippa. May I come in?"

Audrey opened the door. "Please."

Philippa offered a warm smile, then came in to give her a swift but strong hug. "How are you?"

"Better after a bath. Thank you for loaning me your maid." Like Miranda and Fox at Bassett Manor, they kept a relatively small staff and didn't have a spare ladies' maid. "And this dressing gown and nightrail, and . . . I could go on, but I'll stop."

"Of course." She closed the door and walked with Audrey into the bedchamber. "Have you given any thought to what you'd like to do?"

"I'm not sure. Can I just stay here forever?" She smiled weakly as she perched on the edge of her bed. "Not really."

"You could if you wanted to," Philippa said, sitting beside her. "Will your parents mind?"

Philippa was a good enough friend to know that Audrey's parents gave little thought to her other than to be disappointed by her failure to attract a husband—a failure her father had been assured of for years, which only made his disappointment both puzzling and frustrating. Would they mind if she disappeared? Given the way they'd stopped her from running to America two years prior, she supposed so. Still, removing herself to quiet spinsterhood in Cornwall might just be acceptable to them. The question was—would it be acceptable to Audrey? It would have to be. The dream she'd had of running away with Ethan was dead.

"Ethan and I pretended we were eloping to America." She wasn't sure why she shared this, but her emotions just seemed too great.

Philippa's eyes widened. "Oh." Then her gaze narrowed shrewdly. "Is that all it really was, pretend?"

Audrey recalled the kisses they'd shared in his bedchamber, the waltz outside the assembly, the spirited evening with Fox and Miranda. Those had been the happiest two days of her life. "Somewhat."

"You didn't know what sort of man he was then."

Audrey looked at her friend. "I did. But I believed he was trying to change. I still think he is. He doesn't want to return to his criminal life. Philippa, if you only knew what he was forced to endure. He was left alone to fend for himself at a young age."

Philippa's gaze was kind. "I'm sure he's had a difficult life, and I can't fault him for trying to change. Lady Jocelyn Carlyle told me something last month when we were in London. We were talking about Lydia and Jason. Jocelyn asked if I knew Mr. Locke—Ethan. The manner in which she asked led me to believe she might know him as I'd known him—as Jagger."

"And did she?"

"Yes. He'd been involved somehow in a theft ring that had stolen something of Jocelyn's. Her husband—Lord Carlyle is a former magistrate—helped to recover the item. Apparently Lord Aldridge had been behind the theft. He'd given the piece to his wife, which is how Jocelyn had discovered it. Facing exposure, Aldridge had tried to find a way to avoid any charges against him. However, his criminal cohorts prevented him from going to the authorities by killing him. Jocelyn said she and her husband witnessed the entire thing."

Audrey inhaled sharply. "How awful."

Philippa nodded. "Indeed. Jagger was there too, and he stopped the criminal from killing Jocelyn and Carlyle."

Audrey's chest expanded. "See, he *is* trying to change."

"Maybe, but it's going to be a long while before I'll forgive him. I can't forget what he's done." She touched Audrey's hand. "Can you?"

No, but neither could she forget his touch, his kiss, the way he looked at her. All of it was intertwined to make him the complicated gentleman criminal known as Ethan Jagger Locke Lockwood.

Philippa gave her hand a pat and stood. "Sleep on it. Jagger plans to leave in the morning. Audrey, what sort of life would you have had with him?"

Was he really going to leave? Though she'd told him he should—without her—the reality of it cut into her heart. "What sort of life do I have now? I have no idea what awaits me in London. What's more, I'm not certain I care. I chose to leave with him. I preferred an unknown adventure to known tedium. I had no marriage prospects. My father won't finance any more Seasons for me. He wants me to become a lady's companion. He says it's the best I can do."

Philippa's eyes shone with pity. "Oh, Audrey, I had no idea."

No one did, because Audrey had never shared the true humiliation that was her life. To her parents, especially her father, she was at best a pawn, and at worst, a hindrance. She'd long ago accepted her lot, but that had been when she'd assumed she'd marry and establish herself as someone's wife and mother. But with no marriage proposal, year after year, that expectation had withered and died. When the blacksmith's son had told her of his desire to go to America, she'd leapt at the opportunity to reinvent herself in a new place. Her parents had convinced her it had been reckless, though as she'd resumed her stagnant life she'd decided it hadn't been, not when she truly believed there was nothing beneficial about her life in London. That's why when the chance came up again—with Ethan—she hadn't hesitated. And this time she wouldn't have to go back to her useless existence. Her reputation would be tarnished enough that it would likely be impossible.

Audrey forced a smile, her lips feeling tight and thin. "It's all right. I'm sure things will work out for the best. They did for you, didn't they?" As they had for Lydia and Olivia, Audrey's other dear friends. So many happy endings; it seemed unlikely she would find one too.

With a last empathetic look, Philippa turned and left. Audrey lay back and stared at the canopy overhead. It was hung with a rich, gold velvet, with drapes that pooled on the floor at each post. The bed itself was a massive piece of furniture, rather masculine in its size, but the gold hangings and stitched coverlet gave it a feminine touch. She ran her fingers over the outline of a leaf. Who had worked this thread and when? Had she lived here? Mayhap she'd been a spinster like Audrey would be—doomed to a life alone and without love. Had anyone even missed her after she'd passed? Would anyone miss Audrey?

She didn't know how long she sat there nursing her maudlin thoughts, but the click of her door opening and closing drew her out of her reverie. "Philippa?"

Ethan moved further into the chamber. "No."

He prowled like a cat, his booted feet moving without sound. He wore only his shirtsleeves, the collar open at his throat. His dark hair was carelessly rumpled, as if he'd been lying down, but he'd shaved his face, leaving every contour and dimple naked and overwhelmingly attractive. His gray eyes raked her from head to foot with a sense of possession.

Her entire body came alive, her seconds-ago sadness immediately cast aside. "Why are you here?" She ought to tell him to leave, but she couldn't bring herself to banish him.

"I know you said you didn't want to see me, but I can't leave tomorrow without . . ." He looked away and it was the first time he'd appeared uncertain, anxious.

Her heart leapt at the change in him, but she cautioned herself not to capitulate to her attraction to him. Just because she didn't want to be alone didn't mean she should accept *him*. Even if she wanted him. Which she absolutely did.

He refocused on her, his chin set as if he was working up his courage. She would've smiled if she hadn't been wound like a clock.

"I can't leave tomorrow without seeing if there's any chance you would still come with me."

She felt like her heart might beat out of her chest.

He stepped toward her, his gait slow and purposeful. "I know I've given you every reason to hate me, but I want to leave my past behind and the best way I can see to do that is to start somewhere new with you—somewhere we could both be safe. If you want me, that is."

The urge to wrap her arms around him and kiss him senseless was so great that it paralyzed her. Or maybe that was her doubt and her fear keeping her fixed to the edge of the bed.

"What do you mean, 'somewhere new'?" Her voice sounded distant, strange. Her breath caught.

"Anywhere you want."

Five days ago she'd wanted nothing more, but that had been before she'd watched him kill—again—with such brutal precision. Before she'd learned what he'd done to Philippa. Before she'd truly understood the horrors he was capable of. She couldn't bring herself to talk about those things just yet. "But you wanted to return to London and fight for your innocence."

"I did." He went to the hearth, where the fire had burned low. He picked up a poker and stirred the coals, coaxing the flames into an active dance. "There is every chance I would hang." He replaced the poker and turned back toward her, his eyes bleak. She'd never seen him look like that—forlorn and lost. She imagined that was how he must've looked after his mother had died.

She stood from the bed and took a step toward him.

"How can I face the end of my life," he said softly, each word rustling over her like a lover's caress, "when I feel as if it's just beginning?"

Audrey threw herself into his arms and kissed him hard on the mouth. She twined her hands around his neck and kneaded his flesh. She never wanted to let him go.

His lips opened over hers and their tongues met in a clash of fire and need. He slanted his head and lifted her flush against him. She pressed her chest to his, reveling in the feel of his heated flesh. She shouldn't want him. She should push him away. She couldn't breathe.

She ripped her mouth from his and would've stepped back, but he held her fast.

"Don't leave me," he croaked.

Audrey fought to inhale and exhale. She stared up into his desperate eyes and felt his despair in her bones. "I don't know if I can—"

He cupped her face and stroked his thumbs along her cheeks. "Audrey, I'm not the man I was six months ago. Hell," he closed his eyes briefly, "pardon. I'm not even the man I was six days ago. Because of you."

Her legs felt weak. Hope expanded in her chest.

"I don't want to be bad anymore. I've had enough of corruption and death. When I think of what I did to Philippa—" He inhaled sharply, then let go of her face. He stepped back. "It's too late," he whispered.

Her face must have reflected something to cause his

reaction. "No. I want to believe you. I think you do want to change. Philippa told me you saved Lady Carlyle and her husband."

His eyes widened for the barest second, but she caught it. "Lady Carlyle told her that?"

Audrey nodded. "Is it true?"

"Carlyle and his wife, though she wasn't his wife then, had been kidnapped by the man who was running Lord Aldridge's theft gang. His name was Nicky Blue." He recalled the vivid blue eyes of his onetime right hand. "He was a friend of mine once—as much of a friend as someone like me can have. But he was a bloodthirsty wretch, which is why I knew he'd kill Carlyle and his wife."

"You didn't let him."

He shook his head, his mouth twisting in a cold, but wry smile. "For the first time in my life, I ignored the code of survival. I risked myself to save someone else. Do you want to know the worst of it? I almost regret doing it, because you see, if I hadn't, Gin Jimmy might not have determined that I was double-crossing him. At least, that's the only thing I can figure." He wiped his hand over his face. "I spent all summer plotting how to escape being Ethan Jagger, and Gin Jimmy must have somehow suspected me, despite my careful planning."

Audrey thought she understood. "You think he sensed a change in you."

He shrugged. "Maybe. He'd sent me into Society to ensure Lady Aldridge didn't know anything about her husband's theft ring. He didn't expect me to like it. He had no idea it was what I wanted. But then, I didn't know how badly I wanted it either."

She heard the longing in his voice. He wanted the life he'd been denied, a life as the son and brother of a viscount. Yet, he was willing to walk away from the chance of having it in order to start over with her. One might argue he was simply saving himself from the noose, but he'd been ready to return to London. Something had changed his mind. She had to know what that something was.

She breached the gap between them and laid her palm against his chest. Her fingers touched his bare skin, while the heel of her hand rested against his shirt. His heart beat strong and fast beneath her hand, like a wild animal locked within a cage.

"Why would you forgo that life to be with me?"

His gaze was fierce. He laid his hand over hers, trapping her fingers against him. "Because I love you."

CHAPTER 14

*E*than watched her eyes widen and her mouth open with surprise. Regardless of how she felt, joy coursed through him. He didn't remember the last time he'd felt so full, maybe never. Giving her his love gave him hope that perhaps his life wouldn't be a waste. He'd heard the opposite so many times over the past dozen or so years that he'd almost grown to believe it.

He lifted her hand and pressed his mouth to her palm. His kiss was soft, but he licked her flesh and felt her shiver. He moved up to her wrist and kissed her again, his mouth open and wet so that he could suckle her softness. He wanted to taste every inch of her.

Her eyes slitted as he pushed up the sleeve of her dressing gown. He ascended her forearm until he reached the gentle indentation of the inside of her elbow. She twitched when he tongued her there.

He straightened. "Look at me, Audrey. I will stop whenever you ask me to."

She shook her head, her eyes still half-closed. "Don't stop." She unhooked the front of her dressing gown and let the front gap open to reveal her nightrail beneath.

It was the most chaste offer he'd ever received, but by far the most provocative. A tremor ran though his body at the thought of what she was truly offering. Her life, and his, would be irrevocably changed. It was why he'd kept his hands to himself since they'd left London. Well, for the most part.

"Does this mean . . . you'll come with me?" He was almost afraid to ask, but he had to know. This was an action that, once taken, could not be reversed.

She gazed at him with hope. "If you truly mean to stop being a criminal, yes."

"I do." Happiness, true bliss, was just within his grasp. "You'll have to marry me, though." He'd never imagined that would come to pass, and Christ, he'd bungled the proposal horribly. He took her hand and dropped to his knees. "Audrey, please be my wife and I will spend my life trying to deserve you. You make me yearn to be decent and," he stopped before his voice could crack and took a sustaining breath, "good."

She smiled down at him. "Yes." With her free hand she leaned down and cupped his cheek. "You have made me the happiest woman alive. I know you've struggled and I understand what you've done in order to survive. And I am so glad and relieved you want to be different. I know you can be, Ethan. I've seen the man no one else has."

Her confidence filled him with awe. He wasn't sure he'd ever deserve her, but he was going to try his damnedest.

She tugged on his hand. "Stand up. Please. You can't make love to me from down there."

Just because he was giving up his criminal activities didn't mean he had to abandon his wicked nature, at least not when it pertained to giving her pleasure. He clasped her ankle beneath her gown, eliciting a gasp from her. "On the contrary. I can make spectacular love to you from down here."

Her cheeks pinked and he hoped she never, ever stopped blushing.

"I can see you're trying to puzzle that out." He slid

his hand up her calf, his fingers sliding along her flesh until he wrapped his hand around her knee. His thumb found the curve at the back and she twitched as she'd done with her elbow. "You're ticklish."

"A bit," she said breathlessly.

"Back up to the bed." He inclined his head.

With one small step back, her buttocks hit the mattress.

He let go of her hand and slid his hand up her other leg until he was lightly clasping both of her knees. "Now, be a love and lift your nightrail."

She pulled the cotton up to his hands, exposing her ankles and calves.

"Very pretty," he said, appreciating the view. "Higher, please."

The garment climbed slowly, revealing inch after tantalizing inch of her thighs. His hands followed the movement, all the while caressing her softness. She paused just before revealing what he wanted to see most. He looked up at her, saw that her eyes were a mix of desire and trepidation. She wanted this, but didn't precisely know what "this" was.

He grasped her thighs firmly but gently. "I shall stop whenever you ask." She nodded in response. He pushed the nightrail up to expose her mound and the delicate chocolate curls. "Beautiful."

She still held on to the nightrail and didn't try to lower it. He traced his hands down over her hips and slid them between her thighs. "Open wider, my love."

Her legs trembled as she followed his command. He pressed a kiss to her inner thigh, a chaste brushing of his lips against her smooth, pale skin. But then he caught the scent of her arousal and he couldn't help himself. He opened his mouth and deepened the kiss, licking at her and drawing on her flesh, while his hands kneaded her. She slumped against the bed, which was why he'd positioned her there. He'd meant to put her on the edge of it, at least, but he hadn't gotten there yet, and damn, he might not.

His cock raged but he ignored his own wants, beyond wanting to give her pleasure. For that was what he most desired—to show her the wonders of her body. He glided his hand up to her entrance and grazed his thumb along her pink flesh. She twitched again, but her thighs opened farther. *Good girl.*

He wanted to bury his tongue in her wet heat, but he urged himself to go slow. They had all night—no, they had a lifetime—before them. He used his thumb to stroke her, gently at first so she could become accustomed to his touch. When she grew slick, he found her clitoris and flicked it softly. Her gasp made him smile against her thigh, where he continued to lave kisses upon her flesh.

When his mouth was just below her sheath, he slid his finger inside of her. She was tight, but there didn't seem to be a barrier as there had been with his first experience—his only virginal partner. Was Audrey not a virgin then? He'd assumed she was, but there had been the blacksmith's son. Jealousy knifed through him.

"Audrey," his voice sounded dark and pained, "have you done this before?" He looked up at her, his breath halting.

Her gaze locked with his and there was panic reflected in their blue-green depths. "I—" She nodded. "Not like this. Geoffrey, the blacksmith's son, he . . ." She looked away. "You know."

Ethan stood and cupped her face, forcing her to look at him. "Did he rape you?" Rage coursed through him.

"No, though I did think we were going to wait until we were properly wed." She rushed to add, "I didn't want him like I want you. He was a means to an end and I liked him well enough. I didn't realize there would be more to it until I met you, that I would feel so . . . hungry."

Laughter threatened Ethan's fury. "I'm going to hunt down that prick and tear him apart."

She frowned at him. "No, you're not. You don't do that anymore. Besides, he didn't hurt me." Her eyes softened. "Are you disappointed I'm not untouched?"

Ethan slid his hands into her hair. "Never. I want you any way you'll allow me. Don't for a minute think you're somehow a lesser woman—not to me, not to anyone. People have disregarded you for far too long. You are beautiful and strong, and the most desirable female I have ever encountered."

Her lips spread into a smile. "Would you mind going back to . . . ?"

He loved that she asked him, even if she couldn't say the words. And he hadn't even started what he really meant to do. He kissed her deeply, his tongue probing the hot recesses of her mouth as he tipped her head back. She kissed him in return, her hands coming around him and digging into his spine.

He drew his mouth from hers, but didn't retreat. "Lie back." He lifted her onto the bed and she reclined. He hastily removed his boots and stockings before climbing onto the bed beside her. He drew the bed curtains closed on either side, leaving the base of the bed open to the glow of the fire. He wanted to see her sprawled before him. Her dark hair fanned against the white pillow, her legs were slightly parted, bare up to her mid-thighs, where the nightrail had shifted when she'd moved.

He caught her gaze with his and held it while he pushed her nightrail back up. And when his fingers teased her opening, her nostrils flared. Then as his middle finger slid up into her, slowly but effortlessly amidst her wetness, her legs parted, inviting him further. He buried himself as far as he could go, then withdrew gradually. Her eyelids fluttered and her mouth opened. He repeated the action several times, never increasing his speed. With each stroke, she reacted in some way. When her hips began to move, he took that as indication to go a bit faster. He thumbed her clitoris and she thrust to meet his finger.

He kneeled between her legs and put his mouth on her. She gasped loudly, her body tensing. She was so hot and wet. He settled her thighs over his shoulders, opening her to his attentions. He licked her, savoring her soft, slick flesh. She cried out. Her muscles clenched. She was very close, and he'd only just begun his feast. He wanted to prolong this for her, but didn't know if he could. With each lick and suck, her hips came further off the bed. Her cries became more erratic, more desperate. Her fingers tangled into his hair and she tugged when he closed over her clitoris and sucked hard. He pumped two fingers into her and felt her begin to spasm. Her thighs quivered and he heard his name spill from her lips over and over. It was the sweetest sound he'd ever heard. At last he was Ethan, a man and a lover instead of Jagger, the criminal.

Her orgasm rocked through her, and he kept up his lovemaking until he felt her go still. His own lust raged hard, but he rested his head against the softness of her lower belly and inhaled the lavender scent from her bath.

"Ethan," her tremulous voice broke the silence, "I had no idea. This is probably a silly question, but does that only happen when you use your mouth? Or, is it possible when you put your . . . your *penis* inside me? Geoffrey did that, but it didn't feel like what just happened."

God, how he loved her innocence. His world had been full of corruption and decay for far too long. She was sweet and honest, and she was a balm to his soul.

He rose and looked at her beautiful flushed face. "If

a gentleman is a considerate lover, you would feel like that in any instance of lovemaking. Geoffrey sounds like an inexperienced, or perhaps just callous, ass."

"I see. What do you mean, any 'instance'?"

"There are many ways in which to find satisfaction with your lover. I could've just used my hand, but I'm afraid I was desperate to taste you." He knew he was shocking her, but he couldn't help but add, "Better than honey too."

She didn't look away from him. In fact, her eyes narrowed slightly, perhaps as her desire began to ignite again. "And I could do that to you? With my hand, or with my mouth?"

Ethan's cock hardened to granite at the thought of her doing either of those things. "Yes." The word was barely more than an exhalation.

"Would you mind taking your shirt off? I like looking at you without it."

He was enjoying playing with her far more than he'd ever imagined. "You'll have to remove it."

She gave him a saucy look, then brought herself up to kneel so that they were facing each other in the middle of the bed. She found the hem of his shirt and drew it over his head, Her gaze fixed on his exposed chest and then her hands splayed over him. "I never thought a man could look so . . . delicious." She ran her thumbs over his nipples.

He gritted his teeth against a powerful surge of lust. "Careful, Audrey."

She lifted her gaze to his and gave him a saucy smile. "Don't I get my turn?"

Oh, God. She didn't mean to put her mouth on him?

She shrugged out of her dressing gown and cast it aside. Then she pulled her nightrail over her head and tossed it away, too. Her naked breasts were plump and pale in the firelight, their nipples pink and peaked. He leaned forward to taste one, but she pushed him backward until he was lying flat and had to stretch his legs out toward the pillows.

Her hands trailed down his chest and paused at his waistband. Then she found the buttons of his fall and slid them open one by agonizing one.

"Audrey," he groaned.

Her lips came down against his chest. She kissed and licked swirls around his nipples and then south along his ribcage. She opened her mouth and suckled him as she worked his breeches down his hips.

She absolutely meant to mimic what he'd done.

Her movements stilled with his breeches trapped around his thighs. He looked down and saw her contemplating his cock. It rose hard and proud, seeking her touch. Gingerly, her fingertip brushed the head. Ethan squeezed his eyes shut; the sight of her touching him was nearly his undoing.

"I can use my hand," she wrapped her palm around him, encasing him in her soft heat. If she stroked him . . . "Or I could use my mouth." He felt something wet and delicate against the tip of his cock.

He tortured himself and looked. Her tongue, pink and perfect, was laving him. He didn't know where he found the ability to speak, but said, "Or you could use both."

"Oh!" She grinned up at him, her eyes narrowing seductively. "I see." Her hand squeezed around him with the perfect grip, sliding down to the base and then back up to the head. Then her mouth came down over him and somehow, bewilderingly and amazingly, the tutor became the student.

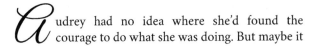

*A*udrey had no idea where she'd found the courage to do what she was doing. But maybe it wasn't courage, it was simply need. She wanted to give him what he'd given her.

She didn't know if she was doing any of it right, but focused on doing what felt good. He was so hard, yet his skin was like the softest silk. And at his tip, moisture seeped out, just as she'd grown wet when he'd touched her. Their bodies, it seemed, while quite disparate, had their similarities too.

When she'd moved her hand along his shaft, he'd moaned, so she took that as encouragement. She copied what he'd done to her, moving slowly at first and then quickening her pace. His hips thrust into her hand, and, strangely, she wanted to rotate her own hips in response.

"Audrey, my breeches. I'm rather . . . restricted." His words were clipped with an underlying desperation.

She smiled, enjoying the power she never knew she possessed. She quickly divested him of his breeches and returned to her task—both for her own pleasure and his.

She wrapped her hand around his sex and guided him to her lips. She slid her tongue down his length and drew him deep into her mouth. His hands twisted in her hair and his moans filled the room. She withdrew, then pitched forward again; this time his hips met her. He tasted of salt and man, something she never imagined she would've found desirable and yet she couldn't get enough.

Suddenly, his hands dragged her away from him. "Audrey, you have to stop."

She gazed up at him, sensing he'd been close to achieving what had happened to her. "Why? I want you to . . ."

"Orgasm. That's the word." He grimaced like he was in pain. "I desperately want to come—that's another word—but, I'd rather do it inside of you."

"Oh. Can't you just do both?" She'd felt her own . . .

orgasm building again while she'd been attending to him. She was amazed she could feel like that from what she was doing to him. But he was so beautiful and the sounds he was making spurred her own desire.

He laughed. Then he reached up to cup the back of her neck and drew her down to kiss him. His tongue speared into her and all of a sudden she wanted exactly what he wanted—him inside of her. She lifted her head and looked down at him. "Show me what to do."

"Straddle me." He put a hand on her hip and guided her into position. His sex nudged her opening, tantalizing her.

She pressed down, seeking the friction of him against her. She gasped as his hand came up to her breast. He pulled on her flesh, tweaking her nipple. Sensation shot straight to her core and she swiveled her hips down.

His hand moved between them. "Help me put my cock inside you. Audrey, look at me."

She'd blushed—for the thousandth time tonight—at his language, not because it was crude, but because she found it strangely . . . erotic. Her gaze met his and her body reacted to the stark desire in his eyes. "Yes." She put her hand over his, but he shifted so that her fingers wrapped around his hot length.

He parted her and thrust gently upward. "Guide me."

She positioned him and slid her body down over his cock. Thinking the word made her feel bold and powerful. Then he filled her and she didn't think at all.

He gripped her hips and held her on him for a long moment. But she wanted to move. She rose and fell, slipping over him like a well-made glove.

His fingers ground into her skin. "You are so beautiful."

She looked down at herself, the firelight playing over her breasts and felt a moment's shyness. But then his thumb was on that most sensitive place between her legs and she threw her head back and moaned. She widened her legs and moved faster.

He increased his pressure on her and her orgasm built. She pitched forward and his mouth found her breast. His tongue and teeth teased her until she thought she might burst. "Ethan, I can't—"

He wrapped his arm around her waist and clasped her tight. Then he flipped so that he was on top of her, his cock never leaving her. He came up over her and fanned her hair out, his pause giving her a moment to catch her breath as she hovered at the edge of the cataclysm.

He smiled at her. The glow of the fire made his eyes look like liquid silver. "What can't you do, my love?"

"Hold on. You make me want to let go of everything."

"Then let go." He kissed her softly and pumped into her with swift precision.

She arched up, meeting his thrusts and kissed him back.

"Wrap your legs around me," he said into her mouth.

She complied and he sank deeper inside of her. One more thrust and she threw her head back against the bed, her eyes closing in ecstasy.

He continued to move, which only intensified the sensations within her. There was light and bliss and an overwhelming satisfaction. She made awful, hideous sounds, but couldn't help herself. Then he shouted and buried his face into her neck.

They lay like that for several minutes. She loved his weight and size on top of her. As a taller than average woman, she rarely felt delicate or very feminine, but he made her feel both of those things. As well as desirable and . . . loved.

He'd said he loved her. Did she love him in return? She wasn't certain—her mind was still awhirl with everything that had happened, how drastically her life had altered in just a fortnight.

He shifted finally and guided her underneath the bedclothes. Then he parted the drapes and stepped from the bed.

She grabbed his arm. "You're not leaving?"

He smiled at her. "No. Just getting something for you to clean yourself."

How thoughtful. And how utterly mundane. Maybe they could have a normal life together. Yes, she thought they could. After seeing him at the orphanage with Fox, she knew there was a side to him that even he probably didn't know—or was only just beginning to discover.

He returned with a towel, which she used to clean between her legs. He waited patiently for her to finish, then disposed of the article after completing his own brief toilet.

When he climbed back into the bed and closed the curtains, she yawned widely. She offered a weak smile, suddenly feeling bone-tired. "Pardon."

He lay on his back and drew her against his chest. She heard his heart beating and was already drifting off when he said, "Sleep well, my love. Tomorrow, our future awaits."

CHAPTER 15

*D*espite the most satisfying sleep of his existence, Ethan woke early as always. It seemed he couldn't escape his training. Sleeping late meant having your meager possessions stolen or perhaps your throat slit. There were plenty of occasions when he hadn't risked sleeping at all.

But all of that seemed so long ago, so far away now as he watched Audrey in slumber. Her dark lashes fanned against her cheeks, which were pale as porcelain. Her nose had a gentle, but regal slope. And her lips were dark pink and lush, cushioned against each other just waiting for his kiss.

Her hair was a wild tangle of dark curls. He'd longed to touch it again, bury his face in its softness, and inhale her scent. But now that wasn't enough. He'd been to heaven and back, and he was forever changed.

Where would they go? America? The continent? Somewhere more obscure? Maybe an island in the tropics. He'd heard of men who owned plantations there. Or perhaps they needn't go so far. Surely they could start anew in a remote area of Scotland or Wales.

A piece of him still longed to return to London. He regretted having to forfeit his dream of taking his place as a Lockwood, especially since he and Jason had seemed to forge a brotherly relationship—or at least the promise of one. But his dream hadn't accounted for a woman like Audrey. He'd never imagined he'd wed or even want to. She was an unexpected gift—a treasure he wouldn't deny.

He had to admit a certain relief about not having to fight Teague or Jimmy. Guaranteeing Audrey's safety was paramount, which was why he needed to make certain that wherever they went, neither Bow Street nor Gin Jimmy's men would follow. He rather thought Teague would give up at some point, if he hadn't already. However, Jimmy was a tenacious bastard, and he had a particular hatred for those he thought had personally wronged him. And since he'd trusted Ethan like no other and knew Ethan had betrayed him, he would take extreme measures to ensure Ethan's demise.

Audrey stirred beside him, a sigh escaping her kiss-ready lips. He evicted thoughts of Jimmy and Teague from his mind. He didn't want them here, not with her.

He leaned down and pressed his mouth against hers softly. She opened her eyes, which for a moment reflected surprise. Then her lips curved into a smile. "Is it morning?" she asked.

"Close enough. I thought it best if I returned to my room."

"Why? I don't want to hide from Philippa and Sevrin. I plan to tell Philippa that we're leaving together."

He didn't see any point in lying to them either. Still, did he want to be obvious about their behavior since they hadn't yet exchanged vows? "We'll tell them this morning, but I prefer not to shock the maid when she comes to wake you."

"I don't even know if a maid will come. They employ a limited staff." She scooted closer to him and slipped her arms around his middle, squeezing one beneath him to accomplish her goal.

He turned so that he was half-lying on her. He kissed the sensitive spot beneath her ear. "I'm happy to play lady's maid if you require assistance."

She giggled. "Somehow I think your 'assistance' might be more of a hindrance."

He drew back and gave her a look of mock affront. "Did I not provide service on our journey?"

She wriggled beneath him, bringing her hips into contact with his. "You did. My apologies."

His cock grew against her, but she didn't draw away. He resumed kissing her neck and stroked her breast.

She sighed softly and kneaded his back. "Where will we go?"

He moved his lips past her collarbone. "We have several choices. America, if you still wish. Anywhere, really."

"But we don't have any funds."

Hopefully, Sevrin would help him on that front. "Let me worry about money." He drew her nipple into his mouth and suckled her while he massaged her flesh.

She moved her hand up and twisted her fingers into his hair, holding him against her. "I think America is the best choice. You can be anything you want there—or so Geoffrey said."

"I think I'd prefer you didn't mention that bounder again. His opinions don't hold much weight with me."

"You're right, of course. Would you prefer to go somewhere else?"

He paused in his attentions and looked up at her. "Audrey, either you are thinking way too hard or I am not performing my duties properly. Why aren't you lost in the throes of ecstasy?"

Her lips lifted in a seductive smile. "I'm quite enjoying your attentions." She pushed his head back to her breast.

He nipped her softly and she arched into his mouth. He closed his mouth around her, drawing on her and sending shocks of pleasure to her core. She squirmed beneath him, opening her legs.

Accepting her invitation, he moved one hand between her thighs and caressed her slick softness. Her body came up off the bed, seeking more of him wherever he touched her.

He increased his pressure on her breast, laving and suckling her insistently, as if he could devour her whole. He slipped his fingers inside of her moist sheath. She cried out and bucked as he pumped into her.

She rotated toward him. "I want you. Now. Please."

He pushed her back against the bed and rose above her. Her hand came between them—his beautiful intrepid girl—and guided him home.

Where last night he'd taken his time to bring her pleasure and ensure her satisfaction, this morning he was more confident in her abilities to find what she sought. Which gave him the freedom to do what he'd asked of her last night—to let go.

He drove into her, but still held back. He didn't want to hurt or frighten her. But, Christ, he wanted to fuck her until his head exploded. Nothing in his life had felt as good as Audrey. Her laugh, her kisses, her simultaneously innocent and brazen touch.

She spread her legs wider and wrapped them around his hips, squeezing him with her muscles. She drew his head down and kissed him, her mouth open and wet. "Faster, please," she breathed against his lips.

It was all he needed. He braced his hands on either side of her head and slid his length to the hilt, then retreated only to plunge forward again. He moved fast and hard. Her hands clenched his biceps and her cries grew louder and higher.

"Ethan!" She tensed with her orgasm and Ethan rushed to join her. He called out as he came, then went rigid as shocks of pleasure jerked through his body.

He rolled to the side, taking her with him. "Thank you."

She kissed the underside of his chin. "Why? I should be thanking you."

He took deep breaths to regulate the frenzied beating of his heart. "We can thank each other. You're amazing."

"Am I?"

He heard the pride as well as the sliver of doubt in her voice. He brushed her hair back from her face and kissed her, exploring her mouth with sensual precision. He drew back and looked into her eyes. "You are spectacular. I have never been happier in all of my life."

She smiled and stroked his cheek. "When can we leave for America? I can't wait to start our new lives together."

"We need to talk to Sevrin and Philippa first."

Her smile faded. "Yes, but I think Philippa will try to dissuade me from going with you."

Sevrin probably wouldn't be terribly supportive, either. "As she should. She's a good friend."

"She'll change her opinion of you when she understands who you truly are." She flattened her palm against his face, her touch soft yet firm. "Ethan, you have to let your guard down now—with some people. Please. You trusted me, didn't you?"

He did. He marveled at that even now. "I will do my best. This is all new for me. And you must accept that you are special." He covered her hand against his cheek and drew her palm to his mouth for a fierce kiss. "You know that, don't you? You are something no one has ever been for me."

Her eyes met his and held. "I know, and I won't ever let you down."

She kissed him and he was lost to the wonder of her once more.

~

*A*fter making love to her again, Ethan had reluctantly left her chamber an hour or so after sunrise. Audrey completed a quick and solitary toilet and hurried downstairs to join the others. She found Ethan and Sevrin in the breakfast room. Both men rose from the table as she entered.

Ethan pulled out the chair beside his for her. "I've just told Sevrin of our change in plans."

Sevrin frowned at her. "You're certain you wish to leave with him? You're not under any sort of duress, are you?"

Audrey tried not to look affronted. She had, after all, given him the distinct impression that she and Ethan were parting ways. "No. I want to be with Ethan. I was . . . angry yesterday."

"I've sent the footman to fetch Philippa. She will undoubtedly want to participate in this conversation."

She sat and gave Ethan a quick smile over her shoulder before turning to their host. "That would be lovely. But do save us all the effort of disagreement. Nothing you can say will change my mind."

"Audrey!" Philippa sailed into the room in her morning gown, something she might not have normally worn in Ethan's presence. "Is it true that you're going with Jagger?"

Audrey's pulse began to pick up speed in anticipation of the coming conflict. "His name is Locke, and yes, I'm going with him. We're going to be married."

Philippa's amber eyes widened, then focused on her husband in a communication that clearly said, "Do something."

Sevrin shrugged. "Please sit, sweetheart." He indicated the chair beside him, which Ned, the footman, pulled out for her.

She sat but crossed her arms and fixed Audrey with an insistent stare. "What happened?"

Sevrin touched Philippa's hand. "Sweetheart, do you really want to know the answer to that?" The dryness of his tone nearly made Audrey laugh. She snuck a look at Ethan, whose lips were twitching. "Now," Sevrin continued, "do we have to understand her choice or like it? No. But there are plenty of people who thought your choosing me over Allred was sheer foolishness, so perhaps we ought not judge."

Philippa shot her husband a surprised look, but then her shoulders seemed to relax as she sat back against her chair. "I see your point."

Audrey also began to relax. "Philippa, I hope you'll come to see the Ethan I know. He deeply regrets what he did to you. I know you can't forget what happened, but perhaps in time you can forgive him."

"He has an awful lot to prove," Philippa said.

"They'll be leaving in a few days," Ambrose said. "I'm going to talk to Sedley about taking them to Guernsey."

"Who's Sedley?" Audrey asked.

"He owns several boats in Portscatho."

Audrey turned to Ethan. "And why Guernsey?" It was a small island near the northern coast of France.

"Sevrin suggested it," Ethan said after swallowing a bite of egg. "It doesn't follow the same laws as England, so we should be safe there. And it's much closer than America."

Did that mean he wanted to try to come back at some point? She couldn't fault him for wanting that, not when he wanted to get to know his brother.

Ethan smiled at Audrey. "We can be married there immediately, as well."

"Is that what you want?" Philippa asked.

Audrey smiled back at Ethan, her chest expanding with emotions she could barely contain. She'd been hesitant to declare her love—she hadn't tried to love anyone in such a long time. "Yes," she said, then added softly, "I love him."

His gray eyes reflected surprise and joy and astonishment. She took his hand and squeezed it. He seemed to fight a battle, then capitulated and brought her hand to his mouth for a gentle kiss.

Sevrin coughed discreetly. "Call me tenderhearted, but I can't fault anyone who finds true love."

Philippa exhaled, drawing Audrey to finally look away from Ethan. "I shall endeavor to support you, my dear friend, since this is clearly what you want. We'll need to take a trip to Truro to outfit you with a trousseau. Are you going to write to your parents?"

"I should, but I don't want them to know where we've gone."

Ethan still held her hand. "You should send a note telling them you're safe and happy, that they needn't worry."

Both Philippa and Sevrin looked at him as if surprised he'd suggest such a thing.

"I realize I haven't given you reason to think I'm a thoughtful person," he drawled wryly, "but hopefully you'll see that I can be." The last part was uttered with such sincerity that Audrey didn't know how they couldn't.

Philippa looked at Audrey with concern. "Are you certain you wish to leave your life behind?"

Audrey straightened her shoulders. "I already did when I chose to leave London with Ethan. There's nothing for me there." She added softly, "You know that, Philippa."

There was a beat of silence before Sevrin said, "Then it's settled, I'll go and speak with Sedley today, and Philippa will take Audrey into Truro tomorrow."

Audrey didn't want to wait. What if they could leave tomorrow? "It's early, why can't we go today?"

Ethan laughed. "My bride is in a hurry."

Sevrin chuckled. "I know how that feels."

Philippa blushed and shook her head at him before addressing Audrey. "Yes, we can go today. We need a little alone time, I think, so I can hear just how Mr. Locke changed your mind." That she referred to him as Mr. Locke and not Jagger was progress.

CHAPTER 16

After visiting Sedley and arranging for passage to Guernsey the following day, Ethan and Sevrin strolled back through Portscatho toward Beckwith. It was a fine autumn day, the sea breeze was cool, but the sun overhead provided enough warmth, as did their exercise. But then Ethan thought this might just be the most splendid day of his life.

He looked at Sevrin's profile as they walked, still uncertain if they were friends or not. He wasn't sure he'd ever had a true friend. "I can't thank you enough for helping me. The truth is, I can't quite believe it, either."

Sevrin glanced at him. "Neither can I. No, that's not precisely true. I'm trying to practice forgiveness—for myself as much as for you. I have my own bad decisions and regrettable actions to overcome."

This wasn't the first time Sevrin had inferred his past was less than exemplary, but then Ethan had heard he'd ruined his brother's fiancée or some such. And then today, with Sedley, there'd been some underlying current. "Something to do with Sedley?"

They turned onto the main street of Portscatho. "You could say that," Sevrin said. "Mrs. Sedley was once engaged to marry my brother."

Shit. That was definitely *something.* "I'd heard the rumor that you'd dallied with your brother's fiancée. That's her?"

Sevrin shot him a pained look and gave a subtle nod. "I'll never fully recover from what I did to him. He died, indirectly, because of my callous indiscretion."

His message came through very clearly: Ethan might not recover from his past deeds either. "I'm aware I have to live with the things I've done. How do you manage it?"

Sevrin inhaled. "Fighting. At first."

Ethan began to understand why Sevrin had fought. He'd wanted Sevrin as his prizefighter because he'd been damned good—good enough to win the title— but he'd suddenly stopped. Ethan had hoped to coax him out of retirement, but he'd refused, which was why Ethan had used Philippa to persuade him to agree. "If the fighting soothed your pain, why did you stop?"

"Because it also brought me glory. I didn't deserve that."

Ethan's neck prickled. He suspected he didn't deserve this amazing day, the feelings of joy inside of him, or the love of Audrey. But could he even consider doing what Sevrin had done—deny himself that which made him happy because he didn't deserve it? What purpose did it serve? "Do you fight anymore? Obviously, I'm aware you turned Ackley's training over to one of your fighting club men." Sevrin had found Ethan a prize-fighter—Ackley—and had trained him until marrying Philippa.

He shook his head. "Not since Philippa and I wed. I occasionally spar with Ned, but it's purely educational."

"Pity, you were awfully good." Ethan enjoyed a good fight. He'd wanted a prizefighter because it was a legitimate way to make money and it had been his father's favorite sport. He used to take Ethan and Jason to bouts when they were lads. Those were some of the best memories of Ethan's life.

They came upon the one of the town's inns just as a man stepped out into the street. Ethan recognized him immediately. "Hell."

Teague had just covered his balding pate with his hat when his gaze connected with Ethan's. He strode toward him purposefully. "You can't mean to run again." He shouted toward the inn, "Lewis!"

The second Runner came from the inn. He wasn't as large as Teague, but he was tall and fit. Ethan didn't think he could take both of them on. He glanced at Sevrin. He wouldn't help Ethan fight, but would he join the Runners?

Teague drew his pistol and Lewis did the same. Teague inclined his head at his cohort, who circled around to Ethan's side.

Deep furrows carved into Sevrin's brow. "What do you mean to do with Locke?"

"I'm arresting him for the murder of the Marquess of Wolverton and transporting him back to Bow Street."

At Sevrin's intake of breath, Ethan shot him a dark look. "I didn't kill Wolverton."

"The evidence against you is enough. My testimony alone will commit you to trial." Teague flicked a glance at Sevrin. "I saw him standing over the body, holding a bloody knife, on the terrace at Lockwood House."

Ethan could see the doubt in Sevrin's gaze. "Teague, use the logic you're so fond of. Jimmy was wearing the livery of the dead footman you seem to have conveniently forgotten. Jimmy had to have killed him, donned the costume, and committed the murder against Wolverton. I was simply in the wrong place at the wrong time."

Teague appeared unconvinced. "Nothing with you is as simple as you'd have it seem. You're Jimmy's most trusted man. I'm certain you worked together. In fact, I suspect it was you who anonymously informed us Jimmy would be at Wolverton House—that way we'd be busy while you and he killed Wolverton at Lockwood House. Don't worry, we'll be taking him down, too."

If they could bloody find him, which they wouldn't be likely to do. Jimmy knew and was welcome in just about every rookery in London. The denizens of those places wouldn't help Bow Street.

"You should go," Sevrin said quietly. "We'll follow you tomorrow."

The world careened sideways as Ethan saw his options disappearing. Hadn't he planned to return to London anyway? Before he'd glimpsed a dream life with Audrey. *Audrey.* His knees nearly buckled. "I don't want to leave without seeing Audrey."

Sevrin clasped his shoulder. "It's all right. I'll take care of her. And I'll send a note to your brother."

It was more than Ethan could hope for. Far more than he likely deserved. He turned to Teague, hating that the man would see this as a victory. "I'll go, but I promise to disappoint you. I'll prove my innocence."

Teague nodded at Lewis, who went to one of their horses and came back with a pair of shackles. His eyes gleamed with satisfaction. "How could this possibly disappoint me?"

"Is that really necessary?" Sevrin asked. "He said he'll go with you."

Teague's glower didn't move from Ethan. "I don't trust him."

Sevrin moved toward Lewis. "You can't mean to keep him locked up for several days. That's brutal. Ja—Locke," he corrected, "tell them you won't run."

"I won't run." He looked at Sevrin. "Thank you. You'll bring Audrey?"

Sevrin nodded. "We'll figure this out. Don't run."

Teague scoffed. "You don't trust him either."

Sevrin turned to him. "No, I'm trying to make him understand that he can trust *me,* that he can rely on someone. I don't think he knows how to do that."

It seemed Ethan had a friend at last. He only hoped he'd be around long enough to appreciate it. No, he wouldn't think like that. He would prove his innocence. He simply couldn't contemplate the alternative.

Sevrin looked at the pair of horses they had tied outside the inn. "How are you transporting him?"

"We'll get a cart and I'll drive. I'll arrange to have my mount returned to London," Teague said.

"Why don't you come back to Beckwith with us?" Sevrin said. "I'll provide your transportation and you can leave in the morning."

Ethan wanted to hug Sevrin, or at least thank him profusely.

Teague shook his head. "I want to get back to London as quickly as possible."

"Then let me ride a horse," Ethan said, hating the idea of being confined to a cart for the next five or six days. "I won't bolt. And we'll get back much faster."

Teague shook his head. "No. We'll find something here in town."

Sevrin inclined his head toward Ethan. "I can procure something comfortable."

In a short while, Sevrin had obtained a curricle with a single horse and gave Teague instructions to change the horse once a day. Teague wasn't a particularly good driver, but though he hadn't shackled Ethan's hands, he also refused to let him take the reins. They rode out together, with Lewis traveling on horseback beside them. Sevrin had agreed to bring Teague's mount back to London.

Ethan looked back at Sevrin and tried to find a thread of hope. But it was far easier to believe that his dreams for a happy future had just gone up in flames.

~

*I*t was late afternoon before Audrey and Philippa returned to Beckwith. They'd spent a productive day gathering supplies for her and Ethan's trip to Guernsey. She'd purchased some clothing, but it would require alteration once they arrived at their destination. She wondered what they would do there and looked forward to discussing it with Ethan. Hopefully, he would've worked out their transportation as well as how to obtain his money from London so they would have a means to live.

Philippa had quizzed her about why she'd changed her mind and Audrey had explained that Ethan was indeed trying to change and that all he really needed was for someone to have faith in him—and she did.

"How long will you stay in Guernsey?" Philippa asked as the coach came to a stop in Beckwith's drive.

"I have no idea." Nor did she particularly care. She was just happy to have the chance to start a life with the man she loved. "You and Sevrin must visit us." The voyage wasn't that long.

Ned, who had accompanied them on their errands, helped them from the coach.

The front door of the house opened and Sevrin stalked toward them, his face a dark mask. Audrey's stomach fell straight through her toes. "What is it?" she breathed. But the absence of Ethan told her all that really mattered: He was gone.

"Come inside."

"No," Philippa said. "Tell her now. Did he leave?"

"Yes, but not of his own accord. Bow Street found him." Sevrin looked to Audrey. "He didn't want to leave without seeing you, but he wasn't given a choice."

Part of her was glad he would have the opportunity to prove his innocence, but the rest of her was devastated their plans had been ruined. There was always a chance he would be found guilty . . . She straightened and blinked against sudden tears.

She walked toward the house. "When can we leave?"

"Tomorrow," Sevrin said, trailing behind her.

She paused at the door, wanting to protest, but knew it was pointless to depart today. They would barely have enough light to make it back to Truro, let alone anywhere on the way to London. She nodded as defeat seeped into her bones. *No.* She'd find a way to save him from hanging. He said he hadn't done it, and she believed him.

Sevrin and Philippa followed her inside. She removed her gloves and bonnet with shaking hands. "I know you don't have much faith in Ethan, if any, but he's innocent of this crime."

"What do you know of it?" Sevrin asked.

Audrey fought the embarrassment that rose to her cheeks. She hated that she didn't know much of anything. "He said he was innocent and I believe him."

Philippa gave her a sad look. "I hope you're not wrong to place your trust in him."

"He told me the same thing," Sevrin said, leading them into the hall where he rang for refreshment. "He said he was in the wrong place at the wrong time. Lockwood House, to be exact." Sevrin glanced at Philippa. Lockwood House held special meaning for them.

And maybe it did for Audrey too . . . Her mind turned. This murder had to have happened the night they'd left London. It was why he'd fled. *She'd* been at Lockwood House that night.

It had been an odd evening, unlike any of the others she'd spent there. She'd been in the card room watching the hazard table when a footman had come in from the terrace. A few moments later, Lord Lockwood had gone out onto the terrace and shortly thereafter another man had followed him. There had been an urgency and tension to all of their movements. She'd grown nervous. Well, more nervous than sneaking into Lockwood House typically made her, and she'd departed quickly. But the important thing was that she'd been there.

She knew what she had to do and she didn't hesitate. "I was at Lockwood House that night. I know what happened."

Sevrin snapped his gaze to her. "You were?"

Philippa was also staring at her. "Audrey, what were you doing there?"

Audrey fought the blush that rose up her neck. "After you made it seem so easy to get in, I decided to try it for myself. I went once in a face-covering mask." But she'd garnered too much attention from the attendees. People inviting her to do things she could scarcely imagine. "After that, I went dressed as a gentleman."

Philippa blinked. Then she smiled and shook her head. "Shocking."

"Did you see the murder?" Sevrin asked, his voice heavy with concern. "Can you identify the man who killed Wolverton?"

The Marquess of Wolverton had been the one killed? No wonder Bow Street had followed Ethan to the end of England. One didn't kill a peer and get away with it. Not that he'd done it, but Bow Street thought he had. "I can. It wasn't Ethan."

"I don't understand." Philippa crossed her arms over her chest. "Why wouldn't you have gone back to London together if you could prove his innocence?"

Audrey exhaled. She'd have to tell them the truth—or at least part of it. "We didn't discuss the specifics of what he'd done. I didn't realize who he was accused of murdering until now."

But how she wished they had. If he'd been honest with her, she could've told him she'd been there, that she would give the testimony that would save him from hanging. Her neck chilled. If she'd been honest with him about why she'd been dressed as a gentleman, he would've realized she was there that night and maybe he would've told her his truth. They'd both been foolish, and now they were paying the price.

"You didn't really see anything, did you?" Sevrin asked quietly.

"I saw enough. And I *was* there. I'll be able to prove it. I won a large sum of money at hazard." Which she and Ethan had spent on their travels.

Philippa gasped. "Audrey!"

Sevrin moved toward Audrey and pinned her with a serious stare. "Ethan says Gin Jimmy killed Wolverton. He was dressed in Lockwood livery."

Audrey nodded slowly. "I saw him leaving the terrace." She recalled Lord Lockwood and the man—now that she thought about it, she was sure that had been Teague, the Bow Street Runner—had gone onto the terrace. "Was Wolverton killed on the terrace?"

"Yes."

Audrey's heart sang. She hadn't seen Gin Jimmy commit the murder, but she absolutely believed he had. "I'm going to say I saw Gin Jimmy kill Wolverton."

Philippa came to her side and touched her arm. "You're going to lie?"

She'd do that and more. "I'll do whatever is necessary to save the man I love."

Audrey barely slept that night and finally gave up trying just before sunrise. She dressed and went downstairs just as the sun was creeping over the horizon. Where was Ethan? Was he sleeping? Was he as distraught as her? Was he well?

Her heart clenched and she fought to take a deep breath. She went through the solar to a small room that led to the back terrace. She grabbed a bonnet and a wrap hanging from a hook and went out into the cool morning. Sea mist dampened her cheeks as she awkwardly tied the ribbon beneath her chin. The wrap was large and soft, something Mrs. Gates had knitted, Philippa had told her. It was also warm and comforting. She tried to imagine Ethan's arms around her in place of it.

She was anxious to leave. Sevrin had promised they would depart early, but until they were actually on the road moving toward London, she wouldn't relax. Hell, she probably wouldn't even relax then. Listen to her, *swearing*. She smiled, missing Ethan and his foul but delectable mouth.

She walked through the yard to where there was a gate in the wall. Philippa had told her it led to a path that wound along the cliff side and then down to the beach. Audrey had hoped she and Ethan could walk to the beach together before they left for Guernsey. Now, alone, she went to the edge and looked out at the waves. Waves she ought to have been riding to her new life. With Ethan.

They could still have that life. He wouldn't hang before she got to London—she wasn't even a full day behind him. She'd tell her story, and he'd be freed. Maybe Bow Street would even apprehend Gin Jimmy, which would solve that problem too. Free from pursuit, they could stay in London; he could be close to his brother. But what sort of life would they have? He'd been marginally accepted as the curious long-lost brother of the scandalous and allegedly mad Lord Lockwood, but once the ton became aware of his criminal background, he'd be ostracized. And her reputation, such as it was, had to be ruined by now.

It didn't matter to her where they lived, so long as they were together.

The breeze rustled the grass at her feet and the shrubbery dotting the cliff side. It was a bit noisy, but soothingly so. She could imagine living here, actually.

When the hands grabbed her arms, she inhaled

sharply. When the palm came over her mouth, she jumped. When the voice hissed in her ear, "Don't say nothin' or we'll just save ourselves the trouble o' haulin' ye back to London and slit yer throat right 'ere," her stomach curled in on itself and her knees gave out.

The smell of unwashed flesh overcame the soft, fresh sea air and filled her nose until she thought she might pass out. She turned her head to see the assailant to her right. He was a bit shorter than her, with greasy black hair and a pockmarked face. The man on her left was taller with a short crop of sandy hair and small, vicious eyes. His lips spread in a nasty grin. "I'm Perkins and that's Bird. If ye keep yer mouth shut and yer hands to yerself, ye'll make it to London in one piece. Can ye do that?"

She nodded. Bird's hand loosened over her mouth, but both men kept a tight hold on her arms. "Do you work for Gin Jimmy?"

Perkins' grin widened. "We do."

Her knees shook. How could she help Ethan if she was Gin Jimmy's captive? And would she be just a captive? "What are you going to do with me?"

"Gin Jimmy wants ye," Perkins said. "He wanted yer man too, but that damned Runner got to 'im first. No matter, Jimmy'll get him one way or another."

They knew Ethan had gone with Teague. And they wanted her anyway. Which had to mean they planned to use her to lure Ethan into some sort of trap where Gin Jimmy could exact his revenge. Audrey lifted her chin. "He's in custody, and I'm the only person who can free him."

The criminals exchanged looks and then laughed. "Ye don't know Gin Jimmy!" Bird cackled. "Yer man'll get out and come right for ye."

Perkins sobered and gave her a hard look. "Time to go. Remember, don't scream or do nothin' else to draw attention. I'd hate for ye to get to London in more than one piece."

Audrey's blood ran colder than the Thames in winter. As they dragged her toward their pair of horses, she wondered how she was going to endure the journey to London. She quickly realized that was only the beginning of this nightmare.

CHAPTER 17

*E*than lay on his bed in his basement cell at Bow Street and stared at the ceiling. Two other prisoners lay on their beds, to which they were each shackled. Ethan had spent the last night the same as the previous five: frantic with worry about Audrey.

Was she well? Was she on her way to London? Did she even want to come to London now that he'd been arrested?

The door opened and Teague walked into the windowless room. He was a large, beefy man, which made the low ceiling seem even lower.

"Sleep well?" Teague asked, though his sarcastic tone said he didn't actually give a damn.

Ethan sat up. "Let's get this over with."

Teague gazed at him with stark superiority. "In a hurry to get to Newgate?"

Which is where he'd go to await trial if the magistrates found the evidence against Ethan sufficient. Teague unlocked the shackle around Ethan's ankle.

Ethan massaged his lower leg before drawing his boots on. "Has my brother arrived?"

"He is, in fact, waiting in the courtroom. Carlyle, too." Teague said the last with a tone of irritation.

Carlyle had come? Ethan didn't know if he was

friend or foe. Ethan had saved his life, but Carlyle had made no secret of the fact that if he had to choose between Ethan and the law, the law would always win out. Perhaps Jason had convinced him to come, but Ethan didn't know why.

"I've waited a long time for this day," Teague said slowly, deliberately. "But I won't truly celebrate until the hood is placed over your head and you're swinging from the rope."

Ethan understood the man's anger and sadness over the loss of his sister, as well as he understood the need for revenge. However, at no time in the long years in which he'd hated his brother had he wished for Jason's demise. He only wanted him to feel the pain of loneliness Ethan had endured. "It's a dangerous thing to want another man's death."

Teague's head snapped up. "As if you haven't wanted that."

Ethan stood. "I have, but I've only killed when I had to, for my own survival. We're human, Teague. It's the one thing we fight for from the moment we enter this godforsaken world."

Teague was quiet a long moment. "I'm a man of the law. I want you to pay the price for what you've done—and that's hanging." He moved toward Ethan, holding his gaze as his eyes narrowed. "Yes, you've survived. But you have to live with your actions. How do you do that?"

Ethan allowed the remorse and regret he worked so hard to repress wash over him like a cleansing wave. Only he didn't feel clean. He'd never feel clean. "Not very well, I'm afraid. Do I look as if I'm living a dream life?"

In truth, he'd been so close. Closer than he'd ever imagined. But Teague only reminded him that he didn't deserve it. And maybe that's why it hadn't come to pass.

Teague opened the door and held it open for him. "Let's go."

Ethan picked up his coat from the bed and shrugged into its wrinkled folds. He was a rumpled mess from traveling so many days, but there was nothing he could do about it save knot his cravat the best he could, which he'd done earlier.

He paused beside Teague and looked him in the eye. "I didn't do this."

Teague bared his teeth. "I don't believe you." He jerked his head toward the door.

Ethan kept his head up as he preceded Teague from the cell. They went upstairs to the ground floor and made their way to the courtroom.

Several people stood about the room. They were prosecutors or witnesses, perhaps even spectators who'd heard Gin Jimmy's closest ally was appearing today. Or, they'd learned Mr. Ethan Locke wasn't all he'd purported to be.

Ethan stepped over the threshold and looked for his brother. Relief sagged through him when he saw him standing near the dock. Jason pivoted toward him, the nasty scar Ethan had caused standing out on his left cheek. Ethan suppressed a wave of self-loathing. He couldn't indulge any unnecessary emotion today. Everything inside him needed to be directed to gaining his freedom.

Ethan recognized Carlyle standing beside Jason, but there were two other men with them.

Carlyle gave Ethan a quick nod and gestured to a thickset fellow. "Allow me to introduce my friend, the solicitor Jeremy Bates. He's brought along a colleague to stand with you today. Lockwood has apprised him of the situation."

The fourth man, a young, slender gentleman, inclined his head toward Ethan. "Mr. Harworth at your service. Shall we proceed?" He gestured for Ethan to precede him up to the raised dock against the wall on the right side of the room. The magistrates' table was opposite, with the well of the court between them. This is where witnesses gave their testimony and where Teague took himself. Jason and Carlyle joined him in the well.

The three magistrates were seated at the table. The one in the center, a portly fellow with a ruddy complexion scrutinized Ethan. "Ethan Jagger?"

"Ethan Lockwood, your worship" Jason answered.

Ethan grabbed the railing in front of him for support. So much for suppressing emotion. His knees nearly buckled from Jason's declaration. He looked down at Jason, but his brother was glaring at the magistrates. *Glaring.* Ethan nearly smiled at how good that felt.

"Indeed?" the magistrate asked, while the one to the left scribbled a note. "Teague, is this the correct man?"

Teague sent Ethan a harassed look. "Yes, he is. He has several aliases, your worship."

The magistrate nodded. "We'll address him as Mr. Lockwood then. Mr. Lockwood, you are charged with murdering the Marquess of Wolverton."

"I am not guilty of that crime," Ethan said. Harworth elbowed him discreetly and he added, "Your worship."

The magistrate on the right cleared his throat. "Mr. Teague, you have evidence to present?"

"I do. I witnessed Mr. Jagger, pardon, Mr. *Lockwood,* standing over the marquess's body holding the knife used to stab him to his death." Teague glanced at Jason. "Lord Lockwood witnessed the same scene."

The magistrate turned his attention to Jason. "Is this true?"

"Yes, your worship," Jason said coldly. "However, I did not witness him stabbing Wolverton. He merely picked up the knife." He glowered at Teague. "Mr. Teague didn't witness the murder, either."

"Is this true, Teague?" the magistrate in the middle asked.

"It is, but Mr. Jagger, pardon, Mr. *Lockwood,* is a known criminal. He claims Gin Jimmy, a crime lord of some fame, committed the murder, but I believe they worked in tandem. I know they were cohorts. Your worship, I have other evidence that ties Mr. *Lockwood* to the murder of Lady Aldridge."

The magistrate's dark brows—at odds with his gray hair—rose. "Are you charging him with that today also?"

Teague grimaced, and the flesh around his mouth paled. "Unfortunately, no. The primary witness has gone missing."

That would've been Oak. What had happened to him?

The magistrate on the right grunted, while the one on the left wrote more notes. The magistrate in the center turned his attention to Lord Carlyle. "Lord Carlyle, what are you doing here today?"

"I came to hear the evidence, your worship. It is my belief that Gin Jimmy committed the murder of Wolverton, as well as the murder of Lord Lockwood's footman, without the assistance of Mr. Lockwood."

Teague gestured to the magistrate's table. "That knife is the weapon Mr. Lockwood was holding over Wolverton's corpse. Upon inspection, you will see it is inscribed with a J." Teague turned his head and smirked at Ethan. "For Jagger."

Ethan sneered. "It's for Jimmy, you half-wit."

Mr. Harworth touched Ethan's arm briefly before addressing the magistrates. "The inscription on the knife is not conclusive evidence that it belongs to Mr. Lockwood."

The center magistrate picked up the weapon and examined it. "Is this your knife, Mr. Jagger?" That he'd reverted to Ethan's criminal name tensed Ethan's muscles. He didn't dare correct him and was relieved when no one else did either. He wanted to be recognized as a Lockwood, but he wanted his freedom more.

"No, your worship."

"And you didn't use it to kill Lord Wolverton?"

"No, your worship."

The magistrate frowned. He exchanged glances with the other two magistrates, who were also frowning. They spoke to each other in low tones, their discussion impossible to hear from Ethan's location.

Ethan's attention was drawn to the waiting area to the left as a pair of men made their way rather close to the dock. He recognized Sevrin, who was accompanied by his friend, the Earl of Saxton. Ethan looked for Audrey, who surely would be with him, but couldn't find her in the crowd. He felt a moment's relief—he wasn't sure he wanted her to see him like this—but it was short-lived as he registered the lines around Sevrin's mouth. Something was wrong.

At last the magistrate in the center addressed the room. "As much as it pains me, Teague, I'm not sure you have quite enough to commit him to trial."

"I'm an eyewitness. Surely that should be enough." Teague sounded desperate.

Sevrin went up to the dock and whispered to Ethan and the barrister, "There's a witness who saw the murder and will testify that it wasn't Mr. Locke."

Mr. Harworth leaned down toward Sevrin. "Where is he?"

Sevrin glanced at Ethan and the lines around his mouth deepened. "Unfortunately, she's unavailable."

She.

Ethan didn't have to wonder who Sevrin referenced. He bit the side of his mouth to keep from exploding. *What the hell had happened?*

Harworth frowned. "When will she be available?"

Sevrin's expression was pained. "That will depend.

She's an estimable member of Society. Will that help his cause?"

"What are you discussing?" one of the magistrates asked in a booming voice.

Harworth straightened. "We beg your pardon, your worships. We're discussing another witness who is currently unavailable. She saw who committed the murder and will testify that it was not Mr. Lockwood."

The magistrate on the left made more notes while the one on the right asked, "Who is this witness?"

"Miss Audrey Cheswick," Sevrin answered. "Her grandfather is Lord Farringdon."

The magistrates exchanged looks again and then nods. The one on the right addressed Teague. "You don't have enough to charge Mr. Lockwood with the murder of Wolverton, especially if this other, quite credible, witness is able to give testimony." He looked up at Ethan. "Mr. Lockwood, you are free to go."

Mr. Harworth clapped Ethan on the shoulder and escorted him from the dock. Ethan was bursting with nervous energy about whatever had happened to Audrey.

Jason and Carlyle came out of the well, followed by Teague, who paused only long enough to say, "I'll find a way to see you hang." Then he stormed from the courtroom.

Ethan didn't take even a moment's respite to celebrate. He turned toward Sevrin. "Where's Audrey?"

Sevrin looked even more pained than he had in the dock. "I don't know. She disappeared the morning after you left."

Ethan wanted to wrap his hands around Sevrin's neck because he was the closest person he could punish. The earth was falling out from beneath him and he was going to tumble into a black abyss. "What the fuck do you mean by 'disappeared'?"

"She was just gone. No one saw her leave. It ap-

peared she rose early—some of her clothing was gone
—and went for a walk. There was a wrap by the door to
the terrace and it's missing, as if she went out that way
and took the wrap with her. I think she went to the cliff
side path. We searched, but there was no sign of her."

Jason wrapped his hand around Ethan's elbow, the
contact giving him a physical support he hadn't realized he needed. "What do you think happened to her?"

"Gin Jimmy." Ethan's insides hardened with resolve.
Audrey wanted Ethan to be done with hurting people,
but he was going to carve Jimmy's heart out if he'd
hurt her.

"You think she's here in London?" Carlyle asked.
The four men were standing around Ethan now, each
one watching him intently like he was some sort of
caged animal on display as a curiosity. Others were
watching him too, despite the fact that the court pro-
ceedings had continued at the other end of the room.

"I can't imagine she'd be anywhere else." Unless
they'd done something with her along the way. No, he
wouldn't let himself think that. Not yet. He turned to
Sevrin and worked to keep the despair out of his voice.
"You're certain she didn't fall or meet any other sort of
disaster on the path?"

Sevrin shook his head. "There was no sign of that."

Ethan ran his hand through his hair and fought to
rip it from his head. He wanted to tear the room apart,
lash out at these men who were just standing there
doing nothing.

But what could they do?

"I have to find her." He moved toward the door, but
Sevrin caught his arm.

"Wait. Let us help you."

Ethan's lip curled as he contemplated the four aris-
tocrats. "How the hell are you lot going to help me?"

Carlyle adjusted his cravat. "I'll try not to be offended that you would think I couldn't help you. After

all, I owe you, and you know my contacts are equal to yours."

Ethan grunted. "I doubt that. But I take your point. Please find out whatever you can."

"Shall we reconvene at Lockwood House this afternoon?"

Hours from now. "I can't wait that long." Ethan heard the anguish in his tone and wanted to shout his frustration.

Jason probed him with an earnest stare. "Be smart, Ethan. You'll be much better served with a plan. You seem to be the master of them."

He was referring to the plan Ethan had been orchestrating to take down Gin Jimmy in order to free himself and join Society. The plan Ethan had refused to share with his brother. He looked at Jason and their unspoken exchange was clear: Jason would help him, but Ethan had to trust him.

Ethan forced himself to exhale and push some of the tension from his shoulders. "What do you propose?"

Jason's eyes flashed briefly with surprise. Then he too seemed to relax. "Let's see what Carlyle learns."

"We'll have to flush him out," Ethan said, his mind working. He knew Gin Jimmy better than anyone. The man rarely left his comfortable rookery in the heart of the Seven Dials and he was untouchable there. If he'd taken Audrey—and Ethan absolutely believed he had—that was the only place he'd keep her. "I know where she is, but if I go in there, I'm dead."

"He's laid a trap," Sevrin said.

"Then we'll have to lay our own." Saxton drew everyone's attention. His pale blue gaze was cunning. "Lockwood—that's bloody confusing." He focused on Ethan to differentiate between the brothers. "If we can lure him away from her, will you have a chance or are you dead either way?"

"I might have a chance," Ethan said slowly. There

were those who were loyal to Ethan, who would support the overthrow of Gin Jimmy, but they'd want Ethan to lead them instead. And Ethan wanted no part of that. "It depends on what Gin Jimmy's told them in my absence. I don't know how much allegiance I still command."

"I'll find out," Carlyle said, striding toward the door. "See you at Lockwood House. You can update me on the plan then."

"Carlyle," Ethan called. The man paused and turned back. "Confirm that she's there—the Cup and Burrow's his place—that she's safe."

Carlyle nodded and left before Ethan could say the most important thing of all: Thank you.

"Did you have a specific trap in mind, Sax?" Sevrin asked.

Saxton shrugged. "It seems like the one thing that could coax Jimmy out of his lair is the thing he wants most."

"Me." Ethan shook his head. "I have to get into his stronghold." Not only because he needed to be the one to save Audrey—and he *needed* to be that man—but because it was also imperative that he take Jimmy down for good. And that would require help, which he could only get by turning the men's allegiance from Jimmy to him.

Saxton lips spread in a shrewd smile. "Not you. The other Lockwood." He inclined his head toward Jason. "Perhaps we can use your similarity in build and coloring to draw Jimmy out. Your scar, however, could be a problem."

Sevrin shook his head. "Not if we covered it. I got pretty good at disguising my injuries from the Black Horse."

"You *tried*," Saxton said. "Let's employ an expert. I'm certain Olivia can put her experience from the theater to good use. It won't be perfect, but we should be able to mask the scar enough to fool people at a distance." Saxton looked to Ethan. "Will that work?"

"It could." Ethan envisioned Jason dressed like him and situated in a dark corner of the Brazen Bride flanked by a few of Ethan's men. It would sufficiently dupe anyone watching into thinking that Ethan was there, which would hopefully draw Jimmy out. Ethan decided he needed to weigh the odds and knew exactly what he could say to lure his former mentor from his den.

The question was, could he bare himself to Jason? He wouldn't have to, he reasoned. He could write a message that would bring Jimmy from his den without telling Jason what it said. He glanced at his brother. His *brother*. His neck tingled uncomfortably. No, the time for secrets had passed. It was time to trust and discover faith—if he could.

"Let's go to Lockwood House where we can sort this all out." Jason slapped him on the shoulder in an exceedingly brotherly manner. "I'm not asking you to relax, but you can bathe, change your clothes, and have a glass of whisky. As my butler North would say, you need fortification."

No, what he needed was Audrey. If anything had happened to her . . . He wouldn't be able to bear it. To have happiness within his grasp only to have it be torn away would kill him. But did he deserve anything else?

∾

*A*fter a brutal six-day journey that had seen her bounced around in a stolen cart, racing over hillsides on a stolen horse, and ushered into London in a rundown—and, yes, stolen—carriage, Audrey was simply glad to be still. Even though it meant she was locked in a windowless room in a flash house in St.

Giles. She wasn't sure what a flash house was, but it wasn't good.

The ground floor had been somewhat like a pub or tavern, but filled with a class of folk Audrey had never encountered. Men, women, children—all filthy and possibly drunk—had gaped and leered at her as Perkins and Bird had dragged her inside. A woman had taken her from them and brought her upstairs to the third floor, a warren of rooms from which came intermittent and disturbing sounds. Crying. Shouting. Darker sounds of a more . . . intimate nature.

The woman, Mother Dean she'd called herself, had drafted two younger women to help Audrey. They'd set up a bath and brought her fresh clothes, though Audrey would've preferred to have her old clothing, wretched as it was after the nearly incessant travel. Her new costume didn't fit properly. As with most gowns that weren't tailored for her, this was too short and too tight in the bodice. It also revealed much more of her bosom than she'd ever exposed.

The room she'd been placed in was small, little more than an alcove beneath the stairs leading to the uppermost floor. The now-tepid bath sat in the corner while Audrey perched on a wooden chair. One of the young women, Ellie, who'd helped her bathe and dress, was styling her hair, and the other had gone to fetch cosmetics.

"I'd prefer not to apply anything to my face." The gown was degrading enough.

"It's expected of the girls 'ere at the Cup and Burrow." Ellie stuck pin after pin into Audrey's hair. "How do ye manage these curls?"

"It's a bit of a trial. What do you mean the 'girls'?" Audrey had a pretty good guess but asked anyway.

"The Cup and Burrow's a flash house. The cup is for the gin and the burrow's for what's between yer legs."

Audrey's gut tightened with fear as her guess was affirmed. "How many girls are here?"

Ellie jabbed a pin into Audrey's hair, scratching her head. "Depends. As many as forty sometimes. We get new girls often, but not all of 'em work out."

"What happens to them?"

"Out on their arse, unless there's another need for 'em. I can usually tell who'll wash out. I tend to 'em when they come in, like I'm doing for ye, if they need it. Most of 'em arrive lookin' as they ought. Not like ye." She stuck another pin into Audrey's curls. "Ye won't last a day."

Audrey suppressed a shudder. "I'm not one of the 'girls.'" God, what if she were? No, she'd cling to the hope that Gin Jimmy was only using her as bait to get Ethan. "But if I were, what would happen to me next?"

"Ye'll be allowed to settle in for a day or so. And if ye're smart, ye'll drink a lot of gin to make things easier." She laughed, which gave the room a subtle scent of the gin she spoke of. She gave a final pat to Audrey's hair, then moved around in front of her. "Ye'll do. After we get yer face done, I'll take ye downstairs to the common room for somethin' to eat."

The second woman came in. Beneath the kohl around her eyes and the unnatural shade of red on her lips, she looked far younger than Ellie, though Audrey suspected they were of a similar age.

Ellie stared at the other young woman. "Nan, where's yer cosmetics basket?"

"I was told to bring 'er downstairs immediately. Mother Dean wants to see you, Ellie."

Ellie went to the door and paused, looking back at Audrey. "Remember what I said about the gin." She gave Ellie a knowing smile and quit the room, leaving laughter in her wake.

Audrey got up from the chair, her legs trembling. "Where are you taking me? I'm not one of the . . . girls."

Nan smiled softly. "I know. I'm taking you to Gin Jimmy. Is it true you're Jagger's woman?"

Though the label was somewhat crude, it gave Audrey a silly thrill. "Yes. You know him?"

The young woman's smile turned shy as she nodded. She suddenly looked quite young. "I'm not one of the 'girls' either, and I have Jagger to thank. I came 'ere to be one. I didn't have no money and there was nothin' left to sell. It was starve or come 'ere. I was lucky that 'e was in the common room that first night. 'E could tell I didn't want to be 'ere. I kept refusin' the gin."

Audrey was desperate to hear why she was grateful to Ethan. "What did he do?"

"'E told Mother Dean I'd make a good maid. They were short one at the time. It was just a few months ago."

"And you haven't had to sell yourself?"

Nan shook her head almost violently, then suddenly took Audrey's hand. "It's terrible what's goin' to happen to Jagger. I wish there was somethin' I could do."

Audrey's skin prickled. "What's going to happen to him?"

"I don't know for sure, but from what I hear Gin Jimmy's angrier than anyone's ever seen 'im." That didn't sound good at all. "Come on, we 'ave to get downstairs." She gave Audrey a pitying look, then turned and led her back down to the ground floor. Instead of going to the front of the flash house, where the common room was located, they turned to the back of the building. They entered an extravagantly decorated room. The walls were hung with silk, the furniture ornate and expensive, if a bit mismatched. There was a dais at the opposite end with a large chair surrounded by lush pillows littering the floor. It was a reception area fit for a king who prized decadence and self-importance.

A stout man with a shock of white hair came from a

door in the corner and climbed the dais to sit in the chair. Audrey recognized his face—the man who'd been wearing the livery at Lockwood House: Gin Jimmy.

He was dressed in clothing that suited his surroundings—a dark velvet frock coat and a garish silk waistcoat with alternating red and gold stripes. Lace from the cuffs of his shirt draped over his hand, which were covered in brightly jeweled rings. He looked like an aging dandy.

"Miss Cheswick at last. Ye know who I am?" He held his hand out just as a boy rushed to his side with a gold goblet.

"Gin Jimmy." She noted the men who'd clustered at the sides of the dais. Rough-looking men like Perkins and Bird, who were standing a few feet away.

"Ye've done well," Gin Jimmy said to them. "Ye've earned yer keep." He inclined his head at the man closest to the dais, a surprisingly young fellow with spectacles. He withdrew two pouches from his coat and tossed them at Perkins and Bird.

They each caught their pay, bowed their heads, and left. Bird flashed her a nasty leer as he passed.

Audrey suppressed a shiver. They hadn't touched her beyond moving her here and there, but the danger surrounding her was seeping into her bones by degrees. She glanced behind her for a supportive look from Nan, but the maid was gone.

"Were ye comfortable upstairs?" Gin Jimmy asked before taking a draught from his gaudy chalice.

"Not particularly."

Gin Jimmy laughed. "Ye've got fire. No wonder my boy Jagger likes ye. But at least I didn't put ye to work. I'm thinkin' ye'd rather not do that."

A chill settled over her. "No. Thank you."

"Polite too." Gin Jimmy chuckled, shaking his head. "What's happened to my boy? He's traded a good life for a bit of Society fluff. Question is, can ye keep his attention? At least long enough for him to come after ye?"

Audrey looked at the group of men with their pistols and knives and was glad Ethan couldn't walk into this trap. "He can't. He's been arrested by Bow Street."

Gin Jimmy took another swig from his cup and handed it back to the boy who'd kneeled on one of the pillows. "That won't stop him."

Audrey couldn't contain her curiosity—or her worry. "What do you mean?"

He lifted a velvet-clad shoulder and Audrey noticed a sparkle in his earlobe, an earring. "Jagger's a cunning lad. He'll find a way to get out. And if he doesn't"—he glanced at his small army and grinned, stirring them to grin and chuckle in return—"they'll try him and sentence him to hang." His tone had turned cold, vicious. His eyes shrank to terrifying slits.

Audrey clasped her hands together to keep them from shaking, but it was no use. A shudder shook her frame. She couldn't countenance either of those outcomes. "What do you plan to do with me?"

"We'll just wait fer a bit. I'm not lettin' Bow Street rob me of sendin' 'im to 'is maker. If necessary, we'll get 'im out and then 'e'll come for ye."

She tried to show bravado. "He may not." Could Jimmy tell she was lying?

He scrutinized her a long moment. "I think 'e will. 'E dragged ye all over England. Aye, 'e'll come fer ye, and then I'll gut 'im. I'm going to 'ave some luncheon. Ye must be famished." He made the observation as if he hadn't just promised to murder the man she loved.

Audrey could only stare at the garish fiend. But then her stomach growled, prompting everyone in the room —save the boy—to laugh.

"Stay and eat then." He stood and walked down the steps of the dais toward her. She fought the urge to turn and run. He held out his hand. "Come, dearie. Let us share a meal and ye can tell me all about our boy Jagger."

Audrey didn't want to tell him a thing. "I'd rather not."

Gin Jimmy's eyes hardened. "Ye ought not turn down my generosity. Wouldn't want ye to end up in a room upstairs."

His threat had the desired effect. Audrey could scarcely breathe through her fear. She gave him her shaking hand. He took it and she steeled herself against the rush of revulsion as he led her to a baroque table at the side of the room. The boy rushed to hold a chair for her.

After Gin Jimmy was seated at the head of the table and she on his right side, the crime lord snapped his fingers. A young woman rushed forward and curtseyed to him. Her gown was even more revealing than Audrey's. The woman, little more than a girl really, was a tiny thing, but her breasts had been pushed up until they swelled above the neckline nonetheless.

"Fetch Marie," Gin Jimmy said to her.

She dashed from the room and came back a moment later with a very attractive woman. She was curvaceous, with blazing red hair and full lips. Her attire was equally scandalous, but for some bizarre reason it suited her. She didn't look nearly as awkward as Audrey felt.

"Marie," Gin Jimmy said, "this is Miss Cheswick. She's Jagger's new plaything. Miss Cheswick, this is Marie." His eyes narrowed with devious intent. "She's Jagger's old plaything."

Guffaws sounded from the gallery of men near the dais. Gin Jimmy laughed with them, then inclined his head for them to take seats at the table.

Audrey stared at Marie, who was beautiful, despite her vivid attire. Jealousy pricked her, but she quashed it. Thinking of Ethan with another woman was pointless. He loved *her*. And he would come for her. But no! She didn't want him to walk into a trap.

Marie sauntered toward her. "Can't see what Jagger'd want with ye. But I s'pose it was all part of his act." She leaned down and sneered in Audrey's face. "Can't pretend to be a fancy gent without a fancy gel on yer arm."

Audrey opened her mouth to tell Marie she was far more than arm decoration, but Gin Jimmy snapped his fingers again and more scantily-clad women appeared bearing trenchers of food. As a steaming plate was placed before her, Audrey struggled between hunger and nausea. She looked around at the men attacking their meals and wondered how she was ever going to escape this nightmare. She wanted to pray for Ethan to find her, but couldn't bear to see him killed. Neither could she contemplate him hanging. If a more hopeless situation existed, Audrey couldn't imagine it. All she could do was fight for her survival. With that thought, she picked up a piece of bread and ate.

CHAPTER 18

*D*espite a bath, fresh clothing from his own apartment at the Bevelstoke fetched by a pair of Jason's footmen, and two glasses of whisky, Ethan didn't feel remotely fortified.

They were still waiting for Carlyle to arrive, so Ethan had asked Jason to meet him in the office. Ethan paced the room like a caged animal, occasionally looking up at the portrait of their father, which strangely gave him a modicum of solace. Father had loved him, had wanted the best for him despite his illegitimacy. He would've hated what had happened to Ethan, what Ethan had done. The solace melted into shame.

Jason came into the office and shut the door. "Carlyle's not here yet."

"I know. But there are . . . elements to the plan I wanted to share with you alone."

Jason blinked at him, appearing astonished, as he sat behind his desk. "You want to share something with me?"

Ethan stopped his pacing to glare at his brother. "Is now really the time for sarcasm?"

Jason held up a hand. "My apologies. I'm just shocked."

"If you're going to pretend to be me, I may as well tell you why you're going where you're going."

"And where's that?" Jason asked.

"A flash house off Portugal Street—the Brazen Bride."

Jason sat back in his chair and studied Ethan. "Why is this particular place important?"

"It's where I first met Jimmy." Memories rushed over him. He immediately smelled the filth and the putridity and the cheap perfumes that were used to hide the overwhelming stench of desperation and decay. He'd wanted to cry at the loss of the comforts he'd known, but such weakness had been beaten out of him right after his mother had died. "After you turned me away, I went to Davis. He'd been Mother's final protector." Ethan didn't look at Jason while he spoke, but went to the bookshelves that lined two walls of the room and sightlessly studied the spines. He didn't want to see the play of emotions cross Jason's face. And if there weren't any, he didn't want to see that either.

"He was a thief-taker, but corrupt," Ethan continued. "I didn't know that at first and I was simply glad to have a roof over my head, which he'd arranged for me at the Brazen Bride."

"You went to live in a flash house." It wasn't a question, but a statement toned with disbelief.

Ethan glanced at Jason, but didn't let his gaze linger. "That's where I met Jimmy—back when he was just Jimmy Gare." Ethan recalled the younger version of Jimmy, with his red-blond hair shot with only a few strands of white and his jovial grin. Something inside of Ethan bent, but he ignored the reaction. "He took a liking to me, I don't know why." Though he could guess. He'd been young, vulnerable, and desperate for someone to treat him with kindness. Davis had helped him, but he could be cruel, demanding. He beat Ethan and his crew when they didn't score enough. "I worked in Davis's theft gang, and Jimmy's gangs were rivals. Davis was setting me up with a job so that he could take the bounty for catching me and the crew. Jimmy helped me foil his plan, and it was Davis who was arrested and hanged."

Jason's intake of air sounded like a thunderclap. "Jesus, Ethan. How old were you?"

Ethan shrugged. He didn't want Jason's pity. "Barely fifteen. After that, I joined one of Jimmy's gangs and eventually took it over." Why not tell him the whole truth like he'd told Audrey? "I had to kill the leader of the gang. It was that or be killed. Jimmy congratulated me and encouraged my leadership." Jimmy had taken Ethan under his wing and brought him up through the ranks. He'd risen along with Jimmy as he'd grown his criminal empire. "Eventually I oversaw all of Jimmy's thieving operations, but I refused to become involved with any of his brothels or gin shops. I figured one vice was enough to see me to hell."

"Why are you telling me all of this?"

Now Ethan turned. "Because the Brazen Bride is where my life changed. It's where I left my life as Ethan Lockwood behind and became Ethan Jagger. It's where Gin Jimmy found me, thoroughly corrupted me, and treated me like his son. I would've done anything to please him." And he had. Thankfully, he hadn't had to kill, only on occasion to protect himself, as with the leader of the gang, but he'd ensured plenty of people had carried out Jimmy's death sentences. Ethan might not have wielded the weapons, but he felt the blood on his hands just the same.

Jason stood and came around his desk. He strode toward Ethan, stopping only a foot away. "I don't know what to say. All this time I hated you for giving me a stupid scar and ruining my reputation, when your life has been nothing but an open wound. Would that you had a scar, for that would mean your injury is old and healed." He pulled Ethan into a hug. "I wish I could go back and make my mother take you in."

For a moment, Ethan just stood there. Jimmy had hugged him at first. But the outward affection had decreased as Ethan had gotten older, which made sense. Men like them didn't show their emotions, particularly between each other. Yet, Ethan had always known Jimmy cared for him, as much as a bastard like him could care for anyone. It was the one thing that had kept Ethan human.

"We're going to get Audrey back," Jason said, pounding his fist against Ethan's back. "And we're going to eliminate Jimmy from your life. He isn't your family, Ethan. *I am.*"

Ethan closed his eyes and hugged his brother. The tension in his chest splintered and emotion swept through him. He squeezed his eyelids tight and held on.

A moment later, a discreet cough broke them apart. Jason's butler, North, stood just over the threshold. "Lord Carlyle is here, along with Lord Sevrin and Lord and Lady Saxton. Lady Lockwood will be pouring tea for them in the drawing room."

Ethan looked at Jason. "You included Lydia?"

Jason moved toward the door. "Of course. Audrey is her dearest friend, and you know my wife, she's not to be deterred."

Ethan followed him, glad for this trifling conversation after the weight of his revelations. "Your wife? You were married by special license while I was gone?"

"I'm afraid we couldn't wait for the banns to be read. I had to get her away from her vicious aunt."

"Yes, I'm sure that's the only reason for your haste." Ethan gave him a knowing look. "I'm still sorry to have missed the occasion."

Jason turned and clapped his shoulder. "We'll celebrate at your wedding."

Ethan silently prayed that would come to pass, but

didn't want to dwell on it. Instead, he recalled something from earlier that day. "Do you know what happened to Oak? He was going to testify that I'd paid him to poison Lady Aldridge."

Jason shrugged. "He might've gotten on a ship bound for the Orient or some faraway place. You could ask Scot."

Gratitude—an emotion Ethan reserved for very few occasions and even fewer people—swelled within him.

They went to the drawing room, where Carlyle, Saxton, Lady Saxton, Sevrin, and Lady Lockwood were already seated. North's twin, and Jason's manservant, Scot, was just delivering the tea tray. Instead of departing, he took an empty chair.

Ethan's gaze settled on Scot, and on his brother, North, who lingered near the door.

"We need all the help we can get," Jason said, sitting beside his wife on a plush settee. He indicated for Ethan to take the chair angled beside him, then turned his attention to the former magistrate. "Carlyle, what did you learn?"

Carlyle inched forward in his chair opposite Ethan. "She's at the Cup and Burrow. Arrived sometime this morning." He looked to Ethan. "There are men stationed at all of your usual haunts, including the Bevelstoke." Carlyle glanced at Jason. "Because Jason's retainers went there to obtain your things, Jimmy is undoubtedly aware that you are no longer at Bow Street."

"Does he know Ethan's here?" Jason took his wife's hand. "Is it safe?"

"I've asked Bow Street to post a couple of Runners outside, just in case."

Ethan's insides churned with anxiety. "It doesn't matter, I won't be staying. We need to act. Do you know if Audrey is all right?"

"Not specifically, no." Carlyle grimaced apologetically. "I agree we need to move quickly."

Ethan removed a piece of parchment from his coat. "I drafted this letter to Jimmy, asking him to meet me at the Brazen Bride. I've used . . . language that should be enough to draw him forth."

Sevrin leaned forward. "What does that mean?"

Jason jumped to answer before Ethan could. "They share a common background. The Brazen Bride is where they met and Ethan believes the location holds enough personal meaning that Jimmy won't be able to deny Ethan's request." He shot Ethan a questioning look. Ethan nodded imperceptibly, relieved that Jason understood and that Ethan didn't need to explain anything to the rest of them.

Carlyle took the paper. "I'll see that it's delivered."

"I, of course, won't be at the Brazen Bride; Jason will be. In addition to covering his scar, he'll wear some of my clothing, which I had his footmen bring from my apartment—things that are known to belong to me." Ethan allowed a small smile. "I'm quite known for my style." He flashed his left hand, which bore three of his rings, including the one inscribed with L that he'd had made after he'd amassed some of his wealth.

"I'll go with his lordship," Scot said.

Carlyle opened his mouth, but Jason cut him off. "Scot has some experience in the underworld. I wouldn't take anyone else."

Carlyle nodded. "I'll be waiting nearby, watching for Jimmy so that we can apprehend him. I'll have some of my old constable friends with me." He turned to Ethan. "We'll send a message to you as soon as we arrest him so you know you're free and clear."

"What can we do?" Sevrin asked, indicating himself and Saxton. "You know I can fight, but you should know Saxton's nearly as skilled."

"Nearly?" Saxton sounded mildly affronted. On any other afternoon, Ethan would've laughed.

"This can go several ways," Ethan said slowly. He'd thought this through every way possible over the past hours. In the best scenario, Jimmy went to the Brazen Bride and was arrested. In the worst, Jimmy never left the Cup and Burrow, and Ethan was forced into his trap. "You can help Carlyle. Or you can wait for me outside St. Giles." The rat's castle was no place for men like them. They'd be eaten alive.

Saxton frowned. "If we dress appropriately, why can't we go in with you? Can't we pass for your lackeys?"

"I can't endanger you that way." He looked at Sevrin. "Lady Sevrin," he glanced at Saxton's wife, "and I'm sure Lady Saxton, would never forgive me. Please, don't." Ethan hoped Sevrin knew how sincerely he meant it.

Sevrin stared at him a long moment before settling back in his chair with a slight nod. He looked over at Saxton and shook his head.

Saxton scowled, but nodded his assent. "We'll be waiting for you and if you take too long, we're coming in after you with a bloody army."

Ethan appreciated the support. He opened his mouth to say something and was surprised to find a lump in his throat that he simply couldn't speak past.

Carlyle stood. "Then we're ready." He tucked the missive into his coat. "Lockwood, you'll get to the Brazen Bride within the hour. Jagger—pardon, what the hell do we call you?"

"Ethan is fine." His voice sounded cracked and dry. He coughed as he got to his feet, eager to get to Audrey now that the moment was at hand. "I know the stakes."

Everyone else got up and moved to leave. Lydia Lockwood touched his hand. "Mr. Locke." She shook her head. "Ethan. Please bring Audrey back safe." She swallowed and nodded. "I know you will." She gave him a wobbly smile that was probably as much to fortify herself as it was for Ethan.

He took her hand between his. "If I don't bring her back, you'll know that I'm dead."

Lydia nodded and stood on her toes to kiss his cheek. "Don't let it end that way," she whispered.

Ethan turned and walked past Jason, who clapped him on the shoulder again and said, "See you soon, brother."

"Ethan, I'll walk out with you," Carlyle called, following him from the drawing room.

They moved through the hall and a footman let them out.

Carlyle turned when they were outside. "You're not going to wait to hear that we've arrested Jimmy, are you?"

"No."

Carlyle nodded grimly. "How will you get Miss Cheswick out?"

"I still have a contingent of loyal men. I'll collect them first. With their help, I'll hopefully be able to convince those at the Cup and Burrow that I'm not the enemy."

"That Jimmy is."

"Yes."

Carlyle walked toward the street. "You think they'll just let you walk out of there with Miss Cheswick?"

Ethan didn't want to contemplate the alternative, but he had to. He fell into step beside Carlyle. "If they don't, you're going to have to go in after her."

"Understood. Hopefully, we'll get Jimmy and you'll extract Miss Cheswick."

"We both know things rarely go as planned—which is why contingency plans must be prepared." Ethan withdrew an envelope from his coat. "Will you have this delivered to Bow Street?"

Carlyle accepted the missive. "You've plotted quite thoroughly."

He had to; there were too many variables. "Just promise me that no matter what happens, you'll make sure Audrey is safe. You owe me, and that's the only thing I want."

Carlyle pressed his lips together. "I'll never forget what you did for me and Jocelyn. You have my word that Audrey will be safe."

Ethan relaxed, but only slightly. Until he saw with his own eyes that she was whole, he wouldn't be free of this hellish torment.

~

*A*fter managing to take a small amount of sustenance at Gin Jimmy's raucous "luncheon," Audrey sat in the corner of his reception room, with Marie at her side. She'd hoped she'd be allowed to return to her dismal closet, but Gin Jimmy had ordered them to sit and keep him company while he discussed business matters with his men. They were gathered around the garish table and spoke low enough that Audrey couldn't hear them.

"Ye know ye won't be leavin' the Cup an' Burrow?" Marie asked her.

Audrey looked askance at the woman, noting the smirk twisting her reddened lips. It was becoming increasingly difficult to remain silent. At the best of times, Audrey liked to talk and at the worst, she rambled in an attempt to mask, and perhaps settle, her nerves. She pressed her lips together to keep from asking why. The woman was just trying to provoke her.

"Whether Jagger comes to get ye or not, ye won't be leavin'. 'Course I'm hopin' Jimmy doesn't kill 'im. That'd be a real shame." Her voice had taken on a dreamlike quality.

Audrey bit the inside of her cheek to keep from talking to Marie, though she burned with questions. This was a glimpse into Ethan's world. But did she really want to see it?

Marie tsked. "Do ye talk at all? Heh, maybe not. Jagger wasn't much for talkin' anyhow. Leastwise in the bedroom. Or wherever." She gave Audrey a wicked look. "Jagger ever take ye to 'is bed? Or anywhere else?"

She stared at Marie, appalled at her prurient curiosity. "That's none of your concern."

"I'm guessin' no then. Too bad for ye."

Audrey glared at the beauty. "Ethan is not going to die, and I'm not going to stay."

Marie's eyes crinkled at the corners as she laughed.

Audrey turned her chair away from Marie. She didn't want to endure her taunts, at least not to her face. A boy dashed into the chamber and went straight to Gin Jimmy. He handed him a piece of paper and Jimmy opened it immediately. The conversation at the table slowed.

Audrey found herself leaning forward anxiously. She could tell the message was somehow important, given the creases lining Gin Jimmy's wide forehead.

He stood from the table and gestured to some of the men. Then he addressed the boy who'd brought the note. "Fetch Perkins and Bird. They're to watch the prisoner, along with the men I leave in this room."

The boy tore off. Gin Jimmy strode over to where Audrey was sitting and pinned her with a malevolent stare. She clutched the seat of her chair for something solid to hold on to.

"Yer man wants to see me. Seems he's sorry about everything and wants to resume his place. He says I can do whatever I want with ye."

Audrey couldn't keep her jaw from hanging open. Marie's laughter raked her spine. Gin Jimmy's eyes twinkled with merriment. "'E did recommend I return ye to yer house, so as not to provoke the upper crust. But I don't know . . ." He tapped his stubby forefinger against his lips. "Ye'd make an awfully fine addition to me stable, and then Jagger could enjoy ye whenever 'e liked."

He leaned down and bared his teeth at her. "Except Jagger won't be here to enjoy ye. I'm going to bury my knife in his gut and pull out 'is entrails. Then I'm going to force 'em down 'is throat. Question is, should I do all of that in front of ye?" He glanced at Marie. "What do ye think?"

Marie smiled at him, but Audrey detected an underlying quiver. "Whatever would please ye most, Jimmy."

Jimmy nodded. "I'll have to think on it. In the meantime, ye sit tight, Miss Cheswick. And don't miss me." He flashed a smile, revealing a gold tooth. Then he spun around and addressed everyone. "If Miss Cheswick isn't exactly where I left her when I return, I'll burn the place down with the lot of ye locked inside."

He quit the room with more than half of his men trailing behind him.

Audrey slumped in her chair. Every bit of resistance leaked from her frame until she felt like a bag of hollow bones.

Perkins and Bird came into the room. Bird waved at her before joining the men at the table. Audrey strained to hear what they discussed, but only caught intermittent words: Jagger, guards, common room, kill.

Had Ethan really told Jimmy to dispose of Audrey at his own discretion? It was wholly feasible that Jimmy had lied to frighten her. She couldn't believe Ethan wouldn't care what became of her.

"I'm sorry for ye," Marie said softly. "But Jagger doesn't stay too long with any woman."

Ethan . . . he wouldn't cast her aside. Not when he'd declared his love and proposed marriage. She couldn't contain herself any longer. Maybe she just needed to hear the words, even from her own mouth. "I think it was Shakespeare who said thieves could not be true to one another, but Ethan is true to me. He loves me and we're going to be married."

Marie's mouth gaped open. She snapped it closed and patted Audrey's knee. "Ye poor dearie. Is that what he told ye to spread yer legs?"

Audrey opened her mouth to retort, but realized he *had* told her those things before he'd made love to her. But no, that wasn't the reason he'd said them. It *wasn't*. "It's not like that."

Marie's gaze was condescending, and her tone was thick with pity. "Jagger's not one of yer Society lords. Ye said so yerself—thieves have no honor."

Audrey didn't want to hear anymore. She folded her arms across her chest and tucked herself into as small of a silhouette as possible.

She wasn't sure how long she sat like that, but it seemed an interminable length. A commotion sounded from outside the room. Audrey leapt to her feet in fear.

The door swung open and several men strode inside. They looked similar to the men who'd risen from the table. Every one of them had drawn a pistol or some sort of blade.

"Ho there, lads!"

Audrey recognized that voice, but she almost didn't realize it was Ethan. He was immaculately garbed, but more flamboyantly than she'd ever seen him. His coat was a vivid blue and his waistcoat a bright green and bronze. His cravat was intricately tied and sported a glimmering diamond within its crisp folds. He carried a walking stick with an ornate handle and his hands were covered in gaudy rings. His ink-black hair was coiffed so perfectly that he would look at ease in any ballroom in London. His gray gaze swept the room with superiority as if he were the king instead of Gin Jimmy.

She lunged forward, intending to protect him, but

he shot her a quelling stare. She'd seen him look cold before, but his eyes held a frigidity she hadn't witnessed. It chilled her to the core.

"Ye got a lot of cheek strollin' in here so brazen-like," Perkins said, his pistol pointed at Ethan's chest.

"Why? I've always been welcome at the Cup and Burrow—for far longer than any of you." He glowered at Perkins and, flanked by two of the burliest men Audrey had ever seen, strolled toward the dais. He climbed the stairs and turned, the men he'd arrived with still clustered about him.

Audrey looked at the men who'd moved out from the table and were now staring at Ethan with their weapons drawn. Why hadn't anyone shot him? Was it because he'd brought his own soldiers? She looked at them—at least ten men—and wondered where he'd found them. But she knew. They were *his* soldiers. He was nearly equal to Gin Jimmy in terms of status in this world.

Marie let out a hiss of breath beside her. She'd also risen. "There's no one like Jagger. In bed or out. Jes' look at 'im."

Audrey suppressed an urge to drive a sharp elbow into Marie's side. She didn't want to hear about Ethan's prowess. She couldn't deny, however, that he was the most attractive man she'd ever met, and that even now amidst the danger and what Marie had said about him, she was drawn to him like no other.

"Listen up, lads." Ethan's voice commanded the room. "I don't know what Jimmy's told you, but I had to leave London to avoid being arrested." There were a few murmurs. "Thankfully, there will not be any charges and I am a free man." He grinned widely and there were cheers from his men—and from a few of Jimmy's.

Audrey sagged with relief, glad that at least that threat had passed.

Ethan's smile faded and his features hardened. "But I'm not really. None of us are. As long as Jimmy runs things, none of us are truly free. Tell me, what did he threaten if anything happened to his hostage?"

One of Jimmy's men stepped forward. "He'd lock us all inside and burn the Cup and Burrow to the ground."

Ethan studied the jewel-encrusted handle of his walking stick for a long moment. When he looked out at the men once more, he seemed to pierce each of them with a direct stare. "And what do we know of Jimmy's threats?"

"They always come to pass." Marie's voice jarred Audrey.

Ethan glanced in their direction, but he didn't acknowledge Audrey at all. "Very true, Marie. Why don't you come up here with me?" He smiled encouragingly.

Audrey's stomach turned and ice shot to her extremities. She backed her knees against the chair for a modicum of support.

Marie sauntered to the dais. When she climbed up beside him, he pointed to one of the pillows.

She kneeled on a round, purple cushion and sat back on her heels. She looked like a dog doing her master's bidding. Then she cast Audrey a haughty glance. Audrey felt sick.

"If you prefer Jimmy's style of dictatorship, then by all means do his bidding," Ethan arched his brow in challenge, "if you can. Or, if you'd prefer the freedom to choose your own jobs and whether you want to risk your life on any given day, follow me."

"Does that mean you're going to be our leader?" a young man asked, his pistol drooping in his grip.

Ethan angled his body toward the criminal who'd spoken. "No. I've no wish to lead. I only want to be left alone."

Audrey's chest expanded. She'd thought for a moment that he meant to take over Gin Jimmy's place.

He'd marched in here so confidently and the men clearly admired and respected him. She could see his importance and what his position had to mean to him.

One of his men standing at the foot of the dais turned and looked at him. "Ye should be our leader." He pivoted back and raised his arms. "Who here wants Jagger as our leader?"

All of his men shouted their agreement, and at least three or four of Jimmy's men joined in. The others looked around, doubt etched in their worn and battered faces.

Marie leaned forward and wrapped her hand around Ethan's knee. She gazed up at him longingly. Audrey moved forward without thinking.

Bird was at her side in a matter of seconds. He slid his arm around her waist and pulled her toward the door. "I don't care what anyone says. I'm followin' Jimmy's orders."

Ethan's face darkened. He strode from the dais toward Audrey and Bird. Bird put a dagger to her throat. "Don't come any nearer."

Ethan drew the handle of his walking stick up to reveal a long, vicious blade. He raised his hand to throw it.

Audrey shouted, "Don't!" She didn't want him to kill again. Not even for her.

Ethan's voice ground between his teeth, deceptively soft, but with a rasp that betrayed his emotion. At least to her. "He's going to kill you, Audrey."

Audrey craned her neck to look at Bird. "Let me go. There's no need for anyone to die."

"Kill 'im!" someone shouted, though it wasn't clear who the "him" was.

Audrey fought to keep her shaking body still as the tip of the knife pressed into her flesh. "Then he's no better than Gin Jimmy, is he?"

"I'll second that!" Boomed a familiar voice. All heads

turned to see Gin Jimmy reenter with an even larger band of men than what he'd left with. "Jagger's no better than me. 'E don't even come close." His gaze settled on Ethan with cold fury.

Bird's grip loosened as he pivoted to look at Gin Jimmy. Audrey took her chance and slipped from his grasp. Ethan reached out and pulled her against him, her chest crashing against his. He wrapped his arm around her and held her tight.

She breathed in the familiar scent of him: spice, sandalwood, and something indescribably Ethan. He was safety. He was shelter. He was home. She snaked her arms about his waist and turned her head to look at Jimmy.

The vicious criminal's laugh filled the room. "How quaint." He walked toward Audrey and Ethan, his blue eyes like cold glass. "Tell yer men to hold. Else we'll have a battle on our 'ands, and I don't think ye have enough might to win."

It was true. It might've been a balanced fight, but Jimmy had returned with too many men. Ethan and his gang were outnumbered.

Ethan glanced at his men, who'd assumed a battle-ready position with their weapons at the base of the dais. He tightened his grip around Audrey. "There's only one deal I'll make."

Jimmy scrutinized them, his gaze lingering on Audrey. "Aye. I figured as much. Yer men can escort her out. But ye stay."

"No!" Audrey moved her body so she was shielding Ethan. "Let us both go. We'll leave London. We'll leave England!" She'd say or do anything to appease him, though her heart knew he would never agree.

Jimmy smiled at her, but it wasn't pleasant. "I can't let Jagger go. He failed me, ye see. And I gave 'im everything I 'ad to give. He was like my son." His gaze hardened and moved from her to Ethan. "Say yer good-byes then."

Jimmy stalked toward the dais and motioned to his men. They shadowed Ethan's gang and drove them toward the door.

Bird grabbed Ethan's knife out of his hand with a wicked grin. He also took the bottom part of the walking stick and sheathed the blade. Then he tossed the implement to Perkins.

Ethan turned her around in his arms. "Audrey. My love."

She grabbed the lapels of his coat. "I won't leave you." Tears streaked from her eyes.

He wiped at her cheeks with his thumbs while he cupped her face. "You must. It's the only way you'll be safe."

"Don't ask me to do this." She could barely speak past the rawness in her throat.

His eyes chilled for the barest moment. "I'm not asking you." His grip grew fierce and his fingers tangled into her hair. "My beautiful, brave Audrey. The time I spent with you was the happiest of my life. I will cherish every moment forever. Death will not part us. I'll be with you always." He touched her chest. "In your heart."

Audrey clutched at his neck as a sob escaped her.

He leaned down, his mouth against hers "Shhh. Don't cry for me. I wasn't meant for more than this. You were my greatest gift, a boon I never deserved, but shall be ever grateful for. Now, kiss me so that I have the taste of you on my lips when I meet my maker."

He crushed his mouth over hers with sweet savagery. His fingers dug into her scalp and his other hand wrapped around her back to pull her tight against him. She opened for him, meeting his tongue in a frenzied need to have as much of him as she could. But it was bittersweet for she knew it would never be enough.

Something pulled at him, but he resisted. He broke their kiss and pressed his cheek against hers. He whispered beside her ear, "I love you," and then he was gone from her, dragged away by Bird and another man.

Ethan's men encircled her. She moved toward Ethan, but one of them grabbed her arm and held her back.

She watched as Ethan was marched to the dais, where Jimmy had taken his throne.

Audrey was pulled toward the doorway. She dug her feet into the floorboards, but it was no use. Two men had her firmly, but gently, by the arms, and hauled her, at last picking her up.

"Ethan!" She couldn't stop the tears, could barely see his handsome face as he watched her go. His expression was stoic, but his eyes were like thunder.

The men who'd escorted him pushed him to his knees in front of Gin Jimmy. With a final, tortured look, Ethan turned from her.

And then she couldn't see him anymore, and her heart shattered into jagged, irreparable pieces.

CHAPTER 19

*P*ain unlike anything Ethan had ever known ripped through him. And Jimmy hadn't even touched him yet.

His mind scrambled for a way out of this, but he didn't see any. Some of the men here supported him, but not enough to go against Gin Jimmy. Like Ethan, they would choose self-preservation above all else. He'd known the plan was a risk and his primary goal had been achieved: Audrey was safe.

Ethan recognized the men in his peripheral vision and registered the apprehension in Marie's face before looking up at the man who'd guided him these many years.

Jimmy's familiar blue eyes were sad. He shook his head. "I hate what I must do, my boy."

Ethan didn't think there was a point in trying to persuade him otherwise. Jimmy was ruthlessly decisive, never wavering to change his course even if he suspected he should.

Jimmy stood abruptly and flicked a glance at the men who'd dragged Ethan up to the dais. "Bring him."

Hands roughly grabbed and lifted him and propelled him behind Jimmy into his private chambers that lay behind what he liked to call his "throne room."

Ethan had been in these rooms many times. As a member of Jimmy's innermost circle, he'd been invited to countless dinners and parties. He even had a favorite seat—his gaze shot to the chestnut-colored wing-backed chair situated near the fireplace.

"Lock 'im up," Jimmy said, pointing toward the chain that hung from a metal loop on the wall near the fireplace. He went to a sideboard and poured himself a glass of gin, then took his favorite chair, a plush russet companion to Ethan's.

One of the men picked up the chain. There were two shackles: one for his wrist and another for his ankle. He'd seen Jimmy use them many times. Until today, he'd never imagined being confined in their grasp.

Jimmy waved his hand at Ethan. "Give me that jewel in his neckcloth. And the ones on 'is fingers."

One of the men pulled the diamond stickpin from his cravat while the other stripped the rings from him. Ethan didn't care about any of it, save the ring with the L. But he wouldn't ask for it. While one of the men deposited the jewelry in Jimmy's outstretched hand, the other removed Ethan's coat and then his boots, as the first man returned to place the metal cuffs around Ethan's left wrist and left ankle.

There was enough slack for him to sit against the wall, but he couldn't get far enough to reach anything that could be used as a weapon, nor could he sit in his chair. It was a humiliating prison, but that was what Jimmy intended. It was also what Ethan had expected.

The men left Ethan and positioned themselves on either side of the door. The only other way out of the apartment was through a doorway that led to a corridor connected to several things, including the outside, which was heavily guarded on the exterior.

Jimmy took a hearty drink of gin. "I knew ye weren't at the Brazen Bride, but I pretended to go so ye'd make yer move. The letter almost got to me." His tone carried the barest hint of regret. "Almost."

Though Ethan hadn't expected the ruse to work, he'd still hoped for it. "How did you know?"

"You ran with the girl. She's important to ye. I knew ye'd want to come and get 'er." His lips lifted, but there was a touch of sadness in his eyes. "I counted on it."

Hope began to spark in Ethan. Was there a chance he'd show mercy? Ethan nearly laughed. In all the years he'd known Gin Jimmy, he'd never witnessed even a measure of softness.

"I just can't comprehend why ye turned on me." Jimmy sounded almost forlorn. He opened his palm. "Look at all the jewels ye have. Ye're a wealthy man. Didn't I give ye everything ye could want?"

Perhaps Ethan's letter *had* worked. He'd penned words he'd hoped would play to Jimmy's ego and arrogance—thanking him, appreciating him, even begging him. That part, imploring Jimmy to forgive him, had filled him with gall. He swallowed and tried to appear humble, something he hadn't attempted in a very long time. "You did, and that's why I wanted to try to make things right." There was no use saying he wanted to regain his place, not after he'd obviously come for Audrey and Audrey alone.

Jimmy didn't seem to register Ethan's words or the plea in his voice. "I made sure ye found yer way—even at the beginning. I knew ye'd take out Four-Finger Tom if ye were pushed 'ard enough, and if ye thought it was the only way to survive."

Ethan shouldn't have been surprised, but the bitterness of realizing how he'd been manipulated by first Davis and then Jimmy burned like acid on his tongue. "You encouraged him to berate me, to target me as weak."

"I thought ye'd be a better leader than Tom. And I

was right." Jimmy raised his glass and toasted him before taking another drink. "Weren't ye happy?"

Happy? He was a thief, a predator, a self-serving bastard who not only put his survival above all else, he wasn't even aware of anything else. Until he was. That's when it had all changed. "For a time."

"It was going into Society, wasn't it? The lure of the prestige was too great." Jimmy shook his head as he deposited Ethan's jewelry on a small table beside his chair. "I should've recognized that about ye. It's one of the qualities I liked best in ye—yer drive to have the most respect, the most admiration."

"Actually it was before that." Ethan wasn't sure why he opened himself up, but once he'd started with Audrey, he found it to be a balm for his battered soul. And if there was ever a time to unburden himself, it was now, when his end might be unavoidable.

"I know you wondered why I got the prizefighter. I did it for my father. He used to take me to bouts." Sponsoring the pugilist had allowed Ethan to reminisce about the life he'd led before he'd been forced into the streets. In turn, that had made him think about the life he might have had.

Add to that his growing discomfort with the things he'd done, and he'd been ripe for a change of heart. He realized he could pinpoint the exact moment his stomach had begun to sour. One of his men, a particularly ruthless bloke called Swan, had kidnapped Lady Philippa. Though Ethan hadn't been a part of it, he'd felt fully responsible. He'd had Swan abduct her once before—to watch Sevrin's fight. Swan's subsequent abduction had made him sick—and it had given him pause.

It wasn't as if Ethan hadn't known these things happened. Hell, they happened all around him. You couldn't walk through St. Giles without seeing a woman selling herself or a man trying to somehow degrade a woman. But with Philippa, Ethan had exposed her to that. *Ethan.* After that, things began to change for him and he'd started to think about a life where he didn't steal and he didn't reside in a flash house.

Jimmy studied him intently. "The prizefighter made ye want to turn against me?"

"I never would've turned against you if you would've let me go." When Jimmy had ordered him to take up his identity as Jason's half-brother to keep an eye on Lady Aldridge and Wolverton, Ethan had suggested he might not want to return to thievery after that. Jimmy had thought he was jesting. He'd laughed, but there'd been a sharpness to his response that Ethan had interpreted as a warning: Ethan had better be joking about such nonsense for his defection would never be tolerated.

Jimmy leaned back and crossed his ankles. "Ye didn't ask."

Ethan barked a laugh. "Christ, Jimmy, you're the most brutal man in London. You don't suffer anything you perceive as betrayal." He leaned as far forward as the chain would allow and narrowed his eyes. "Tell me right now that you would've allowed me to live my life if I'd never come back to you." Ethan watched Jimmy's mouth purse, his chest rise and fall. Ethan settled back against the wall, his lip curling. "I didn't think so."

Jimmy shot forward in his chair. "Aye, that's betrayal. But I shouldn't have been surprised. I knew I couldn't trust ye with everything. Ye fancied yerself better than a number of my operations." His expression turned pained, making him look like what he was—a fifty-year-old man who'd lived a rough life. "Ye were my greatest hope, and my biggest disappointment."

Though Ethan didn't want to be the things Jimmy wanted, his criticism still stung. "You've chained me up like so many others. Do you have a spectacle planned?"

Ethan thought of the countless times Jimmy had

shackled some poor soul to the wall because of an offense—real or otherwise—though he'd never remained long enough to see what had happened. He'd been disgusted by the pleasure some took at another's degradation. He understood they existed in a brutal world, but there was no need to glorify it. On the contrary, it was nice to find moments when he could imagine things were different, but then he supposed that's why he'd wanted to leave.

Jimmy studied him, his mouth twisting into a thoughtful pout. It was his thinking expression and Ethan recognized it well. "If yer plan had worked today, I would've been taken by Bow Street, tried, and likely hanged. Seems like ye deserve the same."

Ice settled into Ethan's veins, sent a chill to every corner of his body. He'd expected it, but hearing it pronounced made him realize just how tenuous his life was at present. So many things could go wrong . . . indeed, so many already had. "You're going to try me and hang me?"

Jimmy settled back into his chair and lifted a shoulder before tossing back the rest of his gin in a quick gulp. "Provided ye're found guilty."

Ethan struggled to find his voice. "When?" The word came out clipped and harsh.

"Tomorrow." Jimmy looked at one of the men near the door. "Tell White I want a scaffold set up outside by morning. Nothing fancy, but it has to be elevated. I think there'll be quite a crowd." The man nodded and left.

Ethan held his breath. "Do you plan to try me out there too?"

Jimmy chortled. "'Course I do! The point is to show them that even the best placed man can fall"—he bared his teeth—"when they try to fuck me. The skirts'll turn out by the 'undreds to weep over ye. Except the one ye really want. Unless ye want me to send for 'er?"

Ethan pulled at his chain. He wanted to wrap it around Jimmy's throat and squeeze the life out of him just for referring to Audrey. "Don't ever speak of her."

Jimmy stood up and moved closer to him. "I'm sorry it has to end like this. Ye were a good lad, Ethan Jagger." He kicked Ethan in the stomach, doubling him over as pain radiated outward through his body. Then he pulled Ethan's head up by his hair. "I'll speak of whoever I want whenever I want. If I want to fetch yer precious gel and sell 'er to the highest bidder, I will. And ye'll be too dead to stop me."

He let go of Ethan roughly, shoving his head toward the wall. "Try to get a little rest, if ye can. But maybe it doesn't matter. Tomorrow ye'll get the chance to sleep for all eternity."

Jimmy turned and quit the room, going back out to his men. Three more guards came in and assumed places about the chamber. Even if Ethan could break free of the shackles, he'd never get past the four men who were armed to their teeth. They were also older, quite set in their ways and methods, and they had absolutely no loyalty to Ethan.

He reclined against the wall, leaning his head back. He loosened his cravat and idly wondered if he could use it as a weapon. He supposed he could slip it around someone's neck like a noose if they wandered close enough.

A noose.

He massaged his neck and swallowed. A vision of Audrey swam before him and the pain slicing through him made Jimmy's kick feel like a caress in comparison.

He wondered what torture would await him before he'd be granted the "trial," but decided it didn't signify. The waiting and the expectation were torment enough.

He brought his knees up to his chest and wrapped his arms around his calves. Somewhere Audrey was safe and whole, and in the end, that was the only thing that mattered.

~

*D*arkness had fallen when Ethan's men ushered Audrey outside of the flash house and through the rotten streets of St. Giles. They moved quickly, never pausing, and they surrounded her on all sides so that she saw very little. But the stench of filth and decay was impossible to ignore. Still, she barely registered its acridity because she was too distraught over leaving Ethan. Twice she tried to turn back, but his men kept her on the path out of the rookery. When they got to a busy enough thoroughfare, they hailed a hack, and two of them climbed inside with her.

When they asked her for an address, she didn't even pause before saying, "Lockwood House." She wasn't ready to face her grandfather, or even worse, her parents.

The hack moved through the streets, jarring and bouncing her, reminding her of the awful journey to London. She squirmed on the seat, her insides in utter turmoil. She couldn't breathe, her throat was raw, and her face was hot and puffy from crying. At last, the cab came to a stop outside Lockwood House.

One of the men who'd ridden with her, Eddy, jumped out and helped her descend. The second, Fitzgibbons, followed her and stood staring at her for a long moment.

"Come inside." Audrey moved up the walk toward the house. "You should be a part of the planning to rescue him."

"Miss." Fitzgibbons looked at her pityingly. "He's probably already dead. I'm sorry to have to say that, but Jimmy's not one to make empty threats. He does what he says."

"I'm sorry, Miss," Eddy added. He tried to offer her a smile, but it was so weak it could only be called a half-smirk.

Audrey couldn't believe he was dead. She wouldn't.

A hack drew up behind hers and stopped. Lord Sevrin climbed out. "Miss Cheswick?" Lord Saxton followed him.

"Sevrin!" Audrey bolted toward him. "We have to save Ethan. Gin Jimmy's going to kill him." She watched Sevrin look behind her, saw his lips turn down. "Don't listen to them." They hadn't said anything aloud, but based on Sevrin's reaction, she assumed they'd communicated something.

"Let's get off the street," Saxton said, going toward the house.

"Come," Sevrin said to Eddy and Fitzgibbons.

The two men exchanged looks then nodded.

The door to Lockwood House opened and Audrey allowed herself to be swept through the entry hall and into the drawing room. The last time Audrey had been here had been during Lockwood's last vice party. The space looked completely different now without its adornment of silks and contingent of masked guests.

Lydia jumped to her feet. "Audrey!" She rushed forward and hugged her friend. Audrey swayed into her embrace. Every muscle in her body sagged.

They stood like that for a moment before Lydia guided her to the settee. "North, please bring some tea."

Audrey collapsed onto the cushion and let Lydia hold her hand. She felt cold and numb.

Lydia looked up at Sevrin and Saxton. "What happened? Where's Jason?"

"We weren't with him," Saxton said. "We were waiting outside St. Giles for Ethan's word. One of his men informed us that he'd turned himself over to Jimmy in exchange for Audrey's release."

Lydia inhaled sharply. "Then Carlyle wasn't able to apprehend Jimmy?"

Audrey glanced between all of them. "What do you mean?"

"Ethan sent Jimmy a note to lure him out of his lair," Lydia said.

That had to have been the message the boy had delivered.

Audrey nodded. "Yes, Jimmy left for a time." That's when Ethan had arrived. "But he came back. The plan must not have worked."

Lydia's face blanched. "Jason was waiting for him, disguised as Ethan in case Jimmy sent anyone in advance to determine if Ethan was actually there—which he wasn't." She looked at Sevrin and Saxton. "Do you think Jason . . . ?"

Audrey felt the tension in her friend's frame and heard the worry in her question. Had Jimmy gotten to Jason, discovered he wasn't Ethan and killed him? Audrey didn't think it was possible to feel any worse. She couldn't bear it if they lost both Ethan and his brother in the same day.

"I don't know," Sevrin said darkly. He turned to Saxton and they spoke in low tones.

"Don't whisper," Audrey snapped, unable—and unwilling—to keep her emotions in check. "We have a right to know everything you do."

Sevrin nodded and came further into the room, though he didn't sit. "We don't know anything. We were just wondering if we should go to the Brazen Bride to determine what happened."

"What's the Brazen Bride?" Audrey asked.

Sevrin braced his hands on his hips. "The flash house where Ethan met Jimmy. It's where he asked Jimmy to come. Lord Carlyle went there with several constables to arrest him."

"Yes, let's go and see what happened," Audrey said, half rising from the settee.

The sound of the front door opening carried into the drawing room and was succeeded by heavy footfalls across the marble tiles. Audrey held her breath until Lockwood stepped over the threshold.

Lydia let go of her hand and ran to him. She leapt into his arms and wrapped her hands around his neck. "Jason!"

Lockwood held her tightly and kissed her forehead. Audrey looked away, unable to suffer the tender moment. All she could see was Ethan's regret-filled gaze, and all she could taste was his bittersweet kiss.

Lord Carlyle came into the drawing room, trailed by a man Audrey recognized as one of Lockwood's retainers. "A trio of Ethan's men found us in Portugal Street and told us what happened with Jimmy. Miss Cheswick, I'm so glad you're safe. It was what he wanted."

He spoke as if Ethan were already gone. Panic threatened to suffocate her. "He may not be dead. We have to try to rescue him."

Fitzgibbons removed his hat and clenched it between his massive hands. "There's likely nothin' to be done." He flicked his gaze around the room. "Even if Jagger's not dead yet, 'e's 'eavily guarded."

Audrey's chest twisted anew and her throat constricted painfully. "We have to try."

"Yes, we do," Lockwood said, his gaze finding Audrey's and giving her a sliver of hope. It was enough to know she wasn't alone in wanting to try to save Ethan.

Lydia turned in his embrace so she could see Audrey. "Yes, we have to try."

Carlyle nodded slowly. "We must remember that Ethan is different—to Jimmy. Lockwood, do you know what the letter said? Are there any clues we can use to help us?"

"He appealed to their father-son relationship."

Father-son? Ethan hadn't told her anything about that. An ache opened up in her chest as she realized there would be countless things she'd never know about him because he wouldn't have the chance to tell her.

Carlyle cocked his head to the side. "Then it's also possible that Jimmy might behave differently in this situation since his emotions are involved."

"And you think that's a good thing?" Saxton's tone was laced with doubt.

"I don't know what to think. But I'll find out." Carlyle turned to the retainer who'd come in with him. "Scot, can you see if you can learn anything through any of your contacts?"

Scot gave a swift nod. "Meet back here in a couple of hours?"

"As quickly as possible. If there's a chance to pull off a rescue attempt, we'll need to move fast."

"Carlyle, do you need any help?" Sevrin asked.

Carlyle frowned. "Ethan didn't want you getting too involved."

"He's not here to argue with me about it. Let's go."

Saxton straightened his coat and turned toward the door. "I'll come with you."

"Wait," Lockwood said, releasing Lydia and moving toward them. "You can't expect me to stay here and do nothing."

Carlyle inclined his head toward Audrey and Lydia. "I don't think you'll be doing 'nothing.' We'll be back as soon as we can."

They all departed and Lockwood spun about to glare at nothing in particular.

North set the tea service on the table. Audrey had no idea when he'd entered.

"I'll bring some whisky, my lord."

Jason dropped himself on the other settee. "Bring the damn bottle."

Lydia returned to Audrey and took her hand again. "We're going to save him." If her declaration lacked certainty, Audrey didn't comment on it. She had to hold on to whatever hope she could find.

Audrey felt a strip of smoothness on her friend's finger. She looked down at the wedding band on Lydia's hand. "You were married," she said softly, her heart aching because she would likely never know that joy.

Lydia smiled sadly. "Yes. I'm sorry you couldn't be there."

North came in with a bottle of whisky and handed a glass of the amber liquid to Lockwood. He raised the glass. "I told Ethan we'd celebrate at your wedding,"

Audrey jumped to her feet, suddenly unable to tolerate company. "Do you mind if I go upstairs?"

"Not at all," Lydia said. "I'll have North show you to the yellow room."

"It's all right, I know where it is." Audrey nearly smiled at the shocked look on Lydia's face.

"Were you actually here that night Wolverton was killed?" Lockwood asked, incredulous. "When Sevrin showed up at Bow Street earlier and said you'd been a witness to the murder, I assumed it was a lie."

"I may have exaggerated what I saw, but I was here. Dressed as a gentleman." The familiar blush that should've stolen up her neck as she revealed this information didn't come. Perhaps she was just too emotionally exhausted to care. "I've been to four of your vice parties, actually. I'm quite familiar with the layout of the house." Both Lockwood and Lydia gaped at her. "Don't look so scandalized, I didn't partake of any of the offerings, save the gambling."

Lydia shook her head. "It's just . . . I'm shocked."

"I'm not always what I seem." Her voice cracked.

Ethan had known that about her. From their very first waltzing lesson, he'd seen right to her core, had declared she was worth more than anyone had ever realized. She'd fallen half in love with him right then.

She turned to go, but Lydia halted her at the doorway. "Should we notify your grandfather or your parents that you're here?"

Audrey turned. She'd barely given them a second thought, including her grandfather, which sparked a pang of shame. "Not yet. What do they think happened when I disappeared?"

"Your grandfather insisted you'd been kidnapped by a dark-haired criminal. Ethan, I imagine. But then Bow Street told them a few days later that you seemed to be traveling with him without duress. The whole affair has been kept very quiet."

"I'm sure no one has even registered my absence." Audrey forced a weak smile. "Except you."

Lydia's gaze was soft, but not quite pitying, thank goodness. They both knew that Society hadn't ever paid much attention to her and wouldn't notice if she'd fallen off the face of the earth.

"Please fetch me when they return." Audrey turned and made her way upstairs on legs that should not have been able to support her. But she wouldn't crumple. Not yet. She would fight for Ethan until she was certain he was gone. And then she didn't know what she'd do at all.

CHAPTER 20

*E*than's warm palm skimmed up her thigh, parting her legs. His bare chest pressed into her side as his lips nibbled the sensitive flesh beneath her ear. Audrey rotated to her back while his fingers played between her legs, coaxing her easy response. She sighed softly. His tongue traced whorls along her neck and licked at her collarbone.

She reached up to guide his head to her breast, but her hand found nothing. Her eyes flew open and she felt a rush of cool air.

She was alone.

With a jerk, she sat up on the bed, surprised she'd managed to doze off. Judging by the length of candle that had burned, she'd slept a long time—longer than she would've thought possible. Why hadn't anyone awakened her?

She jumped up and smoothed her hand over the wrinkles of the dress one of the maids had brought her before she'd lain down. If her gown was that rumpled, her hair had to be a fright, but she didn't give a whit about her appearance. She practically ran from the room and down the stairs.

The drawing room had been converted once again. Though there still weren't any silks draping the corners, the round table that sat in the center during vice parties had been moved into place. However, instead of displaying a female in some state of undress, it was surrounded by the men, their heads bent.

Audrey cleared her throat and they all turned. "What's going on, and why wasn't I awakened when you all returned?" Anger coursed through her. It felt good after so many hours of despair and helplessness.

Lydia came forward, along with Philippa and Olivia, Saxton's wife. A fourth woman lingered near the settee. Audrey recognized her as Lady Carlyle.

"I'm sorry, dear." Lydia said, putting her arm around Audrey and drawing her into the room. "We thought you should sleep as long as possible. We were going to rouse you soon. Would you like a tray of food?"

Her stomach growled, but she didn't think she could eat. "Something to drink, perhaps."

Lydia nodded and turned away.

Philippa hugged her. "I'm so sorry. I'm just glad you're all right. I was so distraught when you disappeared."

Audrey knew her abduction from Beckwith had to have frightened Philippa to death, especially given her own kidnapping. She hugged Philippa back. "I'm all right. They didn't hurt me."

"Thank God." Philippa stepped back, her eyes glistening.

Audrey shared a sympathetic gaze with Olivia before moving toward the table. "What are you discussing?"

They all turned and blocked whatever they were looking at.

Lockwood came to her side and tried to guide her to the settee. "You should sit down."

She shook off his arm and welcomed the rush of frustrated fury. "Please don't patronize me. Tell me what you know."

He nodded. "The good news is that he's still alive."

Relief poured through her, but was short-lived as she realized it couldn't be that simple. "And the bad news?"

Lockwood exchanged glances with Carlyle, who came to stand before Audrey. He opened his mouth, then shut it again. He clearly didn't want to tell her, but eventually said, "Jimmy plans to hang him in the morning."

The world felt as if it were falling away beneath her feet. "Hang him?" He should have escaped that threat when Bow Street had dropped the charges.

Philippa touched her arm. "They're working on a plan to rescue him."

"Yes," Carlyle said. "And we'll need your help to describe where he is. I've been in many places in St. Giles, but never the Cup and Burrow. It's heavily guarded, because it's Jimmy's stronghold."

Audrey relaxed a little, eager to be helpful and appreciative that they were letting her be. "I know how to get there and where he is inside—or at least where he was. I'm very good at direction." She'd proven that more than once while she and Ethan were running across southwestern England.

Carlyle smiled at her. "Excellent." He looked toward the others. "I'm fairly certain we can get in one by one if we're smart. The challenge will be getting Ethan out of there. We'll be quite outnumbered, even with Ethan's loyal followers."

She'd seen their reactions to Ethan and believed he had more support than they realized. "When Ethan arrived at the Cup and Burrow today, he tried to convince Jimmy's men that they'd be better off without him. Some of them seemed swayed. If people knew we were attempting a rescue, they might help us."

Carlyle pressed his lips together. "We don't have

much time to rally troops. It's already nearing midnight."

So late? "We have to try."

Lockwood stepped away from the table. "I agree. We can go back to the Brazen Bride and spread the word from there."

"It's risky," Carlyle said, stroking his chin and staring at the table, which had a hand-drawn map sprawled across its top. "If Jimmy hears that we're attempting to save Ethan, he may just kill him straightaway."

Audrey tensed. The situation seemed hopeless. No, she wouldn't give up. She'd told Ethan she was optimistic, and she would hold on to that—he deserved nothing less.

Scot set his palms on the table and leaned forward, addressing everyone. "We have to target who we tell and instruct them to spread the word at the latest possible moment."

"Yes, we'll have to map out a plan for that." Carlyle went back to the table. He seemed to be in charge. "First, however, we need to determine our entrance strategy. We can't exactly march in through the front door."

"I don't think going in is our best option," Scot said slowly, glancing around. "Even if we could find a way, getting out would be near impossible. We'd have a better chance out in the open, when they bring Ethan outside to walk him to the scaffold."

"Unfortunately, I think you're right," Carlyle said. He glanced at Audrey, who was listening to their discussion as if they were at the end of a long tunnel. She could hear them, but there was this dark, hollow space separating her from everyone. "It would, however, be helpful if we could get a person or two into the Cup and Burrow in order to do as Audrey suggested and sway some of them to our cause. It would be even better if we could somehow smuggle information, or even a small weapon, in to Ethan so that he can be prepared when we make our move."

Audrey strode toward the table, suddenly realizing her purpose. "I can do it." Everyone was staring at her, some of them with widened eyes. "There's a way to get in—if you're a . . . prostitute. They take in new girls through a back stairway. I was kept in a room where they put the women after they first arrive. If I disguise myself, I could get in."

Lydia had come back with a glass of sherry. She moved to Audrey and grabbed her hand. "No, no. That's far too dangerous."

Yes, but it was a good plan and she couldn't sit around Lockwood House waiting for the outcome. She needed to be a part of this. If they weren't successful, if Ethan died, and she'd done nothing but wring her hands, she'd never be able to live with herself. "I can do this. I remember those who seemed sympathetic."

"I'll go with her," Scot said, drawing everyone's attention. "I'll drop her off at the back and then go inside for a pint."

Sevrin nodded at him. "I could go too. I'm as comfortable in a tavern as I am in a ballroom. More so, actually."

Philippa sent him a pained gaze. "Ambrose."

Sevrin went and murmured something in Philippa's ear, then kissed her cheek.

Audrey wanted these people to help Ethan, but she couldn't understand why they would offer. His brother, yes, but the rest of them? "Why are you doing this?" she asked of no one in particular.

They all glanced between one another, but it was Lady Carlyle who spoke. "He saved my life. And Daniel's. I can't sit by while he's hanged."

Sevrin put his arm around Philippa's shoulders. "I was lucky enough to find someone who had faith in me, who gave me the second chance I needed. I can't turn my back on Ethan knowing he wants to change." He looked at Saxton. "I can't begin to fathom why Sax is helping, but I would venture to say he just doesn't like being left out."

Saxton's pale eyes gleamed. "Just so."

A surge of emotion welled up in Audrey. "I can't thank you all enough." She took the sherry from Lydia's hand and toasted them all before taking a sustaining drink.

"If I thought Daniel would let me, I'd go with you." Lady Carlyle cracked a smile. "But I'm certain he would say it's too dangerous."

Carlyle went and put his arm around his wife. "St. Giles is no place for any of us, which is why we need to get in and out as quickly as possible. And we need to blend in—that will be the key to our success or failure. If we look like we belong there, we'll be fine. That is my gravest concern with supporting any of us going. Scot appears to be able to comport himself quite well with the criminal element." He shot Lockwood's retainer a speculative glance, to which Scot merely shrugged. "And I daresay Sevrin would be able to make a place for himself. The rest of you lot . . ." He shook his head. "There's an issue of liability. We need to be focused on getting Ethan and getting out. Only those who can defend themselves should go." Carlyle's apologetic gaze settled on Audrey.

She refused to be left behind. "I can shoot. Probably better than some of you."

"A gun will not protect you for long, Miss Cheswick. I know it will be difficult to remain here, but I think you must."

All the years of being shoved to the background, of her opinions and desires being ignored, erupted inside of her. She advanced on Carlyle, her lip curling. "Either you include me in your plan or I'll find a way to get there myself. Wouldn't it be better if we were all working together?"

Carlyle blinked at her, then exchanged a questioning look with his wife.

"She should go," Lockwood said, sounding quietly authoritative. Perhaps Carlyle wasn't in charge after all. "Just as I'm going to go. Ethan saved Lydia from Jimmy, and I mean to return the favor." His gaze took on a tinge of sadness and regret. "He deserves recompense . . . for so many things."

Carlyle seemed to understand there was no point in arguing further. He nodded swiftly and turned back to the table. "Then let us prepare ourselves. We need to get moving. Ladies, can you put together an appropriate costume for Miss Cheswick?"

"The clothing from my husband's parties remains upstairs," Lydia said. "I haven't had a chance to clean out all of the rooms. I'm certain we can find something suitable."

"I believe I know just where to look." Philippa directed a half-smile at her husband.

"And I can make any necessary alterations," Olivia said. She was an accomplished seamstress and designer. "Plus, I have some experience with how real prostitutes dress. When I'm finished with Audrey, she will look as though she belongs at the Cup and Burrow." She'd confided to Audrey that she'd resided next to a brothel before she'd gone to live with Saxton's aunt, Lady Merriweather.

Lydia, Philippa, and Olivia left while Lady Carlyle moved to stand beside Audrey. She offered an encouraging smile. "What will you do once you get inside?"

Audrey exchanged looks with Lockwood and Carlyle. "There's a young woman, Nan, who serves as a maid. She's particularly"—what was the right word? —"grateful to Ethan. She will help me." Audrey felt certain Nan would participate in a rescue effort, especially when it included her. She resolved to take the young woman with her when they escaped St. Giles.

"Won't they recognize you from earlier?" Lady Carlyle asked.

"If I make up my face and dress differently, I don't think they'll know it's me."

"Olivia will ensure Miss Cheswick is beyond recognition," Saxton said.

"What a peculiar lot of people you are," Lady Carlyle marveled. "When this is all finished and everything is back to normal, I'm hosting a dinner party so that I can hear every one of your interesting stories." She smiled warmly at Audrey.

Audrey appreciated Lady Carlyle's optimism more than she could say.

Carlyle fixed her with a steady stare. "Now, Miss Cheswick, tell us everything you know about the Cup and Burrow."

❧

*T*hat evening Ethan was subjected to the typical humiliations Jimmy inflicted on those who crossed him. Ethan's dinner was tossed to him in pieces, as if he were a dog, and when he had to relieve himself, he was given a chamber pot and no privacy. Jimmy and the men at his table, meanwhile, enjoyed plenty of food, wine, and ale and threw disparaging comments at Ethan. Marie served them and cast intermittent pitying glances toward Ethan.

Ethan didn't let the mistreatment get to him. If his plan worked, it would be a small price to pay. He also tried *not* to think about what would happen if it didn't work.

Jimmy motioned for one of the guards to come to him. The guard leaned down while Jimmy whispered something in his ear. He nodded and left. Jimmy's gaze settled on Ethan a moment, as it had frequently throughout the night. This time lasted longer than the others but ended the same, with a regretful headshake.

Ethan wondered what that was about, but reasoned it maybe had nothing to do with him. He leaned his head back against the wall and stared at the ceiling. There was a grayish stain in the nearest corner. He'd spent a good portion of the last several hours trying to determine its cause. It was better than contemplating his future. He wouldn't let himself think past tomorrow morning.

The guard returned with two other men who came directly to him. Ethan recognized them, but only recalled the name of the smaller man—George. They unshackled him and led him to the other doorway. Ethan glanced over at Jimmy, but he was turned away talking to whoever sat on his right.

Ethan had only been through this door to go outside, but he knew it also led to a room where Jimmy sent men to be beaten. Was Ethan to be punished before he was tried and hanged? His muscles tensed, and he weighed whether he could take out the two men before they subdued him. But Ethan had no weapons—they'd been stripped from him with his boots—and the guards were armed to the teeth.

"What's going on?" Ethan asked.

George shook his head. "Ye're a lucky bastard. Jimmy's sendin' ye a girl." He led Ethan down a short corridor to another door.

"I don't want a girl." Particularly if she wasn't going to aid his cause. He certainly didn't want to shag anyone other than Audrey.

George turned and looked at Ethan as if he were daft. "I'm not tellin' Jimmy ye don't want his generosity."

Why was Jimmy doing this? Was it because he was so drunk? It was when he was most vulnerable—at least emotionally. Was he allowing sentimentality to guide his actions? Perhaps there was still a way Ethan could somehow turn this to his advantage. If he could find a way out of here tonight, he'd save everyone a lot of trouble on the morrow.

George opened the door to a very small room with only a pallet on the floor and a flickering sconce. There was also another ring on the wall to which was affixed a length of chain and a shackle. It seemed Jimmy's generosity only extended so far.

Ethan turned, hoping there was a way to get past the other guard, but he was huge and filled the doorway. He also gave Ethan an impassive glower that somehow verbalized there was no way to get through him.

But Ethan hadn't survived as long as he had without taking risks.

He launched himself at the man's middle, hoping to take him down and somehow clamber over him. If he could get to the doorway in the middle of the short corridor, he could find his way out of the maze that was the Cup and Burrow.

However, the giant didn't fall. He clasped his arms around Ethan and slammed him into the doorframe. Pain radiated along Ethan's spine. He wanted to strike out, but his arms were pinned. Instead, he kicked—ineffectively—at the man's legs.

The brute carried him into the chamber like he was a sack of stolen goods. When Ethan was near enough to the chain, George took his right hand and shackled him to the wall. The man dropped him to the pallet and stepped back. Ethan lunged for him, but the chain kept him from getting close enough.

George had also retreated. "Try anything like that again and I'll have to tell Jimmy. I always liked ye, Jagger, but ye know where my loyalties must lie. We'll be right outside so we can let yer girl in. Try to enjoy 'er."

He gave Ethan a final resigned look, then they left, locking the door behind them.

Ethan had no intention of enjoying anything. But perhaps this *was* the torture Jimmy intended. He knew Ethan loved Audrey, that he was willing to sacrifice his life to save her. So what would be more degrading than to send a woman to entice him, to perhaps even force him?

A shudder wracked his aching frame. He'd endured many long nights, especially in his youth when he'd had to sleep with one eye open in order to preserve himself. This night, however, might just be the longest he'd ever endured.

CHAPTER 21

*A*udrey and Scot made their way through St. Giles with only mild looks of interest directed their way. Or, more accurately, *her* way. Though she wore a cloak to cover the alarming décolletage of her gown, its vivid scarlet hue was still visible at the hem. The lurid color stuck out in the grime of St. Giles like a beacon on a dark night. And despite the bonnet that covered her hair and should've provided a bit of shade for her face, every now and then a lantern cast its illumination over her heavily made-up features. At these times, those who caught sight of her stared. Olivia had done a wonderful job making her look . . . different, and in a surprisingly inoffensive way.

They approached the Cup and Burrow. Audrey's pace quickened as her insides tightened. "Around the back," she murmured to Scot.

He took her hand and led her down a narrow alley, which boasted a half dozen or so slumbering men. They didn't stir as Audrey and Scot picked past them. Audrey brought her hand to her nose as they neared the last—he smelled as if he'd soiled himself.

They came to a door and Scot halted. "This has to be it." He turned to look at her, but his face was barely discernible in the meager light that spilled down the alley-way. "You ready?"

She nodded. She didn't want to think about it too long. Leaving Scot's company filled her with fear, but she knew he wouldn't be far—just in the common room. She also knew that Jason, Sevrin, Carlyle, and Saxton were nearby too, or would be.

Audrey unclasped her cloak and gave it to Scot, who would dispose of it before he went into the Cup and Burrow. "I'll see you soon," she said brightly, in an effort to buoy her confidence.

"Aye, and remember, I'll be only a scream away." He squeezed her hand and departed down the alley. He lingered at the end while she rapped on the door.

It took several attempts before the door opened. Audrey's shoulders drooped in relief as she cast a final glance at Scot before stepping inside.

"Wot ye doin' at this hour?" Mother Dean, the Cup and Burrow's mistress, blinked at Audrey and rubbed her reddened eyes.

"I came to work. Ye ain't goin' to turn me away, are ye?" Audrey had worked on her speech with Olivia, trying to emulate the women Olivia had known in her past. Audrey passed a hand over her bodice and rested it against her hip. She thrust her chest out for good measure.

Mother Dean held up her lantern and scrutinized Audrey for a long moment. Her gaze rested on Audrey's face, and Audrey held her breath waiting to see if she'd recognize her from their brief meeting the previous day.

After several blinks, Mother Dean nodded. "All right then." She rang a bell and after a lengthy wait, Nan appeared, carrying a candle.

Audrey suppressed a relieved grin. Her happiness faded as Mother Dean cuffed Nan. "Took ye long enough."

Nan massaged her ear and murmured an apology.

"Take 'er to the common room." Mother Dean gave Audrey one last assessing glance. She grinned suddenly. "Aye, ye're goin' to make me a pretty penny. Just look at 'er titties, Nan!" She laughed and disappeared the way she'd come.

Nan glanced at Audrey before pivoting away from her. "Come along then. I need to fetch a girl on our way."

Audrey touched Nan's shoulder. "Nan, it's me, Audrey. Jagger's . . . woman."

Nan swung around and leaned toward her, scrutinizing Audrey's face by the light of the sconce flickering a short distance away. Her eyes widened. "I didn't recognize you." Her gaze turned appreciative. "Who made up your face?"

"I can trust you to help me, can't I, Nan?"

Nan's shoulders arched and her features tightened with fear. She backed up a step. "Please don't ask me to do nothin'."

Audrey's hope was dwindling fast. "Nan, you'd help Jagger if you could, wouldn't you? We have a plan to rescue him—and you. Wouldn't you like to leave St. Giles?"

Nan's shoulders relaxed and she moved closer, until she was barely a hand width away. "I'd like that above all else, but how do you mean to do it?"

"I can't get into the specifics, but there will be a time, when they take Jagger outside tomorrow morning, for those who support him to come forward and assist with his liberation." Audrey spoke with as much detachment as she could muster, though discussing his impending execution made her want to toss up her accounts.

Nan raised a hand to her mouth. "Bloody 'ell."

"Nan, you must only tell people you absolutely trust. We can't let Gin Jimmy know of this plan."

After a series of violent nods, Nan lowered her hand. "I understand, and I'll do what I can What're you goin' to do now?"

"I'd like to get to Eth—er, Jagger." She needed to tell him about their plan and give him the knife stashed in her boot.

Nan shook her head sadly. "I can't get directly to 'im. 'E's in the 'eart o' Jimmy's den." She looked down and fidgeted with the candlestick. "I could get you close. I'm supposed to take a girl to Jimmy."

Before she could think better of it, Audrey said, "Take me."

Nan's head shot up and she gaped at Audrey. "You can't mean it."

"Yes, I do. Just get me over there and I'll figure out a way to get to Ethan." Armed with a knife in her boot and a pistol against her thigh, she was optimistic about her chances. Perhaps foolishly so, but Ethan's life was at stake and she wouldn't let him go without a fight. "Could I beg one more favor of you? There's a man in the common room. Athletic looking fellow, attractive, dark hair, very nice blue eyes, goes by the name Scot. Could you let him know where I am?"

Loud voices came from the other end of the corridor. Nan jumped. "We should go. I'll take you the back way." She led Audrey through a doorway and along a narrow passage. At the end, she slowly opened a door. The hinges creaked their arrival like a warning bell.

"Wot took ye so long?" thundered a deep voice.

"We just got a new girl in. I had to get 'er." Nan's voice trembled and Audrey prayed the young woman wouldn't give her away.

Audrey stepped into a small hallway with several doors leading from it. Filling the close space was a huge man with a mane of dark, scraggly hair, and a chest as wide as two Nans. He raked her with a lustful stare, his focus settling on the too-tight and too-low bodice of her gown. Her fingers itched to grasp the pistol strapped to her thigh.

The man chuckled, a low sound that rumbled in Audrey's chest. "Lucky prick. Let's see 'im say no to this one." He inclined his head toward a door, which was being unlocked by a much smaller man.

Fear and bile rose up Audrey's throat. She could go into that room to God-knew-what awaited her or she could take on two men and try to find Ethan. She hesitated too long. The hulking brute of a man grabbed her wrist and pulled her forward, propelling her toward the now open door. The smaller man pushed her inside and before she could regain her footing, the door closed behind her. She spun about and tried to push it open, but the lock clicked.

"Audrey?"

Relief poured through her at the sound of her name in that familiar voice. She pivoted and took in the pallet, the chain, and the man. Her heart tripped.

Ethan.

She rushed forward and threw her arms around his neck. His hands came around her back. She felt the chain graze her waist and realized he was shackled to the wall.

She drew back but couldn't let him go. She clasped his shoulders as she studied his face. He looked untouched, his face as handsome as ever. "You're all right?"

"No." The word was low and dark.

She clutched at him, digging her fingers into the silk of his waistcoat. "What have they done to you?" She moved one hand down over his chest, lightly rubbing as she searched for some sign of injury.

His hand came over hers, stilling her movements. "I'm not all right because you're here. Why the hell have you come back?" He hissed the question at her instead of yelling it, but his fury was evident in the set of his mouth and the glacial tint to his eyes.

"To save you."

"Keep your voice down!" Again, he spoke quietly but with a clear tone of angry authority. "You can't save me."

She touched his face, her heart aching at the sacrifice he'd been ready to make for her. "I'm not alone."

He ran his hand through his black hair, tousling it and reminding her of what he looked like in the morning. "Blood of Christ. I suppose my brother's involved. Tell me he isn't here."

"No. They'll come tomorrow"—she refused to think about all the things that could go wrong—"when they take you outside."

"You came alone?"

She didn't think he could sound any angrier, but she'd been mistaken. "Jason's manservant, Scot, escorted me here."

"I know who Scot is," he growled. "And he'll be the first one I thrash if their ridiculous plan works. Though, given that you've ended up in here with me, I have to assume it won't."

Audrey pressed her lips together. It was a good thing she was used to having enough optimism for the both of them. "I can see how it's going to be for the rest of our lives. You always seeing how things will fail, and me patiently explaining to you how they will not. How together we can overcome anything."

His features relaxed a bit as some of the ire dissipated in his eyes. He exhaled. "Audrey, I would dearly love for you to spend the rest of our lives proving me utterly wrongheaded. However, you must accept that may not be possible."

Where was the man who survived at any cost? "I accept no such thing. You think our plan isn't working, but I'm here. With you. Just as I intended to be."

"An utterly foolish move."

"No. I'm *not* foolish." She lifted her skirt and pulled the knife from her boot. Then she flashed the pistol against her thigh. "I'm armed."

He sucked in air between his teeth. "Holy hell, Audrey."

"I came to inform you of the plan and to give you a knife. The pistol is for me." She dropped her skirt and held the blade in her palm. "There will be an uprising of support for you. When they march you outside, we'll get you away from Gin Jimmy."

He seemed to relax a bit. "Yes, that is how I hoped it might work. Minus your participation. I'm going to gleefully kill Carlyle."

She caressed his cheek. "You'll do no such thing. You're a new man, remember?"

He took the knife from her. "I doubt there'll be an 'uprising' of any kind."

She hated his defeatism. "Try to have some faith—I know it's not something you're used to. I saw how many of Jimmy's men were conflicted when you were trying to persuade them to your cause. I'm confident we'll be able to rouse enough support to free you."

He cradled the side of her face and leaned in close. "And what if you don't?" he whispered, so near she could almost taste him. "If the plan fails and I am hanged, what will happen to you, my love? What danger have you put yourself in for me? I don't deserve your kindness. Or your love."

Her heart was creaking beneath the weight of his words, but she wouldn't show it. "Still, you have it. My love—all I have to give is yours."

"Audrey," he breathed. "Jimmy isn't going to let me go without a fight. He's ruthless on his best day, but to him, my defection—if you want to call it that, and he does—is personal. Is one of you prepared to kill him? Because that's what it will take to set me free."

She knew he was asking if *she* was prepared to kill him. "Why is it so personal?"

Ethan let go of her and backed up against the wall. He turned the knife between his fingers, his movements adept and strangely soothing to watch. "He was the only person who believed in me, even if it was for the wrong reasons. He taught me how to defend myself and how to be a damned good thief. There are many times he saved my life—and I his. He was as much a father to me as my own before he died."

She heard the pain and also the nostalgia in his voice. How difficult it must be to have loved—or maybe even still love—someone so horrible. But he hadn't been horrible to Ethan. At least not until now. "You're certain he wouldn't have just allowed you to leave?"

"No, and he affirmed that last night. I regret that it took me so long to see that relationship for what it was . . ." He shook his head, his hand stilled. "Twisted."

She resisted the urge to touch him, sensing he needed space, if just for a moment. "He was all you had. I understand, Ethan. Stop blaming yourself for past mistakes. What's important is who you are now."

"Your faith in me is relentless." He pierced her with his familiar, provocative stare. "Tell me this plan of yours."

"I have a helper inside the Cup and Burrow. She's seeking assistance for us right now."

He arched a brow at her.

Audrey swatted at his shoulder. "Stop being so skeptical! Will you accept for even a moment that other people might have your best interests at heart and others will rise to the occasion? Or must you believe the worst of everyone?"

His brow climbed even higher. "Since I think you know how I'll answer that, I'll just be quiet." This banter reminded her of their time together after they'd fled London. She didn't want it to end.

He held up the knife. "The weapon is a nice addition. I do thank you for that. While I appreciate the plan, I should like to launch a surprise attack when they open the door. However, that won't be for quite some time. I believe you're supposed to provide an experience that will carry me to my eternal rest."

"I shall provide a lifetime of them." She swayed toward him, angling her chest first up and then down to draw his attention. As planned, his eyes locked on her bared flesh. She grazed her breasts against his chest. She curled her hand around his neck and brushed her lips against his jaw.

"Since I am without footwear at present, I'm going to put this back in yours." He leaned down and hiked her skirt to her knee, then slid the knife between her stocking and the edge of her boot. "Do you know, there's something quite thrilling about you bedecked in weaponry. It brings to mind your scandalous gentleman's attire when we first began this adventure. Wholly unexpected yet strangely alluring." He pressed a soft kiss to her neck.

Need poured through her like a torrent. She curled her fingers around his forearm and brought them down to the cold metal around his wrist. "I don't suppose there's any way we can get this off."

"There's nothing in this room save the pallet. And while your weapons are helpful—and attractive," he said with a sultry smile, "they won't pick the lock." His smile spread into a wide grin as he fixated on her hair.

She smoothed her hand over the curls, unsurprised that a few had sprung free, as usual. "What?"

"Your lovely, necessary, terribly useful hairpins."

She withdrew one from her hair and held it out to him.

He slid the hairpin into the lock and worked it around. "They should've shackled my left hand because then I probably wouldn't be able to do this."

"Because you're left-handed." She remembered the first time she noticed that, during their first waltzing lesson. He'd compared himself to the devil. At the time, she'd thought he was merely being flirtatious, but now she knew he'd meant it. Beneath all of his arrogance and showmanship, his true opinion of himself was poor indeed.

The lock clicked and the shackle fell open. He caught it as he looked up at her and smiled, then quickly put his finger to his lips. "We don't want them knowing I'm no longer confined," he said extra quietly.

She nodded as she took the metal from his wrist and set it gently on the floor. "It's a good thing you're such an expert thief, else you'd still be wearing this."

"You could argue that if I hadn't been an expert thief, I wouldn't be here in the first place." He took her hand and pulled her against him. His mouth crushed over hers in a fierce kiss.

Her body responded instantly. She twined her arms around his neck and kissed him back, eager for his touch and amazed that she could want him so desperately despite the danger they faced. But maybe that was the source of her need. He gave her strength and courage and made her feel like she could do anything, be anyone.

He spun her about so that her back was against the wall. He dragged his mouth from hers, nipping at her lower lip. "You look so different. Who applied your cosmetics?"

"Olivia—Saxton's wife. She worked in the theater for a short time."

"You look rather exotic. Add in the weapons and this gown . . . it's almost like you're someone else." His gaze dipped to her breasts. "You may have to wear this costume for me again."

Her pulse quickened and warmth suffused her—he was beginning to have hope! "Only in the privacy of our bedroom. I'm not terribly fond of putting myself on public display."

"Neither am I. Though I am beyond grateful that you would do that for me." He kissed her throat and stroked his tongue along the underside of her chin. "What happened to my shy, blushing Audrey?"

She tipped her head back against the wall and closed her eyes, giving herself over to the sensations he was igniting. "It seems you've changed me."

He trailed his mouth down her neck and brought his hand beneath her breast. He curved his palm around her and brushed his thumb over the edge of her gown, grazing her flesh. Then his mouth was there, sucking at the top of her breast. She arched forward, offering herself to his attention. But she wanted more. "My gown," she breathed.

"We can't disrobe," he said against her flesh. "We need to be ready. Hell, we probably shouldn't even be doing this." He palmed her breast, then dipped his fingers inside of her bodice to find the stiff peak. His mouth, hot and open, was back at her throat while he pulled at her nipple.

Heat streamed to her core. Had he said they shouldn't be making love? She tugged at his hair as she held his head close to her. "Please, don't stop."

"I couldn't if I wanted to." His teeth tugged at her ear. "Which I don't." His hand left her breast, but for good reason. He hiked her skirt up, baring her calf, her knee, her thigh. "Hold this."

She complied, clasping her bunched up skirt at her waist while his fingers found her center. She moaned as he stroked her flesh. Already her orgasm was building. "I'm finding it difficult to be quiet."

"So don't be. These are the sounds they expect to hear. Let's give them a show." He thrust his finger inside of her and she gasped. "Yes, like that, only louder."

"More." She let herself go, moaning and encouraging him.

His hand left her and she opened her eyes, afraid that someone had perhaps interrupted them. But no, he was opening his fall and then his hot flesh was nudging against her. He lifted her against the wall. "Wrap your legs around me."

She braced her hands on his shoulders and did as he bade, encircling his waist with her legs. He positioned himself at her entrance and drove inside of her, pinning her to the wall. She cried out as he filled her.

His hand came up and cupped the back of her neck, his fingers digging into her flesh. "Look at me, Audrey."

She opened her eyes and saw her own need and desire reflected in his gaze. And love. "I love you," she whispered.

He kissed her, his lips playing over hers softly at first, and then he thrust his tongue inside of her, mimicking the stroke of his cock. He drove up into her, his flesh rubbing against her, coaxing her release.

Pleasure unfurled within her, slowly at first and then at lightning speed. He tore his mouth from hers and slammed her against the wall with his thrusts. Her orgasm broke over her. All she could see was light. All she felt was ecstasy. All she heard were his moans and the relentless sound of him moving inside of her. He stiffened and shouted his release. Then he buried his face in her neck.

~

*E*than's legs quivered as his orgasm subsided. He inhaled Audrey's delicious scent—a combination of lavender and spice—and was overwhelmed with the gift of her. He wished he could give her the fairy-tale ending she deserved, but he'd settle for just getting her out of St. Giles alive. And if, by some chance, he got out too, he'd choke every one of those pricks who'd put her in danger.

He continued to hold her, as tremors coursed through her body. Or maybe they were his. He wasn't quite sure where she ended and he began. He kissed her neck as he slowly withdrew from her. Gently, he eased her legs from his waist and guided them to the floor.

She gripped his shoulders until she found her footing, then she kissed him soundly and thoroughly. He couldn't help but smile into her mouth.

When he drew back, she regarded him with a satisfied gaze. He had nothing to offer her to tidy herself—they'd taken his cravat hours ago. He supposed he could offer his waistcoat. Now that he was unshackled, he could remove it. He rebuttoned his fall. "Do you need anything to clean up?"

She shook her head, and still there was no blush. Not only did she look different, she really *was* different. "I'm fine. Petticoats can serve multiple purposes." She sank down to the pallet.

He went to the door and listened. He couldn't hear anything from the corridor, but knew George and the hulk had to be out there. His mind began to play scenarios where he took on the brute while Audrey attacked George. He glanced back at her and wondered if she could do that.

He joined her on the pallet, tucking her into the crook of his arm as he propped himself back against the wall. She curled beside him, laying her head upon his shoulder and bringing her knees up so they nuzzled his thighs.

She traced her fingertips over the buttons of his waistcoat. "What will we do when this is all behind us?"

How he hoped there would be an opportunity for them to find out. He would expend all of his energy to see her to safety, and if he was somehow saved . . . well, he didn't expect it. Not that he would say that. She'd made her opinion on his cynicism clear. Instead, he decided to indulge her fantasy. And it wasn't a trial. Thinking of a future with her, even if it was hopeless, gave him comfort. It was how he'd spent many of the long days since he'd been arrested.

"This may surprise you, but I actually liked Wootton Bassett. Not the town specifically, since we didn't really see much of it, but I enjoyed the time we spent with Fox and Miranda. Their life is simple and . . . purposeful."

Her hand stilled, her palm flattening against his chest. "Yes, it is. You liked that?"

He nodded. "What Fox does there with the orphanage is astonishing. He impacts so many lives. Without him, those children would suffer terribly."

"Like you did."

"Worse. Many of them are younger than I was. I shudder to think what would've happened to me if I'd been orphaned at a younger age." Because of his pretty face, he undoubtedly would've been forced into prostitution. That path had been suggested to him several times.

She tucked her hand beneath his waistcoat and pressed her hand over his heart. "Me too."

"When we stayed with the hermit, I liked that story."

"What, me being your sister? I'm afraid I didn't care for that part."

He chuckled and kissed her head. "No, I don't care for that part either. I did, however, enjoy pretending to be a schoolmaster. Do you think . . ." Oh, now he really was fantasizing.

She lifted her head and looked up at him. "Do I think what? That you could teach?" She reached up and touched his cheek, directing his gaze down to hers. "I think you can do anything you put your mind to. Especially if I help you."

"When you tell me that, I believe it." He tipped her chin up and kissed her.

A few moments later, she settled back against him with a contented sigh. "Do you envision opening a school at Stipple's End? I think the Foxcrofts would love that. I know they'd like to enlarge the orphanage, but they need more help. I think Miranda's invitation for us to stay was genuine."

"Yes, that's what I was hoping. Provided they forgive us for lying to them and for taking one of their horses."

"We only borrowed her. I'm sure Posy returned to Wootton Bassett when she ran off." Audrey yawned. "And that's what we'll do. After we're married, of course."

"Of course." He tucked a wayward curl behind her ear. "Sleep if you want. I'll be right here."

A few minutes later he heard the even tone of her breathing as she drifted into slumber. He hated that she'd come back for him, but he couldn't regret this time he'd had with her.

The sound of the door jarred him awake. *Shit*, he hadn't meant to fall asleep. He shook Audrey, then pulled the knife from her boot. "Wake up."

He jumped to his feet and rushed toward the door, anxious energy pumping through him.

The brute came in first. Ethan didn't hesitate. He charged forward, knife in hand, but his opponent was viciously strong. He rushed at Ethan and knocked him off balance, sending him crashing backward into the wall. Pain exploded in Ethan's skull, but he pitched forward in an effort to take the big man down. The man's fist landed against Ethan's wrist, and Ethan dropped the knife.

Audrey's shriek filled the small room. George had her by the hair and was drawing a knife from his belt.

Ethan put up his hands. "Stop! Let her go. She isn't part of this."

George dragged her toward the door.

Where the fuck was her pistol?

She tried to reach down—presumably for her gun—but George yanked her hair, pulling her upright. "Ethan!"

The larger man grabbed Ethan's arm in a vise-like grip.

Ethan tried to pull free to get to Audrey, but it was pointless. "George, she's just a worthless whore."

"Then what do ye care if she dies? The Jagger I know would put 'is own survival before anyone else's, but then she didn't call ye Jagger jes' then, did she? I don't think she's a worthless whore at all."

Too late Ethan realized their mistake.

"You're wrong," Audrey said, ever his defender. "Jagger would lay down his life for the people he cares about, or for those who can't help themselves." Her gaze connected with his. "I know this about him."

Ethan's heart warmed at her confidence, but it wasn't helping their cause at all. The more she said about him, the clearer it became that she wasn't some indiscriminate prostitute from upstairs. "She doesn't know shit, George. Just take her back to the common room so she can find another bloke." He gave her a meaningful stare.

"Ollie, lock 'im up again," George said. He kept his hand twisted in Audrey's hair and his knife against her throat. Ethan longed to drive that knife into his heart for daring to touch her.

Ollie tugged him toward the shackle, but Ethan made it hard for him. He kicked out at him and threw his fist into his gut, which felt as though it were made of iron. Ollie slammed him into the wall as he reached down for the shackle. He slapped the metal around Ethan's wrist. "Damn, ye got a key, George?"

"Reach into my waistcoat pocket there, lovely. That's right. Now toss the key to Ollie. There's a girl."

Ethan couldn't tell what was happening because Ollie had him shoved against the wall so that all he could see was the corner. He tried to twist his neck, but Ollie only dug his arm harder across his shoulder blades.

"Bitch!" The report of a pistol sounded. Ollie's hold loosened enough for Ethan to turn around and see Audrey holding her smoking pistol over George who appeared to be bleeding from his hip.

Ethan tried to get to her, but Ollie held him back. Running boots echoed from the corridor and then a pair of faces appeared in the door.

One of them said, "What the 'ell happened?"

"She shot George," Ollie said.

"Take 'er to Jimmy," the new arrival said. The second man came into the room and clasped her wrist. She cried out as he easily took the pistol from her fingers. She tried to pull away and her gaze met Ethan's.

His heart twisted as he watched her dragged from the room. His hope that she'd make it out of the Cup and Burrow withered and died. When Ollie's fist found his gut once more, he crumpled to the floor and prayed that Audrey wouldn't suffer.

CHAPTER 22

*A*udrey kicked and thrashed at the man who pulled her away from Ethan, but it was no use. As soon as he got her into the corridor, the second man picked up her feet and carried her.

"Keep yer mouth shut." Another pair of men passed them. "Fetch George. The bitch shot 'im."

They carried her through another doorway and then dumped her to the floor near a large table. She blinked as she pushed herself up to a sitting position.

"Miss Cheswick?" Jimmy stood from the table and stared at her. "Didn't I let ye leave?"

"Yes." She got to her feet on quaking legs.

"Ye should've stayed gone. I won't be so nice a second time." He scrutinized her appearance. "Particularly when ye look as if ye belong 'ere. Doesn't she, lads?" He laughed and the rest joined in. When the laughter died down, he nodded at the two men who'd carried her. Each man grabbed one of her arms and held her still.

Jimmy came around the table, his hands clasped behind his back. He stopped just in front of her. "Now, why did ye come back?"

She smelled the gin on his breath and fought not to recoil. "To see Ethan."

Jimmy's hand snapped across her cheek so fast, she didn't see it coming. But the pain lingered, setting her cheek afire. "Don't make me hit ye again. I really don't like hurtin' women."

Her eyes watered. She struggled to think of what to say. "I came to see him and you." She cringed, waiting for his hand to strike again and when it didn't, she rushed onward. "He was like a son to you. I can't believe you want to hurt him. He only wants to be happy. With me. Can't you let him do that?"

He squinted at her a long moment. "'E won't be happy with ye. I've seen 'im with women over the years. 'E'll tire of ye soon enough. Then 'e'll move on to his next Society conquest. 'E's fooled ye like 'e fooled me."

She didn't believe that for a moment, but wouldn't try to convince him otherwise. "Fine, then let him do that. Why does he have to be a criminal? Why won't you just let him be free?"

Jimmy wrapped his hand around her neck and she worried she'd gone too far. He leaned close. "'E *is* a criminal. 'E's exactly what I made 'im and that's all 'e'll ever be." Spittle shot from his mouth and landed on her cheek.

He let go of her, shoving her back as he removed his hand. The men tightened their grips on her arms. She swallowed, anxious about what would happen next. She hoped and prayed they still had a chance once they got outside.

Jimmy strolled back to his place at the head of the table and looked down. "I suppose I'm done with my breakfast." He swept the plate from the table. Because it was metal, it didn't break, but hit the floor with a loud thud. "Get 'im ready. 'E's got a trial to attend."

Several men stood from the table and disappeared through the doorway toward the room where Ethan was being held. Audrey tensed.

"And ye shot one of my best men." Jimmy shook his

head. He came back toward her and didn't stop until he'd clasped her chin in a firm, painful grip. "Ye're goin' to have a front-row seat at Jagger's trial and hangin', and then I'm goin' to work ye upstairs until ye can't walk. Do ye know how much money I'll make off Jagger's lovey?" His gaze dipped to her breasts and he dug his fingers into her flesh. "Let's hope ye fuck as well as ye look. Eh, it doesn't matter, does it, lads? They'll pay for the novelty, not the skill." He sneered in her face and let her go before turning away from her.

Stark fear like she'd never known turned her limbs to jelly. If not for the men holding her up, she would've sagged to the floor.

Long minutes passed during which Jimmy retook his seat. He stared moodily at the table. To Audrey he looked upset, disturbed perhaps. She couldn't stop herself from trying to persuade him to change his mind.

"Jimmy, it's not too late to let Ethan go."

"Shut 'er the fuck up, will you?" He turned to the corner where Marie sat on a small stool. Audrey hadn't even noticed her. "Find somethin' to gag 'er."

Marie pulled a long, white cloth out of her pocket as she came toward Audrey. She didn't say a word as she put it in Audrey's mouth and tied it at the back of her head.

Ethan's scent filled her nostrils and she realized it was his cravat. She heard the sound of boots and turned her head just as Ethan was led into the room. There was a bruise blooming on his cheek and blood trickled from his lip.

"Clean 'im up, Marie, and put 'is boots on."

Marie went to a washbasin and dampened a cloth, which she used to cleanse Ethan's lip. He stared stoically at Audrey, his eyes cold and dispassionate. She sensed he was working to mask his emotions and wished she could do the same. But a tear leaked from her eye, and she realized that was hopeless.

Next, Marie fetched his boots from somewhere behind Audrey. She put his feet into them and the act reminded Audrey of when she'd helped him after he'd been wounded.

"Bind 'is hands."

One of the men came forward with a rope. Ethan stuck his hands out without being asked. The rope was circled around his wrists and bound tightly.

Another tear snaked from Audrey's eye, and her throat nearly closed with anguish.

Jimmy stood and straightened his coat. "Let's go. 'Im first."

The men flanking Ethan grabbed his arms and nudged him forward. He moved toward Audrey. "It's all right. You're going to be all right." He said the last so softly, she had to strain to hear.

Then he turned and walked from the room.

Jimmy jerked his head toward the men holding Audrey and they brought her forward. Jimmy took the place of the man on her right. "I want ye right beside me when we watch 'im swing."

The doorway wasn't big enough to allow them all to pass through together, so Jimmy went first and he pulled her over the threshold. They moved through his throne room and into a corridor that emptied into the nearly empty common room. Audrey searched the tables and corners for Scot, but didn't see anyone save a slattern leaning against one wall and a man passed out across a tabletop. Everyone must have gone outside to watch the hanging.

Emotion gathered in her chest, and she struggled to breathe. Tears came fast now, tracking down her heated cheeks. They moved outside into the late morning. Gray skies and drizzle met them; still, it was much brighter than the interior of the Cup and Burrow, and Audrey had to blink several times.

They moved into the street, which was lined with

what looked to be hundreds of people. All of St. Giles's denizens had turned out. The crowd was thick and raucous, with shouting and singing and the smell of food mingled with decay and impending death.

Audrey looked ahead of her and fixed on Ethan's back. The dark green and bronze silk of his waistcoat rippled over his back as he walked. Then she caught sight of the scaffold and the rope.

Blackness edged her vision and she fell to the street.

⁓

*E*than heard Jimmy swear and turned his head to see Audrey being dragged to her feet. Her eyes rolled back in her head. Jimmy slapped her hard.

Ethan lunged toward him, aching to inflict pain and damage, but the men holding him kept him from moving. "Don't touch her, Jimmy!"

Jimmy turned and looked at him, his eyes dark and narrowed. "I'll do whatever I like to 'er. Especially after ye're dead." He grabbed Audrey's chin and shook her until she blinked. "Keep yer wits about ye, gel. The best part's comin' up."

He waved them all forward and the procession continued.

Because he had no choice, Ethan turned and walked toward the scaffold, but he didn't look at it. Instead, he scanned the crowd in search of Jason or Carlyle or Sevrin or any of the idiots who'd launched this futile plan.

At last his gaze settled on Scot. He was standing in the front of the crowd. As Ethan drew close enough, he mouthed, "Save her."

Scot nodded imperceptibly, and Ethan had to trust that he would. Next, he caught sight of Sevrin, then Carlyle. Finally, he saw Jason, who was standing very near the scaffold. His familiar gray eyes were impassive.

They briefly met Ethan's, softened slightly, and then moved on.

Love for his brother swelled in Ethan's chest. At this perhaps eleventh hour of his life, he finally had the family he'd sought. And he'd put all of them in harm's way.

The sound of a pistol cocking behind Ethan drew the men holding him to turn. Ethan spun with them and things seemed to happen in slow motion. In his peripheral vision, he saw men moving, but his gaze focused on the man holding the gun.

Teague.

And he was pointing it at Jimmy. Other men around him had also drawn pistols, but no one had fired yet.

"You don't get to hang him."

Jimmy smiled malevolently. "That yer job, Runner?"

"Damned right it is. And you sure as hell don't get to brutalize women."

Ethan kicked at the men holding him and pulled to get free. From the corner of his eye, he saw Jason move and then he heard the report of a pistol as Teague fired his weapon.

"Audrey!" In the ensuing commotion, Ethan got one of his arms free and punched the man still holding him. It was enough to make him release his grip on Ethan.

Ethan watched Audrey go down, but saw that it was Scot who'd knocked her to the ground, not Teague's bullet, which had appeared to go wide.

Jimmy lifted his pistol and pointed it at Teague. Ethan didn't think. He tackled the Runner as the gun fired. They both fell.

Burning pain sliced into Ethan's shoulder. Audrey's scream rent the air. His head hit the cobblestones and blackness descended.

CHAPTER 23

*A*udrey watched the bullet hit Ethan in the shoulder as he tackled Teague to the ground. She pushed at Scot and her hand brushed the hilt of a knife tied to his waist. She unsheathed it, taking it from him as she'd taken the pistol from George back at the Cup and Burrow.

There was fighting all around her, but she looked for the shock of white hair. Rain fell into her eyes and she swiped at her face, pulling the cravat from where it had dislodged from her mouth when she'd fallen. She managed to roll out from under Scot, who was now engaged with one of the men who'd been behind Jimmy.

She struggled to find her feet as she searched for Jimmy. At last, she found him, not far away. He was fighting his way toward where Ethan lay.

She clutched the knife in her hand and wove through the melee. Jimmy spun and saw her, his gaze falling on the blade. His lip curled and he struck fast and sure, knocking the knife from her hand and forcing her backward. He advanced on her, a knife in his own hand.

"Audrey!" Jason called her name from behind Jimmy. He dodged between two men and tossed her a pistol.

She caught it with both hands, cocked the hammer, and fired. At this range, there was no missing and thankfully there was also no misfire. She watched Jimmy's eyes widen as the bullet slammed into his chest.

He fell back. Jason stood over him and pressed his boot into his neck.

Jimmy sputtered. Blood gurgled from his mouth, came forth in a greater torrent as Jason applied more pressure.

It was more than Audrey needed to see. She dropped the pistol and ran to Ethan.

Teague held him in his lap, his hand pressed to the wound in Ethan's shoulder. "Help me."

She squatted down and lifted Ethan by the bicep of his unwounded arm while Teague hefted him. When Teague had gained his footing, he lifted Ethan over his shoulder.

Jason came forward and led them through the throng. Audrey followed Teague, her gaze fixed on Ethan's ashen face.

Vaguely, she was aware of someone close behind her. A quick look back revealed it was Sevrin.

They wound their way from the crowded street, down a narrow alley to another street. What should have been a difficult passage was surprisingly easy.

"The hack is up there," Sevrin said close to her ear.

She looked ahead and saw a hackney coach waiting. The Earl of Saxton was standing outside, though he was dressed liked one of St. Giles' roughest men.

Teague got to the hack and Saxton helped him lay Ethan facedown on one of the seats. However, it wasn't long enough to hold his entire frame and his legs slumped off the side. Audrey went to climb in after him, but Teague grabbed her arm.

"I'm done. Tell him . . . tell him thank you."

Audrey nodded and looked at Saxton, who helped her into the hack. She lifted Ethan's head and shoulders and eased into the corner of the seat, settling his head on her lap. Jason entered behind her. He bent Ethan's legs so they'd fit onto the seat and then installed himself opposite. He handed Audrey a kerchief, which she pressed to the wound in Ethan's shoulder.

She looked down at Ethan's face, so pale against the lurid scarlet of her skirt. With her free hand, she stroked his dark hair back and tried to swallow through the lump in her throat.

His eyes blinked and he looked up at her. "Are you an angel?"

She choked through a laugh. "No. But I think there must be one on your shoulder. The uninjured one."

Jason leaned forward. "Ethan?"

Ethan closed his eyes again. "Is that my brother?"

She stroked his head. "Yes."

He flinched from where she held the cloth to his shoulder. "What happened to Jimmy?" he asked through gritted teeth.

"Audrey shot him," Jason answered. His gaze found hers across the hack and he nodded approvingly, gratefully.

Ethan opened his eyes again and twisted his neck to get a better look at her. "Is he dead?"

"Yes."

"Are you all right?"

Her heart swelled with love for him. "Yes. I feel . . . unremorseful."

His lips curved into a smile and his lids shuttered his eyes once more. "Good girl."

They rode the rest of the way in silence. Once they arrived at Lockwood House, North met them and helped Jason carry Ethan inside. It was then that they realized the bullet must've gone straight through, as he was also bleeding from the front of his shoulder.

Jason and North conveyed Ethan upstairs to the bedchamber Audrey had slept in the day before. They sat him on the edge of the bed where Audrey quickly cut his clothing from his torso.

Jason held a cloth to his back while Audrey pressed one to his front and prayed the doctor would arrive soon.

North gave Ethan a glass of whisky, which he downed in one swallow. He thrust it back, his hand shaking. "Another."

As Ethan finished the second glass only slightly more slowly, the physician arrived with Scot.

He allowed Audrey to assist as he probed the wound, cleansed it, and then sutured both the front and back. The physician proclaimed him lucky since the bullet hadn't done significant damage and then told them all to pray infection wouldn't set in. He dispensed laudanum, instructed Audrey on how to bandage the wound, and said he'd return the following day.

Ethan touched the puckered wound on his chest and winced. "I don't suppose there's any way to get some of that poultice from the innkeeper's wife in Hounslow?"

"Unnecessary," said Sevrin, stepping into the room. "I stopped by the Black Horse and brought some of Tom's. Works wonders." He handed it to Audrey.

She accepted the small pot with tears in her eyes. "Thank you." She looked at each of them in turn—the Carlyles, Saxtons, Sevrins, Scot, North, Lydia, and Jason. "I'll be forever indebted to you for saving Ethan."

"*We. We'll* be forever indebted." He held his hand out to her.

She went and took his hand, squeezing his fingers. "We."

She didn't look away from him as she heard the room empty. When the door clicked shut, she opened the pot and wrinkled her nose. "What a horrid smell."

He let go of her hand. "If it's going to drive you away, leave it off."

"Never. Now, lean forward a bit." She set about liberally applying it to his back. "I was surprised to see Teague today."

"I wasn't. I asked him to come."

She paused. "You did?"

He turned his head to look at her. "He was part of my contingency plan."

"You asked for help. And you put your faith in him." She didn't bother masking her surprise—or her delight. "I'm glad. Now I understand why you leapt in front of him. He asked me to tell you 'thank you.'"

His head drooped forward. "He lost his sister, and he risks his life to do good. He deserved to live."

"So do you."

"I'm not quite as certain of that, but I will try." He did his best to straighten as she applied the ointment to his front. "What I would like to know is how we escaped St. Giles."

"I'm not quite certain of that, but it did seem remarkably easy. It was as if people helped us along the way. They moved, they ushered us along, they wanted to see you safe." She wiped her hand on a towel and grabbed the linen North had brought for bandages. It was quite long, so she was able to wrap it around him several times. He sucked in air and cursed under his breath as he lifted his arm to aid her efforts.

When she was finished, she helped him lie back against the pillows. She sat on the edge of the bed facing him. "Do you know what I think?" At his questioning look, she smiled, feeling confident that she was right. "I think you were never really alone. You thought you were without friends, but you've always had people who cared about you, even in that world."

His face darkened. "Like Gin Jimmy."

"No." She touched his face and ran her thumb over his lips. "Not like Gin Jimmy. People who genuinely cared about you." She closed her eyes and swore.

"Audrey, did you just curse?"

She looked at him and gave him a lopsided smile. "Apparently I did. But with good cause. I forgot about Nan. She's a maid at the Cup and Burrow, and I said I'd take her out of there with us."

"I remember Nan."

"Of course you do. You helped her. You showed her kindness and mercy when no one else would. And I'm willing to bet she wasn't the first one."

He turned his head and pressed a kiss into her palm. "Your faith in me has made all the difference."

"Maybe, but I still think you were doing something right all along."

His eyes found hers. "I don't know if that's true, but I definitely got something right now."

"I would say so." She leaned forward and brushed her lips over his. He tried to prolong the kiss, but she drew back with a smile. "You need to rest. I don't even know how you're conscious after what happened."

He clutched her hand. "I've spent too much time in the dark, my love. I want every moment with you that I can grasp."

"And you shall have them. I promise to be here when you wake."

His forehead creased with doubt. "You won't leave me?"

She brushed his hair back and kissed his forehead. "Ethan, my dearest love, no one is ever going to leave you again."

EPILOGUE

The summer sun beat through the linen of Ethan's shirt, heating him to the extent that he sought the flagon of water beneath the tree twenty yards distant. As he slaked his thirst, he watched the men dig the foundation for the new school at Stipple's End.

Pride and excitement mingled in his veins as he thought of the changes he was bringing to the orphanage. Fox had been thrilled to bring Ethan and Audrey into the fold. Together, they'd planned to enlarge Stipple's End. Within the next two years, they hoped to double the staff as well as the number of beds, in addition to the new school that would prepare the children for futures they might never have dreamed of.

Like the future Ethan was now living.

The investments he'd begun making eight years ago —right after he'd ventured to Lockwood House and fought with Jason—had made him a wealthy man, and he couldn't spend the funds on anything other than improving the lives of others. He'd been given a second chance and was committed to giving them to as many people as he could.

A child sprinted across the field toward him. Instinctively, he tensed. He'd relaxed since moving to the country, but some reflexes were still ingrained.

It was Hal, a nine-year-old boy from the orphanage. "Ethan!" The panicked tone of his voice did nothing to ease Ethan's anxiety.

He set the flagon down. "What is it?"

"It's Mrs. Lockwood." The children had learned to call Ethan by his given name, as they addressed Fox so intimately, but they still called Audrey Mrs. Lockwood, as they called Miranda Lady Miranda. "She needs you at home!"

The mild sense of apprehension that had struck him upon noticing Hal coming toward him bloomed into full fear. Thank God he had a horse here. "Is she all right?"

Hal was breathing heavily from his run. "I think so?" He didn't look certain and that was enough to send Ethan dashing for his horse.

A scant ten minutes later, he was riding up the lane to their small house. Nan, whom they'd rescued from the Cup and Burrow and brought to the country with them as their housekeeper, met him at the door. She smiled. "Good afternoon, Mr. Lockwood."

Ethan blinked at her lack of visible distress. Was there a problem or not? "Where's Mrs. Lockwood?"

"Upstairs. She's just—"

Ethan didn't wait for further explanation. He ran inside and took the stairs two at a time. He went straight for their bedroom in the back corner, but found it empty. Voices from the opposite end of the house drew him to turn and retrace his steps past the stairs to the large guest chamber they'd only recently finished furnishing.

Audrey stood inside, her hand resting on the gentle

curve of her increasing belly. She laughed at something Jason said, then her gaze found Ethan's. "There you are!"

He gestured to his brother as he went into the bedchamber. "This is why you sent for me? I thought there was something wrong. The baby or something." His voice trailed off as he realized how unjustifiably worried he sounded.

Audrey slid her arm around his waist. "Of course not. The baby's fine—and not due for another four months as well you know. Lydia, on the other hand, does not have that much time." She inclined her head to the corner, where Jason's wife was sitting with her feet propped up. She and Jason had come to the country to birth their child sometime within the next month.

Lydia's hands rested on her rather swollen midsection. "Hello, Ethan. Thank you for letting us come to stay."

"You know you're welcome anytime." Ethan moved to hug his brother, happy to see him after several months apart.

As they parted, Jason glanced around the newly refurbished room with its warm gold and ivory hues. "The house looks good."

"Audrey's been working on it night and day."

"Someone has to pay attention to *our* house instead of the orphans'." She slid a look at Lydia. "I begin to understand some of Miranda's frustration about the lack of improvements to Bassett Manor. Fox and Ethan spend the majority of their efforts on Stipple's End."

Jason slapped Ethan's back. "And now there's a school along with it. How's that coming?"

"We're just getting started. It's amazing how quickly it's all come together. I'll show it to you—now, if you're not too tired."

Jason grinned. "How can I refuse your eager invitation?" He turned to Lydia. "You'll be all right?"

She waved her hand at them, smiling. "Go."

Ethan brushed a kiss against Audrey's cheek and left with Jason.

When they reached the base of the stairs, Jason paused. "Just a moment. I brought something for you."

Ethan couldn't imagine what that could be as he followed Jason into the sitting room at the front of the house. A wrapped package stood against the wall. Jason tore the paper away to reveal the painting of their father from his office at Lockwood House.

"I thought you should have it," Jason said. "You liked him better than I did."

No mention of whom the viscount had preferred. And Ethan realized it didn't matter. It had never mattered. What mattered was that he was their father, and it was thanks to him that they had each other. Ethan looked at Jason and nodded. "Thank you."

As they rode toward the site of the school, Jason asked, "You really are happy out here?"

Ethan cast him a sidelong glance. "It's shocking."

"I don't know if I could do it, at least not full time. I'm happy to visit though, especially since it's likely to be the only time I'll see you. Is there any chance you'll come to London?"

"I'm sure we will—to visit you and Audrey's grandfather." Lord Farringdon didn't entirely approve of Ethan, but he was thrilled to see his granddaughter happily married. Her joy was his, and that was all Ethan cared about.

Her parents, on the other hand, were less pleasant. They'd attended the wedding by special license, but their emotions could only be described as a mingling of disappointment, over her choice, and relief, because she was finally married. Audrey was happy to see them as little as possible, if ever, and Ethan wasn't inclined to persuade her differently.

"That's good," Jason said. "I'm sure the cousins will want to see each other."

Ethan slowed his horse as they neared the building site. "I'd like them to grow up together."

They climbed down from their horses, and Jason touched his arm. "I would too."

Later that night, after a laughter-filled dinner that included Fox and Miranda, as well as the Knotts, Ethan climbed into bed with his wife and drew her into his arms.

She snuggled her backside against his groin as he stroked her belly.

"Are you trying to tempt me, Mrs. Lockwood?"

"Every moment." She turned her head and pressed a quick kiss to his neck. "It's good to have Jason and Lydia here. I'm so happy they're going to have their baby with us."

They hadn't wanted to have the baby in London, and Jason's country seat wasn't an option since his mother resided there. Her fragile mental condition wouldn't tolerate the upheaval. He'd discussed with Ethan that it was perhaps time to move her to a dower house, but he had to build one first. He acknowledged it was past time to do that, now that he had his own family to consider.

"Yes, I'm glad they're here." The relationship he and Jason had forged over the past several months meant almost as much to Ethan as his marriage to Audrey.

The baby kicked at Ethan's palm, startling him. He didn't know if he'd ever become accustomed to that feeling—the jolt of fierce love and possession that overcame him every time he thought of the child he and Audrey had created.

"Our son is glad too," she said, turning in his arms.

The moonlight filtering through the gap in the curtains illuminated her beloved face, framed by the dark, haphazard curls he loved so well.

"I am not convinced he isn't a she, but I won't argue with you. I'll be happy with whoever it is. I only pray she takes more after you than me."

Audrey frowned. "Why? You have many wonderful traits. And I'd be quite happy if she had your quicksilver eyes," she touched his temple, "or your black-as-midnight hair." She slid her fingers into his hair and pulled his head down to kiss him.

"Fine, I'll yield my appearance is my best quality."

"Ha! That's not true. You're charming and hardworking and dependable." She gazed up at him earnestly. "You have to stop thinking of yourself the way you were. You're not a criminal anymore."

No, he wasn't. He'd once thought it impossible to leave that life behind, but now it seemed a distant memory. "Fine, I will also yield my apparent reformation." He rotated so that he was leaning over her and he untied the top of her gown. "Do you remember how I used to watch you while you undressed when we were running from Bow Street?"

"Yes." She'd become a bit breathless.

He pulled the neckline of her gown to reveal the swell of her breast. He kissed her soft flesh, loving the taste and feel of her. "That wasn't very gentlemanly of me, and I'm afraid I still don't regret it. Those are the qualities I should hope our child will not inherit."

She tugged at his head. "But those are some of the qualities I like best about you."

He looked up at her and arched his brow. "Indeed? You like that I'm an unreformed scoundrel?"

Her eyes narrowed as her lips spread into a seductive smile. "Oh yes. I love that scoundrel and you must promise to stay that way."

He grinned at her as his heart swelled so full of love and joy that he felt it might burst from his chest. "Then I vow to be a scoundrel. *Your* scoundrel. Ever after."

The end

Want to catch up with a few of your favorite characters from the Secrets and Scandals series? Check out the Legendary Rogues series featuring four intrepid heroines and adventurous heroes embark on exciting quests across Regency England and Wales!

Need more Regency romance? Check out my other historical series:

The Untouchables
Twelve of Society's most elite bachelors and the wallflowers, bluestockings, and widows who bring them to their knees!

The Spitfire Society
Meet the smart, independent women who've decided they don't need Society's rules, their families' expectations, or, most importantly, a husband. But just because they don't need a man doesn't mean they might not want one...

Wicked Dukes Club
Six books written by me and my BFF, NYT Bestselling Author Erica Ridley. Meet the unforgettable men of London's most notorious tavern, The Wicked Duke. Seductively handsome, with charm and wit to spare, one night with these rakes and rogues will never be enough...

Secrets and Scandals
Six epic stories set in London's glittering ballrooms and England's lush countryside, and the first one, Her Wicked Ways, is free!

Would you like to know when my next book is available? Sign up for my reader club at http://www.darcyburke.com/readerclub, follow me on social media:

Facebook: http://facebook.com/DarcyBurkeFans
Twitter at @darcyburke
Instagram at darcyburkeauthor
Pinterest at darcyburkewrite

and on BookBub to be notified of deals and new releases.

*L*et's keep in touch! I have two fun Facebook groups:

Darcy's Duchesses for historical readers
Burke's Book Lovers for contemporary readers

I'm also a member of the Jewels of Historical Romance. I hope you'll visit our Facebook group, the Jewels Salon. Read on for links to our Fabulous Firsts collections, two six book anthologies featuring starters for our most beloved series—each set is just 99c!

I hope you'll consider leaving a review at your favorite online vendor or networking site!

If you like contemporary romance, I hope you'll check out my Ribbon Ridge series available from Avon Impulse, and the continuation of Ribbon Ridge in So Hot.

Thank you again for reading and for your support.

xoxox,
Darcy

One Night to Remember by Erica Ridley

One Night of Temptation by Darcy Burke

Secrets and Scandals

Her Wicked Ways

His Wicked Heart

To Seduce a Scoundrel

To Love a Thief (a novella)

Never Love a Scoundrel

Scoundrel Ever After

Legendary Rogues

Lady of Desire

Romancing the Earl

Lord of Fortune

Captivating the Scoundrel

Contemporary Romance

Ribbon Ridge

Where the Heart Is (a prequel novella)

Only in My Dreams

Yours to Hold

When Love Happens

The Idea of You

When We Kiss

You're Still the One

Ribbon Ridge: So Hot

So Good

So Right
So Wrong

PRAISE FOR DARCY BURKE

The Untouchables Series

THE FORBIDDEN DUKE

"I LOVED this story!!" 5 Stars

-Historical Romance Lover

"This is a wonderful read and I can't wait to see what comes next in this amazing series..." 5 Stars

-Teatime and Books

THE DUKE of DARING

"You will not be able to put it down once you start. Such a good read."

-Books Need TLC

"An unconventional beauty set on life as a spinster meets the one man who might change her mind, only to find his painful past makes it impossible to love. A wonderfully emotional journey from attraction, to friendship, to a love that conquers all."

-Bronwen Evans, *USA Today* Bestselling Author

THE DUKE of DECEPTION

"...an enjoyable, well-paced story ... Ned and Aquilla are an engaging, well-matched couple – strong, caring and compassionate; and ...it's easy to believe that they will continue to be happy together long after the book is ended."

"This is my favorite so far in the series! They had chemistry from the moment they met...their passion leaps off the pages."

-Sassy Book Lover

THE DUKE of DESIRE

"Masterfully written with great characterization...with a flourish toward characters, secrets, and romance... Must read addition to "The Untouchables" series!"

-My Book Addiction and More

"If you are looking for a truly endearing story about two people who take the path least travelled to find the other, with a side of 'YAH THAT'S HOT!' then this book is absolutely for you!"

-The Reading Café

THE DUKE of DEFIANCE

"This story was so beautifully written, and it hooked me from page one. I couldn't put the book down and just had to read it in one sitting even though it meant reading into the wee hours of the morning."

-Buried Under Romance

"I loved the Duke of Defiance! This is the kind of book

you hate when it is over and I had to make myself stop reading just so I wouldn't have to leave the fun of Knighton's (aka Bran) and Joanna's story!"

-Behind Closed Doors Book Review

THE DUKE of DANGER

"The sparks fly between them right from the start... the HEA is certainly very hard-won, and well-deserved."

-All About Romance

"Another book hangover by Darcy! Every time I pick a favorite in this series, she tops it. The ending was perfect and made me want more."

-Sassy Book Lover

THE DUKE of ICE

"Each book gets better and better, and this novel was no exception. I think this one may be my fave yet! 5 out 5 for this reader!"

-Front Porch Romance

"An incredibly emotional story...I dare anyone to stop reading once the second half gets under way because this is intense!"

-Buried Under Romance

THE DUKE of RUIN

"This is a fast paced novel that held me until the last page."

" ...everything I could ask for in a historical romance... impossible to stop reading."

THE DUKE of LIES

"THE DUKE OF LIES is a work of genius! The characters are wonderfully complex, engaging; there is much mystery, and so many, many lies from so many people; I couldn't wait to see it all uncovered."

"..the epitome of romantic [with]...a bit of danger/action. The main characters are mature, fierce, passionate, and full of surprises. If you are a hopeless romantic and you love reading stories that'll leave you feeling like you're walking on clouds then you need to read this book or maybe even this entire series."

THE DUKE of SEDUCTION

"There were tears in my eyes for much of the last 10% of this book. So good!"

"An absolute joy to read... I always recommend Darcy!"

-Brittany and Elizabeth's Book Boutique

THE DUKE of KISSES

"Don't miss this magnificent read. It has some comedic fun, heartfelt relationships, heartbreaking moments, and horrifying danger."

-The Reading Café

"...my favorite story in the series. Fans of Regency romances will definitely enjoy this book."

-Two Ends of the Pen

THE DUKE of DISTRACTION

"Count on Burke to break a heart as only she can. This couple will get under the skin before they steal your heart."

-Hopeless Romantic

"Darcy Burke never disappoints. Her storytelling is just so magical and filled with passion. You will fall in love with the characters and the world she creates!"

-Teatime and Books

Secrets & Scandals Series

HER WICKED WAYS

"A bad girl heroine steals both the show and a highwayman's heart in Darcy Burke's deliciously wicked debut."

–Courtney Milan, *NYT* Bestselling Author

"…fast paced, very sexy, with engaging characters."

–Smexybooks

HIS WICKED HEART

"Intense and intriguing. Cinderella meets *Fight Club* in a historical romance packed with passion, action and secrets."

–Anna Campbell, Seven Nights in a Rogue's Bed

"A romance…to make you smile and sigh…a wonderful read!"

–Rogues Under the Covers

TO SEDUCE A SCOUNDREL

"Darcy Burke pulls no punches with this sexy, romantic page-turner. Sevrin and Philippa's story grabs you from the first scene and doesn't let go. *To Seduce a Scoundrel* is simply delicious!"

–Tessa Dare, NYT Bestselling Author

"I was captivated on the first page and didn't let go until this glorious book was finished!"

–Romancing the Book

TO LOVE A THIEF

"With refreshing circumstances surrounding both the hero and the heroine, a nice little mystery, and a touch of heat, this novella was a perfect way to pass the day."

NEVER LOVE A SCOUNDREL

SCOUNDREL EVER AFTER

Legendary Rogues Series

LADY of DESIRE

"A fast-paced mixture of adventure and romance, very much in the mould of *Romancing the Stone* or *Indiana Jones*."

-*All About Romance*

"...gave me such a book hangover! ...addictive...one of the most entertaining stories I've read this year!"

-*Adria's Romance Reviews*

ROMANCING the EARL

"Once again Darcy Burke takes an interesting story and...turns it into magic. An exceptionally well-written book."

-*Bodice Rippers, Femme Fatale, and Fantasy*

"...A fast paced story that was exciting and interesting. This is a definite must add to your book lists!"

-*Kilts and Swords*

LORD of FORTUNE

"I don't think I know enough superlatives to describe this book! It is wonderfully, magically delicious. It sucked me in from the very first sentence and didn't turn me loose—not even at the end ..."

-*Flippin Pages*

"If you love a deep, passionate romance with a bit of mystery, then this is the book for you!"

CAPTIVATING the SCOUNDREL

"I am in absolute awe of this story. Gideon and Daphne stole all of my heart and then some. This book was such a delight to read."

-Beneath the Covers Blog

"Darcy knows how to end a series with a bang! Daphne and Gideon are a mix of enemies and allies turned lovers that will have you on the edge of your seat at every turn."

-Sassy Booklover

Contemporary Romance

Ribbon Ridge Series

A contemporary family saga featuring the Archer family of sextuplets who return to their small Oregon wine country town to confront tragedy and find love...

The "multilayered plot keeps readers invested in the story line, and the explicit sensuality adds to the excitement that will have readers craving the next Ribbon Ridge offering."

-Library Journal Starred Review on YOURS TO HOLD

"Darcy Burke writes a uniquely touching and heart-warming series about the love, pain, and joys of family as well as the love that feeds your soul when you meet "the one."

I can't tell you how much I love this series. Each book gets better and better.

"Darcy Burke's Ribbon Ridge series is one of my all-time favorites. Fall in love with the Archer family, I know I did."

Ribbon Ridge: So Hot

SO GOOD

" ...worth the read with its well-written words, beautiful descriptions, and likeable characters...they are flirty, sexy and a match made in wine heaven."

"I absolutely love the characters in this book and the families. I honestly could not put it down and finished it in a day."

SO RIGHT

"This is another great story by Darcy Burke. Painting pictures with her words that make you want to sit and stare at them for hours. I love the banter between the characters and the general sense of fun and friendliness."

SO WRONG

ACKNOWLEDGMENTS

I want to thank my readers for their support and enjoyment of this series. That so many of you were eager to read Jagger's book inspired and motivated me in the best ways possible. Finishing the series was bittersweet, but there are lots of great things ahead!

Thank you to the #plotbunnies: Elisabeth Naughton, Rachel Grant, and Joan Swan for their endless help with the Book That Would Not End. Finding just the right way to finish Ethan and Audrey's story (and the series) took many, many tries and discussions. I couldn't have done it without you.

A massive thank-you to my writing rock and critique partner extraordinaire, Erica Ridley. She brings the hilarity and the honesty, and I would *not* want to do this without her.

Big hugs and kisses to my family who put up with my insane schedule and love me anyway. You make every day a blessing. Thank you.

ABOUT THE AUTHOR

Darcy Burke is the USA Today Bestselling Author of sexy, emotional historical and contemporary romance. Darcy wrote her first book at age 11, a happily ever after about a swan addicted to magic and the female swan who loved him, with exceedingly poor illustrations. Join her Reader Club at http://www.darcyburke.com/readerclub.

A native Oregonian, Darcy lives on the edge of wine country with her guitar-strumming husband, their two hilarious kids who seem to have inherited the writing gene. They're a crazy cat family with two Bengal cats, a small, fame-seeking cat named after a fruit, and an older rescue Maine Coon who is the master of chill and five a.m. serenading. In her "spare" time Darcy is a serial volunteer enrolled in a 12-step program where one learns to say "no," but she keeps having to start over. Her happy places are Disneyland and Labor Day weekend at the Gorge. Visit Darcy online at http://www.darcyburke.com and follow her social media: Facebook at http://www.facebook.com/darcyburkefans, Twitter @darcyburke at http://www.twitter.com/darcyburke, Instagram at http://www.

instagram/darcyburkeauthor, and Pinterest at http://
www.pinterest.com/darcyburkewrite.

Printed in Great Britain
by Amazon